Also by Frances Brody

Dying in the Wool
Murder in the Afternoon

Praise for Frances Brody

'The 1920s are a fascinating and under-used period for new crime fiction, so it's a particular pleasure to have Frances setting her story at that time. Kate Shackleton is a splendid heroine . . . I'm looking forward to the next book in the series!'   —Ann Granger

'Brody's winning tale of textile industry shenanigans is shot through with local colour.'   —*Independent*

'The story, with its secure setting in the richly-detailed woollen industry, is an excellent read.'
—*Mystery Women*

'The background detail of milling and dyeing is spot on . . . as is her ear for the West Riding accent and dialect.'
—*Country Life*

'An enjoyable and gripping mystery story.'
—*CrimeSquad.com*

A Medal for Murder

Frances Brody

MINOTAUR BOOKS

A THOMAS DUNNE BOOK

NEW YORK

This is a work of fiction. All of the characters, organizations, and events portrayed in this novel are either products of the author's imagination or are used fictitiously.

A THOMAS DUNNE BOOK FOR MINOTAUR BOOKS.
An imprint of St. Martin's Publishing Group.

www.thomasdunnebooks.com
www.minotaurbooks.com

Library of Congress Cataloging-in-Publication Data

Brody, Frances.
A medal for murder / Frances Brody.—1st Minotaur Books paperback ed.
    p. cm.
"A Thomas Dunne book."
ISBN 978-0-312-62240-4 (hardcover)
ISBN 978-1-250-02261-5 (e-book)
1. Women private investigators—England—Fiction. 2. Murder—Investigation—Fiction. 3. Mystery fiction. I. Title.
PR6113.C577M43 2013
823'.92—dc23

                                                        2012034638

First published in Great Britain by Piatkus

First Minotaur Books Paperback Edition: February 2013

10 9 8 7 6 5 4 3 2 1

For my sister Patricia

# Prologue

It took the best part of an afternoon to cut out the letters. In spite of touching the pastry brush into the jar so carefully, glue still coated fingertips and had to be peeled off. Glue made your head ache, but your hopes soar.

The sheet of paper turned stiff when dry. It would be ludicrous if a letter fell off. In the end, there it was:

**ONE THOUSAND POUNDS TO HAVE LUCY
BACK ALIVE
AWAIT INSTRUCTIONS
CALL POLICE SHE WILL DIE**

She would, too. Failure means curtains, success a new beginning.

Act One, Scene One.

1

The Pawnbroker

On a muggy August Friday morning, we set out in my 1910 blue Jowett convertible for our 9.30 a.m. appointment.

Jim Sykes, my assistant, is an ex-policeman who endearingly believes he does not look at all like an ex-policeman. He just happens to be lean, mean, and alert as a territorial tom cat. During a ten-day holiday in Robin Hood's Bay with his wife and family, he caught the sun, along with a carefree air that I suspected would not last long.

I braked sharply to let a crazed old woman, raising her stick to stop traffic, hurtle across Woodhouse Lane.

A rag-and-bone cart drew alongside, drawn by a patient shire horse. The lad seated beside the driver pointed at me. He called to Sykes, 'Didn't no one tell you women can't drive?'

Sykes raised his goggles and drew a finger across his throat as he gave the lad a hard stare.

'Let it go,' I said, accelerating away. 'That's threatening behaviour.'

'Threaten? I'll throttle him.'

Sykes finds it hard to let anything go. If he were a duck, the water on his back would sink him.

We bore up manfully as I drove into Leeds city centre and parked outside the double-fronted jeweller's shop on Lower Briggate. Three gold balls above the shop announced its pawnbroker status.

In the plate-glass window, I caught a glimpse of myself. What is the stylish lady detective wearing this season, under her motoring coat? A brown and turquoise silk crepe dress and jacket, copied from a Coco Chanel model, cloche hat and summer gloves echoing the brown. My mother frowns on brown, saying it is too much like wartime khaki sludge, but it suits my pale colouring and chestnut hair.

Jewellers' shops have a subdued air, like churches and banks. This one smelled of lavender polish and chamois leather. The young assistant with neatly combed fair hair and dark suit could easily have worked in a counting house. Head bent in concentration, he showed a tray of rings to a young couple.

Mr Moony, a thin grey-suited man with shining tonsured head, gave us a Mona Lisa smile. He saved the introductions for the small back room.

'One moment!' He disappeared into the shop and returned carrying a chair for me. I am five feet two inches tall. Mr Moony's courtesy in giving me the chair meant that he and Sykes, on high buffets, towered over me. Sykes handled the moment impeccably, concentrating mightily on taking out notebook and pencil.

I prompted Mr Moony to tell us about the incident, which took place last Monday, 21 August, 1922.

He sighed and stroked his chin. 'In my thirty years here, we've never had such a thing happen, or in my

4

father's time before me.' As he began to tell his tale, he gripped the seat of the buffet. His knuckles turned white. He spoke fluently, having already told the story to the police. 'At about noon, I went out for a stroll and came back half an hour later. My assistant, young Mr Hall, then took a stroll about. I insist on the efficacy of stretching the legs in the middle of the day.' He paused, as if half-expecting some criticism for his theory.

'I do just the same, Mr Moony,' I heard myself lie. 'Only yesterday, I walked from Woodhouse Ridge to Adel Crags.'

The energetic fib refocused Mr Moony on his tale.

'While I was alone here, the chap came in. My one consolation is that I and not young Hall bore the brunt of the outrage.'

On the name Hall, Sykes nudged my ankle with his foot. I kicked him. As if I would not think to ask.

'Has Mr Hall been with you long?'

A five-minute testimonial for young Albert Hall followed. I hoped Sykes was noting this while I concentrated on trying not to get the giggles. What Mrs Hall mother would name her son Albert? Call me Bert. Call me Al. Call me anything but a memorial to the late queen's consort and lost love.

Having fully exonerated his assistant, Mr Moony took a deep breath before continuing his story, eyes narrowing as he remembered the distressing scene. 'The man was about five foot six inches tall, slightly built, something of a stoop, a youngish fellow. He wore a darkish raincoat and a homburg. Had an item to put into pledge, that was his story. Swung out a twenty-two carat gold watch chain and asked for twelve shillings. I completed the paperwork, took the chain and handed him the money. Transaction completed, I placed the chain in a bag.'

'Can you remember any other details, Mr Moony?'

'It was a warm day. The chap dabbed at his brow with a hanky. And there was this smell when he pulled out the handkerchief . . .' He frowned.

'What kind of smell?'

'Something heady.'

'Hair lotion?'

'No. Like polish and roses. The police took no notice of that. The officer who came had no sense of smell, said it could have been the polish on my counters. He claimed a person has a heightened sense of awareness when something unusual or bad happens.'

'So you completed the transaction,' I prompted.

'Yes. I counted out the twelve shillings, put the chain in the bag . . .'

'And then?'

'We wished each other good day. He turned to leave the premises. As he did so, I moved to put the bagged item in the safe. The shop bell did not ring immediately. I glanced back, to see whether some item had caught his eye. That sometimes happens, you know.'

Mr Moony stopped, as though reluctant to bring the event back to life. His eye twitched and it took him a few seconds to bring it under control.

I said, 'The police must have been gratified to have so good an account. And what happened next?'

Mr Moony gulped. A great sigh escaped before he could continue. 'He was not by the door at all. He was behind me. Before I had time to close the safe, his hands were round my throat, he'd taken the chain back, flung me to the floor and grabbed everything he could from the safe. By the

6

time I recovered myself, he was gone. I telephoned the police. A constable was here within minutes. But they've had no luck finding him, or the missing articles. Naturally he gave a false address, in Headingley Lane. The police checked. I noticed you live in Headingley, Mrs Shackleton. I know it seems absurd, but my wife took that as a good sign.'

'Let us hope so.'

Sykes looked up from his notebook. 'Mr Moony, is there anything else that you can tell us, about his features, his colouring, manner, the way he talked?'

Mr Moony shrugged. 'I've tried so hard to picture him that I may well be imagining. But there was something fine about him. I can't put my finger on it. Something refined, so that when he pounced, I was taken completely by surprise. It feels ridiculous to say that and somehow I can't expound on it. There was something of the clerk about him. Perhaps the stoop made me think that. I can't be certain.'

'Local accent?' Sykes asked.

'Well-spoken, in a neutral sort of way. Not local I wouldn't say.'

'And the police will have looked for fingerprints?' I asked.

'Yes, but they drew a blank. To tell you the truth, I have no great hopes of their finding him, or the pledges he took. And that's the terrible thing. If he'd smashed the display case and taken new items, that would have been bad enough. This is worse. It's the trust, you see. My customers will come back to redeem their pledges. What on earth can I say to them?'

Sykes and I exchanged a look. It seemed a slightly unusual job if we were being asked to provide the

7

jeweller with a suitable form of words for his disappointed customers. 'Is that why we're here, Mr Moony?' I asked.

'Well, it would be wonderful if you could find the blighter.'

Sounding more confident than I felt, I said, 'Mr Sykes and I will do our best to recover the goods.'

'The more days go by, the less likely it seems.' Mr Moony reached onto the workbench and took a folder from under a pair of jeweller's pliers. 'This contains a copy of what I gave the police, a list of items taken: set of gold cufflinks and tie pin; three watch chains, two pocket watches, four rings and a bracelet. There's a detailed description next to each item you'll see. It's a terrible thing to lose trust as a pawnbroker. Some of those pieces have great sentimental value. If I have lost them, then I need to inform their owners and make recompense. That calls for discretion. Two of the individuals involved are distressed gentlewomen who have utter confidence in me. One entrusted me with her late mother's ring. I thought that if you, Mrs Shackleton, might be so good as to call in person on the ladies, showing the greatest tact ... and ... explain the situation ...'

I could see why old ladies would trust Mr Moony – the gentle manner, old-world courtesy, his thoughtfulness.

I hid my surprise at being asked to convey messages to Mr Moony's customers. Not exactly what a detective might be expected to do. 'And Mr Sykes here would call on the gentlemen? Is that your wish?'

Mr Moony looked relieved. 'Precisely. Then when they come here on the due date, I can arrange compensation.'

I glanced at the list of names and addresses. 'They are not all local people.'

Mr Moony smiled. 'I am the highest class pawnbroker in the vicinity of the railway station. Gentlefolk sometimes find it embarrassing to go to a local establishment.'

'Then we can begin right away, Mr Moony.' I looked to Sykes for his confirmation.

Sykes nodded. 'Of course.'

'Thank you. What will you think it best to say?'

I tried to imagine myself knocking on doors and explaining the situation. 'Simply the truth about the robbery, without any extraneous details, and to say that if they will come to you with the ticket on the due date, some settlement will be reached, or a replacement item offered. Would that be the best approach?'

'Yes, yes, I think so.' He allowed a note of hope. 'Of course if you or the police do retrieve the goods, then that would be the best outcome.'

'Have the police come back to you?' Sykes asked.

Mr Moony's mournful sigh hit the floor and bounced back. 'Only to say there is nothing to report.' He lowered his head, as if overcome by the shame and embarrassment of his situation. When he looked up, I noticed a kind of desperation around his eyes. He ran his tongue across his thin lips. 'These are the worst, the lowest days of my life. I cannot believe I was so lax as to let this happen to me.'

'I'll take a look around the shop, if I may.' Sykes exited quickly, leaving me to reassure Mr Moony and urge him not to blame himself.

'The watch chain the thief brought to pawn, was there anything distinctive about it?'

'Didn't I say? It had a gold coin attached. That's not so very unusual, but this was a South African coin, a gold pond.'

'That's something to go on,' I said, trying to sound encouraging.

Only several hundred thousand British men had served or worked in South Africa. That narrowed it down.

We discussed terms. Mr Moony had already written a generous cheque as a retainer. I tucked the cheque into my satchel and assured him we would do our very best. He walked us to the shop door.

When the door closed firmly behind us, the memory came back to me of my last visit to Moony's jewellers. I went there to buy a gift for my husband Gerald, before he left for his army training. A surgeon, he had enlisted at the start of the Great War, in a blaze of patriotism and courage. He went missing, presumed dead, in 1918. His disappearance is the mystery I have never solved. He could be alive somewhere, ill or with loss of memory. Because he left me well provided, I can afford to solve other mysteries that barely touch my heart. I bought Gerald a silver hip flask. I carry his old one in my satchel.

Sykes interrupted my thoughts. 'Shall I drive?' he asked.

'No you shan't. Ignore the funny looks and smart remarks. It will be good for your character to glimpse what we women have to put up with.'

2

In Harrogate

In Harrogate, hurricanes hardly ever happen.

Following Sykes's directions as he read the street map, I drove out of the town centre, onto Beckett Street and along Harehills Road. Dorset Mount was a respectable red-brick terraced street behind a block of shops. I parked by the shops, feeling a great reluctance to confront some poor woman about a very private transaction.

Sykes stayed with the car. I was just a little too well dressed for the area and felt self-conscious tapping along the pavement in my new strappy brown shoes. The back door seemed the more discreet option. As luck would have it, a plump, pleasant-looking woman stood in the yard, busy with a sweeping brush.

'Mrs Simons?'

Her hand went to her heart. 'It's Solly,' she said. 'Something's happened.'

'No, nothing's happened. No one's hurt.'

She loosened her grip on the broom and came to the wall. 'What is it?'

'May I step into the yard a moment?'

She opened the gate. Standing by her coalhouse door,

I gave her the barest facts about the robbery at Moony's pawnbrokers. She took the news better than I had expected.

'Poor Mr Moony. If he makes it up to me, that is enough. Worse things happen.'

'They won't all take it so well, Mrs Shackleton,' Sykes said glumly, when we were back in my dining room office. He looked at the newly delivered rosewood filing cabinet.

'It is for our case files,' I explained.

'Well, I hope that you are not tempting fate, and that we will have more cases.'

'Mr Sykes, do you have to be such a Job's comforter?'

The truth is that the pawnbroker's assignment is only my second professional case. Before that my missing person enquiries were undertaken as a kindness to other women who, like me, looked for answers at the end of the Great War.

We set Mr Moony's list of stolen goods on the table between us. Mr Sykes frowned as he copied down the names and addresses of the men whose pawned items had been stolen, with the dates they were due to be redeemed.

I did the same with the women's names, putting a tick against Mrs Simons, today's date, and a note of her response. There were now four people left on my list, and six for Sykes. Pawning was clearly a democratic activity, with the sexes engaged almost equally.

'What do you make of the fact that the thief gave a false address in Headingley, Mr Sykes? Does he know the area, I wonder?'

Sykes blew a doubtful sound. He is a man of many

12

non-verbal noises that convey a great deal. This particular exhalation seemed to suggest that he did not believe the thief lived in Headingley. 'Hard to say. It's likely he lives somewhere else entirely, and said Headingley to throw Mr Moony off the scent.'

At that moment my housekeeper, Mrs Sugden, came in with a tray bearing an early lunch of pork pie, tomatoes and cucumber, and a pot of tea. 'You better eat, if you're off to Harrogate, Mrs Shackleton.'

Specs on the end of her nose, Mrs Sugden glanced at my notebook. She is the soul of discretion, except when it comes to informing on me to my mother. 'That was kept q.t.,' she said with surprise. 'I didn't know old Moony had been robbed.'

Sykes scowled. This was not how he was used to working in the force.

'It wouldn't be good for his business if it got out, Mrs Sugden,' I said, passing a plate to Mr Sykes.

When Mrs Sugden had gone, Sykes said, 'It'll be worth my checking with a pal of mine in Millgarth Station. He's the desk sergeant. We were at school together. He'll let me know if there are any leads on our refined gentleman jewel thief, or any attempt to sell on the goods.'

'What about the assistant, Mr Hall?'

'I'll make enquiries. And after that I shall be off to Chapel Allerton, to see this Mr Bing, who'll be expecting to redeem his watch chain next Tuesday.'

'My next call will be in Harrogate, to Mrs deVries.'

Mr Moony had described her as a gentlewoman who, once a year, each summer, pawned her mother's ring. Breaking the news of its loss was not a prospect I relished. But since it was due to be redeemed the following Monday, there was no alternative. Fortunately I was going there anyway so could combine business and pleasure. I bit into the pork pie, which was very good.

'Ah yes,' Sykes said. 'You're off to the theatre.' And then, trying to sound casual, 'Will you be taking the motor?'

'No. It's all yours today. If you don't mind waiting half an hour while I change my shoes and pack a bag, you can give me a lift to the station. There's a train just after one o'clock.'

Sykes looked pleased at the thought of having the car. 'I don't mind waiting.' He speared a pickled onion. 'Harrogate, eh? It's a pity our good gentlewoman didn't pawn her ring closer to home. There's never any crime in Harrogate.'

3

Adaptation

Adaptation: the act of adjusting or adapting

As the guard blew his whistle for the train to leave Leeds station, I took out my book. The carriage door flew open. A waft of smoke from the platform mingled with the scent of violets. Murmuring relief at having caught the train, a slim, familiar figure, about forty years of age, set down a cream silk parasol. She undid the top button of her green satin jacket. 'So 'ot, so vairy 'ot today.' She was speaking to herself in a breathless voice, setting down her bag and packages, spreading her belongings across the seats opposite.

She sat down with a heavy sigh, drew a Venetian fan, ivory and silk, from her bag, flicked it open and put it to instant use. The train let out a hoot of steam.

Of course! That perfect profile, the sleek upswept hair, and those dainty shoes. The Belgian woman was one of the performers in the amateur production I was to see that evening. The play's director, a flamboyant woman I met at a party, had coaxed me into taking photographs of her cast. It was an enjoyable task. The camera fell in love with them.

This Belgian woman and her husband played an

English alderman and his wife. She padded out for the role, in order to look like a stout Potteries matron. Meriel, my director acquaintance, said she had coached them mightily, and sometimes their diction was excellent.

The woman felt my gaze as I tried to remember her name, recognising me as she did so. 'Ah, the photographer, Mrs . . .'

'Shackleton. And you are the alderman's lady in the play, but in real life . . .'

'Ah, real life, real life. Far too much of it. But yes, I am Madam Geerts. Olivia Geerts. Please, take a Parma Violet.'

I prefer pear drops but one should enter Harrogate with a fragrant tongue. 'Thank you.' Would it be rude to ignore her, and read my novel? She smiled, and answered the question for me.

'You read the book of the play, I see. *Anna of the Five Towns.*'

'Yes, just one more chapter. And I'll be intrigued to see how Meriel adapted this story for the stage. Not an easy task I shouldn't think.'

She wafted her fan. 'I shall not disturb you. Please to read. I look out of the window.'

As we neared Harrogate, I snapped the book shut. 'How awful! It's the wrong ending. It was bad enough that one of the characters hanged himself.'

'That scene, it is cut. We do not now see this man cut down from the rope by 'is son.' Madam Geerts sighed. 'An ill-fated man. But this heroine of the story, such a tiresome girl. I want to shake her. Say, Speak! Stand up for yourself!'

She made me laugh. I knew exactly what she meant.

Anna of the Five Towns is a Cinderella story without a fairy godmother. Anna is the daughter of a miser. She inherits a fortune on her twenty-first birthday. But the miser holds power over his daughter. She hardly dare draw a crooked sixpence. Anna makes a good match, with the town's up-and-coming businessman. Too late she discovers her heart belongs to young Willie Price, the doomed son of her ruined tenant. The older Mr Price hangs himself in despair. My brief telling makes the story sound melodramatic. It pulses with real life. Anna's kingdom is her sparkling kitchen. Her feelings are fine and sensitive, with a natural distaste for hypocrisy. She cannot give her thoughts words, even to herself. Not the most promising material for a stage play.

Madam Geerts tucked away her fan and fastened her jacket. The train rattled to a halt. She leaned across the carriage and took my hands in hers. At first I thought this some expression of sympathy regarding the heart-breaking end of the novel.

She gave me a piercing stare. 'Please. Do not mention to a soul that I am on this train.' Although we were alone in the carriage, she dropped her voice to a whisper. 'As a married lady, you know it is best female medical matters stay secret. My 'usband Monsieur Geerts. If 'e know I am on the Leeds train 'e will get the wrong end of the pole. 'e is a jealous man. Always where 'ave you been, who seen, what done. Ahhh! You cannot imagine.'

I smiled. 'I wouldn't dream of mentioning that I saw you. It won't arise.'

She leaned confidentially close. 'You are a woman of the world. To you . . .'

Mercifully, a guard opened the carriage door at that moment, saving me from her medical details.

'We will see you tonight?' she asked as we parted at the barrier. 'You come to our final performance?'

'Wouldn't miss it for the world.'

I handed in my overnight bag to Left Luggage. Turning up on the doorstep of the unfortunate Mrs deVries to break the news of the loss from the pawnbroker's shop of her mother's ring would be hard enough. I did not want to create the impression that I had come to move in with her.

Making my way through the crush of arriving and departing visitors, I went into the station bookstore. Amid guides to the Spa, I found a street map of Harrogate. By coincidence, Mrs deVries lived on the same road as my theatre director acquaintance, who had offered to put me up for the night.

Consulting the map, I estimated that St Clement's Road was about a mile from the station. The map deceived me. In the heat of the afternoon, sun blazing in a cloudless sky, I felt myself begin to wilt as I walked up West Park. A silk crepe outfit is not the best choice for a hot afternoon. I had changed my strappy brown shoes for a pair of black buckles with Cuban heels, to double for this evening's visit to the theatre. Now they were crippling me. You are not here to sit under the shade of a tree on The Stray, I told myself. But it was tempting. The expanse of green, the scent of grass and the tiny daisies, stirred happy memories. Mother and I came to Harrogate before she had the twins, my brothers. Dad was attending a police conference and mother and I tagged along for the enjoyment. Dad must have escaped for an hour. I remembered the three of us sitting on the grass together. I had rolled over and over down an enormous hill, in a great adventure of watching the sky and the earth change places, as the grass prickled my arms and legs. Now I saw no enormous hill, only a gentle slope.

By the time I reached St Clement's Road, my feet felt twice their size. I ignored the pain and instead pictured myself, in a few more moments, knocking on the door of number 92. Even with Mr Moony's business card to wave under Mrs deVries's nose, the interview could prove awkward. Ideally, she would be alone, ask me in and I could rest my poor feet while tactfully explaining the sad situation regarding the loss of her pawned ring.

Just my luck that the numbers started at one. Not until I had walked the length of the street did I realise that there was no number 92.

I paused by Meriel Jamieson's garden wall. The house was a four-storey semi-detached of red brick, probably built around the middle of the last century. Some of the houses on the street were well cared for, with glossily painted doors and window frames, elegant drapes at the windows, tubs of geraniums, petunias in window boxes and the small front gardens immaculately manicured.

Meriel's house had peeling paintwork. One of the steps leading to the front door was cracked. Nettles and thistles grew in the garden where two neglected rose bushes fought for space.

In the hope that Meriel might still be at home, and I could rest my feet, I climbed the seven steps to the front door. There were two bells and two name plates: *Capt. Wolfendale* and *Miss Fell*. No Miss Jamieson. From the bay window, a suit of armour looked out at me. By taking two steps down, I could glance into the room without being seen. Two men were seated at a low table in front of the fireplace, heads bent over what could have been a game of chess. This must be the Captain Wolfendale of the name plate. Better not disturb him and his fellow player. Meriel had not lived in Harrogate for long. Perhaps she did not have a name plate.

The door opened suddenly. A Pekinese thrust its small head out. As the door opened wider, I saw that the leash attached to its collar was held by an elderly lady with a round, pleasing face. Her left hand flew to her heart. 'Goodness! You startled me.' She closed the door behind her.

'Sorry if I made you jump. I'm looking for Miss Jamieson.'

'Miss Jamieson has the lower ground floor flat.' The woman's voice was cultured, even a little affected. 'She is not at home. I saw her leave earlier.'

So much for dreams of resting my tortured feet. 'Oh well, never mind.' The Pekinese sniffed at my shoes, as if it knew they were too tight. 'I'll be meeting her later. I'm here to see the play.'

'Ah, then we shall perhaps bump into each other. I shall be there myself. You are in for a treat, Miss . . .'

'Mrs Shackleton. I took the photographs.'

'So you did! I have heard all about you.' Her voice now took on a much more friendly tone.

We came down the steps together and stood for a moment on the pavement.

'I had better get myself back to town, to meet Miss Jamieson.' I bobbed down and patted the Pekinese's small silky head, suitably ingratiating myself and softening up its owner for my question. 'Miss Fell, before you go ...' The dog tugged at its lead. 'A friend of my mother's lives somewhere nearby, only I don't have the address. Her name is Mrs deVries.'

Miss Fell stared at me, unable to hide her surprise, or was it shock? She knew Mrs deVries, I felt sure of that. The dog began to pull. Miss Fell let herself be dragged across the street at speed, turning briefly to call back to me, 'Sorry! Never heard of her.'

She was lying. But why? Then an odd thought struck me. This was number 29 St Clement's Road. Mrs deVries lived at the non-existent 92. The number transposed.

Pulling in my skirt to avoid being accosted by a giant thistle, I decided to take a look at this lower ground floor flat where I was to spend the night. I stepped onto the narrow path and down three steps to a basement door. This, too, had a name plate: "Root – Watch Mender".

This was the strikingly handsome young man who was in the cast of *Anna of the Five Towns*. By bringing him onto the stage from the shady obscurity of his basement room, Meriel had done the female population of Harrogate a great favour. I passed by his door. At the rear of the building, Meriel had her own entrance, but no name plate. Looking through the window, I saw a dimly lit cellar room with narrow bed and chaise longue. Miss Fell was right. Meriel had already left.

As I walked back, I noticed Dan Root. He sat with his back to me, facing the fireplace, like a boy waiting for Father Christmas to come down the chimney. He was a broad-shouldered, solitary figure wearing white shirt, dark trousers and waistcoat.

I remembered him as extremely charming and very

photogenic. His good looks would not have been out of place on the London stage or in the picture palaces, though heroes there were invariably dark. This Adonis was blond, but with honey-coloured skin and a smile to set hearts racing.

He turned suddenly, as if he had felt my eyes on him. How embarrassing, to be caught staring through his window. He came to the door as he was, still wearing his watch mender's apron.

Think quickly, I told myself. 'Sorry to be staring. I thought I might spot Meriel. We've arranged to meet in the Valley Gardens, only I thought I might have caught her before she left.'

At least he remembered me. 'Mrs Shackleton, not here to take another photograph then?' He drew a watch from his waistcoat pocket. 'She set off half an hour ago. Said something about calling at the theatre first.'

The gold coin on his watch caught my eye but his movement was too quick for me to identify it. I could hardly ask him, Is that a South African pond and did you rob a pawnbroker this week?

He gave a charming smile. 'I'm sorry. I would ask you in, or offer to walk you there, but I have a mass of work to get on with.'

'That's all right.'

'Goodbye then,' he said, somewhat abruptly.

'Goodbye.'

Now I felt a complete idiot. He probably had females beating a path to his door all the time. "This watch has lost three hours in the last ten minutes. I'm sure you can fix it for me, handsome Mr Root."

Annoyed with my lack of success, I hobbled back to

town and by twists and turns found Crispin's Boot Company on Cambridge Street. Reluctantly, I bought a pair of low-heeled lace-ups that an old lady would be proud of. The assistant, a young woman of about my age, looked tired and seemed glad to have made a sale. When I asked directions to the Post Office, she walked me to the door. 'You're practically there, madam. It's just round the corner there.'

She had wrapped my own shoes, and I walked to the Post Office looking decidedly less elegant.

The street directory showed no deVries on St Clement's Road, or the adjacent streets. Nor was she in the secondary index of telephone subscribers. This did not surprise me. Not everyone takes to the luxury of the telephone, especially if their economic circumstances lead to pawning precious possessions.

Picking up a telegram form, I composed my message to Sykes. *No luck St Clement's Road STOP Confirm correct address*

At the counter, I paid the elderly clerk for my nine words, giving Meriel's address for the reply.

I bumped into Meriel close by the Valley Gardens. She greeted me with an extravagant hug. Her large oval face and expressive eyes lit with delight. I wear my hair bobbed. Hers is long, loosely pinned and fixed with combs. Her floating skirt, voluminous sleeved blouse and a waistcoat embroidered in purple silks gave her an exotic, gypsy look.

For the time being, I gave up all thoughts of work as we strolled the footpath, past the bandstand where the orchestra played a marching tune. A little girl did cartwheels on the grass. A child's hoop spun across our path. 'We'll take that as a lucky hoop,' Meriel said. 'At least the weather's brightened up. The Agricultural Show was a bit of a washout last week, and the golf course flooded — something about a burst pipe.'

'That must have put a damper on for the tourists.'

'Oh they just keep sipping the waters and bathing. And none of it has harmed my production. Excellent box office.'

We reached the tea-room and sat down. Meriel turned her face to the sun while the waiter cleared the table and set down menus. She closed her eyes. 'This reminds me of glorious days when my mother sang in La Scala. I would sit out in the afternoons while she rested.'

Then she glanced at me over the top of her menu. 'You're so trim,' she said accusingly. 'You could have any number of these delicious ices. I tried the pistachio last week, and they have the most amazing selection of cakes and éclairs.'

The band began to play a Viennese waltz. Before the tune finished, the waiter jotted down our orders.

'It's lovely here, Meriel.' I felt relaxed and glad to be alive.

'They have excellent musicians. Harrogate city fathers believe music banishes anxious cares and encourages a cheerful outlook. And I do feel cheerful. Look at this.' She thrust a newspaper under my nose. Just like home then, with Mrs Sugden devouring tales of folly and crime. But this was Harrogate after all. The item in Wednesday's *Herald* comprised a list of names — this week's visitors to the Spa, set out according to which hotel they stayed in. She pointed to a name. 'See! There he is.'

'Burrington Wheatley?'

'The very one.' She glanced around the tables, as if to make sure the man himself was not within hearing distance. 'A funny butterball of a man with a face the colour of a blazing cinder, pure white hair, snowy moustache and flyaway black eyebrows. You can't mistake him.' As she spoke, she drew moustache and eyebrows on her face with her fingertips, to drive home her description.

A suspicion sprouted. 'Why would I not want to mistake him?'

The waiter set down our salads. Meriel waited. 'Because, dear Kate, I want you to praise me to the sky when you sit next to him this evening. He is the well-known Manchester theatre impresario.'

'What does an impresario do?'

She looked at me as though I were the worst kind of innocent. 'He produces plays of course, tours productions across the country, into the best venues. If he likes my work . . . Well, let us say this could be the making of me. Clap till your hands hurt. An hurrah or two would not go amiss.'

I said doubtfully, 'I didn't know I was to be your standard bearer.'

She closed her eyes, stretched her neck and pulled back her shoulders. 'My life is going to change. I can feel it in my toes.'

As we ate, we caught up with news of a mutual friend at whose fancy dress party we had met last New Year's Eve.

Meriel ordered more bread, and surreptitiously slipped a slice into her bag, along with a tomato. 'Harrogate has been lucky for me. Who would have thought I could have a spell at the Opera House for an

25

amateur production at the height of the season? It is too good to be true. I tried to get a foot in the door in London, and it just did not happen. I was assistant to an assistant wardrobe mistress. Every moment was torture – an utter squandering of my talents.'

I listened to her accounts of costume making until the young waiter set down our cakes and ices. The ice cream was already melting in the heat of the afternoon.

Meriel asked the waiter's name, then said, 'Well now, Malcolm, can you tell me what's playing at the Opera House this week?'

'Why, it's an adaptation of an Arnold Bennett novel, madam. *Anna of the Five Towns.*'

'What have you heard about it?' she demanded.

He blushed and looked for a means of escape.

'Well?'

'I'm not sure of the tale,' he admitted. 'But I was told that the best-looking lass in Harrogate is taking a good part.'

'Thank you. That is an excellent recommendation.' His answer seemed to satisfy her. 'It doesn't matter what they say, Kate, as long as they are talking.' She turned the page in the newspaper. 'Read this review.'

I scanned the piece. Her production had indeed earned a glowing review.

Meriel dabbed a dribble of ice cream from her chin. 'You know why I chose this story, *Anna of the Five Towns*?'

'It does seem a difficult choice. I would have gone for a ready-made play myself.' I bit into my chocolate éclair.

'I chose it because it reveals hypocrisy, meanness, oppression, tyranny.' She waved her spoon, flicking a dash of ice cream onto the hat of the woman at the next table. Given the meltiness, it was an impressive hit. As Meriel talked about the play, she drew a good deal of attention to our table.

The café was busy. While customers were not exactly being hurried out, we were encouraged not to dawdle. The waiter brought the bill. Meriel snatched it from me. 'This is my treat.'

She opened her copious bag and began a search. 'Do you know, I've left my dratted purse in the theatre. How annoying!'

I took the bill from her.

'But what I was saying, Kate, about *Anna of the Five Towns*, it has a heroine who has no way of fighting back because she has always lived under tyranny and does not have the language or the ability to fight her corner, and say what she wants. And in Lucy Wolfendale, I have the most perfect Anna.'

'You have cast someone similar in character?'

'Heavens no! Lucy could not be more different.'

At the theatre, I made a beeline for the box office, while Meriel chatted to the doorman.

The white-haired bespectacled box office attendant handed me my complimentary ticket for that evening. I thanked her and asked, 'Do you know whether a Mrs deVries has booked to see the play? I came across from Leeds without her address and hoped she may be here tonight.' It was a good try, but failed.

The woman shook her head. 'Half Harrogate's seen the show, but that name rings no bells.' She frowned. 'deVries? Sounds Belgian. The Belgies form a bit of a clique if you ask me.'

4

Is This a Dagger?

The final curtain fell on *Anna of the Five Towns*. The cast had taken bow after bow, to rapturous applause.

Bravos greeted the young leading lady as she stepped forward, a young man on either side of her: one who had won her hand, and one who had died tragically. *Anna* took a solitary bow.

Mr Burrington Wheatley, Meriel's velvet-clad impresario who sat to my right, applauded loudly.

At the interval, he and I had moved from the front row of the stalls to the back, to escape an obnoxious fellow theatregoer who arrived late, blew cigar smoke up at the cast, and gave me his running commentary while rustling a bag of mint humbugs.

When the applause subsided, Mr Wheatley and I squeezed out of the auditorium, pausing in the crush of the lobby at the foot of the stairs that led to the dress circle and bar. He turned to me. 'The girl who played Anna . . .'

'Lucy Wolfendale.' I remembered her from our photographic session.

'She'll leave a trail of broken hearts and empty

wallets in her wake, rely upon it. An actress like that comes along once in a generation. She is a natural.'

A growl came from behind. It was the humbug-eating cigar smoker we had escaped from earlier. With a good deal of annoyance, he snarled, 'An exquisite creature like Miss Lucy Wolfendale comes along not once in a generation but once in a lifetime.'

Mr Wheatley gave me an amused wink. He said, 'I comment only on her acting abilities, sir. I mount theatrical productions that tour the provinces. I would have Miss Wolfendale in my company tomorrow.'

The cigar smoker's nose twitched with distaste. He kept in step as we climbed the broad staircase. 'Miss Wolfendale will tread no one's boards. Her future is here.'

Mr Wheatley raised a mischievous eyebrow. 'You're her father?'

'Her father?' The cigar smoker stopped in his tracks. For a moment I thought he would strike Mr Wheatley. He bit on the cigar. Out of the side of his mouth, he said coldly, 'I am Lawrence Milner, an old family friend. Miss Wolfendale is a respectable girl. A turn on the amateur dramatic stage with friends might be acceptable. The professional theatre is out of the question.'

Attempting to defuse the situation, I said, 'The young chaps were very good.'

'One of them is my son, Rodney,' Lawrence Milner said. 'And he will have no more time for this sort of thing.'

He had made that point during the play, and the likeness was clear. Younger and older Milners had the same reddish-blond hair.

I decided to ignore him. 'Did you not think, Mr

29

Wheatley, that Dylan Ashton acted the part of Willie superbly? He seemed entirely in love with Anna.'

'That wasn't acting,' Mr Wheatley murmured in a kindly voice.

Mr Milner pushed past us and elbowed his way towards the bar.

Mr Wheatley took my arm. 'Miss Jamieson's talent as a director is to know what to cut and what to play.'

'Oh and what did she cut?'

Meriel and I were the last to leave the theatre. She had to make sure nothing had been left in the dressing rooms. She thanked the doorman effusively, as we followed him to the stage door, saying she would never forget all his small kindnesses.

'A tip wouldn't go amiss,' she whispered to me. 'With all the junk in this bag, I can't find my purse.'

The instant we left the theatre and stepped into the little back street, great drops of warm summer rain turned to stair rods. I hurried into the nearest shop doorway, diving into my overfull bag. 'I've an umbrella here somewhere.'

Meriel pulled a hood over her head. 'You'll have to let me carry the brolly. I'm taller.'

My heel touched something. I looked down, stepping back with a sudden gasp, fearing I had trodden on some sleeping tramp.

'Is he drunk?' Meriel took the umbrella from my hand, opening it with a swish.

Bending, I touched the man's warm cheek. He had lost his hat. Light reddish-blond hair fell onto his fore-head. His jacket was undone, and missing a button. Later, I wondered how I could have focused on such small details. Perhaps something in me wanted not to look at the hilt of a dagger that protruded from his chest. By the glow of the alley gas lamp, I noticed a streak of blood, trespassing onto the starched white dress shirt.

I stared blankly, wondering for a moment whether this was some tom-fool stage trick with a retracting dagger. The figure might leap at us and start to laugh. He did not. In the soft shadowy light, the features came into focus. The jut of the jaw, the broad nose. It was a handsome face, frozen in a look of angry surprise, as if his lips had not expected to be deprived so soon of their cigar.

'It's that fellow . . . the one who sat next to me. He's dead.'

Meriel shrieked. 'Not my Mr Wheatley!'

Pushing my bag into Meriel's hands, I felt for a pulse on the man's neck, knowing the gesture to be futile.

Meriel backed away, fear in her voice. 'It's Lawrence Milner.' I stood up and as we faced each other, I saw terror in her eyes. She said quickly, 'That's his motor, just on the Parade there.' She hurried to look, as though what we saw in the doorway might be some trick of the light and the real Mr Milner would be alive and sitting at the wheel.

'Somebody has slashed the tyres,' she called.

But that would no longer concern Mr Milner.

I waited for her to walk back up the alley. 'Ghastly, ghastly,' was all she could say. The body lay behind me. Meriel blocked my way. For a long moment, I felt para-lysed.

One of us had to do something. Meriel seemed to have lost her grip.

'Stay here, Meriel. I'll get the doorman to call the police.'

At that, she turned, and ran back towards the stage door, calling, 'I'll tell him.'

She had taken the umbrella. I had the choice of standing in the lashing rain, back to the window, or sharing the doorway with the dead man. I chose the lashing rain.

 Exit on a Bike

Lucy Wolfendale had triumphed in the part of Anna Tellwright. The applause made her feel as if she were floating. She felt her spirit inhabit the entire theatre, reaching out to everyone there, buoyed up on their applause. Afterwards, she wanted to drink champagne, and dance in some magnificent ballroom. Instead, she had made do with a glass of sherry in the theatre bar, while warding off the sick-making attentions of Rodney Milner's lecherous old goat of a father. Ugh.

If it were not for her good friends, she would have gone mad.

Now here she was at close on midnight, on the back of a bicycle. Droplets of rain hit the back of her neck and trickled down her spine.

'I didn't imagine it would pelt it down for my big adventure.' Lucy leaned into Dylan's back. 'I can't bear being on a bicycle in the rain.'

Dylan did not answer straight away. He pedalled along the bumpy road as if the devil were after them.

At the turning for Stonehook Road, he slowed down. 'It's not going to let up. Do you want to turn back?'

'No!'

They continued in silence along the winding road. The rain stopped as suddenly as it had begun. Finally the tower loomed in the dark field, lit by the moon. Seeing it at night gave Lucy a jolt. It looked so very different. Menacing.

Dylan slowed down. He brought the bicycle to a stop by the side of the road.

Lucy climbed off, shaking away the raindrops. She hopped from foot to foot. 'Just a mo ... Let me ...' She leaned on his shoulder, shaking her leg. 'Oh, oh, oh! Pins and needles!'

The hem of her skirt was soaked from wheel splashes.

Dylan leaned the bike against the hawthorn hedge. He unclipped the lamp from the handlebars. 'There's still time to change your mind.'

'Don't be a big baby.' She took the lamp from him and began to look for the gap in the hedge. 'My mind's made up.'

He followed, reaching out to stop her. 'Do you have to? Why not be at home when the postman comes in the morning? Intercept the note before your granddad sees it?'

'Dylan! Then I'd be a soppy drip.' She shook free of him. Let him be a coward if he wanted. He looked the part, only a little taller than she was, skinny, and with something of the child about him still. 'I can't see the gap,' she called. 'We'll have to climb the gate.' Lamp in one hand, she put a foot on the second bar of the gate. 'Don't go all useless on me. You said you'd help.'

'That was on a sunny day,' he said lamely. 'It seemed a good idea.'

She was on one side of the gate, he on the other, not

34

moving. She put her hand on his. 'I have to do this. I only want what is mine.'

It was that June Sunday afternoon when they rehearsed together. She had sworn him to secrecy. When she told him she wanted to train as an actress, and had applied to the Royal Academy of Dramatic Art, she hardly dared hope anything would come of it. When she was offered an audition, she feared she would not find a good enough lie to cover her two-day disappearance, or she would not scrimp together the fare to London. Her grandfather was such a miser, like the miser in the play. But being Lucy, she did find the money. Being Lucy, she was offered a place at RADA, and she intended to take it up.

On her twenty-first birthday she had asked her grandfather outright for the legacy she knew to be hers. He refused.

Lucy got the idea for the ransom note from one of Miss Fell's library books. A thousand pounds would pay her fees at RADA, and her board and lodgings in London.

Now here she was on this wet August night, struggling to make her dream come true, and with only Dylan to help. He was turning out to be a wet blanket, a cowardy custard.

'What if your grandfather works out that you sent the ransom note?'

'Well then, let him. He'll know I mean it.' She began to stride across the field.

Dylan climbed after her, hurrying to catch up. 'He'll call the police.'

She turned. The moon lit their way. She saw that Dylan was looking at the ground, trying to avoid stepping on buttercups and daisies. 'Granddad won't call the police. He will pay up because he is afraid.'

'Of what?' Dylan asked.

They were so close that Lucy had the sudden picture in her mind of the two of them as a pair of bedraggled scarecrows in a field. They would cling together against all the birds of prey in the world. But she would have to do the protecting. Dylan had not one ounce of courage or initiative in his body.

'I'm not sure what Granddad is afraid of. Scandal I suppose.'

Even as a little girl she had known that her grandfather did not want to draw attention to himself. Her low heels sunk into the soft ground. Dampness from the grass tickled her ankles through her stockings.

Lucy shone a light on the lock in the old oak door. Dylan inserted the heavy iron key and turned it. With a noisy creak, the door opened. They stood stock still. Lucy shuddered. 'It's black as pitch in here.'

'That's what I'm saying. You're not going to like it. It will be scary at night . . .'

She stepped inside. The beam from the lamp showed cracked floorboards, and a dark void beneath. He said, 'Stop! The boards are giving way. There's a ten-foot drop to nowhere.'

She tugged at his sleeve. 'Then let's go up the stairs. Don't look down.'

Dylan sniffed. 'That stench! This lower floor must have been used to store something that rotted. That's why the floorboards are breaking, cracking.'

A straight staircase with two missing treads led to the floor above.

'Steady, Lucy!'

'Don't fuss.'

A mullion window, its glass cracked, let in a smidgen of moonlight.

When her eyes became accustomed to the gloom, Lucy saw that everything was in place, just as she had left it: blankets, bottle of water, biscuit tin with food, candles and matches. She struck a match and lit a candle.

Dylan took a sharp breath. 'This place would go up like a tinderbox. I wish I'd never . . .'

'It will be all right.' She lit a second candle and let the grease drip to the floor, then fixed the candle in its own wax.

'It's madness,' Dylan moaned.

'Sometimes madness is best. And you won't say that when it's all over. I'm only demanding my due. One thousand pounds might sound a lot, but not if you say it quickly. For heaven's sake, if a fictional character like Anna Tellwright in the play can come into fifty thousand pounds . . . And there'll be something for you, for helping me.'

'I don't want any money.'

'Nothing bad is going to happen. Anyway, I can let myself out at any time, so stop worrying.' She reached out a hand. 'Let's look at the moon. Let's count the stars. Let's dance on the battlements. Is that what they're called?' She led the way to a narrow spiral stair-case. 'Come up to the top. I've brought a compass. I'll give you the lie of the land.'

He followed reluctantly. 'I know the lie of the land, and I don't feel like dancing.'

'You see, these stairs are quite firm.'

They reached the top of the tower.

'Isn't it glorious?' She flung out her arms. 'You can see for miles.'

The moon lit the surrounding fields. To the east, the blur of a copse formed a dark backdrop. Stars glittered for attention. Hay-making had been going on in a distant field and the scent still hung in the air. Dylan said, 'Whoever built this tower came up here to look at the stars.'

'Or to dance with his true love.' She held out her arms and began to sing. 'If you were the only boy in the world, and I were the only girl, nothing else would matter in the world today . . . Come on! Dance with me!'

'I'm dreaming,' he said, reaching out, one arm around her waist, another on her shoulder. 'I shall wake up soon.'

'Go on dreaming, but sing.'

'If you were the only girl in the world . . .'

They danced around the roof of the tower.

'When I'm an actress, you must come to any stage door in the world and ask to see me. I'll never forget my friend in need, Dylan. I feel I've loved you, like Anna loved Willie. Something true and forever.'

'Then . . .'

'Shh.' She put a finger to his lips. 'I'll remember you forever, wherever life takes me.' She laughed. 'We gave old Milner the slip all right. He was determined to give me a lift . . .'

'That's not all he was determined about,' Dylan said.

'And your face!'

'Don't talk about him.'

'He's odious. If I were a man and a character actor, I would study him. As it is . . .' She made a sound of

38

pretend vomiting. 'Can you imagine that he and my granddad actually thought I would marry him?'

'Yes, I can imagine.'

'What century, what country in their mind are they living in?'

'No one can force you to marry. People can say "I do not" as well as they say "I do". Anyway, don't think about that. It will give you nightmares.'

'You should go now, Dylan.'

'Let me stay and look after you. I'll watch you as you sleep.'

'You've done enough. You need to be fine and frisky for work tomorrow. The girls will be swarming to the window of Croker & Company to catch a glimpse of you.'

'I doubt it.' Reluctantly, he turned up his collar.

She followed him down the stairs.

He would not take the lantern. 'The moon will be out again soon. Goodnight, Lucy.'

'Goodnight.' She turned the key in the lock, went back up the stairs and watched him cross the field. At the gate, he looked back and waved.

For a moment she thought he would turn tail and hurry back to her.

Yesterday Lucy had purloined her grandfather's army groundsheet and khaki blankets. She had borrowed a bike and brought what she needed to the tower. Her chosen spot was by the wall on the top floor, the level below the parapet. Her tapestry shoulder bag formed a pillow.

She had taken a big gamble, she knew that. What if, when Granddad opened the ransom note, he set aside the habit of a lifetime and went to the authorities? Well, they would not find her. No one would. This place had been abandoned years ago.

Of course tomorrow was Saturday and he could not go to the bank. But she had thought of that. Let him sweat. Let him fester all day Saturday and all through Sunday. Let him run mad in his mind. He would be knocking on the door of the bank first thing Monday morning.

She frowned. Of course it was always possible that he really did not have her legacy, that he had gambled it away, or spent it, that he had been leading her up the garden path all these years, saying there was something substantial for her in that dim distant future that had arrived with the break of dawn on the 6th of August this year, her twenty-first birthday.

In that case, he had better know how to get some money, because she would have it. She would live her life, away from him and his weapons, uniforms, medals, his ancient nonsense.

Something touched Lucy's face in the darkness. Something scuttled by her hair, a stealthy creature pitter-pattering. She lay very still. The tower moved and breathed. Its nooks and crannies held the scent of long-ago harvests. She could taste dust and hay-making in the back of her throat. The grey stone walls reeked of eternity, and the wooden floor of pity and decay.

'Fallen into disuse,' was how Dylan said he would describe it if the tower found its way into the files of Croker & Company, House Agents.

She had chosen the tower as her hiding place after elimination of other possibilities. Dylan would have risked his job if he hid her in his rooms above the house

40

agent's offices. Girl friends would not understand her determination and need for secrecy. They had mothers who would not keep her confidence.

There was another reason that had nothing to do with logic or sense. All through her childhood, Lucy adored fairy tales. She felt the ring of truth that chimed with something in her own soul. A fairy tale girl, miller's daughter or princess, would somehow find her true self, would be granted her deepest wish. But before that, a trial must be endured, a solitary struggle with no certainty of success.

Without being able to put it into words, Lucy knew that if she could pass three nights in this tower, the future would fall into the palm of her hand. And it must be three nights, the magical number three. Tonight, Friday, her grandfather would sleep soundly, suspecting nothing. On Saturday morning, when the note dropped onto the doormat, he would begin to stew. All Saturday he would plot and plan how to get the money, the thousand pounds. He would take out his bank books and do calculations. The thought of parting with the smallest sum always gave him the runs. When a bill arrived, the lavatory flushed so often, the house rattled. How glad she was to be out of there, out of that mausoleum, and soon it would be forever. Granddad would lie awake all Saturday night. Sunday, he would stride the room. The only person he might possibly confide in would be Mr Milner, his partner in board games, his partner in the plan to ruin her life. If so, let them rustle up the money between them. On Monday morning, Granddad would go to the bank. Monday at noon would come her deliverance.

Poor old Granddad. Part of her could not help but

feel sorry for him. But he should not have been so tight-fisted. He had lived his life. Now she must live hers.

She pulled the blanket tighter. To send herself back to sleep, she pictured all the fairy story towers that ever were.

She dreamed of cobwebs. She dreamed of silken hair flowing into the sky and intertwining with stars. She dreamed of a dwarf grandfather who tore himself in two. She dreamed of being Anna in the play, inheriting a fortune and yet not knowing how to live. Now she boarded a train.

The hoot of her dream train became an owl. She woke, paralysed.

Someone was standing there, filling the space by the staircase. Lucy wanted to speak, to move, to stand up and demand to know, Who are you? But no sound came. She could not move so much as a finger.

When she woke again, the figure had gone. She wondered was it one of those dreams, when you know for sure that you are awake and there is someone there, and yet you must be asleep or you would be able to move your hand. You would be able to speak.

She sat up.

'Is someone there? Dylan!'

No one answered.

She drew on shoes, and called again, 'Is anyone there?' half expecting a dwarf to lasso her with a length of silk, a witch to cackle curses.

She climbed the rickety spiral staircase to the roof of the tower, and stepped out onto its battlements. Beyond the sulky moon a distant haystack made the shape of a witch's house. The scent of clover floated in from another time, a distant century. Over by the wood, something moved – perhaps a fox going about its stealthy business, or a deer feeling safe in the hour before dawn.

Soon, very soon, her life would begin, properly, for the very first time.

6

Corpsing: forgetting one's lines

It was a terrible way for a life to end, in a shop doorway on a rainy night. For what seemed an endless time, I waited for Meriel to come back and say the police were on their way.

I walked from the alley to the road where Mr Milner's car was parked. A couple passed by on the other side of the street, she laughing at his joke. He glanced across, murmuring something to her. She looked at me, a woman alone, loitering. They hurried on their way. It was obvious what they thought.

The night had turned cold. I returned to the alley, keeping my distance from the doorway. Future shoppers and shop workers might sometimes feel a chill as they crossed that threshold where the body lay. The doorway might hold a memory of the dreadful act, and of Mr Milner's final moments.

It was no use. I had to look again at the lifeless man. He seemed to move. I forced myself to check once more for a pulse. Not a murmur of life, not half a breath. He was cold now. All that remained was a well-dressed shell.

The dagger had pierced his heart. It had entered so deep that only the hilt was visible. The dark bloody stain formed an almost symmetrical pattern. I turned away, and walked back down the alley. Why did no one come?

Mr Milner's top hat lay on the kerb, beside his car. The slashes to the tyres seemed incongruous. Was it not enough to murder a man without attacking the rubber on his wheels? It struck me as an act of rage, or madness.

I began to shake, and to look all around. The murderer might still be here, in another doorway, out of sight. I should have hailed that passing couple. An odd thought struck me. The murderer was in the car, crouched and waiting, ready to pounce. A small cry startled me. The sound was my own. *Someone come. Someone come soon.* I had seen men die from their wounds in hospital, from fever, but not this. Not in a peaceful spa town, in a shop doorway.

I dared to look into the car for the lurking murderer. There was no one. In the gutter, near the rear wheel, lay some small glinting item. I bobbed down. It was a cufflink. Evidence. What a marvel our minds are that we can feel and think in so many ways at once. The world threatened to spin away from me. I walked back up the alley. My and Meriel's bags were still where she had dropped them. I sat on mine.

I am not going to faint. Head between knees. What if he comes up behind me? I won't faint. I don't faint.

After what seemed an age, Meriel and the doorman appeared. I called to them. 'Stay clear of the doorway. The police will want to examine the scene.'

The doorman peered at Milner's body. Then the three of us walked to the road and waited.

45

A uniformed sergeant and police constable arrived first, striding into view like two creatures from the underworld, everything black, including their jackets with the night buttons. The constable was the younger of the two, pale-faced, clean-shaven and gangly. The older man wore a small neat moustache, and walked with his feet turned out. The sergeant strode into the alley. As we were giving our names and addresses to the constable, I heard the sound of hooves. A pony and trap came into view and drew to a halt. A portly figure, in top hat and tail coat, stepped onto the pavement.

'Evening, doctor.' The constable produced a flash-light, and led the doctor into the alley. I felt a sudden moment of panic. What if Milner had not been dead? Perhaps I had made a mistake. Immediate attention might have saved him.

Their slow, returning footsteps gave no sign of urgency.

The medical man's breath smelled of whisky. He took out a tiny notebook and pencil from an inside pocket. 'Can you tell me what time you saw the deceased, madam?'

I felt foolish at not having checked my watch. 'We stopped to sort out an umbrella,' I said lamely.

'It was about half past eleven,' Meriel supplied. 'Mr Milner was still warm. You said so, didn't you, Kate? Mrs Shackleton was a nurse. She checked for a pulse.'

The doctor jotted down the time.

Meriel let out a shuddering groan. 'I can't bear it. Poor man. I suppose the only consolation is that he saw a good play before he died.'

'Do you think she's in shock?' the doctor asked quietly.

I was grateful that he did not seem to notice I had begun to shake again. In as calm a voice as I could muster, I said, 'Probably.'

The sergeant commandeered the pony and trap, leaving the constable to guard the scene.

'Are you taking us home?' Meriel asked as he helped us into the trap.

The sergeant spoke to the driver: 'Raglan Street!'

'I live on St Clement's Road . . .' Meriel began.

'If it's all the same to you, ladies,' the sergeant said in a gentle voice, 'I'd like to take you to the station and give you a cup of tea.'

7

Curtain Up on the Case

'Shocking business for you ladies.' The elderly sergeant led us into a bleak room at the back of the police station. We sat on benches, at a table marked with cigarette burns and tea stains.

'You are shivering.' He placed an old army blanket around my shoulders.

Meriel squeezed my hand. 'Kate is the brave one. She stayed by the body.'

I envied Meriel in that moment. She seemed to have detached herself from what had happened, as though finding the body had become one more made up scene, an epilogue to her production.

The constable disappeared, returning with thick white cups of strong sweet tea. Shakily, I delved into my satchel for Gerald's old hip flask. How I wished Gerald could be here now.

I unscrewed the top of the flask. There was a decent amount of brandy – enough for a good splash in each of our cups. *Here's to you, Gerald, wherever you are. Lost in this world, or the next. Wouldn't it be wonderful if, one day, you just walked back into my life?*

The constable stayed in the room with us, saying in a friendly voice, 'Don't mind me.'

'We're not under arrest are we?' Meriel asked.

'Oh no, miss. It's just that statements will be required.'

We sipped our drinks and waited, listening to the loud tick of the big round clock on the wall. With infinite slowness, the hands of the clock moved to midnight. Was that all? It seemed indecent to want to be out of there. But how much could there be to state in our 'statements'? We would be unlikely to forget the horror of finding a body after just one night's sleep, or wakefulness.

Meriel leaned towards me, picking at a thread on her cape. 'This is horrible. It's like one of those German films where everything . . . oh you know.'

That glimmer of fear I had noticed earlier returned, perhaps a fear of having been close to the dead. Straight away, she began to take deep breaths. After a moment, she said, more to herself than to me, 'I made a good impression on Mr Wheatley.'

'You did.'

'He said to call him BW. Do you really think I made a good impression?'

'Meriel, for heaven's sake!' I closed my eyes, momentarily not having the strength to find the right words, unable to tell whether this was crassness or insecurity. At least analysing Meriel took my thoughts from my own reaction. She escapes into the theatre, I told myself, in the way an inebriate drowns in the bottle.

'Your face, Kate! I'm only trying to make conversation, to take our minds off things. Did I tell you he invited me to lunch tomorrow?'

She had. 'Yes.'

'He plans to do an Ibsen and asked me which one. What do you think to that?'

I was saved the need to answer by the sound of foot-steps, and voices in the corridor.

Our guarding sergeant snapped to attention as the door opened. 'Ladies.' The man was dressed in a good, dark suit, spotless shirt and dark-green tie. There was something familiar about him, about the eyes, hazel flecked with green. His light-coloured hair held a neat side parting and was cut short. Late-night stubble covered his chin. He looked a little tired.

'I'm Inspector Charles, of Scotland Yard.' He stepped forward and shook each of our hands in turn as we offered our names.

Everything about the moment felt unreal, as if it might dissolve and turn out to be as ephemeral as the drama played out on the stage only hours ago.

Meriel held onto his hand. 'Goodness, you must be the murder squad. You can't have appeared from London.'

He paused for a moment before he answered, as if deciding how much to say. 'I would have been on the night train to London now. It's not often I'm called North, but this will be my third investigation in Yorkshire recently. I hope it won't become a habit.'

He looked at me when he said this, and I realised he was the same man who had appeared on the scene at Bridgestead when I was working on behalf of Tabitha Braithwaite. That was my first professional case, just a few months ago. I had investigated the mysterious disappearance of Joshua Braithwaite, a millionaire mill owner, and Tabitha's much-loved father.

As I remembered, Inspector Charles had wanted me out of the way. I wondered afterwards whether he held me responsible for the local bobby being less than meticulous in securing the scene of crime.

The inspector nodded to the sergeant who hovered behind him. 'Sergeant, take Miss Jamieson's statement, please. Keep it short.' He then turned to me. 'Mrs Shackleton?'

'Yes.'

'If you'll come with me, please.'

I followed him into the corridor and to a room where a fire had been lit. He drew chairs near the fire. 'I'm sorry you were kept waiting.'

I felt too numb to respond. At this rate, the young, pale-faced constable who sat at a table by the wall, notebook at the ready, would have little to write.

'I appreciate that you kept the scene clear once you found the body. And thank you for spotting the cufflink. I had a case a few weeks ago where the fool of a village bobby and some female photographer marched all over the house. It's a miracle there was a scrap of evidence left.'

Oh he remembered me all right. My hackles rose. 'If you're referring to Bridgestead—,' I said, about to remind him of one or two points.

'But that was then, and this is now,' he said quickly.

It made me wonder whether he had thrown out the challenge to rouse me from my half-stupid state.

He picked up a small evidence bag and tipped a cufflink onto a sheet of paper. It was just over half an inch square, with a gold edge and a banded agate centre in white, black and brown. 'In good condition, no scratches, but some wear on the back.'

51

'It's quite distinctively marked,' I said. 'You think it might belong to the killer?' The cufflink was not expensive enough to be Mr Milner's. It was of a type that could be bought in any gentleman's outfitters, or a jewellery store at the lower end of the market.

'It's possible, and it may indicate a scuffle,' the inspector said. 'Is it familiar?'

I shook my head. It struck me that one only notices cufflinks if they are particularly flashy, or if you are in love with the man.

'Did you know Mr Milner before this evening?'

'No. I sat next to him for the first act of the play, and then moved to the rear stalls.'

He raised an eyebrow. 'Because?'

'I don't like to sit on the front row, and he was not an ideal theatregoer. His son was in the production. Mr Milner gave a running commentary.'

'What sort of commentary?'

When someone is a bore and their comments unwelcome, it is suprising how much one shuts out. But I could still hear some of Milner's words in my head.

'He was critical of his son's performance. He said that at Rodney's age, he was serving in South Africa.'

'Anything else?'

'Tonight was the last night. Mr Milner had seen the play several times. I'm afraid he rather put my back up, so I wasn't very sympathetic to the poor man. He said he hoped Rodney would not be treading the boards again anytime soon. That he was better at selling motor cars.'

The young constable eagerly scribbled this down. He was not sufficiently experienced to feign lack of interest.

I produced the programme from my bag and opened it at the page of Mr Milner's advertisement.

MILNER & SON'S MOTOR WORKS
(Established 1903)
Summerfield Avenue
Harrogate
\-
Sole District Agent
Austin   De Dion   Ford   Wolseley
Any make of car supplied
Official Repairers to Royal Automobile Club, etc.,
Agents A.A.
Tyres – Petrol – Accessories
Telegrams "Motor"   Telephone 417

The inspector took the programme. 'Do you mind if I keep this?'

'Please do.'

Inspector Charles turned to the cast list. 'This must be his son, Rodney Milner, playing Henry Mynor.'

'Yes. Rodney plays the up-and-coming businessman, the chap who gets the girl.'

There was something reassuring about the inspector's presence. He was thoughtful, unhurried as he looked at the names.

'Do you suspect one of the cast, or a theatre patron?' I asked.

He stretched his legs. 'It's far too soon,' he said gently, as though I had not asked a stupid question. 'One must keep an open mind. It's not theft. His wallet was not taken.'

'Oh,' I said rather stupidly. Mr Milner struck me as a man who would carry a wad of money.

He made a steeple of his hands. 'Mrs Shackleton, if Mr Milner was not at the theatre because of his son's less than scintillating stage performance, why was he there?'

The voice in my head said, Never speak ill of the dead. 'To sell cars in the bar afterwards? I'm not sure.' It seemed treacherous to damn Milner for a lecher as well as the worst kind of theatregoer. But it had to be said. 'He admired Lucy Wolfendale, the young leading lady. He offered to escort her home, but she joined her friends.'

Scratch, scratch went the constable's pencil.

'Go on.'

'Mr Milner struck me as a man who would persist. I felt sorry for Lucy and kept him talking. I was relieved when we were joined by Madam Geerts.'

The inspector interrupted me. 'Madam Geerts?'

The constable, busy at his notes, had pricked up his ears. He looked at me, expectantly. I know that the police are meant to keep information confidential, but this fellow looked a little too keen for my liking. Something made me hold back the fact that Madam Geerts, with the subtlety of a hungry shark, had clutched Milner's arm and whisked him away.

'She and her husband are in the play,' I said, in a voice that sounded to me over-prim. 'I left Mr Milner with Madam Geerts, and that was the last time I spoke to him.'

The inspector picked up on my insinuation immediately. It was the last time I had spoken to Mr Milner, but not the last time I saw him.

The inspector turned to the constable who had paused in his note-taking. 'That will be all. Call a cab will you?'

'Right, sir!'

When the constable had gone, the inspector gazed at me candidly. 'Mrs Shackleton, you are an observant woman

54

and your impressions will be valuable. It would be unfair to keep you here any longer after your ordeal. But would you be willing to give me a written statement tomorrow, regarding what took place after the performance?'

'Of course. Only I have no wish to embarrass people . . .'

'Like Madam Geerts?'

'Yes.' He did not miss a trick. A man to watch.

He sighed and said gently, 'If something is not relevant, believe me I won't waste valuable time on it. Please tell me now.'

Relieved that the constable had left the room, I took a breath and began. 'They went off together, Mr Milner and Madam Geerts. She first, he following a few moments later.' I felt myself blush in case he thought I had followed them, which I had not. 'Afterwards, I went to a dressing room, to collect my overnight bag that had been brought from the station Left Luggage. It's a bit of a maze backstage. I opened the wrong door, and saw Mr Milner and Madam Geerts. Fortunately they did not see me. They were too busy.'

'Go on.'

'I think the legal term is *in flagrante delicto*.'

I was pleased with that – so much better than saying they were at it.

He leaned forward. 'Might anyone else have come across them?'

At that moment, the constable opened the door. 'Transport's here, sir.'

The inspector escorted me into the street where the pony and trap waited. Meriel was already seated, and our bags in place.

'Mrs Shackleton, may I?' With great gentleness,

Inspector Charles took my arm, helping me into the trap.

A constable climbed into the vehicle with us. Perhaps we were considered important witnesses, in need of police protection.

8

Wee Willie Wolfendale

A single light burned in the ground floor flat at 29 St Clement's Road.

'Coming home under constabulary escort,' Meriel murmured. 'My blithering nuisance of a landlord is going to love this if he's looking out of his window.'

'Here you are, ladies. I'll wait while you're inside.' The constable jumped from the trap and took our bags before handing us down.

I suddenly remembered that I was supposed to be passing on a message.

'Meriel, Lucy Wolfendale asked me to tell her grandfather that she'd be staying with . . . I forget the name, one of the other actresses.'

'Alison?'

'That's it. I'm sure it would be better coming from you.'

'And I'm sure it wouldn't,' Meriel said emphatically.

'I've never met the man.' I felt exhausted and wanted more than anything to fall into bed.

On the ground floor, a window flew open, flooding the garden with light. A face appeared, under a Wee Willie Winkie nightcap.

Meriel groaned and dashed into the garden out of sight, saying 'You better give the old boy Lucy's message. I'll leave the door on the latch.'

She had already begun to walk round the garden, towards the back of the house.

'Meriel!' I pleaded.

She paused, keeping close to the wall, shaking her head. 'Lucy asked you to tell him because she knows what he's like with me. He's got very petty about the rent. I've told him I'll catch up. He only has to look at me and pounds, shillings and pence signs light up his eyes.'

The face at the window took on a voice and called, 'Lucy? Is that you?'

My mind had gone blank. 'I've forgotten his name.'

'Same as Lucy. Wolfendale. Call him Captain, give him a salute and he'll eat out of your hand.'

The old man watched as I mounted the front steps. Without waiting for me to knock, he opened the door. At the same moment, the driver gee-upped his pony which trotted away, the regular clip-clop of hooves breaking the silence of the night.

There was no light in the hall but a pale glow came from the flat. The elderly gent who peered at me had discarded his nightcap. He wore a shabby army great-coat over striped pyjamas and a pair of ancient brown leather slippers. He was in his seventies, with a short, bulky figure but upright and military in his bearing, and with a twirling moustache. He brushed a hand over his totally bald pate.

In a light-hearted tone I did not feel, I said, 'I'm so sorry to disturb you, Captain Wolfendale. Message from the front line for HQ. Lucy is bivouacking at her

58

friend Alison's this evening. I promised to remind you.'

'It's one in the morning! Why is she sending me a message at this hour?'

We had been asked by the police to say nothing about the murder. I floundered for a reply. 'I apologise for the lateness of the hour. I was at the play earlier this evening and I stayed on to help. There's a touring company coming in tomorrow. You don't notice the time when you're striking camp.'

I like to think that the military jargon impressed. He tilted his head to one side. 'And you are, madam?'

Not having rank and number put me at a disadvantage. 'I'm Mrs Shackleton.'

'Lucy asked you to come here?'

'I'm staying with Miss Jamieson downstairs, just for this evening.'

'Shackleton you say?'

'Yes.'

'Then I have something for you. Please step inside.'

What could he possibly have for me, I wondered. As I entered his flat, with some trepidation, the Pekinese on the floor above began to bark.

The captain looked about for a moment, as if trying to recall where he had put the something he wanted to give me. Then he picked up an envelope from the side-board. 'Took delivery hours ago. Telegram. Nearly turned the boy away. Didn't recognise the name.'

'Thank you.'

It would be Sykes's reply. *Please let me not have made a mistake writing down the address of the unfortunate Mrs deVries.* Sykes would think himself too clever by half if he had to put me right on that. 'Do you mind if I read this straight away?'

'Would you like to sit down?' he asked courteously. 'Sit under the lamp.' He was solicitous. For so many, telegrams and bad news went hand in hand.

'Thank you.'

He moved a few feet off, but hovered expectantly, as though I might suddenly collapse from shock and be in need of reviving. Sykes's message was brief: 'Address correct.'

So the pathetic gentlewoman pawning her mother's diamond ring had given a false address. Perhaps a false name, too. Why?

'Not bad news I hope?' He spoke with a slight rasp, as though recovering from a sore throat.

'No, thank you, Captain. I'll leave you in peace.'

Opening a sideboard drawer, he said, 'Don't go stumbling about outside looking for Miss Jamieson's entrance. Have a torch here. I'll show you the back stairs that lead to her quarters.' He managed to make Meriel's quarters sound disreputable. She would like that.

He shone our way into the dark hall. 'Need to change the gas mantle in the hall here.'

'They don't last two minutes these days,' I agreed.

He lit me along the passage. 'You are not theatrical then?'

'No. I took the photographs for the play.'

'Of course you did. I remember Lucy telling me about you. Jolly good photographs. Slipped into the back of the theatre on Wednesday evening. Lucy took a good part, but so did they all.' He lowered his voice. 'Only, I shan't let the lower rooms to a theatrical again. Nothing personal, you understand, but horses for courses and all that.' He pushed open the door at the end of the hall. 'These back stairs lead to Miss Jamieson's quarters. I'll wait till you are through the bottom door, just to make sure she hasn't bolted it and locked you out.'

Bag in hand I stepped onto the top step. He had not offered to part with his torch but shone a light.

I turned. 'Captain Wolfendale, were you in the Great War?'

Why do I always have to do it? He was a captain, that's why. Same rank as Gerald. Perhaps they had met.

Why do I expect the serendipity of stumbling into someone who will say, Ah yes, Captain Gerald Shackleton, fine fellow, knew him well.

'Sadly not,' said Captain Wolfendale. 'South Africa, that was my last show, and what a show it was.'

'Then you're the second person this evening I've talked to who fought there.'

'Indeed?' he said in a non-committal voice that did not invite further comment.

But in spite of his dismissive tone, I said, 'I sat next to Mr Milner at the theatre.'

Something clicked in my tired brain. When I had looked through the Wolfendales' window earlier, the captain was playing a board game. His opponent had reddish-blond hair, just like Lawrence Milner.

'You'll know him,' I persisted.

'Ah Milner,' the captain said, 'the motoring man. Yes, he was in South Africa. Of course, that's an old war now. People have forgotten all about it.'

'Not everyone has,' I said, thinking of my aunt's old colonel chum who spoke of little else.

'We had to go in there. They denied Englishmen the vote, you see. Had to have South Africa in the Empire,

61

under the rule of law. Otherwise it would have been a free-for-all. Boers, and don't get me wrong, there's good and bad, but they're bible-thumping farmers. You couldn't trust them to manage gold mines and diamonds.'

It was far too late to be having a conversation at the head of the back stairs in the small hours, but it intrigued me that he had no words about Milner, only a general comment on the war — a war that was not forgotten by any means.

'Did you and Mr Milner serve together?' I asked.

'I was all over the show. Started out in '99, supposed to be relieving Kimberley, but that took longer than any of us expected. Brother Boer was a surprising kind of enemy. Bit of a blighter. He'd run up a white flag, and when you got near, pop!'

'Goodnight then, Captain.' I picked my way down the dim narrow staircase. Perhaps it had not been Milner whom I had seen with Captain Wolfendale earlier in the day. But if my guess was correct and they were old comrades, then Milner's death would come as a great shock to the old man.

9

Hard-Bitten

'Hard-bitten Boer farmers with their ancient theology and their inconveniently modern rifles.' —*Arthur Conan Doyle*

South Africa, November, 1899

Corporal Lawrence Milner stuck his head out of the carriage window, sick of this bloody heat, sick of being packed like a sardine. The Doncaster dimwits played cards for farthings. The skeleton from Skipton squeezed his canteen for the last drop of water. Every window on the train was open, to suck in a breath of air. A whole trainload of hot, sweaty blokes, trying to breathe.

What a foul bloody war to be dragged into. Fighting to teach Kruger a lesson. Fighting so that the English in the Transvaal could have a vote. My arse. Milner had never voted in his life, and his father neither. No one had ever said to Milner, here's a vote, lad. If they had, he'd have told them what to do with it. Clear as the nose on your face what it was about. Glory of the British Empire? Glory of the diamond mines. Glory of the gold mines. Make you laugh, if you didn't think the next bullet might have your name on it.

At least Milner was on the train, not like the poor

sods marching on from Belmont and Graspan towards Kimberley.

November. In England there'd be fog, drizzle, grey skies. Here it was supposed to be spring. Upside bloody down, this country. Dust clouds rose from the flat land. Then sodding mountains and more sodding mountains. It was the White Man's burden to simmer in cauldrons for the glory of the Empire. Boer bastards in there waiting to pounce, and the top brass too bloody thick to get it. Brother Boer fights dirty. Shoots and melts away. So much for diamonds, so much for gold. Not a sniff. All Milner got for his pains was dust up his snout and a tongue the size of an ox's. The quicker they gave the Boers it in the neck, the sooner he'd get round to making some money.

The train slowed. Milner rolled a cig. The train screeched to a halt. Cigarette paper stuck to his dry lips. Now he could hear the captain and his arse-licking batman in the next carriage. Milner leaned out to listen. Word was the Boers had dynamited the railway bridge that crossed the Modder River. Milner heard the poncy voice, Captain Wolfendale, saying to his sergeant, 'What do you see out there?'

Milner couldn't help but laugh. The idle bugger of a captain didn't bother to stir to look out of the window. Oh no, his batman could do that for him, when he'd finished licking his arse.

Sergeant Lampton, piping up, doffing his cap with every word. 'Nothing much beyond the settlement. Open land, the veld as they call it. Dusty . . .'

Milner guessed the captain had begun to stir his gin-soaked carcass.

'No welcome party?'

'Not yet, sir.'

'They must have heard the bloody train.'

'Got your dress jacket here, sir.'

Why don't you genuflect, Milner thought. Stroke his cock for him.

'And here's your belt, cap, gaiters.'

'God it's hot.'

'Wet flannel, sir.'

A few minutes later, Milner watched the pair of them step from the train. The sergeant got out first, holding the door, of course. Milner couldn't think of anything worse than to toady to an officer. Captain Wolfendale and Sergeant Lampton were a few feet away. Milner instinctively drew back, so as to earwig without drawing attention to himself. It irked him that the two could now see much more than he could.

A tame ostrich rose up from the acacia shrub and stepped forward as if to greet the new arrivals. 'Come a bit closer and I'll have you on a plate tonight,' Milner muttered. The creature dipped its small neat head from side to side, casting a beady eye over the situation, like a pub landlord watching trouble brew.

All the way down the train, soldiers looked out from carriage windows. It was the waiting that drove you mad.

The captain turned and called out in that jolly wanting-to-be-liked voice, that didn't fool Milner. 'Sorry, men. War should come supplied with a comfortable waiting room, but it never does.'

The drips obliged him by laughing at his little joke. Not Milner.

Milner strained to hear. 'I'll order them off now, sir,' Sergeant Lampton said quietly.

The captain lowered his voice. 'Let the blighters wait. They'll be kicking up dust soon enough.'

So much for which of them was the bigger bastard, Milner thought. He could see why Wolfy wanted to keep them on the train. A small welcoming party hurried across the bridge, led by a major.

The major saluted sharply. 'Captain Wolfendale?'

'The same.'

'Pleased to have you here, sir.'

When the captain had gone, Lampton turned back to the train and gave the order to disembark.

By nightfall, tents were erected, row on row. Men queued for their rations of bully beef, hard biscuit and hot sweet tea. A thunderstorm rolled out a welcome, smacking the tents with sharp pellets of tepid rain.

The sergeant turned his dusty face to the African heavens and ran his tongue over his lips to catch rain drops.

In his tent, the captain wrote his diary. *Men keen to get on with the show.* Through the walls of the tent floated the disembodied voices of the men who'd been first in the queue for food and now had time on their hands. They were singing filthy ditties, arguing the toss as they played dice. A wisp of blue smoke from the camp fire wafted through the tent flap. They were burning acacia bushes and eucalyptus.

A loud argument had blown up, over nothing as usual. A private from Blackburn wanted to lasso the ostrich and bring it along as a mascot. His mate disagreed. The ostrich was definitely a Boer spy, he said.

Sergeant Lampton put his head around the tent flap. 'Everything all right, sir?'

'Shut them up,' the captain ordered. 'Make an example of them.'

The sergeant hesitated.

'Just do it. And then look into what I asked you.'

'Yes, Captain.'

The sergeant took a deep breath, let the tent flap fall behind him. He shut up one private with a punch to his jaw and his mate with a blow to the ribs. 'You're disturbing our captain.'

The men fell silent.

A thin young African lad, wide-eyed and anxious, approached the sergeant. 'Message for Sergeant Lam.'

The sergeant drew him to one side, out of hearing of the men. 'What's the message?'

'For Captain Wolf, a room.'

When the lad did not move, Sergeant Lampton gave him a coin. 'Go!'

'Thank you, baas.'

Sergeant Lampton went back to the captain. 'It's fixed up, sir.'

The captain nodded. He pulled on his jacket.

Sergeant Lampton watched him go, marching towards what passed for a hotel where a Kaffir woman would be waiting. It had always been the same. Gin. The most comfortable room. A woman. In that order.

Mule carts would transport bell tents, blankets, big guns and cooking pots. Each African mule driver carried a concertina. Sergeant Lampton listened to them at night, playing and singing. He imitated their tunes on his mouth organ. It gave him the odd notion that the mules had an ear for music and would serve willingly.

At four o'clock on a muggy, misty morning, under

marching orders, men stoked the fire with acacia brush. Smoke would mislead enemy scouts into thinking that the camp stayed solid, stayed put. A scouting party gave the all-clear. Men would march alongside the railway line carrying rifles, food and ammunition. The train would come back with reinforcements, heavy guns, and engineers who would hop on and off, repairing the line. They would repair the dynamited bridge.

Long before Lord Methuen gave his pep talk – British pluck, British surprise, British Empire – word had passed through the lines that they would be heading for Kimberley.

The colonel told the major. The lieutenant told Captain Wolfendale. Captain Wolfendale told Sergeant Lampton. Sergeant Lampton told Corporal Milner.

'I knew it,' Milner said.

Kimberley had the deepest diamond mine in the world. Its owners scoffed toast and marmalade from gold plates and supped ale from gold tankards. But the Boers had Kimberley under siege.

Captain Wolfendale was ready for the off.

The stationmaster had said that a few Boers were burrowed into the river mud like water rats. Soon see them off. *A scout said six thousand? Six hundred more like.*

Sergeant Lampton despaired of his captain. 'You'll be a sitting duck, Captain, all that gleam and polish. Let me . . .'

The sergeant scooped mud from the river, to take the shine off his captain's buttons, the sparkle from his stars and buckles. The captain frowned. He liked to be pristine.

Soon only the steady, monotonous tramp of thousands of boots could be heard, scudding through stubbly grass and over small rocks. The thickhead bird that started out with them, *hui hui*, had taken flight.

It must have been a tale, about the enemy digging in the mud. What fool would hide in a muddy trench? If the Boers were anywhere, they would be in the hills. Scouts had gone ahead and would signal back when the sun rose and the heliograph messaging could be put to use.

Captain Wolfendale had entered that state of pretending, that he is riding along an English country lane, easy enough with the poplars and the river to his right. And now his horse needs rest in the shade of an English oak. It is ninety degrees in the shade. In the absence of an English oak, the captain halts the column by the foot of a kopje. The sergeant spreads his ground-sheet. The captain sits down, takes a swig of water, pulls a clean hanky from his pocket.

It was when the riders led the horses to water that the firing began. At first it was not clear where the shots came from. A hail of bullets ripped the air. The captain jumped to his feet. A bullet sent him staggering. The sergeant leapt at him, shoved him to the ground shielding him with his body.

A dark patch stained the captain's trouser leg and the shoulder of his jacket. The sergeant saw both stains. One, at least, must be blood. 'Stay down!' The sergeant gave the order now. 'Lie flat.' The sergeant squashed himself into the ground, rifle at the ready, looking for a target.

An Irish corporal made a sudden dash for the river, his horse as cover. Both horse and man fell. Not only was the Boer invisible on the mountains, armed with Mausers that shot at a range of a mile, he was invisible by the river bank.

With no rocks, no sandbags, no wagons for cover, the soldiers were living, breathing target practice, sitting ducks, only they were not sitting but lying flat, some hiding under their blankets.

With the butt of his rifle, his hands, his nails, the sergeant began to dig a dip. The ground was sandy here. If they could survive till nightfall, hold on until dark . . . He urged the captain into the hollow, helping him, so that for a moment they looked like two boys playing on a beach. The shelter was poor but if the captain lies still, the sergeant told him, he may escape another more deadly bullet.

Then the sergeant crawled on his belly away from the river. He passed crafty Corporal Milner, sheltering between the carcass of a dead horse and the body of a fallen comrade.

Bullets bounced from the ground like hailstones. One bullet skimmed Lampton's hair as he edged his way down a dip in the terrain. Smoke and dust dimmed his sight. His throat burned. He blinked and cringed for what he believed would be the last time. It was not supposed to end like this. He should have made NCO, earned a few more bob, respect, not doing the captain's bidding thirty hours out of every twenty-four. A twisted length of railway line crashed through the air and landed by his side. Invisible Brother Boer was north, south and east, but there was a lull to the west.

The sergeant touched the twisted metal of the railway line, for luck.

Shouldn't have left the captain. Must get back to the captain.

Ahead, a young face looked at him, popping up from the camouflage of a trench. For a moment, the young

Boer and the sergeant stared at each other in surprise. Split seconds, rather than the long minutes it felt like.

The sergeant's Lee-Metford has a ten-round firing capability, but the British Army, in its wisdom, has fitted a plate so the soldiers don't go mad and discharge ten rounds at once. Sergeant Lampton can fire one bullet at a time. Is it loaded or not? He can't remember. The sergeant caresses his rifle, and presses the trigger. A moment later he is diving into the trench beside the dead Boer.

Under cover of darkness, he dared to come crawling out again. Miraculously, a shocked horse let him lead it to be tethered. The sliver of a moon obliged, refusing to be more than candlelight in the black sky.

Then the moon did the favour of hiding. Stooping low, the sergeant found his captain. Shoulders tearing, arms pulled to breaking, Lampton carried Wolfendale to the horse and helped him on.

West. The earlier racket and the sudden quiet made him hope that the Boer line gave way there. They travelled on through the early dawn, to where the smell of a burned-out camp fire told Lampton he was near some stopping place. Boer or British, who could tell? 'Rest here,' he said.

But the captain had a second wind. 'On we go.'

The sergeant obeyed. The captain had a sixth sense for comfort, and he was right. There was a farmhouse on the horizon.

The Tommy on the gate said, 'We broke through. Brother Boer's done his vanishing trick.' He helped the sergeant get the captain into the farmhouse. Sergeant Lampton willed himself to stay upright. 'Who's your officer in charge?' he asked.

'Major got it in the neck, sarge.'

So the captain was the highest ranking officer. Two highlanders lifted the captain onto the table. The back of the men's legs bore ugly blisters from lying face down under a burning sun. They held the captain steady while Sergeant Lampton dislodged the bullet from the captain's thigh.

When the general arrived, he shook the captain's hand. 'Brave man for fighting your way through. You'll be mentioned for this.'

The captain smiled. 'Saw a weakness in the enemy's flank, sir. Led the charge through, scattered Boer to the winds.'

'Don't just stand there, sergeant,' the general barked. 'Make yourself useful. Find some food.'

The sergeant waited, half expecting some small acknowledgement from his captain. None came.

10

Closet Drama

Closet drama: a play intended only for reading aloud

Too tired to sleep, I lay on Meriel's narrow bed. The thin mattress was worn through to the springs. The discomfort took me back to my VAD days, when we took roughing it for granted much of the time.

Across the room, Meriel slept soundly on a chaise longue, snoring gently.

A weakness of mine is that people intrigue me, especially those with a story to tell. Meriel was just such a one. We met at the fancy-dress party held by a mutual friend. Our host had allocated characters. On arrival at the party, we were instructed to find our mate. I was Pierrot, the clown, dressed in a rather dull loose white tunic with a ruff at the neck and a boater perched on my head. It did not take long to find Pierrette, the lovable French pantomime figure. Meriel was elegantly dressed in ballet skirt, brightly coloured peasant waistcoat and cocked hat. We drank a little too much of some homemade concoction. Meriel held me in thrall as we sat on the stairs.

She was brought up in concert halls and theatres, travelling with her mother, an opera singer. She picked up several languages and was taught to play the violin and other instruments by various members of the orchestra. The violin was her first love and what she believed she excelled in. Her mother gave up singing when she re-married in Switzerland, just before the Great War. Her step-father was under the impression that the marriage gave him rights to Meriel too. She spent less and less time in their apartment and gravitated towards a Russian émigré theatre group. She fetched and carried, played walk-on parts or lying still parts as a corpse. She learned the ways of actors and directors. Unable to find work in an orchestra, she hovered on the edge of the theatre, sewing costumes, finding props, acting as prompt and understudy, writing up rehearsal schedules, and selling tickets. She made a living when and where she could.

Her story impressed me, hinting at far greater hardships. I felt I understood why she escaped into the theatre, and preferred it to real life. When she asked me would I take photographs for her planned production, I said yes. We clinked glasses and I gave her my address. That would teach me not to drink unidentified liquor in large quantities.

So it was thanks to a fancy-dress party that here I was exhausted, still seeing Mr Milner's face when I closed my eyes. If I were at home, I would get up and go downstairs. But Meriel's room was as far downstairs as you could go without visiting the sewers, or Hades. At least until dawn, there was nowhere else to go.

I guessed the time to be about three in the morning. Saturday. Soon the world would be stirring to life.

At least I was not the only one who could not sleep. Footsteps sounded on the floor above, the captain on the march.

Well, if sleep would not come, there was something else I might do. Inspector Charles had asked for a statement. He should have one. If, without too much noise, I could light the candle from the mantelpiece, set it on the table, and take my writing case from the bag, then I could get on with it.

Do it now, I told myself. Hand it in tomorrow on the way to the railway station, and get home in time to make a couple more visits for Mr Moony. The poor man had already given me his cheque, and he deserved priority.

Enough moonlight came through the curtains for me to see the candle, and matches. Fortunately, Meriel had her back to me. She slept soundly as I took out my writing case. Meriel's theatre programme lay on the table. I used it as a crib, to remind myself of the names of the cast.

Mrs Kate Shackleton, Statement, Saturday, 26 August, 1922

I met Miss Jamieson through a mutual friend last December. About three months ago, she asked if I would do her the favour of taking photographs of the cast of *Anna of the Five Towns*. She then invited me to see the play.

At last night's performance, I sat in the front stalls, next to Mr Burrington Wheatley, a theatre producer from Manchester. Mr Milner arrived about ten minutes into the performance. He took the empty seat on my left. After the interval, I moved to the rear stalls, as did Mr Wheatley. Mr Milner had been rather talkative during the first act.

During and after the performance, Mr Milner expressed admiration for the leading lady, Lucy Wolfendale.

In the theatre bar, Mr Wheatley spoke to Miss Jamieson. He then left for his hotel, The Grand. Miss Jamieson was very much engaged, moving from group to group in the bar, accepting congratulations.

Knowing that I was staying the night with Miss Jamieson, Lucy Wolfendale asked me to remind her grandfather (Miss Jamieson's landlord, Captain Wolfendale) that she would be spending the night with her friend, Alison Hart. (Alison played the part of Beatrice Sutton in the drama.) While Lucy and I were talking, Mr Milner approached and in a rather insistent way said he would give Miss Wolfendale a lift home. She said that she was not ready to go home. It was apparent from her manner that his attentions were most unwelcome. She went back to be with her young friends: Rodney Milner, Alison Hart and Dylan Ashton. They surrounded her in a protective manner and, as far as I am aware, remained together, and left together, along with another young man whose name I do not know.

Out of sympathy for Lucy, and because I thought Mr Milner was being a pest to her, I kept him talking. I got the impression of a vain man, happy to boast about his success. Mr Milner told me that as a young man he joined the police force in South Africa, and signed on with the army at the outbreak of the Boer War. He rose to corporal. Demobbed at the end of the war, he returned to England, to London. He experienced hardship at first, until an old comrade (unnamed) helped him. He came to Harrogate, where he started his business.

We talked until Madam Geerts (she played the alderman's wife) drew Mr Milner away.

At various times, members of the cast went to collect their property from the dressing rooms, which had to be left clear for the next day. I also went to a dressing room, for my overnight bag.

Unfamiliar with the backstage area, I looked in at the wrong door and saw Madam Geerts and Mr Milner in a compromising and intimate situation. Unseen, I closed the door. M. Geerts was coming along the corridor. I felt sorry for him and tried to divert his attention by asking him to help me find my bag. He did so but did not walk back with me to the bar. It is highly likely that M. Geerts interrupted his wife and Mr Milner.

Miss Jamieson and I were, I believe, the last guests to leave the theatre. We left by the stage door at about 11.30 p.m.

I paused. What could I write here? 'The rest you know.' It seemed inadequate. If the inspector hoped for an account of who left the theatre when, he would be disappointed.

It began to rain as we left the theatre. In the stage door alley, I stepped into a shop doorway and there saw Mr Milner, a knife in his chest. Although I could see that he was dead, I felt for a pulse on his neck. Miss Jamieson went back to the theatre for help. Mr Milner's motor was parked on the road at the bottom of the alley, tyres slashed. I noticed a cufflink in the gutter.

Kate Shackleton

By the time I had finished writing, the sun had risen. My intention was to dress and hurry home. But tiredness hit me. I dropped back into bed, like a stone hitting bottom. The faces that floated before my eyes as I fell asleep were Mr Milner's, and Captain Wolfendale's. They were younger, and wore military caps.

11

Noises Off

Noises off: the sound effects needed in a production

Waking suddenly, I had no idea where I was. A dull, leaden sound reverberated in my skull. Then it came back to me. I was in Meriel Jamieson's flat on St Clement's Road, Harrogate. Light found its way through the low cellar window. The thudding was someone walking to and fro in the room above.

Had Harrogate woken to the knowledge that a murder had been committed in her genteel town centre? Poor Rodney Milner. His father might have been a boorish bully, a lecher and a show-off, but it was a terrible end – to be found in a shop doorway with a knife through the heart.

Outside, a street-seller wheeled his barrow across the cobbles, calling out his wares in a jumble of consonants I could not decipher. Bed springs creaked as I moved. The thin check curtains remained closed but I could see well enough. A cobalt-blue jug stood on the window sill, filled with wilting marigolds. Meriel had made an effort to turn this sad room, with its damp patches, into a cheerful refuge. The coconut mats formed stepping stones from the door to the chair by the stove. A crocheted blanket now covered the chaise longue.

The stove had been poked into life. A battered kettle slowly gathered steam. Plates had been set to warm.

As I swung out of bed, the memory of last night's events slowed my movements. I shook off those thoughts. Soon I would get back to Leeds and visit the next person on Mr Moony's list, a Mrs Taylor in Roundhay who had pawned a watch chain.

A note lay on the table.

Gone to buy eggs — M.

A sliver of Sunlight soap sat on the draining board, along with Meriel's damp, well-worn towel. She must have washed and dressed very quietly. The shallow sink, with its single cold tap, was chipped and pock-marked, but spotlessly clean. I washed quickly, and used the dry corners of the towel.

I had not unpacked last night. My fawn linen skirt came from the bag crumpled, but it would have to do. At least the cream blouse did not crease so easily and if today proved as warm as yesterday I would not need the costume jacket.

I combed my hair, peering into the cracked mirror on the window sill, and pinched my cheeks which were paler than usual. Next to the dresser stood a tea chest, its lid half off, piled with skirts and blouses. So she kept her clothes in a tea chest. That would explain her faint whiff of Darjeeling. Another thought began to form, but was banished by loud knocking.

At first I did not know where the sudden pounding came from. Then a shadow darkened the window. I put on my shoes without fastening them and clomped across to the door, turning the knob.

A hefty policeman glared at me. 'Miss Jamieson?'

My heart thumped. Policemen do not batter the door on a Saturday morning at eight o'clock to tell you something to your advantage. Had there been an arrest?

'No, constable. Miss Jamieson is not here.'

'And you are?' the constable asked, eyes narrowing.

'Mrs Shackleton.'

Was Meriel under suspicion? She, along with everyone else from the production, had disappeared for a while towards the end of the evening to gather belongings. Could Meriel be the killer? No. She would have no motive. She would have steered me away from the alley so as not to see the body. Wouldn't she?

The constable's voice became stern. 'Were you in the little park half an hour ago?'

His manner alarmed me. 'No.'

The constable gave me a hard look. 'Municipal flowers are for the enjoyment of the townspeople of Harrogate, not for personal use or gratification, not to be picked at will. Please advise Miss Jamieson she is required to report to the police station.'

I had all on not to burst out laughing, probably from relief that his visit was not connected with the murder. Harrogate municipal life must continue its even course whatever disruptions happen. If someone had the temerity to interfere with flowers, naturally the full weight of the law must be drawn down.

He was not the cream of the constabulary crop, not selected for the tricky task of helping investigate homicide.

I had a sudden mental picture of Meriel, plucking blooms. Like some mad lawyer for the defence, I fetched the vase of wilting marigolds from the table.

81

'These certainly weren't picked within the last half hour.'

Perhaps he was not so dim. Quick as a flash, he said, 'No. Them's some she plucked earlier on. It's not the first time she's been spotted.'

Poor Meriel. After all her hard work on the play, someone should have presented her with a bouquet. I could have kicked myself for not thinking of it.

'I'm sure there must have been some mistake.'

'Ah,' he said slowly, as though having caught me out. 'Then where is Miss Jamieson?'

This was tricky. She's behind you, I could have said, because at that moment she appeared at the top of the steps that led to the basement. She carried a shopping basket, its contents covered with a small white square of cloth on top of which lay a bunch of Belladonna lilies, the soft pink flowers wafting their delightful scent around the waiting policeman.

'Miss Jamieson is . . .'

Meriel is quick on the uptake. I expect one would need to be in order to mount plays, direct actors and produce miracles of drama while living out of a tea chest.

'In the bathroom,' she mouthed, jerking her thumb to indicate she would enter the house through the front door. She disappeared silently.

'She is in the bathroom.'

'The bathroom?' The constable's voice expressed incredulity. He glared beyond me into the poor room, his look betraying disbelief that the occupant of such a dingy cellar could lay claim to the possession of a bathroom.

'Please step inside, Constable. I'll fetch her.'

He trod cautiously into the room, as though expecting a trap, removing his helmet and holding it before his chest like a shield. I picked up Meriel's note from the table and slid it into my pocket.

This drew a suspicious glance. 'Constable, if you are going back to the station, would you oblige me by giving this envelope to Inspector Charles of Scotland Yard?'

I handed him my statement.

In an instant, his manner changed from near bullying to obsequious. 'Well, yes, madam, of course.'

As he tucked the statement into his tunic, I snatched the well-worn towel from the sink. I hurried through the inner door and up the dark stairs to the ground floor. Meriel stood there, as if undecided whether to stay put or continue up to the next floor and disappear into the bathroom. She set down the basket.

I handed her the towel, saying, 'Wind this round your head.'

'Oh well done!' She grabbed the towel and twisted it around her hair.

Kicking off her shoes, she whispered, 'Did someone spot me taking the milk?'

'Not the milk.'

'The eggs then?'

'Not the eggs.'

'Well then for heaven's sake . . .'

'You were seen picking flowers.'

'How bloody petty. Honestly you'd think they'd have better things to do. The flowers are going to die. I might as well have a bit of enjoyment out of them.' She led the way down the stairs, muttering, 'I don't have time to stroll the parks, sniffing and admiring flora. I'm a busy woman. If I'm to have any enjoyment at the ratepayers' expense . . .'

'Shh. He's not deaf!' I hissed, surprised that such a theatrical doyen did not have a better sense of stage whispering.

More loudly, she said, 'Can't a girl wash her hair these days?'

Entering her room, she beamed at the constable. 'Good morning, officer.'

He stepped back from her tea chest as though he had burned his fingers. 'Good morning, miss.' His eyes narrowed with suspicion.

Meriel rubbed her hair.

For a moment I thought he would snatch the towel and feel her hair. His thoughts raced so fast that his eyelids twitched. Was he considering that females of his acquaintance usually washed their hair on a Friday night?

'I'm Meriel Jamieson. This is an old friend, Mrs Shackleton, who kindly came over yesterday to see the last night of my play, *Anna of the Five Towns*. Did you get to see it yourself, officer?'

'I did not see the play, but I saw the posters.' The fog of suspicion began to clear from his broad face. A theatrical female could not be expected to wash her hair to the same timetable as other women. 'A lady made a complaint regarding having seen an individual answering your description stealing flowers in Westerly Park this morning.'

Meriel sighed, rubbing her hair beneath the towel. 'I'm afraid I'm not very remarkable. She must have mistaken me for someone else.'

The kettle began to boil. The constable considered Meriel's offer to join us in a cup of tea.

I was nearest the back stairs, and conscious of a sound behind the inner door. Someone was listening.

'The kettle's nearly boiled,' Meriel said.

Nearly was not good enough. The constable snatched his helmet, and left.

Only when the outer door closed behind the constable did there come a gentle tapping on the inner door. The captain stood in the gloom of the servants' passage. He seemed smaller than the evening before. 'Is everything all right, ladies?'

Meriel unwound the towel from her hair. 'Come in, Captain.'

'What did the constable want? I couldn't catch his words. Hearing not what it was, you know.'

Meriel ran her fingers through her hair. 'He wanted to know had I witnessed a person stealing flowers.'

'Stealing flour?'

'No, flowers, flowers that grow.'

'And had you?'

'Certainly not or I would have reported it at once.' Meriel reached for a comb.

The captain shook his head. With a great effort he said, 'Flowers, fuss and nonsense about flowers. Haven't the constabulary anything better to do? I thought something must have happened to Lucy.'

Meriel paused in her hair combing. 'Is anything wrong, Captain?'

'No, no. Nothing wrong.'

He turned to go. On the first step he seemed to stumble, then regained his balance.

Meriel's eyes widened. She pointed to the top of the stairs. 'The basket!' she mouthed. 'I left it in the hall.'

I nodded that I would get it, and turned to follow the

captain up the steep stairs. He moved painfully slowly, his hand on the wall for balance. At the top he stepped into the hall but did not appear to be in a hurry to go back to his own flat. He turned, and looked at me. Did he wonder why I had shadowed him up the stairs? I picked up the basket, flicking the white cloth over the flowers.

Raising a shaky hand, as if to reach out to me, he said, 'Before you leave, Mrs Shackleton, would you do me the favour of calling in for a confidential word?'

I hesitated, unsure what he could want to talk to me about.

'Just between us. Nothing to do with Miss Jamieson . . .' He nodded towards Meriel's room. 'Private matter, if you don't mind.'

I slid the basket handle along my arm, carefully, remembering that it contained stolen eggs and milk as well as the flowers. 'Yes, Captain. I shall come up after breakfast.' I picked up the shoes that Meriel had kicked off.

And of course my thought was still that the captain would have something private to impart to me. Some news of Gerald. Although I knew that to be ridiculous.

He walked back to his own door slowly, like a man with a long way to go before nightfall.

I carried the basket and shoes downstairs, also moving slowly as though his creeping pace had infected my movements.

Meriel stood over a cast-iron frying pan of spluttering fat. I placed the basket on a chair and handed her the duck eggs.

She cracked the first directly into the pan. 'Isn't it huge? Shall we share?'

'Yes. Will you scramble it?'

'I will. Drop of milk, I think. Will you pour?'

I retrieved the milk and poured a drop into the pan, listening to it sizzle as Meriel stirred.

'Thanks for dealing with our local bobby, Kate. It would have been awkward to explain myself before the bench just as I have my great opportunity with Mr Wheatley. You saved my bacon.'

'There was no need to go out stealing, Meriel! We could have gone out for breakfast. I would have bought you a bunch of flowers.'

'All too, too bourgeois,' Meriel said, with a wave of her hand. 'You are my guest. You must have a good breakfast. I'm honest as a rule, but all my ready cash was eaten up by the production. The theatre's a glutton, Kate. It will swallow my heart one of these days.'

I set plates and cutlery on the table. The faded marigolds bowed their dying heads. I changed the water in the vase and replaced the marigolds with fragrant Belladonna lilies, courtesy of Harrogate Corporation.

'You know BW has invited me for lunch today?' With a look of total concentration, Meriel shared the scrambled duck egg between our two plates.

'You did mention it last night. Twice.'

Meriel pulled a face. 'I could say something in my defence, but you won't want to know.'

'What? What could you say?'

'That life is short and art is long. I must make my mark in the theatre, and if that means being a little, well, ruthless, I suppose, that . . .'

'You were totally insensitive. And now you've been out thieving and I have covered for you. More fool me. It is not something I should do, given my occupation.'

'Oh yes. I'd forgotten about your sleuthing. But, Kate, we had to have *something* for breakfast. I don't want to arrive at the Grand Hotel famished. You behave very oddly if you're hungry, don't you think?'

What am I doing here? I asked myself, as I tucked into the scrambled duck egg and listened to Meriel as she gave me tips about how you shouldn't wash a frying pan but wipe it round with a piece of newspaper.

Her conversation turned to famous people she had met. Wiping her bread round the plate, she said, 'Did I tell you that I once met George Bernard Shaw?'

'No.'

'It was at a buffet supper, and I hoped to talk to him. He could have been helpful in my career. But I couldn't stop thinking about food. I was so hungry that day. He saw me stuffing a cooked chicken into my bag. I wanted to die! He's a vegetarian you know.' She sighed at the lost opportunity. 'He did explain Frederick Alexander's technique – not to me personally, but to the whole room, rising from the sofa, saying you had to imagine a piece of string going through the top of his head all the way down his spine. Have you heard of it?'

'No.'

'It's a method of releasing physical and mental tension from the body through awareness of posture. By re-educating your muscle system, movements become light and easy. The technique would benefit you, Kate. You looked very tense earlier, when you came down the stairs.'

I liked her nerve! Why wouldn't I be tense? It was enough to find a body, without then lying to protect her from arrest for stealing.

She moved from the chair, threw a blanket from the

chaise longue on the floor and laid herself flat. 'You see, with Mr Alexander's technique, you become aware of every part of your body, and the tension floats away.'

'I'll leave you to it, then. Your landlord has asked me to have a word.'

In an instant, she sat bolt upright. 'What about?'

'I think it's about his wartime experiences.'

'Well, while you're up there, I shall practise my Alexander. But I'm surprised if he wants to talk about the war. He doesn't normally. He just marches an awful lot, especially at night when I'm trying to get to sleep.'

I paused at the foot of the stairs. 'It's odd for an old man to bring up a young girl. What happened to Lucy's parents, and the captain's wife?'

Meriel expelled her breath with a whoosh, and closed her eyes. 'Story is they died in darkest Africa. Old granddad up there is the only survivor, worse luck for Lucy.'

12

The Ransom Note

Captain Wolfendale opened his door cautiously. He peered over my shoulder. 'Did you mention to Miss Jamieson that I asked you to come up?'

'She believes you're going to talk to me about the war.'

He nodded. 'Thank you. I thought you would be discreet. Do come in, Mrs Shackleton. Forgive the cloak and dagger.'

I followed the captain into the high-ceilinged drawing room with its elaborate cornices, and small chandelier.

To the right of the doorway stood two large fumed oak cabinets stocked with small arms and medals. A pair of carved Zulu warrior figures guarded the whisky decanter on the sideboard.

On either side of the Adam fireplace stood easy chairs, one of leather, one of worn velvet. Between these chairs, across the hearth, lay a tigerskin rug, the head of the tiger caught in a permanent snarl. Its hard glass eyes glared malignantly at no one in particular and everyone and everything in general. Intricate carved Indian stools and tables were dotted about the room. Swords and animal trophies decorated the walls, including the head of a sad-eyed deer and the tusks of a mighty elephant. Captain Wolfendale stood by the leather chair and motioned me to take the opposite seat. Beyond his shoulder, on top of a cabinet, were more specimens of the taxidermist's art: a mongoose and a curled cobra.

On one side of the bay window, a suit of medieval armour stood guard. On the other side of the window, a boy-sized tailor's dummy wore breeches, a jacket and a bush hat. A gun, that was sure to have a special name, had been taped to the dummy's hand. The armour and the dummy were divided by a flourishing aspidistra in a brass pot.

I took a seat, and waited for him to speak.

It took him a long moment to settle himself, placing his hands cautiously on the chair arms as though this may, after all, be a trick chair. 'My granddaughter told me that as well as taking photographs, you are a private investigator.'

'Yes. She asked me what I do with my time, besides taking photographs.' It was unusual. Often young people are so caught up with their own lives that they do not enquire about their elders. But Lucy Wolfendale was twenty-one, and so old enough to be curious about how other women live their lives.

The captain continued by telling me something I already knew. 'Lucy came of age this month. My job ought to be done now. She should be married.'

Where was this leading, I wondered. I hoped he would not ask my advice.

'Did I say this conversation is in confidence, Mrs Shackleton?'

I hate it when people repeat themselves, and insisting on confidentiality is an insult. 'You did, and it was not necessary.'

'Sorry. Take a look at this.'

He stood up. From the mantelpiece, he took a white envelope which he handed to me. It was postmarked Harrogate, with yesterday's date stamp. Name and address were written in block capitals.

CAPTAIN R. O. WOLFENDALE VC
29 ST CLEMENT'S ROAD
HARROGATE

I was impressed. 'Victoria Cross? You are one of the gallant few, Captain.'

He waved his hand dismissively. 'I want you to read the note.'

I slid out the sheet of paper carefully, holding it by the corner.

In letters cut from a magazine, the message read:

ONE THOUSAND POUNDS TO HAVE LUCY BACK ALIVE
AWAIT INSTRUCTIONS
CALL POLICE SHE WILL DIE

My first reaction was that this looked like a schoolgirl prank. It seemed too preposterous to be real. But then, so did finding the lifeless body of a theatregoer in a shop doorway. There could be no connection. Lucy had been in a huddle with her young friends. No one could have snatched her, could they?

'When did you receive this note?' The chair was soft

and deep. Holding the note, taking in the situation, forced me to try and sit up straight.

'It came with the first post, at seven thirty.' He sat down again, looking across at me. Only the drumming of his fingers on the chair arm betrayed a hint of agitation. 'What do you make of it, Mrs Shackleton?'

'I have no idea what to make of it, Captain Wolfendale.'

He nodded sagely. 'I ask for two reasons. First, because you were the person who brought me the news that Lucy would stay with Alison last night.' The pause that followed hung in the air like an accusation.

'And the second reason?'

'Because you are a private detective.'

'You say I brought you "the news" that Lucy would stay with Alison. Lucy said she wanted me to remind you that she would do so.'

'Reminder!' He shook his head. 'I'm not senile yet. If Lucy had said she was staying with a friend, I would have remembered. When you gave me the message, I expected she would be back this morning, saying "I could have telephoned to you if we'd had a telephone installed." She accuses me of refusing to hobble into the twentieth century. Been after me to get a telephone for months, as though a telephone is one of life's necessities.'

'I can only repeat what she said. I don't know what to make of this note. Do you?'

He shook his head.

'Captain Wolfendale, there's a simple way of checking whether this note, this demand, should be taken seriously. Find out if Lucy is with Alison.'

He pushed himself to his feet. 'And what if she is

93

not there? What then? By the very fact of asking, I would be announcing to Mrs Hart, and Alison, that Lucy did not come home last night. Something like that could shred her reputation. She's sought after you know, will make a good match. But this . . . What's the meaning of it? Has some blighter taken hold of her? Is it to torment me?'

'I'm sorry but I don't know what else to suggest. I brought you the message, but that's all. I hardly know Lucy, or Alison. Kidnap seems most unlikely.'

But so did murder seem unlikely.

He picked up a framed photograph from the table beside him. It was the one I had taken of Lucy, as a publicity picture for the play. 'Look at her,' he said. 'She's a beauty. Her mother was a beauty, but Lucy . . . She really does shine in this photograph. What did you do to make her so . . . translucent?'

When people ask about photographic technique, they rarely want to know the technical details. 'I took the photograph on the day she was wearing her halo,' I said.

He smiled.

'How long have you been Lucy's guardian, Captain?'

'Since her parents died.'

'Has she ever gone missing before?'

'No,' he said emphatically. 'Most certainly not.'

'You've asked my advice. A little background would help.'

He placed the photograph back on the table and sat down. 'Her parents died before she was two years old. She doesn't remember them. Her mother died of influenza, her father in a motor accident in the African veld. A nursemaid brought her to Britain. I was already a widower, so coming to Harrogate when my aunt died and left me this property worked out well. It gave Lucy stability. Miss Fell, my tenant on the floor above, was very helpful. She's a spinster but had brought up younger brothers and sisters.'

'The nursemaid did not stay?'

'Not for very long.'

The envelope and letter remained in my lap. 'Do you take this threat seriously?'

He jumped to his feet as though unable to contain himself. 'How else am I to take it?' He began to pace. 'I can't come up with a thousand pounds. It's absurd.'

'Then put your mind at rest. Walk round to Alison's house, say you were passing. Congratulate Alison on her role. You did see the play?'

And here was my chance for a rapier thrust, because I still wondered why he had been so cagey when I mentioned Mr Milner last night. It would have been natural to say he had been here that afternoon, when I had seen them playing a board game. 'Were you at the performance last night?'

Had he murdered Mr Milner, outraged by the man's pestering of his granddaughter?

'I did not leave the house yesterday,' he said firmly. He placed a hand on the mantelpiece as though for support. 'Saw the play on Wednesday.' Unable to keep still, he made his way to the window, with renewed vigour, as if expecting to see Lucy and Alison in the street. 'You're right, Mrs Shackleton. This is some prank. Some girlish prank. She's with Alison after all. They're going to come in and start joshing me and saying, Now will you have a telephone installed.'

'Captain, let's be clear. I didn't say I thought this a prank. You can only be sure by going to see Alison Hart.'

The captain stood at the window, his back to me, for another long moment. When he turned to face me, he closed his eyes, putting his hand across his forehead, as though blinded by a sudden pain. 'Even if it is a prank, how could she do this to me?'

I was beginning to feel impatient. This was where I should say, Are you consulting me in a professional capacity? In that case, sorry but I am otherwise engaged.

He sighed. 'Mrs Hart is a widow. If I call and the girls are out, well, she's the kind of lady likely to misconstrue my visit.' He looked at his military memorabilia on the sideboard, as if for inspiration. 'I could deal with the renegade Indian or Egyptian. I could deal with the Boer. I don't know what to do about my own granddaughter. Women, the fair sex have not been . . . I'm at a loss in that direction.'

Without attracting his attention, I carefully placed the ransom note and envelope in my satchel. It was possible the paper would need to be checked for fingerprints, but I did not want to alarm him by saying so. He suddenly appeared vulnerable, a frail old man. 'What were the circumstances which led to your being awarded the Victoria Cross, Captain?'

He looked at me quickly. For a few seconds, I thought he would avoid answering.

He waved his arm. 'We attempted to relieve Kimberley. Ambushed by the Boer. I managed to break through the Boer's encirclement, while wounded, and under fire. That was all, and so long ago. I was a different person then. And the truth is, when you reach a certain rank, there are all sorts of things you just don't have to deal with. I had a wonderful batman, never

96

properly appreciated him. He was with me that day. He should have got that medal.'

I stood up and slung the satchel across my shoulder. 'Where does Alison Hart live?'

13

Prompt Corner

Prompt corner: where the prompter installs a copy of the play

I arrived at Alison Hart's house, justifying my dereliction of the pawnbroker's mission by telling myself I would ask whether Mrs Hart knew a Mrs deVries. The garden gate swung open on well-oiled hinges. Paved with green tiles, and not a weed daring to peep through, the garden path took a straight no-nonsense line through a neat garden, the air heavy with the scent of roses. To the left of the path, roses were red. They had been dead-headed so only the brightest and best blooms and buds displayed themselves. To the right of the path, all roses were white.

The green-painted door was decorated with leaded light panels. Elongated tulips in red and mauve entwined and reached longingly for the lintel. I rang the brass bell, and then crossed my fingers. Thick lace curtains defeated my attempt to peer through the bay window.

Mrs Hart answered the door herself. A statuesque woman with a seriously stout neck and definite jaw line, she invited me in as soon as I introduced myself and waved Arnold Bennett's *Anna of the Five Towns*. 'Alison lent me her copy after the cast photography session. I said I'd return it.'

'Alison's not here, but do please come in.'

With a busy, bustling walk that made me feel I was joining a procession, she led me along a hall decorated with heavily embossed blood-red anaglypta. I followed her into the dining room, keeping my eye on the grey bun at the nape of her neck.

A fully extended table took up the centre of the room. It was covered in a heavy-duty cloth and strewn with a cornucopia of sale of work goods. Four chairs were tucked under the table. Four more chairs had been placed either side of the sideboard.

There will come a day when English dining rooms are not full of dead things. But not yet. On the sideboard, a stuffed peacock, its glorious tail fully fanned, glared from beneath a gleaming glass dome, as though demanding an apology.

'So it's the play that brought you,' Mrs Hart sighed. 'Everything comes back to that play.'

Mrs Hart caught me glancing at the peacock. 'Bert died of natural causes,' she explained. 'His heart gave out after an unfortunate encounter with Skippy.' She pulled out a chair for me to sit down, and then rang the bell by the fireplace. 'You will have tea?'

'Not if I'm disturbing you. You seem very busy.'

'I like to be disturbed.' She took the seat opposite me and ordered tea from a flustered maid who appeared in the doorway. 'Alison usually helps me, Lucy too. But I'm on my own today. If you wouldn't mind making cones of the paper squares there, that would be a great help. This is how you do it.'

She picked up a square of greaseproof paper, shaped

it into a cone and twisted the end. I copied the action, as she began to fill the first cone with pink and white marshmallows. 'This is the first time they haven't been here to help. First the play, then needing to get over the play.'

At a closer range, I could examine the contents of the table. As well as the home-made marshmallows, and toffee, there were trays of fairy cakes ready to be transferred to waiting tins, jars of jam, knitted tea cosies, an embroidered table runner and a pious framed sampler extolling the virtues of home and hearth. Clustered together, like upside-down sand pies, were several small bucket-shaped bins. They had been given decoupage treatment, with pictures cut from magazines and old books pasted onto the bins and varnished. One was covered with dogs and puppies, another with cats and kittens, horses and foals, wild flowers and so on. 'You're admiring Alison and Lucy's handiwork,' Mrs Hart said, pausing in her sweet-filling operation. 'Of course it pre-dates rehearsals. Nothing else mattered once rehearsals began.'

'The decoupage must have taken great patience, and a long while to gather all the pictures.'

Mrs Hart smiled fondly. 'That's Alison for you. She sets her mind to something and gets on with it.' She held up a bin that bore pictures of babies and infants. The images covered the entire surface: solemn faces, sleeping, smiling, crying; chubby bodies, toddling, wriggling and lying sinisterly still.

'Now guess,' Mrs Hart challenged. 'What was the original use of these small buckets?'

'I can't imagine.'

'Guess.'

'They were for children to play with at the seaside?'

'Not even close! Guess again.' She waved a tree and ivy covered bin, turning it this way and that as though to give me a clue. 'If you were to ask me animal, vegetable or mineral, the clue would be animal.'

'But the tins are metal.'

'Precisely.'

I wondered whether gathering all this stuff had sent her slightly mad. Perhaps Alison and Lucy had looked respectively at their mother and grandfather and decided to fake a kidnap, raise a thousand pounds and flee the country.

'I give in.'

At that moment, the maid returned carrying a tray that looked far too big for her. I watched as she placed it precariously on the edge of the full table.

Mrs Hart made a space, moving several pairs of misshapen slippers that bore a strong resemblance to greasy felt hats. 'Tell Mrs Shackleton, Annie. She can't guess the original purpose of our decorative bins.'

Annie sighed. 'Offal. They held offal. The butcher saves 'em for us.' She beat a hasty retreat.

Mrs Hart called her back. 'Annie! I know for sure that Alison made several pounds of chocolate bon bons. Do you know where they are?'

Annie took a deep breath as though to savour her own words. 'You know Miss Alison and chocolates, madam. Two guesses where they are.'

Mrs Hart waited until Annie had closed the door. 'Silly girl. As if Alison would scoff the lot.' Mrs Hart stirred the tea in the pot. 'Don't these decoupage tins make perfect work-of-art waste bins?'

'They do. Most ingenious.'

It dawned on me. I would be held captive. She would shortly produce knitting needles, wool and a tea-cosy pattern. I would not be released until I knitted twelve tea cosies. The prison authorities could have learned a thing or two from Mrs Hart. Oakum picking? Child's play!

Not to be rude, I would take tea, sit for several minutes longer, and discuss the play, and Alison's role, while thinking of a way to find clues as to where Lucy and Alison might be.

My intention to enquire after the elusive Mrs deVries evaporated. If she existed, Mrs Hart would undoubtedly know her, and Mrs deVries would not thank me for naming her to such a thorough person.

We agreed how clever it was of Miss Jamieson to turn the story of *Anna of the Five Towns* into a living, breathing play.

'They rehearsed in such odd ways sometimes,' Mrs Hart said, an edge of disapproval creeping in. 'Miss Jamieson is something of a Bohemian I expect. It had me worried at times, though of course Alison and Lucy are so level-headed, and Rodney Milner is a charming young man. But off the three of them trotted, to be in character they called it. Not just learning the words but pretending to be Henry Mynors, Anna Tellwright and Beatrice Sutton. How extraordinary! Off they'd go on a picnic, taking not what they liked but what they imagined their characters would tuck into.'

'Whatever Miss Jamieson did, it worked. The performances were quite extraordinary.'

Mrs Hart smiled. 'My feeling is that Miss Jamieson chose them for their parts very cleverly. For instance, Alison played Beatrice Sutton, who loves chocolates.'

'Is Alison likely to be back soon?' I asked. 'I would have liked to congratulate her again on her performance.'

'She's staying the weekend with Lucy.'

Ah, so that was the way of it. They were providing each other with an alibi. But why?

'Have they been friends long?'

'They were at Harrogate Ladies' College together.' Mrs Hart poured tea. 'Help yourself to a biscuit.'

'Thank you.'

'Of course, Alison insisted on taking a position on leaving college. She has an important post in the solicitor's office. Her father would never have allowed it had he lived.'

'Alison and Lucy must have lots of friends from their college days.'

Mrs Hart returned to filling cones with marshmallows. 'Times move on, and so many of the girls boarded. They write, but really it's just Alison and Lucy now.'

'I expect being in amateur dramatics broadens their social circle.'

Mrs Hart looked down her nose at a slab of toffee. 'Are you any good at hammering toffee into even pieces?'

'I'll have a go.'

'Good, because I'm hopeless. What did you ask?'

'They must have made new friends through being in the play. I'd better not hammer the toffee until I've finished my tea.'

'Good thinking. And it's funny you should say that about the play. Daddy would certainly not have approved of theatricals and on that account I was not entirely enthusiastic about the venture, but something good may have come of it.' She smiled a secret smile.

'Oh?'

'Just between us, I think that play may have cemented a friendship, a friendship that has ripened into courtship, if I dare say so?'

'For Alison or Lucy?'

'Alison. I do think that she and Rodney Milner became close during rehearsals. It was thought that Rodney and Lucy at one time ... but really, those two were always more like brother and sister.'

Rodney Milner. He had been part of the little group encircling Lucy: Rodney, Alison and one other young chap. I hoped that wherever Lucy was, she would be safe, and in company. Perhaps there was a party afoot and it had gone on until the early hours. That would be something to keep quiet about among the polite society of parents and guardians.

I transferred the toffee to the tea tray, set it on the floor, knelt down and began to tap-tap with the confectionery hammer.

'Thank you so much, Mrs Shackleton. It's unusual for me to be on my own on a bazaar day. I do half expect the girls may surprise me and come along this afternoon after all. They love the church bazaar.'

'I'm sure the bazaar will be great fun,' I said.

'I hope so. But of course there's a very serious side to it. We split the takings between church funds and a charity. This year our charity is the home for unmarried mothers.'

'A very worthy cause.'

'I'm glad you think so. Personally, I would have preferred widows and orphans. They at least cannot help their predicament. But perhaps you'll call in? We open the doors at two o'clock.'

'Right, thanks for telling me.' I returned the hammered toffee to the table, and remained standing, to indicate departure. She did not take the hint.

She stuck to her chair. 'Of course not all the committee ladies were entirely happy about our choice. Some of us argued that by supporting such unfortunates we would be condoning immorality, slack values, rewarding sin, not to put too fine a point on it. But there we are. Charity is as charity does. The vicar was all for the fallen women. What about those who don't fall but stumble along as best they can? That's what I'd like to know.'

'I'll put the book over here, shall I?' I set the copy of *Anna of the Five Towns* on the sideboard beside the peacock. 'I'm sorry to have missed Alison.'

'You see at one time, I would have had an ally in Mrs Milner. She was a practical, down-to-earth woman, and very fond of poor motherless Lucy. Of course with Captain Wolfendale and Mr Milner having fought side by side, and Lucy and Rodney being close in age, the families were quite in each other's pockets at one time. Two old soldiers. Though Mr Milner not so old of course, and now a widower . . .'

So she had not heard about the murder. At the thought of it, I stopped hearing what she said. I placed a hand on the table to steady myself. What was going on that both Lucy and Alison had disappeared around the same time as Lawrence Milner's murder? According to Mrs Hart, Alison and Rodney Milner were in love, and Lucy was like a sister to Rodney.

Something stank, and I did not know what. This was

not up to me. I should tell the police. It was possible that last night's shock, which set my every nerve on edge, was making me see connections where none existed. Information. That was what I needed before wasting Inspector Charles's time with red herrings. Was there some connection between the murdered man and the captain?

'Mrs Hart, I believe you have a telephone.'

'I would not be without it, and hang the expense.'

'Would you mind very much if I make a call and reimburse you?'

She hesitated. I took out my purse.

'Of course. This way. It is in what was my husband's study.'

She led me along the hall and into a book-lined room, the shelves bulging with legal tomes. The telephone stood on a desk by the window.

I waited until she had gone and closed the door behind her. Her footsteps retreated along the hall. Had she loitered, I would have put in an innocuous call to my housekeeper.

As it was, I took the chance of finding my London cousin, James, at home. He is Something-in-the-War Office and on close terms with the old colonel who has intimate knowledge of what every British officer who fought in the Boer War had for lunch on the day Ladysmith was relieved. James's wife, Hope, answered. I exchanged the briefest pleasantry imaginable before asking for James. Hope keeps such a discreet silence over everything that you would be hard pressed to get beyond a weather report. Much as I disliked mentioning names over the telephone, I asked James what he could find out about Corporal Lawrence Milner and Captain

Wolfendale. My excuse being, that they were so very brave and one of them would shortly help write the other's obituary. James cottoned on in an instant, saying he would send me a telegram at home.

I left money by the telephone, and then returned to Mrs Hart. She walked me to the door.

'I'll tell Alison you called.'

'Thank you. Good luck with the bazaar.'

All I had to do was report back to Captain Wolfendale that Lucy was not with Alison. After that, it would be up to him. Like Mrs Hart, he would probably blame Meriel and the play, seeing acting on stage as the root of all evil. Certainly amateur dramatics did seem to have revolutionised the lives of Lucy and Alison. Now they were young women who dared.

14

Rehearsal

Nine weeks earlier

Everything seemed to Lucy to be a rehearsal: a rehearsal for the play, a rehearsal for the rest of her life. She dipped her toes in the stream and then slowly slid her feet into the icy water. She was Anna now, on the chapel picnic a year or so before the action of the story. This was how Meriel had instructed them to rehearse. 'Go out somewhere, as your character, and never for a moment be yourself. Go onto The Stray. There you will meet Dylan. But he won't be Dylan. He'll be Willie. This is the situation: the time is a year before our story begins. You are about to set off on the chapel picnic. Just a little way off are the elders of the chapel, your neighbours and their children, your Sunday school charges. But you have wandered away, you and Willie, and find each other. What will you say, as Anna? What will you say as Willie? How will you look at each other, how near will you stand, will you walk?'

They decided not to follow Meriel's instructions to the letter. They agreed that to be seen on The Stray by people who knew them would leave them feeling foolish, and exposed to mockery. It was a fine Sunday. Dylan suggested the spot.

Taking a moment on her own, away from children's games, matrons' bossiness over food hampers and lemonade, Anna Tellwright wandered barefoot on the bank alongside the stream. She conjured up the laughter and cries as her younger sister played games with other children. Playing her part as Anna, Lucy walked with that feeling that if she stepped off the beaten path, stood for a long moment by a certain oak tree, she would latch on to another life, the life that must be out there, waiting for her.

'Anna.'

The voice was soft, almost a whisper.

She looked up. Dylan was Willie to the life. His trousers hitched a little too high, a look on his face that spoke deprivation, hunger, yearning.

'Hello, Willie.'

'Are you enjoying the picnic?'

'I suppose so. The ham is nice.'

'The ladies have put on a very good spread.'

'They have.'

Silence. A long silence. Dylan picked a buttercup. He held it under his own chin, in the way that he thought Willie might. Lucy laughed, as she thought Anna would laugh. 'Someone is meant to do that for you, Willie. How can you see yourself whether you like butter?'

He handed her the buttercup.

'Tilt your head a little.' She held the buttercup close to his throat. 'You like butter, Willie.'

'I do, Anna.' He took back the buttercup and held it under her chin. He could not seem to decide, to read whether the reflection on her throat indicated like or dislike of butter.

'We're not very good at this are we?' Lucy said. 'Meriel would tell us off for not being properly prepared in our characters.'

'What do you think I would say as Willie?'

'I don't know. What do you think I would say as Anna?'

'I think you're very kind. You would put me at my ease because I'm awkward and unsure.'

'I wouldn't know how, being awkward and unsure myself. Everything is in my head. I'm hopeless at conversation.'

He studied her throat. 'It must be that you like butter. I'm sure of it now.' He set the buttercup down carefully among the clover.

Lucy shook out a picnic rug, not in her own careless throw-it-down fashion, but as Anna, straightening the sides, smoothing out the creases with the flat of her hand. She sat down, tucking her legs to one side, patting the space beside her.

Dylan sat as far from her as he could without being off the blanket altogether.

'Are you sitting there as Willie, or as yourself?'

He blew a confused breath through parted lips. 'Perhaps we should just practise our lines. Do you think that would be all right?'

'Dylan, we know our lines. She wants us to . . . What was that word she used? Something the characters.'

'Inhabit. Inhabit the characters. I remember because it made me think of my work and the properties we rent out to people who inhabit a place in the world not their own, which is most of us. But you best not call me Dylan. I'm Willie Price.'

'Before we "inhabit" the characters, just tell me, who are you named after in real life? Is Dylan a family name? If I know that I can put it out of my mind, and you'll be Willie.'

'Don't know. Never thought about it. It's just the name my parents gave me.'

'Where are your parents? You're not from round here are you?'

He blushed at her interest in him. 'No. I'm from where this play is set. From the Potteries, only Ma thought it would be a good idea for me to see a bit of the world. An uncle of hers knows Mr Croker. That's how I got the job as house agent's clerk.'

'Do you get lonely away from your family?'

'To tell you the truth, I like to have the space of the room above the shop. At home I shared with my three brothers. They were all bigger than me, great strapping lads who work in the potteries. My sisters work there too. Paintresses.' He did not say that they had called him the runt of the litter.

'It must be very interesting, to go out and about, looking at houses. Is that what you do?'

'Once a week I collect rents, on a Friday evening and on Saturday morning if people were out the night before. Other times, I'm in the office. I read a book, though I'm not supposed to. It's in the office that I learned my lines by heart.'

She picked a clover. 'I'm not sure that Anna and Willie would have talked like this. I think they just saw each other now and then, and he was only just building up courage to talk to her.'

'If we weren't in this play together, perhaps we wouldn't talk either. You would walk by Croker &

Company and never so much as glance to see who sat behind the desk.'

'Oh I would.'

'No. You wouldn't. I've watched you pass by ever so many times, with a friend, or alone. You never once looked.'

'I shall look next time.' She bit the head off the clover and ate it.

'I'd like that. If you want to step inside, you could pretend to be Lucy looking for a fine house, coming into her fortune.'

'You mean I could pretend to be Anna?'

'Yes, that's what I meant. You could pretend to be Anna.'

'Where would you recommend for her, for Anna?'

He made a little clucking sound of thoughtfulness and stretched his scrawny legs. 'I would recommend that she leave the Potteries altogether and come up here. There's a spot not far off that would be just right for her, and her sister. She could turn it into a most magical place. It would need some work.'

'Take me to see this place. Let's go as Anna and Willie. Then it will be all right.'

'But we said we'd meet the others here, Alison and Rodney Milner.'

Lucy came to a kneeling position, ready to stand. 'They can get on without us. Don't forget that Henry Mynors and Beatrice had an understanding long before Mynors turned his attention to Anna. We'll leave them a note, a message.' She smiled at her own ingenuity, picked up a stick and ran down to the soft sand of the stream's bank. She wrote *Anna & Willie gone for a walk. Do not wait!*

112

Dylan hesitated. 'Is that fair to Alison?'

Lucy laughed. 'But they're not Alison and Rodney. They're Beatrice and the upright Henry Mynors.'

Rodney Milner swerved round the bend on the wrong side of the road. With seconds to spare, a girl on a horse urged her mount onto the verge and practically fell into the hedge.

'Dashed horses!' Rodney complained. 'D'you ride Alison?'

'Not for ages.' She adjusted the motoring goggles. They pressed too hard and made ugly red marks around her eyes and on the bridge of her nose.

'Be glad when the horse has gone the way of the dinosaur. Sooner the better from our point of view.'

'Would you like a peppermint cream, Rodney?'

'Pop one into my mouth, eh? There's a good girl.' He turned to her, opening his lips.

Gently, she placed the peppermint cream on his tongue. 'I thought it was a good idea to bring peppermint creams for the picnic, because of my character being so fond of chocolates. But they're very melty.'

He gave an exaggerated groan of appreciation. 'I love melty. What else have you brought in that picnic basket of yours?'

She pursed her lips. 'You'll have to wait and see.'

'Something delicious I'll be bound.'

'I wonder what Lucy has brought?' Alison said, artlessly, as if not knowing the answer.

'You know Lucy as well as I do,' Rodney smirked. 'She'll come empty-handed. Lucy only ever brings Lucy.'

'But this time she's Anna, and Anna is such a good

housekeeper and so thrifty and all of that. What do you think she'll bring as Anna?'

'I should think her miser father won't let her bring anything. "Leave it to the others," he'll say.'

'Oh but she'll bake.'

'Anna might bake. Lucy won't.'

Alison sucked chocolate from her fingers. 'You know Lucy so well don't you?'

'Too well.'

'What's that supposed to mean?'

Rodney smiled. 'I'm the only man in Harrogate not in love with Lucy.'

'What are you so pleased about today?'

'If you must know, I'm celebrating. That's why I've brought ginger wine for you lovely ladies and dandelion beer for myself, as pillar of the community Henry Mynors, and for Dylan as the pathetic Willie Price. Poor chap can't even be a William.'

'They wouldn't have alcohol at the chapel picnic!'

'In that case, Meriel Jamieson will have to sack me and find another actor, because I'm celebrating.'

'What are you celebrating?'

'Ha ha ha! Who sold more motors than his pater this month?'

'Did you really?' She raised her goggles and gazed at him, eyes wide with admiration.

'I did. Who has sold more motors than his pater for the last three months?'

'Have you?'

'So you must not refuse a toast to Rodney Milner's success before he turns his attention to becoming dull but crafty Henry Mynors.'

'Why do you call him crafty?'

Rodney pulled in to the side of the lane. 'This the spot?'

'I think so.'

He climbed out and helped Alison from the motor. 'I call him crafty because he——' in helping Alison, he first took her hand, then put out his arms to steady her '—— because he chooses Anna the heiress over the bouncing friendly charmer who loves chocolates.'

'You mean Beatrice Sutton?'

'Do I?'

Alison cleared her throat. 'I can't see them. I can't see Lucy or Dylan over by the stream or . . .'

'Then let's go and explore.'

He lifted the picnic basket from the back of the car. 'I think my bottles might fit in here, what do you think?'

'Probably.'

He arranged the bottles in the basket and snapped it shut. 'I see you've brought glasses.'

'I did. But Mother said we should cup our hands and drink water from the stream. She said that's what people on a chapel picnic would do.'

'That's carrying it a bit far in my book. I wonder what else they would and wouldn't do?' He opened the gate to the field and bowed her through.

'I don't know. We shall have to think ourselves into the roles.' Their hands touched as she helped shut the gate. 'You had better call me Beatrice.'

Side by side, they walked to the stile that led to the far field. 'Let me go first,' he said. 'Then I can help you across. Henry and Beatrice are very chummy at this point you know. It wouldn't surprise me if they held hands.'

After climbing the stile, they walked towards the

stream. He saw where Lucy and Dylan had been sitting, where the clover and buttercups lay flat. 'Look. They were here. Or someone was. I was in the Scouts you know.'

'That's a bit mean,' Alison said. 'If they didn't wait, just because we're a little late.'

'Who cares? I don't. Over there?' He nodded to a sheltered spot a little further off.

'Yes.'

They walked closer to the stream, where the bank sloped. 'There are wild violets,' Alison said. 'How lovely!'

He spread the blanket. 'Succulent Miss Beatrice Sutton, may the dashing Mr Henry Mynors tempt you to a titillating glass of ginger wine?'

She laughed at his silliness. 'Do you really think that's how they would talk, if not following the script I mean?'

He winked. 'I think the two of them had a very big secret at one time.'

'What was that?'

'That they were far more chummy-rummy than chapel people ought to be. I think they probably kissed.'

'Really? That's a bit much.' They clinked glasses. 'Anyhow, well done, Rodney, for selling so many cars.'

Rodney sipped his dandelion beer. In a single breath, the bravado deserted him. 'Do you know why I really sold more motors?'

'I don't know.' She gazed at him with rapt attention. 'Why?'

'Because people can't stand my father. They come in when he's not there, usually on Saturday mornings. That's what Dad puts my success down to, the popularity of Saturdays. But they're always so relieved to see me. And when Dad puts in an appearance, honestly, Alison, you think he'd have some idea how people feel about him. He has the hide of a rhinoceros. Probably brought it back from South Africa.'

'Really? Lucy's grandfather was in South Africa.'

'That's how they know each other. It gives them something in common. They play this ridiculous board game sometimes, *Called to Arms.* They shake dice and go to squares called things like *Quick March* and *Conspicuous Bravery Advance to Victoria Cross.*'

Alison giggled.

'I know. It's mad. Grown men.'

Alison prided herself on seeing the best in everyone. 'Your father must have a lot of confidence, to give you so much responsibility. He must think a great deal of you.'

Blushing, suddenly losing his composure, Rodney shook his head. 'He thinks a great deal of himself.'

'But . . .'

Rodney took Alison's hand. 'I don't know how you do it, Alison.'

'What? Do what?' She left her hand in his.

'What you do to me, every time we're together. And when we're not together, I think of you all the time.'

She stared at him, 'But . . . I thought . . .'

'Now I've made a fool of myself. I spoke out of turn. Sorry.'

'No. It's just that, I thought you and Lucy . . . I mean . . .'

He started to laugh. 'No. Did she say that?'

'Of course not. She wouldn't.'

'She wouldn't because it's not true. There's never been anything like that between us, and it's just as well.'

'How do you mean, just as well?'

'Because – well, it's too puke-making to even say. If I tell you something will you keep it just between us?'

Alison nodded. 'You know I will.'

'My father has his eye on her. I can tell. If he gets his way, Lucy will be my step-mother.'

Alison started to laugh. 'Never. Never in this wide world.'

'Oh yes.'

'Does Lucy know?'

'Do you know, I don't think she does. Because it's beyond comprehension, don't you think?'

Alison kept on laughing. 'I'm sorry. I shouldn't laugh, but if he thinks Lucy . . .'

'I know.'

They both began to laugh, rolling about on the picnic blanket, laughing louder and louder until they reached a pitch and Alison had to pull out her handkerchief. She dabbed her eyes, then offered the hanky to Rodney.

Instead, he took her hand. 'I love you, Alison.'

They came upon the round tower beyond the trees and across the meadow.

Lucy gazed at the tower. 'Do you really think Anna would want to live here?'

'She might. It's very remote and romantic.'

'Do you know, you're a bit right there. Only Anna is so practical, I think she might worry about the water supply and the gas pipes. She'd never be able to get the floor clean.'

Dylan looked crestfallen. 'I hadn't thought of that.' He brightened. 'If you come at it from the other side, there's the road, and a meadow to cross. And Anna's such a hard worker that she'd think nothing to having a well dug and coming out to draw her own water. She'd be a great one for old lamps and that sort of thing, having been used to the miser and his mean ways.'

'I like it anyway,' Lucy said. 'Shall we go inside and take a proper look?'

'It's probably dangerous.'

'Let's go in and see. Don't forget who we are.'

Dylan turned the heavy key. The property was not on Croker's books, but keys that fitted another old property would work this lock. Dylan had it in mind to give Mr Croker a report on the state of the place. Perhaps the owner would like to have it taken care of.

In the precise clipped voice that Anna sometimes used, Lucy said, 'This place is awfully dilapidated, Willie.'

Dylan loved the word dilapidated. Lapis, stone, stone falling away. He answered in character, as Willie.

'It is rather dilapidated, Miss Tellwright. Just like my father's works.'

'That does not mean you are allowed to get so far behind with your rent. You must tell Mr Price that.'

'He does understand. Please come up to the office.'

They continued their tour in character until Lucy stood on the battlements looking out across the fields, picking out, in the distance, the figures of Alison and Rodney. She held herself very straight, as Anna Tellwright would.

'Willie.'

'Yes, Miss Tellwright?'

'Do you have your field glasses?'

'I do.'

He handed her the binoculars.

She looked again at the two figures, that now were one.

'May I look, Miss Tellwright?'

'Perhaps not, Willie. We must talk about the rent.' She turned away. 'My grandfather has done me a very bad turn.'

'Don't you mean your father, Miss Tellwright?'

'Of course, that's what I mean, my father, the old miser whom I love and hate in equal measure.'

'And what bad turn has he done you? After all, he has signed over a fortune to you.'

Lucy dropped the character of Anna. She looked across the fields to the far horizon. 'Anna and I don't have much in common really. Except that she is twenty-one and I will be twenty-one on 6th August. My granddad always said I would have an inheritance on my twenty-first birthday. Now he's going back on his word.' Their hands lay side by side on the parapet. Half an inch, and they would touch. 'Oh I should not be blabbing about this. He always says not to tell people our business.'

Dylan did not know what to say. Inheritances and prospects were so far from his experience. He racked his brains, but no words came. Only by hiding behind his character could he speak his deepest thoughts.

'You can tell me. After all, in the play I'm Willie who adores you. And Willie dies, so his lips will be sealed.'

Lucy turned to him and smiled. 'My Aunt Ada – Miss Fell who lives on the floor above – she was my great aunt's companion. Well, there's something fishy. Aunt Ada is sure that a legacy should come to me when I'm of age, from my parents. Only there's nothing I can pin Granddad down on. Whenever I ask now, he puts me

120

off. And I have to get away. I think . . . This sounds too horrible to say.'

'What?'

'Oh, I can't say it to anyone. Not to Rodney, not to Alison because she's sweet on Rodney and would tell him . . . It's Rodney's father, Mr Milner. He's after me. He's always been after me, since I was little. I can see that now. He disgusts me.'

'Mr Milner?'

'He used to lift me up and spin me round and . . .'

Dylan cupped her hand. She left it in his.

'I have to get away.'

'How will you do that?'

'I don't know. But I must. Granddad's so mean, just like the miser in the play, even over the smallest amounts of money. Every little bill has to be gone over with a magnifying glass. And I spend hours doing useless things . . . helping at the dancing class, playing whist with Mrs Hart, making decoupage waste bins for the church fete. I'll go mad if I don't escape. I want to be independent, to earn my own living. I want to train to be an actress.'

15

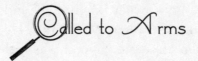alled to Arms

Called to Arms: an early twentieth-century board game

So Lucy's alibi was Alison, and Alison's alibi was Lucy. More and more, the ransom note began to look like something cooked up after reading a Girl's Own mystery story. All they would have needed was a sheet of paper, a pot of glue, scissors and a magazine. Perhaps Lucy and Alison had first made half a dozen decoupage waste bins, and then decided to liven up their lives with a little criminality.

Slowly, I retraced my steps to St Clement's Road, with more questions than answers. Was I wrong to have kept quiet, and let Mrs Hart go on believing that her daughter had spent the night at the Wolfendales?

The way Lucy and Alison had stuck by each other after the performance made me feel sure they were together somewhere. Perhaps I misjudged them and the note delivered to the captain was some foolish joke, played by an envious 'friend' who was not as daring as the two budding thespians. Were Lucy and Alison somewhere having a secretly wonderful time?

After all, they were twenty-one years old. If I had lived either with Captain Wolfendale or Mrs Hart at age twenty-one, I would have wanted to disappear.

But where had they gone?

A pig in the middle is the person who cannot catch the ball. I could not even see the ball, its size, shape, or who was throwing it.

What would I do if I were the captain? Not difficult. If I were seventy years old and a retired army man, I would call the police. Mrs Hart would then be told. A constable would march down the Harts' path between the serried ranks of red and white roses. He would be directed by the Harts' maid to the church hall, there to be devoured by a hundred curious eyes. Some other socially minded lady would need to step in and take charge of twenty-four decoupage waste bins, several pounds of toffee and marshmallows, the small mountain of fairy cakes and the mile and a half of crocheted dressing table runners. Alison's reputation would be trodden underfoot and kicked under the crepe paper-covered trestle tables.

Let that be on someone else's head, not mine.

Captain Wolfendale was watching out for me. Before I had time to mount the front steps he had opened the door. His eyes searched my face. I shook my head. A deep sigh escaped as he waited for me to step inside.

He stood in the doorway, looking left and right. 'I keep expecting to see her coming along the road, hear her feet tip-tapping. Lucy can be a brisk walker when she chooses.'

The door creaked closed. I had not noticed before that it needed oiling.

The drawing room was hot. Even the tigerskin rug looked subdued, its cold eye now ever so slightly sympathetic. I half expected the elephant tusks on the wall to turn floor-wise in sympathy.

The captain did not flinch from stating the obvious. 'Lucy not with Alison then?'

'Mrs Hart thinks Alison is staying here.'

'You didn't . . .?'

'No.'

He frowned. 'Was Mrs Hart curious as to your visit?'

'She wouldn't have expected me to know anything. I returned a borrowed novel, that's all.'

The two of us remained standing. It was up to him now. I would find a way of leaving shortly. This was nothing to do with me. He stood between me and the door. In his stillness, he reminded me for all the world of a lead soldier. His breath came in shallow bursts. Suddenly he put his hand to his heart. 'Could I prevail . . . would you . . . a drop of whisky.'

'Yes of course.' I went to the sideboard. The carved Zulus stared impassively as I unstoppered the decanter and poured the amber liquor into a cut-glass tumbler.

'Soda?'

'A dash.'

I placed the glass on the carved table beside his chair, so that he would sit down.

'You were gone a long time,' he said as he sipped the whisky.

'Mrs Hart wouldn't have thought so. She's a woman who likes company.' I perched on the chair arm opposite him.

'Mrs Hart would be highly agitated if she knew the girls were missing.'

'Captain, I'm sure you'll be able to rely on police discretion, if that seems the best course of action.'

I did not say that the police would hardly welcome a missing persons investigation, not with a murder to solve.

'But you saw what the note said.'

'Yes.' Stay non-committal, I warned myself. The note had been written by someone with a love of suspense novels, or sensational true stories from the other side of the Atlantic. Yet to disregard it would be foolish.

'I want to believe it's a prank.' The captain finished his whisky. 'And at the same, I don't want to believe it's a prank, not if Lucy did it.' His hand began to tremble. 'I thought ... when I saw the bobby this morning, I thought ... I feared the worst. Dashed clodhopper, near giving me a bad turn. I'm my granddaughter's guardian – but it seems I haven't guarded her well enough.' The whisky had done little to revive him. Pale and drawn, he looked on the verge of collapse. 'You saw what the blighters say. "Call police she will die." Daren't risk it. And I don't have a thousand pounds.'

'Someone thinks you do.'

'Then someone is seriously misinformed.' He nodded at the medieval suit of armour. 'He's worth something. Is it a ploy to rob me of what I love best?'

I did not know whether he meant Lucy, or the suit of armour.

I refilled his glass. Slowly, the whisky seemed to restore him a little. 'Whoever's done this nasty trick doesn't know who he's dealing with. I've routed tribes-men. I've outwitted the Boer. Comes to campaigns, this blackmailer has found more than his match. Harm Lucy and I'll run him through. Who is it? Who's taken her?'

'You don't know that someone has taken her. Or why would Alison go missing too?'

He took another gulp of whisky and answered himself as to who had taken Lucy. 'Some damn theatrical type.

Mixing with the wrong sort. Well, let him send me his next set of instructions. I shall rendezvous and shoot the rotter through the mouth.'

'Let's hope it won't come to that.'

We were getting nowhere. If Lucy had been a child, or even fifteen, sixteen, I would have offered to help. But to do any more seemed like interfering. I stood up to go.

Inspector Charles had asked me to say nothing about finding Lawrence Milner's body. But murder cannot stay a secret long. If the captain did not contact the police, and something terrible had happened to Lucy and Alison, something connected with the murder, I would never forgive myself.

'Captain, there's something you should know. Something happened last night that made Miss Jamieson and me so late in coming back after the play.'

'To do with Lucy?'

'No. Nothing I've said about Lucy and Alison changes. You're acquainted with the Milners.'

'Yes.'

He sounded impatient, as though I were about to begin a gossipy conversation.

'Mr Milner was murdered last night.'

His body went slack, as if what little energy he possessed suddenly drained from him. His eyes closed. 'Was he . . .' Then '. . . but who else?' The tick of the clock grew louder. Words deserted him for a long moment.

It seemed odd to me that he said 'but who else'. Did he mean who else was murdered, or who else knew, or who else could have done it?

'Who else what?' I asked.

His hand shook as he drained the whisky glass. 'How was he murdered?'

'I was asked not to say anything. The police are interviewing people. I expect they'll want to talk to Lucy, and the others who were at the theatre last night, and to his friends and associates. You knew him very well, I believe?'

It was phrased innocently but the effect was electric. The old soldier's mouth dropped open, like a baby bird's beak. He did not answer my question but gave me a beseeching look as he changed the subject. 'At one time, I wouldn't have been so useless. I would have acted decisively. I would have marched out there and known what to do. I've grown unused to ... I don't even go out very much any more. Please don't go. Help me. The police won't want to know about Lucy with a murder on their hands, and they could think there's some connection with Lucy and Alison going missing. Do you think they're in danger?'

I looked at Lucy's photograph, her high cheek bones and determined chin. No one would dare to harm such an exquisite creature. Wherever she was, I felt sure she would be safe.

'What is it you want me to do?'

Hope lit his eyes and he leaned forward. His words came out in a great rush. 'You'll help me? What do you charge? I'm not a rich man but I'll find the money to pay you. I'll beg, borrow, steal.'

'That won't be necessary. I'm ...' I did not want to say that I was on another assignment that would easily cover my time. 'If you want me to help, I shall gladly do so for the rest of today. If I'm unsuccessful, you must agree to go to the police.'

'I want you to find her.'

'But is that agreed? If I come to the point where I think it the right thing to do, I'll go to the police myself.'

'Very well. Whatever you say. I agree.'

'Tell me, had you and Lucy quarrelled? Or had she given any indication of being dissatisfied with her lot, of wanting to . . . go on a visit, have a change of scene?'

'Nothing. Nothing of that sort at all.'

'May I take a look at Lucy's room?'

That would give him time to calm down, and me time to think.

'Yes, yes. Come and take a look at her room. I can't look through her things. Never have, never will. Female matters.' He rose creakily to his feet.

I followed him towards the rear of the flat, dodging antlers and tusks, swords and shields, passing other doors that must have been dining room, bedroom, kitchen. We reached the last room, at the back of the house.

'She has the larger of the two bedrooms. Had it done out for her.'

The wallpaper was a pale blue, dotted with forget-me-nots. A white candlewick counterpane covered the bed. The furniture consisted of a dressing table, wardrobe and tallboy in polished walnut – a neat and tidy room, almost as if it were ready for inspection.

'Is it always this tidy, Captain?'

He shook his head. 'Can't answer that one. Not my territory.'

On the bedside table lay a copy of Thomas Hardy's poems and stories, and the novel, *Two on a Tower*.

On the top of the wardrobe was a brown leather suit-case.

'Does she have another suitcase?'

'Only that one.'

Disliking the thought of going through Lucy's things. I sat on the bed, and looked round the room, as though it would deliver up some clue without prompting. 'I still find it hard to picture your family life, Captain.'

He stood in the doorway, hand against the jamb. 'I've made a mess of things.'

'In what way?'

'Oh, in every way. I should have stayed in the army. That was my life.'

'And your wife, what did she think?'

'I didn't ... I didn't believe in having a wife who would travel with me. She stayed at home. I wasn't there when she died.' He lowered his head and covered his face with his hands. 'I had a batman. He did everything for me. Poor man died in London in 1903.'

Was it my imagination, or did he seem more put out by the loss of his batman than the death of his wife? But at least he was talking.

Then he turned to go. 'I'll leave you to look round.'

'No, please stay. Your son was also in South Africa, you said?'

'My son?'

'Lucy's father.'

'Apple of my eye. Didn't realise he'd intended to follow in my footsteps. Unlike me, took his wife with him. She died in the Transvaal of fever, shortly after Lucy was born. I think it made my son careless of his life, with terrible consequences. I resigned my commission, to bring Lucy home. People said put her in an orphanage, but I couldn't do that.'

His telling of his life did not ring true somehow. It

129

combined uncertainty, almost if he were unsure he had ever had a wife, and the glibness of an oft-repeated tale.

I opened the drawers of the dressing table, and the tallboy, disturbing underwear, handkerchiefs and stockings. In the drawer at the bottom of the wardrobe lay neatly folded cardigans and a stole.

The captain stood in the doorway, watching.

'Does she have a desk?' I asked.

'No, no desk.'

'Where does she keep her writing case, papers and books, the script for the play, that sort of thing?'

'Her books are out here, in the hall, on the top shelf. We share the bookcase.'

'I'll look in a moment.' I stayed in the bedroom, bobbed down and pulled a box from under the bed. The captain turned away. 'I'll leave you to it. Don't want to pry.'

On top of the box was a birthday dates book, an address book, and an autograph book dating back to her school days and including the signatures of some of the professional actors who had played in Harrogate.

A fashion magazine caught my eye. I flicked through to see whether it contained any notes.

Paper slipped from the magazine, but it was where the pages had been cut. Words and letters had been snipped. The ransom note had been cut and pasted from this fashion magazine.

I returned to the drawing room and showed the captain the magazine, with its missing letters.

'Good Lord! What does this mean?' His hand trembled as he held the magazine.

I felt sorry for the poor old man. 'It may mean that she composed the note herself. But we shouldn't jump to conclusions.'

He gulped. His voice came out in a whisper. 'She wouldn't do such a thing to me. Some blighter's put her up to it. Some blaggard has her under a spell. By God I'll have him.' He set the magazine down on the table, next to Lucy's photograph. Then he dropped heavily into his chair. His look was piteous, like a little boy lost. 'What do you suggest?'

'I could speak to one or two of the other players who left the theatre at the same time as Lucy and Alison.'

That would include Rodney Milner. Difficult. I did not know him well enough to call and offer condolences, and to begin questioning him about Lucy would be insensitive to say the least. Since Alison had also disappeared, that left only Dylan, the house agent's clerk who had played Willie Price. But my words satisfied the captain.

He nodded, then closed his eyes and bit his lip. 'I have an inkling what this is about. Lucy was twenty-one on the sixth of this month. She expected to come into an inheritance, just like that confounded creature in the play.'

'Are you suggesting that she was copying the heroine of a story? If she were to do that, she would have asked for fifty thousand pounds!'

For the first time since I had met him, the captain laughed.

It was hard to imagine that Lucy could play the scrupulously conscientious Anna Tellwright, and hours later put her grandfather on the rack.

He sighed. 'It's my own fault. When she was growing up, I thought it would give her confidence to think that she had expectations.' He shut his eyes and heaved a sigh.

131

I prompted. 'Does Lucy have expectations? A trust fund, or something of that sort?'

He had recovered slightly. He picked up his pipe from the mantelpiece, poked at the bowl with a pipe cleaner and tapped it against the fireback. He opened a tobacco jar and tore off a strip which he began to stuff into the bowl of his pipe. His state of panic had subsided but his eyes gave him away. He looked puzzled, and lost. 'By Jove, she's shocked me. We'll never recover from this.' He turned to me. 'It must be a prank, don't you think?'

'I don't know. It's best to keep an open mind.'

'Except, except ...' He raised a finger in the air as though testing the direction of wind. 'Could that confounded magazine have been given to her to bring home, and make it look like a prank?'

'It's possible.'

I took out my notebook and pencil and put on my most businesslike voice. 'It will be useful to know some background information. You see Lucy, or whoever composed that note, does seem to think that you have money. If, as you say, you are not a man of means ...'

'It doesn't do in this day and age to let people know if you have to tighten the old belt a notch. By Jove, it doesn't, especially round here. People judge you on what you have, not on what you are. Oh yes, they do that all right. Doesn't matter if a chap distinguishes himself in the service of his country twenty times over, it's his debit and credit balance that counts. How much does he have in the bank? That's what they want to know.'

As gently as I could, I said, 'So you put on a good front as it were?'

'In confidence?'

I slapped the notebook on the chair arm. Who on earth did he think I would blab his finances to? 'Yes, in confidence.'

'I do indeed put on a fine front as you call it. All I have is my pension, such as it is, and the rents from my tenants in this house. Mentioning no names no pack drill, not all of them are up to date.'

'Would Lucy believe that you could come up with such a large amount of money?'

He struck a match, lit his pipe and drew deeply. 'You see, the thing is, because of what I told her as she was growing up, she expected an inheritance, from her parents, when she reached maturity. On her twenty-first birthday, I believe she anticipated some kind of handing over and signatures and all that sort of palaver, as happened in that dratted play. If I'd known the text of that play . . .'

'But if she's twenty-one, then she's of age.'

'I always told her she'd come into her inheritance at maturity, not majority. A man might be mature at twenty-one, a woman perhaps not until she's thirty.'

'Captain, does she or does she not have something to come from her parents, or anyone else, at any age? I assume you're her trustee?' He looked at me blankly. I prompted, 'For instance, sometimes if a woman marries she can claim what she might otherwise have to wait for.'

'By Jove, you're right. She could have run off with someone in the belief that if she married she could make some claim.'

'But we don't think she has run off and married. Not going by the note.'

133

'I knew no good would come of play-acting. Painting her face. Prancing about in front of all those people . . .'

'No one in their right mind would accuse Lucy of prancing. She took her part well.'

'I should have put my foot down.'

I snapped the notebook shut. 'Does Lucy have an inheritance to come, or not?' He was a man who could beat about the bush until it screamed for mercy. 'Have you been stringing her along?'

He sucked on his pipe. After a long moment he met my gaze. 'That's a private matter. Of course she has expectations . . . of a sort.'

'Is there an inheritance?'

'Not exactly. No.'

'Was there?'

'I say, this is pushing things a bit far.'

'Have you used up your granddaughter's inheritance?'

'There was no inheritance! I invented it, to make her feel secure.'

At last he had come out with it. I did not know whether to believe him. But at least his words gave a motive for Lucy's disappearance.

'She thinks money grows on that tree out there.' He walked across to the window, and tapped the suit of armour on its chest. 'When she was small, she asked me to get into this suit of armour, which of course is dashed difficult as a solo task. Then I had to clank about the room and she ran about screaming. I practically broke my neck getting out of it, only to find she was enjoying herself. She liked being scared. She liked being pursued across the flat by a suit of armour.'

'It might have been better to be frank with Lucy.'

'Please be discreet. Lucy's reputation and all that . . .'

'I think perhaps we had better find her first, and let Lucy herself take care of her reputation.'

He bit thoughtfully on the pipe stem. 'Lucy is taking her revenge because she thinks I am withholding something from her. There's not a brass farthing, and that's the truth. I wanted her to feel secure. Is that so terrible?'

'If you'd told her, she would have known how to plan her future. Girls can find jobs these days, can train for various occupations.'

'The prospect of a good marriage to a wealthy man is something, I think.'

I stopped myself from asking whether this wealthy man had been one that she loathed. One who had been knifed in the heart in a shop doorway.

'I'll do my best to find her, Captain Wolfendale.'

For her sake, not yours, you old fraud.

I retrieved Lucy's script from the bookshelf. Alongside the cast list, she had written the names and addresses of the actors.

I showed the names to the captain. 'Who besides Alison might she confide in?'

The captain ran his finger down the names. He stopped at Dan Root, miser, revivalist and ill-fated Mr Price who did away with himself. 'They walked home together sometimes.' The captain told me what I already knew. 'Mr Root lives in the front flat below. But you can rule him out of any shenanigans. Polite young chap. Always on time with his rent. Watchmender. As far as the theatricals, he's a pressed man, not a volunteer. Miss Jamieson roped him in to play half the male parts.'

'What do you know about the other cast members?'

'You'd be better asking the Adventuress about them. Sorry, slipped out. My private nickname for Miss Jamieson.'

'I shall ask Miss Jamieson. But what do you think? The wealthy man ... Lucy's marriage prospect, I daresay he's not in the cast, but will I find his name in the theatre programme?'

I was goading him into admitting that the prospective suitor was Lawrence Milner. Mr Milner's advertisement had helped Meriel with the costs of mounting the production. She had said he paid a premium for his full page announcement that Milner & Sons could supply all your motoring needs.

The captain was no longer looking me in the eye. He glared at the toe of his well-polished boot. 'I know who I don't want her to take up with. Did you see the way she looked at that young house agent's clerk when they parted company in that confounded play?'

'But captain, they were acting their parts. It wasn't real.'

'It looked real enough to me, and to ...'

'To ...?' Had he been at the point of mentioning Milner by name?

'To everybody else in the theatre I should think.'

He was right there. The theatre man, Mr Wheatley, had spotted it too.

The letter box rattled. For a moment neither of us moved.

'Second post,' the captain said. He froze on his chair, knuckles tightening.

'I'll go.'

He nodded.

I walked into the hall. A solitary letter lay on the mat. The envelope was in the same neat block print as the earlier one.

CAPTAIN R. O. WOLFENDALE VC
29 ST CLEMENT'S ROAD
HARROGATE

The only difference was that this time, Captain and VC were underlined. Was this significant? A taunt? The envelope bore a penny stamp and was postmarked Harrogate, 6.25 a.m. I placed it on the open leaf of the bureau. The captain handed me his paper knife. The letter read.

ONE THOUSAND POUNDS TO HAVE LUCY BACK ALIVE
LEAVE CASH NOON MONDAY IN HOLLOW OF OLD OAK TREE TOP OF VALLEY GARDENS THEN GO HOME
CALL POLICE, SHE WILL DIE.

There was a lock of silky dark hair, braided into a slender plait and tied with thread at both ends.

'It's Lucy's hair all right,' said the captain.

'On the envelope, your title and your decoration are underlined this time. What is the significance in that would you say?'

His extraordinary Adam's apple leaped into life as he gulped and swallowed. 'Don't know,' he said in a flat voice tinged with anxiety, or was it fear?

'Does Lucy have contact with anyone who served with you in the army? Or perhaps someone who resents what you represent?' I tried to make some connection. As a schoolgirl, I had heard about Emily Hobhouse and her campaign against the concentration camps in which we British held Boer women and children after their homes and farms had been destroyed. 'Captain, remind me. There was an insulting term for people who did not support the war in South Africa, now what was it?'

'We patriots called them *Screamers*, and *Boer lovers*.'

'Could there be a connection?' I asked.

'There can't be a connection,' he said, too vehemently. 'All that was a lifetime ago.'

'Mr Milner served in the Boer War. He was a corporal I believe.'

'What does any of this have to do with Lucy going missing?' he asked.

'I don't know. Call it instinct. I could be wrong, but I have a feeling there is some kind of link.'

I was feeling my way, guessing. Guessing that the captain had run through Lucy's inheritance from her parents, and that Mr Milner knew. Milner had planned to ride to Lucy's financial rescue, make her an offer she was meant to be grateful for. Did the captain fear he would lose face if Milner revealed what he knew?

I now regretted my promise not to go to the police before the end of the day.

'It's now that matters,' the captain said with a gulp, 'not the past. What matters is sorting this business out before it goes any further. You said you'd help.'

'Very well. I'll talk to one or two of the other actors.'

I would begin with Dylan Ashton, the house agent's clerk who played the besotted doomed youth.

The captain walked me to the door.

In the hall, I turned back. 'The wealthy man who wanted to marry Lucy, were you discussing his proposal yesterday afternoon over a game of *Called to Arms*?'

He stared, uncomprehending. 'What . . .?'

'I saw the game on your table just now, and you were playing yesterday afternoon. A man with reddish-blond hair, and a ruddy neck. Saw you through the window.'

I had him. Every muscle in his face tightened. He was weather-beaten and dark from his years serving in the Empire, but his face darkened still more. It was answer enough. Yesterday afternoon, Captain Wolfendale and Mr Lawrence Milner, formerly Corporal Milner, had sat by the fireplace and played *Called to Arms*.

'Well, Captain?'

'Yes,' he said in almost a whisper. 'Milner was here yesterday. He sometimes calls by, brings me a bottle of whisky and a twist of tobacco. Knows I don't get out much.'

16

Oh I Will Sit

'Oh I will sit me down and weep / For bones in Africa. / For pay and medals, name and rank.' —A.E. Housman

South Africa, September, 1900

Special duties took Captain Wolfendale across country that spring, Kimberley behind him, Ladysmith ahead. The fertile horseshoe of land within the Wittenbergen range was well guarded, in British possession. Now it must be safeguarded. These Boers had a way of living to fight another day. Surrender on Tuesday, re-form on Wednesday, attack on Thursday. But only if they could be fed and watered in the meantime.

In the bright sunshine, watching a lizard sun itself on a boulder as he rode by, he could almost forget that Brother Boer nearly did for him. His shoulder still gave him gyp. His leg went into cramp at a whim.

He sat easy in the saddle, the grey pony trotting patiently, keeping its foothold. His batman, Sergeant Lampton, followed behind, then the small troop of infantry. Thank God so many black Africans had joined the good fight. They could find the way when the captain came to a bend in the river and did not know how to cross. When the game was over, the Kaffirs would expect their reward. You could see it in the energy of their movements, hear it in their voices. At night, they made music, caressing concertinas, singing to the stars. Once he had asked what they sang about, but he couldn't fathom the answer.

The captain waved the line to pause. He took out his field glasses and looked down at the peaceful valley. The farm nestled like a sleeping cat. He could see why Brother Boer would fight to keep this land, fight for what he saw as his birthright. Psalm-singing Brother Boer thought God was on his side. Well, he would soon learn that when push came to shove, the Almighty signed up for the British Empire.

Captain Wolfendale looked back at Sergeant Lampton. 'We take everything we can carry.'

He halted the column further on, letting the horses drink at the river that ran through the valley, ordering the native drivers to unhook the oxen and let them rest and graze. It had been a long trek. The business could wait till morning.

The woman who opened the farmhouse door was about fifty years of age, big and buxom, with a broad Dutch face and a wary smile. She knew better than to argue, looking beyond him to the troop of men, indicating in her guttural voice and with waves of her arm that the men could sleep in the barn. He told her they would pitch their own tents. Don't trust them an inch. *Sleep in our barn. We'll put a match to the straw while you sleep.* Opening the door a little wider, she asked the captain and the sergeant inside. A boy of about ten fetched two mugs. These people never had just one child. There'd be sons, off on commando with their father. There'd be a girl, out of sight. The woman poured milk from a jug into mugs, handing them to the captain and sergeant, waving them to sit at the table.

She spooned stew with dumplings into dishes. They were strange people. He could not tell whether she was hospitable or trying to ingratiate herself. Yet she showed no fear. If he were to believe her gestures, she was complaining that there was little food, little to give or to be commandeered.

The captain looked round the room. It was a typical farmhouse with a sturdy dresser, gleaming pottery, a piano, and what he took to be religious texts framed and hung either side of the door.

Through the open window, he could smell smoke from the fire the men had lit. The Boer boy looked through the window, said something to his mother.

'The men have killed a pig to roast,' Sergeant Lampton said quietly.

The captain nodded.

When they had finished eating, Captain Wolfendale thanked the woman politely. He made a point of ruffling the lad's hair. The boy squirmed. Captain and sergeant pulled on their caps, and left the house.

Early the next morning, the captain knocked on the door again. This time he had half a dozen men with him. The woman opened the door. Behind her was a girl of about sixteen who seemed unsure whether to stay put or to hide. The woman spoke to her daughter, telling her to give the men a jug of milk.

The captain nodded to Corporal Milner to take the jug. Then he said, in his loudest, clearest English, 'You have ten minutes to leave the house and then we shall burn it down.'

The woman did not understand.

He repeated the words.

The girl dropped the jug. It smashed. Milk spread in a puddle across the flagged floor. She translated the captain's words.

In came the six men, carrying straw. Like furniture removers, they began to shift table, chairs and the dresser. Unlike furniture removers, they stacked it in the middle of the room.

'Not yet,' the captain said.

The six men took up positions around the room, idly picking up this item and that. Corporal Milner pulled one of the framed texts from beside the door, dropped it with a clatter, ground it under his heel.

A shot rang out. The boy ran to the window and yelled. His sister joined him.

The girl drew herself up defiantly, turned to her mother and spoke quietly, then back to the captain. 'Why do you kill the bullock?'

The captain pointed to the clock. He held up his fingers. 'Ten minutes.' No one could say he was an unfair man.

The girl and her mother disappeared upstairs.

Milner said, 'I wouldn't mind living here meself.'

One of the straw bringers said, 'Seems a terrible shame.'

'Are we gloomy?' asked Private Clark. 'No we are not.' He pulled out the piano stool, sat down and began to play 'Rule Britannia'. Lampton took out his mouth organ and joined in. At the end of each chorus, the men sang the words at the ceiling, *Britons never ever ever shall be slaves!*

From upstairs came a young sweet voice, singing in Afrikaans. One of their damned hymns.

Private Clark thumped out a music-hall tune as mother and daughter came down, carrying bags, wearing coats and sturdy shoes. The mother and daughter looked straight ahead as they left the house and walked into the yard. The boy helped a bent old woman. Hatred spilled from her currant eyes. She cursed, spit dribbling from her mouth.

'Never mind that, Ma,' the captain said. 'Just get yourselves outside.'

The old grandmother leaned heavily on the boy's arm, still cursing the soldiers as she left.

The captain looked through the window at the burning fields, at the cattle being walked away, at the sacks of oats and barley, being lifted by the mule drivers onto the carts. He would never ask his men to do a job he wouldn't do himself. Striking a match, he lit his pipe. With great care, he held the match out to his batman. Lampton took the match. Every eye was on him as he touched it to the straw in the middle of the room, beneath the stacked furniture. There was a low derisory laugh when it did not take and Lampton had to strike another, breathing soft encouragement on the flame.

There is something about a burning house, as the flames lick up the walls, as the smoke pours out, chased by the wind, as a wooden lintel cracks and drops and a roof collapses in on itself.

The old woman cursed every soldier in sight, her hand on the boy's shoulder. Their faces blank with misery, mother and daughter watched the house burn. It was as if, by not turning their backs, the destruction might be reversed.

Africans had appeared from who knows where, the

144

farm labourers. They stood in silence, watching.

The girl said, in English, 'What do we do now?'

'You should have thought of that before,' the captain said, shrugging his shoulders. 'We know your father and brothers come here for supplies and to use this as a base for going out and cutting the telegraph lines and destroying the railway. Ask *them* what you should do.'

A plume of black smoke rose through the light spring breeze, etching cruel unnatural clouds onto the clear blue sky.

17

The House Agent's Clerk

What would Dylan Ashton have to say for himself, I wondered. Might he have dared let Lucy and Alison stay in his rooms above the house agent's office?

Croker & Company, house agents, occupied a prime position in the town centre. A small poster advertising *Anna of the Five Towns* still held pride of place in a corner of the window. A flyer taped to the glass of the door informed, in neatly printed block script, "Tickets at the box office, or apply within."

A balding gentleman with a perfectly egg-shaped head sat at an important-looking oak desk scanning a ledger. Dylan, slight, his hair oiled into submission, came from the back room carrying a file. He frowned with concentration as he took his seat at a smaller desk opposite the door, where a typewriter held paper. He looked down at the open file, and then began to type.

I stared hard through the window, hoping to attract his attention. I did not relish the thought of waiting until either he or his boss chose to go out for their midday meal. Mr Croker looked like a man whose wife would wrap a potted meat sandwich in a piece of beef sheeting.

Dylan had said that he lived above the premises, so he may not venture out.

Mr Croker raised his head. I tried to look like a woman dissatisfied with her current abode as I perused the information in the window. If Dylan felt my stare, he did not respond. Just when I thought this could not go on for much longer, the telephone rang.

Mr Croker picked up the receiver and began an animated conversation. I stepped inside and approached Dylan and his tap-tapping typewriter. He stopped and looked up.

I smiled warmly. 'Pretend you're helping me with something in the window and step outside.'

His eyes lit with surprised recognition. 'Mrs Shackleton. How lovely to see you.'

Poor boy. I felt quite mean that all I wanted was information, not to pass the time of day or to reward Mr Croker for his advertisement in the theatre programme by becoming a customer.

'A property in the window, Mr Ashton?'

The edge to my voice deflated Dylan in an instant. For a moment, he looked as though he would object. He thought better of it.

'Certainly, madam.'

Dylan followed me into the street, turning his back towards Mr Croker. He ran his tongue over his lower lip. His face was pale, with just a little soreness around the right ear. A sprinkling of fiery spots could have been a skin complaint that erupted now and again. He had cut himself shaving and had taped a plaster under his chin. Something about him inspired pity. The hardness in my voice came with some effort.

'Captain Wolfendale is desperately worried about his

granddaughter who is missing. I think you might be able
to help.'

'Lucy?' he said, the fiery spots on his cheeks growing
a deeper shade of red. 'Why should I know?'

It was the lack of concern in his voice that gave him
away. 'Where is she?'

'I don't know.'

'Lucy is missing, Dylan, and so is Alison. You were
with them last night. Where are they?'

He touched the red blotch on his face as if to soothe
it. 'I tell you, I don't know.'

He was not a good liar.

'Where did they go when they left the theatre?'

He glanced back at his employer who was returning
the telephone to its cradle. 'You'll lose me my job.'

'No I won't. I'm interested in a property . . . unless
you refuse to help me find your friends. Either you'll
help me, or I'll call the police.'

His face clouded with anxiety. 'Lucy's twenty-one.
She can do as she pleases, I think.'

'The police take blackmail very seriously. And your
employer wouldn't like the bad publicity of a clerk who
aids and abets a crime.'

'It's not a crime for a person to want her own
money.'

Straight away, he realised he had said too much.

'You wanted to help her. But after what has
happened, you had better tell me everything you know,
and quickly.'

I guessed that he had heard about the murder.
Something like that does not stay quiet long.

He glanced back into the office, where Mr Croker was
watching us with great interest. 'I gave my word to Lucy.'

'Did you give your word to Alison?'

'No.'

'Then tell me where Alison is.'

'They both went to the Geerts' house.'

'The truth!'

'That is the truth. Madam Geerts, Lucy and Alison went there together.'

'And you?'

He met my look with defiance. 'Mr Geerts walked me back here. We had a drink, upstairs in my flat. That is the truth.'

'Where do the Geerts live?'

'I'm not sure. But they hold their classes in the arcade.' He cast a worried look at his employer.

To let him off the hook, I said, 'Let's go inside, Dylan. You can say I am looking for a cottage to rent and write down some suggestions.'

Mr Croker greeted me warmly and stood over Dylan, suggesting various properties. Dylan wrote down the addresses. He handed me the sheet of paper, which I held by its corner before placing it carefully in my satchel. It would be useful to have Dylan Ashton's fingerprints.

The telephone rang. Mr Croker moved to answer it, saying to me, before he picked up the receiver, 'Would you like to be taken on a viewing?'

'Not yet, thank you. I'll look at some properties from the outside.'

As I made my escape, Mr Croker was saying into the mouthpiece, 'Yes, a shocking business, shocking.'

So news of the murder was spreading.

It was now eleven o'clock. I must make my mind up what to do next.

Everything so far had taken longer than expected. Part of me wanted to simply tell the captain to call on the Geerts's, and I would catch the first train back to Leeds. But now I was intrigued. I wanted to get to the bottom of this. Missing persons are more my special interest than missing jewellery. I would postpone Mr Moony's business just a little while longer. In fact, I might spend one more night in Harrogate. Mr Moony would not expect any report back over the weekend.

Over the road, a cabdriver dropped off his fares. I waved to him. He brought his cab closer, and I climbed in.

'Where to, madam?'

Not knowing any of the hotels, I said the first name that came into my head. 'The Grand Hotel.'

It was probably extravagant, and I could not entirely justify it. Oh go on, the little voice in my head said. Live a little. It's what Gerald would want, and he did leave you enough money not to stint.

At the Grand Hotel, I booked a room and placed a telephone call. I guessed that my housekeeper had been out for her errands and would be putting her feet up with a cup of tea and the newspaper. While I waited in the lobby for the call to come through, I pictured Meriel. She would shortly be gracing the dining room of this very hotel, preparing to enjoy a meal with her impresario, oblivious to the disappearance of her leading lady. Surely she must have had some inkling of what was going on? Would she be on a pre-lunch drink at this very moment? I had a good mind to waylay her and demand that she be the one to go marching round the town,

150

wearing out shoe leather in the search for Lucy Wolfendale.

The porter beckoned me to the reception desk. I took the telephone from him. 'Your call,' the operator announced in a nasal twang that sounded as if she had a clothes peg on her nose.

'Hello, Mrs Sugden.'

'Mrs Shackleton. Is everything all right?'

'Everything is perfectly all right. I'm booked in at the Grand Hotel. I shall extend my stay. It seems a shame to be here and not take the waters.'

'That sounds splendid. It will do you no end of good. Shall I tell your mother?'

I tried not to groan. 'I haven't arranged to see her this weekend.'

'She did telephone.'

'You might get a message to Mr Sykes for me please.'

I wondered how he was getting on with his enquiries about the pawnbroker's stolen goods, and felt a pang of guilt that I would now be putting him to some trouble on a totally unrelated matter.

I heard a shuffling sound as Mrs Sugden reached for paper and pencil.

'Yes? I'm ready to take the message.'

'Please tell him to send the kit as a rail parcel on the first afternoon train. I'll meet the train and collect it.'

The pencil scratched into silence.

'But you said . . .' Mrs Sugden began, and thought better of telling me off for having led her to believe I was staying on in Harrogate simply for rest and recreation.

The kit is our code for the fingerprint set. It had occurred to me that if Lucy and Alison had someone

151

else helping them, it was likely to be Dylan, a poor liar whose very skin burst into a giveaway red rash that betrayed guilt and anxiety. His fingerprints on the list of addresses he had given me would allow me to confirm my suspicion, or eliminate him.

But I believed he was telling me the truth when he said that Lucy and Alison had gone to the Geerts's house. He had seemed surprised that they had gone there, and that made me think it was not the first lie that would have sprung to his lips.

My call to Mrs Sugden was a kind of insurance, a superstitious feeling that if I had the fingerprint kit, I would not need to use it. With a bit of luck, a single visit to Monsieur and Madam Geerts would solve the mystery. Having given my own theatre programme to Inspector Charles, I had taken the precaution of borrowing Lucy's. I opened the programme at the half-page advertisement for the Geerts' dancing school.

Monsieur and Madam Loy Geerts
Dancing School
Ballroom Ballet Tap
Classes and private tuition
Tea dances
(Professional partners)

7 Arcade Buildings, High Harrogate
Telephone 312

18

Stage Fright

The hours dragged. Lucy had done her health and beauty exercises on the battlements. Now she came back down to the floor below. Light filtered through the narrow slit of window. A blackbird perched on the sill. Tilting its head as though showing off its bright yellow beak, it peered at her. She stared up at the cobwebbed beams and into the corners of the tower's ceiling. She counted four nests, three above the beams and one between a beam and the wall.

The floor had grown harder during the night. She had slept in her clothes. Her face felt hot and dry. She reached into the depths of her tapestry bag and took out the small mirror. Looking glass in hand, she ran fingers through her hair, smoothing it into place. Lucy smiled at her reflection. No one would ever suspect her of anything wicked or underhand. She lowered her eyelashes for the demure, angelic look. 'Oh you,' she said aloud. 'You are such a monster, Lucy Wolfendale.'

What time must it be?

She reached for her watch. Eleven o'clock. The romance of the tower had entirely worn off. This place was damp, smelly and very uncomfortable. Only the thought of her brilliant future would keep her here two more nights. Two more nights! I must have been mad, Lucy thought. There should have been another way. I shouldn't have been so quick to make a move the minute we brought down the curtain on *Anna of the Five Towns*. But once you made up your mind, it was best just to do it. The RADA term loomed. A letter had come to Lucy's invented parent, asking for payment of her first fee.

If Granddad was to believe she had been kidnapped, it had to look real. If the plan went madly wrong, then she would look the part, dishevelled and unwashed. Acting distressed would not be difficult. If this scheme went awry she would be more than distressed, she would be furious, thwarted, frustrated, murderous.

Granddad would have had her ransom note by the first post this morning, just after seven. Perhaps even the second note would have arrived by now. The wheels of her future had begun to turn. Soon they would spin and take her far from here.

She yawned, stretched and slowly unfurled herself. Slipping on her shoes against the splinters of the ancient floorboards, she stood. She shook out her blankets, folded them carefully, set them down on the ground sheet and covered them with that. If this was to be her home for two days, she must make the most of it.

Seated on her folded blankets, she drank from her bottle of water, emptying it. Perhaps later she might risk a walk to the stream for a refill. From her Oxo tin she took the last of her bread and cheese. This would have to do, until Dylan brought her more food. He would not come yet. Saturday was a working day for him.

154

The thought of work reminded Lucy of another annoying attitude of her grandfather's. He did not believe that girls and young women of their station in life should work. It was no use telling him that Alison had a job in a solicitor's office. As far as Granddad was concerned, Lucy should marry, settle down, and soon.

A knocking on the door of the tower disturbed her thoughts. Her heart began to thump. She had been so sure no one came here. For a moment she hardly dared breathe. Then she hurried up to the battlements and looked down. Dylan. He took a couple of steps back and waved up at her. 'Let me in!'

She threw down the key. It fell into the long grass. She watched as he bobbed down and searched for it.

Moments later, he bounded up the stairs, empty-handed. She hoped he would have chocolate in his pocket.

He spoke all in a rush. 'I haven't got long. Everything's changed, Lucy. Someone has been asking for you.'

'Who?'

'That woman, that friend of Meriel's.'

'Mrs Shackleton?'

'Yes.'

'Well what about it? Let her ask.'

'She knows.'

'What?'

'She knows I've helped you.'

'Dylan you didn't . . .'

'No. But I could tell. She made it plain. Your grandfather must have set her on to look for you.'

Lucy's eyes widened. She had thought only of the police, and that he would not contact them because of

155

the threat in the note. And now this. 'How dare he send someone looking for me? It could be dangerous. For all he knows I'm in the hands of horrible . . . I don't know, bloodthirsty bandits or something.'

'Well, Mrs Shackleton has worked it out somehow.'

'Oh Lord.' Lucy put a hand to her mouth. 'If they've been in my room he'll have found the magazine I cut the note from. But he never goes in my room.'

'I suppose today was a bit different.'

Lucy stamped her foot. 'Dash and bletheration. I won't give up.' She sat down heavily on the folded blankets. 'Have you brought food?'

He opened his hands and with a stricken look said, 'I'm sorry. I've brought nothing. I came as soon as I could, and I don't have long.' He looked around the tower room. 'I must have been mad to agree. You shouldn't have spent the night here. A tramp could have broken in. Anything could happen. Come back with me now, on the bike.'

'No!'

As he spoke, a distant church bell tolled noon. 'Go home. Say you managed to escape. Anything. Say it was a joke.'

Lucy wound her fob watch thoughtfully as the chimes died away. 'Are you mad? I should have had my inheritance on my twenty-first birthday, just like Anna did in the play. Granddad won't give it to me because he knows I shall leave, but I'll make him.'

Dylan shivered. 'It's so cold in here. It's lovely and warm outside.'

'I don't want a weather report.' She patted the space beside her on the blanket. 'Come and sit beside me, Dylan.'

'No.'

'Why not?'

'Because I have to get back to work, and because if I sit beside you, you'll get round me. You'll make me go on helping you when I know it's no use.'

'At least Granddad didn't go to the police. For all he and Mrs Shackleton know, those magazines could have been put under my bed by someone else. Anyhow, perhaps they didn't find them and she's just guessing by coming to see you.'

Dylan knelt on the ground sheet, facing her. 'Come away from here. Let me cycle you back. I saw gypsies in the lane. This is just the kind of place they'd come to. Rip out the floorboards for firewood.'

'Let them! I'll help. And I would rather run away with the gypsies than give up and go back now.'

'If anything happens to you, it'll be my fault.'

'No it won't. I'd have done this with or without your help. Just forty-eight hours and I'll be free. Mrs Shackleton should be on my side. She does what she pleases with her life. Why shouldn't I?'

'I hurried here soon as I could. Now I have to go. Lucy, give it up. Please.'

'Never.'

Dylan lowered his head. 'Oh God, what have I done? This is all my fault for showing you the tower.'

'Don't be a ninny, Dylan. Just fetch me a flask of tea and a cheese sandwich, or jam, or anything.'

Dylan sat back on his heels. He looked away, through the narrow window. 'There's something I haven't told you.'

Lucy waited. She was becoming impatient. Dylan had seemed the ideal person to help her. Now she wished she had been able to do this all alone.

He said, 'You wanted to get away from Mr Milner didn't you?'

'Don't ask me to go over and over this that and the other. It's too late.'

Dylan gulped. 'There's no need to worry about Mr Milner any more.'

Lucy's eyes widened. 'What do you mean?'

'Mr Milner's dead.'

'That is not clever. If you're saying that so I'll give up . . . I thought better of you.'

'It's true!'

'How? When?'

'Last night, after the theatre. He was found dead in a doorway. It's all over the town.'

'How did he die?'

'Horribly.'

She waited, but he seemed reluctant to say more. 'How?'

'Someone said a gun, someone said a knife. The police are interviewing everyone. I expect they'll want to talk to you and your granddad, so everything's bound to come out.'

Lucy felt some subtle change inside herself, a kind of bracing for what would come next. 'I'm not sorry he's dead. The only thing I'm sorry about is that if Granddad really doesn't have money for my ransom, he could have got it from Mr Milner. Now he won't be able to.'

She saw the shocked expression on Dylan's face. Immediately her own look softened, as she reached out and touched his cheek. 'Poor Dylan. Now you know what I'm really like. It's up to you whether you go on helping me. But I shall stay here until Monday morning, and then I shall go and collect my ransom, if it's there.

If it's not, I don't know what I shall do. But whatever happens, I'll be leaving.'

Slowly, Dylan rose to his feet. He walked back down the uneven stairs, treading heavily, as if hoping the world would give way beneath his feet.

Lucy followed.

He left without speaking.

She locked the door behind him.

He had gone without promising to bring food. She would show him. She would show them all. Lucy needed no one. Lucy would come through. Later, she would go out into the meadow. There was clover in the meadow, she could gather and eat clover. There were blackberries in the hedgerow, the stream not far off.

She felt angry with Dylan for being so ready to give up. Her head had begun to ache. She needed a pee.

Lucy pulled down her drawers and squatted over a gap in the broken boards. And then it happened. The key fell from her hand through the space to the hard ground far below. She pulled up her drawers quickly and looked down, to see whether the key was visible. Down, down, to nothing. Down to a hard earth floor strewn with years of debris, straw, dead leaves, the droppings of rodents.

She hurried back up the stairs, one storey, two, and another to the battlements. She somehow missed her footing, tried to right herself and twisted her ankle. Her cry of pain bounced back to her from the thick stone walls. 'My ankle. Dylan!' she screamed. 'Come back,' knowing he could not hear her now.

He would be pedalling back towards Harrogate.

She pressed her hand into the cool stone wall for support and made a wish, that this was just a trial, like in the fairy stories, and there would be some way through, and she would find it.

If she were Rapunzel, she could let down her long hair. But Lucy's hair was a neat, short bob. Besides, who could climb down her own hair? The thought made her smile. Dylan would come back.

Dylan climbed on his bike. He felt too heavy for the saddle. His leaden feet did not want to push the pedals. He was stupid to have helped Lucy, idiotic for taking her to the tower in the first place. The road dipped on a downward camber as he rounded the bend. The vehicle coming towards him was going too fast, on Dylan's side of the road, taking no account of the bend. The driver did not see him. As Dylan veered towards the grass verge, his eyes locked onto the eyes of the motorist in the last second before the collision. *I'm invisible. I'm dead.*

19

Foxtrot Murder

I mounted the stairs to the arcade mezzanine room where Geerts's dancing school held sway. A reasonably good pianist played a tune I had danced to long ago. What was it? Just as I thought the name would come to me, the music stopped abruptly.

Monsieur Geerts had dropped all attempts to sound like the Potteries burgher he had played in *Anna of the Five Towns*. I hesitated by the door, listening.

'Rrrun smoothly on the toes! Let the music leeft you. For the foxtrot, first slow walk, two counts to a step, one, two! Watch me! Now a trot, you copy the gait of the 'orse, one count, one step. Again! One-two-one, one-two-one. Smile! Trot like 'appy 'orse.'

I pushed the door open a fraction. A dozen young couples, boys and girls aged between thirteen and sixteen, were standing about the room, eyes on Monsieur Geerts, one boy trying not to giggle. A slender young assistant stood beside the dancing master, smiling encouragingly at the couples nearest to her. In the corner by the window, upright as her piano, the grey-haired pianist waited patiently for her cue to begin again. Monsieur Geerts tapped his stick three times. Music filled the room. The happy young horses began their foxtrot. Now I recognised the tune. 'Foxtrot Murder'.

Monsieur Geerts sighed heavily, and then noticed me. 'May I have a word, Monsieur Geerts?'

He waved to his young assistant to take over, and stepped out with me onto the mezzanine.

'Sorry to disturb your class. I'm looking for Lucy Wolfendale. I thought she may be helping with your classes today.' It was a spur of the moment lie. And one name would be enough. Find Lucy, and I would find Alison.

His eyes brightened at Lucy's name. 'Sometimes she does teach a class. She is very good dancer, good with the younger children. They hang on her words, she mesmerises.'

'I can imagine.' He seemed such a nice man. In my statement for Inspector Charles I had pointed him out as someone who could be suspected of murder: the jealous husband. 'Have you taught dancing since you came to this country, Monsieur Geerts?'

'When we first come, as refugees from Belgium, we stay in a room the authorities give us. But a man must do something.' He chuckled, at a fond memory. 'We 'elp with the wounded soldiers, the sick soldiers. Some officer organise a Charlie Chaplin look-alike competition. That is when I get the 'ang of English sense of humour. The soldiers, they look like Chaplin but not move like Chaplin. I show them, this is 'ow you move like Chaplin.'

He twirled his cane and did a few Chaplin steps along the mezzanine landing, then back towards his dance studio, shuffling ahead of me. One moment more and he would disappear back into the land of foxtrot.

'Lucy came to your house after the performance and party last night.'

He shook his head vigorously. 'No, no, no.'

One no would have been enough.

There was no way to keep this tactful. 'She and Alison were seen at your house, and not seen since.'

He tensed, his jaw tightened. 'Who says this?'

'I just need to speak to them. It will save time and trouble if you tell me the truth.'

'Lucy was not at my 'ouse.'

We faced each other for a long moment.

'Monsieur Geerts, I'm sure you don't need more troubles than you already have.'

'What do you mean?'

Inspector Charles had asked me not to say anything, but I felt sure Geerts already knew about Milner's murder, just as Mr Croker had known.

Monsieur Geerts's look was wide-eyed and innocent, as though he was not a man who had been cuckolded by the murder victim.

'Two girls go missing, on the night of Mr Milner's murder.'

He turned pale. 'The police do not think ... Not Lucy ...'

'I do not know what the police think. I have been interviewed, and you will be too. The police will also want to speak to Lucy and Alison. And I think you know where they are. Wouldn't you rather tell me than the Scotland Yard inspector?'

He pushed his hands into his pockets, so that I would not see he was shaking.

'Go back to your class, if you would rather speak to the police about Lucy and Alison.' I turned away, taking a chance that he would not let me go.

Suddenly he was behind me, one-two-one-two. 'Where do you go now? If Lucy is missing, I worry.'

'Where do you suggest I go?'

He ran his tongue across dry lips. His fingers reached for his moustache as though he had been told of clinging crumbs. 'Wait. It is all around the town about Mr Milner. I know the police. Two and two together and they think they tango.'

I waited.

A thin film of sweat broke out on his forehead. 'I 'old nothing against Mr Milner. The advertisement in the play programme for our dancing school, 'e insist to pay for that.'

'My concern is to find Lucy and Alison.'

He shook his head. 'Lucy? I don't know. Alison, go see my wife.'

'I shall. The address, Monsieur Geerts?' I took out my notebook.

He looked at his feet for inspiration, and then gave me his address.

'Thank you.'

His long slender fingers touched my wrist. 'She . . . she 'as not been out of the 'ouse today, my wife, so . . . Mr Milner's death, she does not know.'

In the room behind us, the pianist stopped playing. From the ground floor came the sound of a child's cry. Was Monsieur Geerts asking me to tell his wife about Milner's death, or not to tell her? It seemed he did not know himself.

'My class,' he murmured, and turned away.

Watching my step, looking at my sensibly shod feet, I made my way down the wrought-iron spiral staircase to the ground floor.

I wished I had not known about Mr Milner and Madam Geerts. I wished I hadn't felt obliged to tell the inspector that Monsieur Geerts almost certainly saw them together in the dressing room.

'Good morning, Mrs Shackleton.' The voice startled me out of my reverie. As if I had conjured him up, there was Inspector Charles. 'Don't tell me, you've been enquiring about dancing lessons?'

I smiled in what I hoped was a beguiling fashion. 'I already dance very well.'

He tipped his hat. 'I'm sure you do.' And with that, he mounted the stairs.

Seeing Inspector Charles in the arcade, on his way to question Monsieur Geerts, upset me. Monsieur Geerts would think back to the night before, to seeing me in the corridor at the theatre as he searched the dressing rooms for his wife. He would know that one of two people had betrayed him: his own wife, or me. Put it out of your mind, I said. Scotland Yard are the murder squad, not you. Besides, I had confidence that Inspector Charles would not give me away. And if I knew about Lawrence Milner and Madam Geerts's affair, then others would too.

20

Masking: one actor blocks another from sight

It was a street of identical terraced houses not far from the railway station. Standing at the front door, I could hear the doorbell ringing inside the Geerts's house. No one answered. I made my way round to the back. Pots of mint, chives, parsley and thyme stood in the spotlessly clean yard. I knocked on the door.

Geraniums sat on the window sill, turning leggy, some petals falling onto the scoured sill. The window blind was dropped. Through a small gap at the side of the blind, I could see into the neat kitchen with its square deal table and raffia-backed chairs. There was a cup, saucer and coffee pot on the table.

I knocked on the door again.

Stepping back into the yard, I looked up at the bedroom window. Was it my imagination, or did the blind move?

After one more knock on the door, I searched my satchel for something useful. There it was. Earlier in the summer, when I was on the Braithwaite case, Hector, Tabitha Braithwaite's fiancé, had given me his old scout knife, as a keepsake. I flicked open the blade, slid it under the window catch and edged it back. The sash window lifted easily. Carefully, I moved the pots of geraniums and climbed inside.

The kitchen smelled of coffee, Cherry Blossom boot polish and a faint odour of yeast, like dough left to rise. A sudden bump and a scream came from beyond the door that led from the kitchen. Crashing into the long string of garlic bulbs that swayed from the clothes airer, I crossed the small room in a few strides, kicking the tin bath whose water was still warm enough to be sending up a cloud of steam.

A figure lay at the foot of the stairs, doubled in pain, clutching herself, moaning.

I bent down beside her.

She looked up at me, her eyes full of tears, chubby round face filmed with sweat and distorted in pain. She was barefoot. Her nightgown was damp. Unpinned, her long hair stuck to her forehead and cheeks.

For a few seconds I did not recognise her, perhaps because I expected to see Lucy, or Madam Geerts. A tear fell, and the moaning turned into a sob.

'Alison! What happened? Let me help you up. Can you stand?'

'I think so.'

Aware of another presence, I looked up.

At the top of the stairs, Madam Geerts stood still and erect, frozen as a statue, beautifully dressed in a bias-cut blue linen skirt and white blouse, her hair immaculately coiffured in loops. 'Poor girl,' she said as, in her best dancer's glide, she slowly descended the stairs. 'She fell.'

Alison's sobs turned to a whimper as I helped her to her feet. 'Did you fall?' I asked.

The answer sounded like oh, or no.

Madam Geerts drew herself up to her full height of about four feet eleven inches. She stood three stairs above us, which allowed her to glare down. 'Of course she fell. You say I pushed her?' Madam Geerts moved to Alison's side.

The three of us stood in a tight knot at the bottom of the stairs, scarcely able to move.

Madam Geerts tried to edge Alison up the stairs. 'Don't speak. You must lie down.'

'I hurt, I hurt.'

'Where?' Madam Geerts demanded.

'For heaven's sake, woman,' I said. 'She'll hurt all over. She's just taken a tumble down a dozen stone steps.'

'Fifteen steps,' Alison whined.

'Then march back up fifteen steps,' Madam Geerts commanded.

I ignored her, and helped Alison into the downstairs room that was kitchen and living room. Alison's bare feet splashed into the water that had spilled on the floor from the tin bath.

Madam Geerts followed. 'Who let you in, Mrs Shackleton?'

'Myself.'

'But . . .'

'You must have heard me knocking.' I led Alison to the Windsor chair by the hearth.

'So the Englishman's 'ome is not a castle. There is a law to answer the door?'

'There is a law against pushing a girl down the stairs.'

'Push her? Push her?'

'She . . . she . . .' Alison's voice came out in choking

sobs. 'She didn't . . . I fell. I fell down the stairs and it didn't . . . Did it . . .'

Madam Geerts brushed past me and faced Alison. 'It is best you lie down, Alison.'

I stepped between Madam Geerts and Alison. 'From the way things look here, I don't believe you are in any position to say what it is best for Alison to do.'

Madam Geerts jutted her chin. 'Oh? And what do you insinuate?'

'A hot bath. Alison "falling" down the stairs. A powerful smell of brewers' yeast, but no baking in evidence. What did you buy in Leeds yesterday? Cohosh? Slippery elm? Penny royal? Something to "restore female regularity"? Your visit was a secret from your husband because . . .'

'You are wrong.'

'. . . he would have asked what you were doing there. He would have connected it with Alison's stay, and why you are not at the dancing school this morning.'

Madam Geerts turned pale. 'You know nothing.'

'On the contrary, I know a great deal. I was in the V A D during the war. Soldiers were not the only casualties.'

'Alison is in trouble. I try to help.'

'Shut up, shut up both of you.' Alison rocked back and forth in her chair. 'I'll lie down. I want to lie down.'

My instinct was to gather her up and take her home, but she was in no fit state for that.

Madam Geerts and I looked at each other across Alison's bent head. It was almost a moment of truce, but I was determined not to let her get the upper hand. 'You make some tea. I'll take Alison upstairs.'

169

'It is not tea that she needs,' Madam Geerts barked back, but her bark was sulky. She would do as I said.

'Strong tea, sugar for Alison, no sugar for me.'

Slowly, I led Alison up the narrow stairs. She plodded, as if hoping never to reach the top. To the left of the small landing a door led into the front bedroom.

'I'm in here,' Alison said weakly, turning into a small whitewashed room with a single bed, washstand, small cabinet and a straight-back chair. The room smelled of violets, spearmint and vomit. Its cream window blind was drawn down, but the strong sunshine outside broke through into the gloom and created an unreal air, like a stage set.

I helped Alison into bed. 'Let me brush your hair.'

She had looked so pristine and jolly, playing her part in the play the evening before. Now her hair lay lank and straggling. I propped the pillows so that she could sit up. First I brushed one side of her hair, then the other, plaiting each side. With the plaits over her shoulders, she looked so very young.

Returning the hairbrush to the washstand, I asked, 'What age are you?'

'Twenty-one.'

'Same as Lucy.'

'I'm two months older than Lucy.'

'Alison, I know it doesn't seem like it now, but everything will be all right. Try not to worry.'

Her hands clasped at her chest. Her round moon face looked pale and drawn. She seemed utterly done in. Her breath was laboured but she had stopped crying. On the cabinet beside her bed was a dish of chocolate bon bons, and a glass of water.

'I'm expected in work on Monday,' she wailed. 'What will I do if I'm like this?'

Carefully, I handed her the glass. 'Take a sip. You'll have your tea in a minute and you'll feel better. Don't worry about work for now.'

'If I lose my job . . .'

'Shush.'

Alison emptied the glass. I took it back from her carefully and slid it into my satchel. With a little luck there might be fingerprints and then I would know whether she had helped Lucy write the ransom note.

I pulled up the rattan chair and we sat in silence.

Moments later, Madam Geerts appeared with two cups of tea on a tray. She set the tray on the washstand and handed a cup to each of us. Alison made no move to take hers. Madam Geerts set it on the bedside cabinet. Making one more effort to pull the wool over my eyes, she said to me, 'Alison 'ave too much cherry brandy last night and stay 'ere.'

So that was the way she wanted to play it. I took a sip of sugary tea. 'This is yours, Alison. Take a drink. It will do you more good than Madam Geerts's cherry brandy.'

For Alison's sake, I would stay calm, although I felt like pushing Madam Geerts down her own stairs.

Alison began to drink the tea. I wanted Madam Geerts to leave, so I could talk to Alison. I caught her eye, and we retreated to the landing, closing the door behind us.

'Well?' Madam Geerts asked. 'She drank cherry brandy. She fell down the stairs.'

When I did not answer, she led me into the other room, well out of Alison's earshot.

171

Before she had the chance to tell more lies or try and justify her actions, I said, 'You asked me not to tell your husband you were on the Leeds train. Now I know why. You were at some chemist's shop buying what you needed. Monsieur Geerts might choose to believe your cherry brandy story. Don't insult me with such a tale.'

For once, Madam Geerts seemed speechless. She wrung her hands in a rather dramatic fashion.

Why did I feel so angry? Calm down, I told myself. This is not my business. This foolish woman believes she is doing what is best. 'You know that what you've done is a crime in England? It's classified as an offence against the person, under an Act of 1861.'

She looked towards the window, as though she might be able to fly away. 'For the best. I did it for the best.'

'It's lucky for you that it hasn't worked.' I said that with more conviction than I felt. After all, Alison might still miscarry. And I knew nothing of the circumstances. I thought of Alison's mother, busy with her preparations for the church fair, disapproving of the fact that half the proceeds would go to fallen women. It would not be an easy matter for Alison to admit to being pregnant. And of course she would lose her job in the solicitor's office.

Madam Geerts set her mouth in a stubborn line. 'The young man will not marry her. This I know from 'is father who is against the match, and made this plain to me.'

In an instant I knew that the young man must be Rodney Milner. I could imagine that Lawrence Milner would oppose a match to a widow's daughter who

172

worked for her living. That would not have suited his plans to rise in Harrogate society.

My feelings towards Madam Geerts softened, but for less than a moment. I wanted to tell her that Milner was dead, but remembered Inspector Charles's prohibition. Not that it seemed to carry much weight since half of Harrogate now knew of the murder. But not Madam Geerts.

'I suggest that you empty that bath and clear up any signs of "cherry brandy" . . .'

'Thank you.' She breathed a sigh of relief.

'. . . because it is unlikely I will be your only caller today.'

She frowned. 'What do you mean?'

'Just do as I say.'

'You will not tell?'

'For Alison's sake, not yours. Now tell me, please. Where is Lucy Wolfendale? She came here last night with Alison.'

'She walked with us yes, and came in only for a moment.'

'Who else was with you?'

'Rodney and 'is friend, a fellow who was at the bar. I forget 'is name. 'is father keeps a public house and sometimes the young men play cards there when the place is shut.'

'Did they come in?'

'No. They just escorted us home.'

'Did Lucy leave with them?'

'She came in for a few moments. Drank a quick cherry brandy, far too quick. Then said she would catch up Rodney and this other fellow and ask them to walk her home.'

173

So I would need to call on Rodney Milner. That was not a task I relished.

The only person Madam Geerts had not mentioned was her own husband. That did not look good for him.

'And Monsieur Geerts?' I asked. 'He did not escort you home?'

'He came later.'

'Alone?'

'Why all these questions?'

She was right, of course. It was up to Inspector Charles to find out about Monsieur Geerts's movements.

'I don't like being asked to convey lies. Last night, Lucy asked me to give her grandfather a message. Captain Wolfendale was meant to believe Lucy stayed with Alison, just as Alison's mother believed she was with Lucy.'

Madam Geerts's brow creased with puzzlement. 'She say . . . I do not remember *exactement*. I swear I thought Lucy would go home.'

'Unless she is found soon, there will be a major police search.'

Madam Geerts looked genuinely surprised. She shook her head. 'Yes, I lie to you for Alison. But I do not lie now. If the police come . . . I empty the water.'

Without another word, Madam Geerts hurried down the stairs to empty the tin bath.

When I went back into the small whitewashed room, a cat had found its way onto the counterpane. Alison stroked its head. In a sudden instant, I felt that the words I had spoken to her before would come true. Everything would be all right. Alison's gaze fixed on her hands, and on the cat. Slowly, tears formed. One began to trickle down her cheek. I produced a hanky. She dabbed at her eyes and wiped her nose.

'Do you want me to take you home? I can fetch a taxi cab.'

'No! Please don't. Mother mustn't see me like this. I'll stay here a little longer. Mother thinks I'm with Lucy.'

'Does Lucy know why you are here?'

Alison shook her head. 'Not properly. She thinks I'm just late. First she said I missed my bleeding time because I was nervous about the play. We usually have the curse at the same time. That's how I know I've missed two.'

'But she's your friend. Couldn't you confide?'

'She said I could not be pregnant. It was just once, you see. And she felt guilty because she had left the two of us alone. And when we told Olivia, Madam Geerts, she knew what to do to bring me on. We thought it was just some blockage sort of thing,' Alison said miserably. Her hands went to her belly.

I resisted the urge to reach out and touch Alison's hand.

Her eyes met mine. 'You haven't to say, not to anyone. Swear you won't.'

'I won't say anything.'

'Thank you.' She blew her nose. 'Madam Geerts wanted to help. She explained that I could be pregnant, and that with me in this condition, Rodney could not have married me because of the disgrace.'

'Did Rodney say that?'

'No. He doesn't know. But it is true. His father . . . you see . . . they have a position to keep up, Madam

Geerts explained that. Well, so do I have a position to keep up, and my mother.'

'Some things are more important than appearances. Don't give up hope. If Rodney loves you, you will marry, and sooner than you think. Trust me.' Even to myself I sounded a little like a gypsy whose palm has been crossed with a silver threepenny bit.

She looked at me, puzzled. 'Did I say Rodney's name? I didn't mean to.'

'Babies can be premature. People might talk, but they would soon forget.'

Her eyes lit with hope. It would be better not to mention that people certainly would talk if Rodney Milner married five minutes after his father had been murdered. 'Don't let Olivia Geerts give you anything else.' I reached for the witch hazel from the dresser, along with some cotton wool. 'Dab at your bruises, wherever they're coming up. And if you throw yourself down those stairs once more, I shall personally put an announcement in the *Harrogate Advertiser* about it.'

'But . . .' Her fingers played an agitated tune on the counterpane.

'No buts. Start dabbing. And talk to me about Lucy.'

'Why?' She looked genuinely surprised to be asked.

'I just thought she'd stayed here with you last night. Where is she?'

'She walked here with us, stayed a few minutes, and then went home.' Her eyes widened with alarm. 'Has something happened to her?'

'No, I'm sure not. It's me getting the wrong idea.'

So Dylan knew nothing, Monsieur Geerts knew nothing, and now Alison knew nothing. My confidence in my ability to uncover any information slipped to the soles of my feet. What did I know? I had taken Alison's photograph, watched her act the part of Beatrice Sutton, never guessing that her chubbiness may not have been entirely due to a passion for chocolates. I had to get out of here before I started lecturing, losing my temper with the poor girl, telling her someone would have adopted her baby even if that swine – not that one should speak ill of the dead – did want to prevent his spineless offspring from marrying the woman he loved. I found it hard to believe that Rodney did not know about Alison's condition. But now wasn't the time. And it was not my business.

You are not here to pity, or to judge, I told myself. Think of why you are here, Kate Shackleton.

'Did you and Lucy and Madam Geerts walk here alone last night, Alison?'

'Rodney and his friend George walked us to the door. Lucy only came to keep me company. She said she would run and catch up with the boys.'

'Don't be alarmed, Alison, but Lucy didn't go home last night. Do you have any idea who else she may have stayed with?'

Alison shook her head. 'I can't think who, not old school friends, because then it would have come out that I'm not with her.'

'I'd better go. Just stay calm. Be well. And don't worry about Lucy.' There is no greater way of helping someone to worry than telling them not to. So I lied. 'I'll track her down soon enough. She's probably just being mysterious.'

Madam Geerts sat at the kitchen table. A large ashtray

177

held dozens of pearl beads. She was rethreading a necklace. In a flat voice, she said, 'I wish I 'ad nothing to do with it.'

'Then why did you?'

'It was for the best.'

'Rodney Milner should not get away with it. She's a respectable girl. It would be a reasonable match.'

A pearl rolled onto the floor. She dived down and scrambled about, looking for the lost bead. I waited. She came up for air and set the bead with the others in the ashtray.

'Lawrence thinks . . .' Madam Geerts stopped.

'What does Mr Milner think?' I asked.

'A lovely man, quiet, gentle, a widower you know. 'e says Rodney is not the father. Alison is trying to make a good catch.'

'I find that hard to believe when she has not even told Rodney that she is pregnant.'

She shrugged. 'Perhaps I listened too much to Mr Milner.'

She most certainly had listened to him too much. '*He* asked you to do this?'

'It was for the best, I thought. Now I change my mind. I believe Alison. Mr Milner, perhaps 'e is mistaken.'

Mr Milner, he is dead, but it is not up to me to tell you.

'Madam Geerts, do you have any idea where Lucy may have gone?'

She pursed her lips. 'If I know I tell you. I know nothing. Lucy is good at secrets.'

'So am I, and so are you. We have a secret that could find you disgraced, on trial, your dancing school finished.'

She picked up a handful of beads, and then slowly let them trickle through her fingers back into the dish. 'I think Lucy 'as been offered a place at a drama school.'

'Really? Where?'

Madam Geerts shook her head. 'I'm not sure. I 'eard 'er and Meriel, they talk in a corner. I add two and two. If she run away, I am glad for 'er.'

I bet you are, I thought, and glad for yourself, too. Particularly since Mr Milner couldn't keep his eyes or his hands off Lucy.

The four young people in the play, Alison, Dylan, Lucy and Rodney, had formed a tight little band at last night's party. Perhaps Lucy did catch up with Rodney and his friend, and they would know where I could find her. A chilling thought struck me. Lucy had shown such disgust at being pestered by Milner, perhaps she had been the one to stab him through the heart. Or it could be Rodney, if he had worked out that his father had come between him and Alison. It was time for me to speak to Rodney.

It would be distasteful to question a young man who had just lost his father. On the other hand, offering condolences would be entirely acceptable.

'Where would I find Rodney Milner, Madam Geerts? Perhaps he'll be able to help me find Lucy.'

Madam Geerts hesitated.

I prompted. 'If Lucy has decided to leave home, then that is up to her, but at least her grandfather should know. Or would you prefer that the police search for her?'

'The Milners live on Cow Gate Road,' Madam Geerts said. 'Number 12. But if you seek Rodney, go to the motor car showroom. On Saturdays 'e is always there. Lawrence, Mr Milner, 'e takes Saturday off, to play golf.'

'Thank you.' Soon Olivia Geerts would learn Lawrence Milner's golf club swinging days were over. He would be taking Saturdays off, and every other day, into eternity.

21

Closed Due to Bereavement

I left Madam Geerts's house with the speed that anger gives. My old-lady shoes pounded the pavement as I almost broke into a run, needing to get away.

And then it hit me. I realised where the anger, the throbbing in my heart, had come from. My head had not worked out what was going on when I kicked into the steaming tin bath in the Geerts's kitchen, and heard Alison's cry. My body told me. I was back to that fateful day when Gerald had his army letter, telling him where to report. Should I break the news that I am expecting a child, I had asked myself? He went to work. By the time he came home, the question did not arise. I never spoke about my miscarriage. 'What's the matter?' he had asked. 'Oh it's nothing, just not so very well today.' 'You're upset because I'm going,' he had said. 'Everything will be all right.'

That was the nearest I came to bearing a child, something that I put behind me, like a bad dream. Even as I thought of it, a pain splashed somewhere deep inside me, breaking in angry waves like the rush of a stormy tide.

Everything will be all right. The words I had used to Alison. Gerald's words.

No, Gerald. Everything was not all right.

Before reaching the Milner house, I had to sit on a wall and take deep breaths to steady my nerves. That was then. This was now. No longer a young bride, I was a widow, to all intents and purposes – with a job to do.

The houses were set back from the road, with long gardens that would give the postman something of a trek.

Meriel had said that half the young women in the theatre audience fell for Rodney Milner. He was handsome in the style of a leading young man in a drawing-room comedy, with a strong jaw, thick reddish-blond hair and steady grey eyes. Though a little stilted, his manner on stage suited the character he played: Henry Mynors, self-made businessman. Only occasionally was his ease of manner ruffled. That was when Mr Milner, sitting on the front row, eating humbugs, smoking, made facetious comments at his son's expense.

With some trepidation, I lifted the knocker, a leering gargoyle with the weight and thud of a blacksmith's hammer. Moments later, a matronly woman wearing a large pinafore opened the door. Her mouth was set in a grim line. She blinked red-rimmed eyes. That someone might be crying because of Lawrence Milner's death astonished me into silence. She spoke impatiently.

'Yes?'

'I'm Mrs Shackleton. Is Mr Rodney Milner at home?' I did not want her to think I had come looking for a dead man.

'He's at the showroom.'

'Really?' The surprise must have shown.

'You've heard?' she said. 'About the master.'

In a suitably sombre voice, I said, 'I was the one who found Mr Milner and called the police.'

Her manner changed. 'You knew him then?'

'Only recently, through the play. But because of the circumstances I thought I would call and see Rodney, and offer my condolences.'

'As I say, he's at the showroom. It's closed up for the day of course but the police wanted to look around there, and Master Rodney has the key. He felt he should be there.'

'Will he mind if I call, do you think?'

A tear squeezed from the corner of her eye. She dabbed her apron at it. 'The poor lad's not in any fit way to mind or not mind.'

So the tears were not for Lawrence, but for Rodney.

'You must be getting tired of answering the door this morning.'

She sighed. 'You expect it. Chap from the Chamber of Commerce was here first thing. Don't know how he knew. Miss Jamieson, the theatrical lady, she called, and Captain Wolfendale.'

That was kind of Meriel, I thought. Good for her. She had a heart after all.

'Wait a minute!' The housekeeper narrowed her eyes warily. I might be spinning her a yarn. 'Miss Jamieson said *she* found Mr Milner.'

'We were together,' I said. 'Well, I'm sorry to have disturbed you. I'll go to the showroom.'

As I walked back to the Milners' gate, I wondered was the captain really and truly there to pay condolences, or did he believe that Rodney might lead him to

Lucy? If Wolfendale was so close to Rodney as to come round straight away, it puzzled me that he had been reticent about admitting that Lawrence Milner was his friend. Perhaps some snobbery was involved. After all, a captain does not usually become great friends with a corporal. There was some connection between them. Milner had said that an "old comrade" had helped him when he was down on his luck, and that then he had come to Harrogate and started his business. Curiouser and curiouser. If Wolfendale had stumped up some money, it was odd that he should be penniless when Milner prospered. All in all, I was beginning to wish I had not agreed to help the captain. After all, if he were fit and well enough to come trotting round to see Rodney, he could have searched for Lucy himself. I had only agreed because the old man had looked on the point of collapse.

You have a case of your own to attend to, Kate Shackleton, I said to myself. Missing jewellery from Moony the pawnbroker. Having reminded myself of that obligation, I decided that this afternoon I would call on another of Mr Moony's customers.

Milner & Son's car showroom colonised the corner of Summerfield Avenue and Leeds Road. It was a bold, triangular futuristic building that looked as though it might sally forth and crush all before it. Bricks faced with white porcelain formed a fascia above the plate-glass windows. Above that, on the first floor, were smaller iron-framed windows. Two brand-new Wolseleys vied for attention, displayed at angles to each other. At the back of the showroom stood a couple of older cars, one very much like mine, only more highly polished.

184

The building was so avant-garde that I could not see the way in at first. On the other side of the window, a tired-looking old man in a brown overall stooped as he wielded a broom, sweeping slowly and methodically. He looked up and pointed to the doorway on my left.

The sweeper-up moved to the other side of the door, indicating to a sign that said, *Closed due to bereavement*. By dumb show and exaggerated lip movements, I let him know that I had come to speak to Rodney.

He opened the door.

Inside the showroom, I caught the whiff of polish and leather. The man held his brush close, as though without it he might fall, and stood so near to me that I could hear his short, wheezy breathing and catch the smell of a body pickled in nicotine. 'Afternoon, miss,' he said politely, in a soft Irish accent. 'Mister Rodney's in the office, only he won't want disturbing.'

'It's all right. I know him.' Still, he stood there, the brush tilted at an angle, ready to present arms.

'I'm here to express condolences. I'm the person who found Mr Milner.'

While he was taking in this piece of information, I sidestepped him and made my way to the office, which I could see on the left.

I tapped on the door and opened it. 'Rodney. May I come in?'

Rodney looked every inch the man-about-town. He wore a dark mohair suit, trousers crease so sharp it would slice a finger.

He stood up. As if forgetting his situation for a moment, he switched on a brief semi-professional smile. The smile oozed the assurance that comes from

185

imagining you have the best of everything under life's bonnet. The confident manner said, "I'm in this salesroom by choice, not necessity."

But the practised smile did not reach his eyes, and he let it slip as he offered his hand. 'The police told me you found Dad.'

'I wanted to say how sorry I am, Rodney.'

'Thank you. It must have been a shock for you to see him in that doorway.'

'I should be saying that to you, a shock for you to learn of his death.'

'Won't you sit down? It's strange to be here with that sign on the door. Saturday mornings are sometimes so busy. Today it's like . . . I was going to say like a graveyard . . . I can't take it in.'

'Excuse me, Mister Rodney.' The man in the overall put his head round the door.

'Yes, Owen?'

'Will I fetch you both a cuppa tea?'

Rodney looked at me. I nodded.

'Yes, thank you, Owen.'

'Oh and, sir, will I be in next week?'

'Well, yes,' Rodney said in surprise. 'Not Monday of course. We will be closed as a mark of respect for my father, and then on the day of the funeral, but I don't know when that will be. But I should like you to come in first thing Monday, so that you can ensure the note is on the door. I've spoken to the works manager, but you could be here in case any of the mechanics don't get the message and turn up for work.'

'Thank you, sir.' Owen nodded gravely, but it seemed to me there was something like pleasure or relief in his voice.

At the risk of being nosy, I gave Rodney a questioning look.

'My father sacked him. Said he was too slow. Today was to have been his last day, working out a week's notice. But I shall keep him on. What does it matter if it takes twenty minutes or thirty-five to sweep a showroom or clean a motor?'

It occurred to me that the business might improve, with Milner dead. Unless Mr Milner senior was the one with the business head, and then Rodney may turn into one of those agreeable young men who let an inheritance slip through their fingers.

Weeks ago, when I had taken Rodney's publicity photograph for the play, he had radiated confidence, but almost too vividly, as though it might be a sham — something he put on as he fastened his necktie each morning. It struck me that he was very much at home, sitting in the leather chair, pictures of motor cars on the wall behind him.

'Is this your own office?' I asked.

'It is now. Dad and I shared. When we were here together, mostly I'd sit where you are, or go out into the showroom, or the works, and make myself useful.'

'You enjoy it?'

'Very much. But I didn't kill Dad to take over.'

'Rodney!'

'That's what Inspector Charles seems to think.'

'I'm sure not.'

He waved an arm at an empty shelf on the wall. 'He's had a man take our ledgers away, and bank statements, to check whether Dad owed money, or had made enemies.'

'And had he?'

'Not that I'm aware of. There's a difference in not being liked and having enemies. Dad wasn't liked. But why would anyone kill him?'

Rodney was quiet for a moment. I thought back to the performance of the night before, sitting on the front row of the stalls when the curtain rose. When Mr Milner came in late, noisily, excusing himself, waving a cigar, brushing ash from his trousers, he had settled himself, and suppressed a fit of coughing. On stage, Rodney began to stumble over his lines. 'My son,' Milner had whispered loudly as he puffed out a cloud of smoke. 'He'll say I'm late on purpose.'

As if he read my thoughts, Rodney said, 'He put people's backs up. That was his way. It didn't mean to say he had enemies.'

I racked my brains for something kind to say. 'He's built a superb business. There must be people who envy him that.'

'No other motor business for miles around comes near what we've achieved, but there's no ill-feeling from other traders as far as I know. I can't imagine who would want to kill Dad. They say he wasn't robbed, that his wallet was still in his pocket. If he had been robbed, that at least would be an explanation.'

'Do you have relatives, friends who'll stand by you? It's going to be hard over the coming weeks and months.'

He picked up a pencil and began to fidget with it. 'Mrs Gould, she's our housekeeper ... She ... when my mother died, Dad left a lot of the arrangements to her.'

'When did your mother die, Rodney?'

He gulped. 'Two years ago.'

188

Owen brought in a tray with a teapot, milk jug and sugar and two cups. He set it on the desk. 'Will I go out for biscuits, or to the off licence? Something a little stronger for you, Mr Milner?'

Rodney looked at me.

I shook my head. 'Not for me.'

'No thank you, Owen.'

Now I was glad that I had come. Poor Rodney seemed so very solitary.

I stirred the tea in the pot, and then poured milk into the cups. 'Your mother's death is quite recent. That's so sad for you.'

Rodney concentrated on watching the tea as it came from the pot. When the cups were filled, he said, 'You pour tea just like my mother did. As if you can't trust the spout.'

'Well, you can't always,' I said, 'especially if it's an unknown spout.'

'Can I tell you something?'

'I wish you would. I know what it's like to lose someone close to you.'

'Dad drove Mother to her grave. He treated her badly.'

The stuffing went out of Rodney when he said that. He shrank on his chair. I was sorry to hear it, but not surprised. 'In what way?' I asked.

'Oh . . . bullying . . . he can wear you down. And . . . well, other women. So I feel . . .'

'You were too young to help her?'

'I didn't know how.'

'And now you could, had she lived.'

'If she were still alive now, I'd take the very best care of her. I hated him for it. But I didn't kill him.'

I wished he didn't have to keep on denying he'd killed his father. But I could understand his guilt at having the 'wrong' response. Having hardly known Mr Milner, but disliking him in spite of that, I could not feel sorrow about the man's death, only the shocking manner of it. Not wanting to break the mood, I pushed the sugar basin towards Rodney, and waited. He spooned in two heaped teaspoons and stirred, very slowly.

'I couldn't sleep last night. I woke remembering that once Mother had another chap who cared for her, but she threw him over for Dad.'

'Did she tell you that?'

'No. Mrs Gould, our housekeeper, she told me, after Mother died.'

'I think Mrs Gould answered the door to me earlier.' So her tears had been for Rodney and his mother.

'Last night – well, early hours of this morning, after the police had called – I was turning everything over and over in my thoughts. I even wondered if this old flame had reappeared, heard how badly Dad treated Mother, and took his revenge. Is that far-fetched?'

'Our minds explore all sorts of possibilities, whether we want them to or not.'

I knew that well enough. That was why I liked being a detective. It gave my mind something real to ponder, rather than will-o'-the-wisps and might-have-beens. The trouble with having received a wartime telegram to say my husband was missing presumed dead, is that straight away the imagination turns that around. Missing presumed alive.

We concentrated on drinking our tea in silence.

'Did your mother help start this business?' I asked.

He looked surprised. 'Don't think so. Why?'

'I was just wondering. Mr Milner was a corporal in the army, and still quite young when he came out. Something like this must have taken a lot of capital.'

'It's funny you should say that.' Rodney lit a cigarette. 'Someone else asked me about that recently.'

'Oh? May I ask who?'

He blushed. 'It was Alison. She has a very quick mind, you know. Trained at the secretarial school and did accounts and everything. She works for a solicitor.'

Now I was the one lost for words. What a fool Alison had been not to tell Rodney of her pregnancy, and to confide instead in Olivia Geerts who went trotting off to Rodney's father with the news. I could just imagine the two of them putting their heads together over it.

Keeping as neutral a tone as possible, I asked, 'And what did you tell Alison?'

'Why, that I didn't rightly know. Except Mother once said Dad won money from Captain Wolfendale, and that probably we should be grateful to him. She used to invite the captain, Miss Fell and Lucy to Sunday dinner.'

So I was right. There was a financial link between the captain and Milner. And one that the captain might have reason to resent. I wondered had Mr Charles made that connection?

'Are you very close, you and Lucy?'

He looked at me sharply, picking up straight away on the meaning behind my words. 'Not in that way. We're good pals.'

I was here to ask about Lucy, and here was the perfect moment to do so. But he did not know she was missing, I felt sure of that.

'You must be the only young man in Harrogate not in love with Lucy Wolfendale.'

191

It was a relief to see him forget himself for a moment, and laugh. 'That's exactly what I said to Alison. It is because I know Lucy too well. When you asked me earlier who might stand by me over the next weeks and months, well, Lucy will. And Alison. She and I are very close as you put it. We've talked of becoming engaged.'

'I'm glad. I hope you'll both be very happy.'

'Neither of the girls must have heard yet, or they would have come to see me. They were staying with Madam Geerts last night.'

So much for thinking I would get a new lead on Lucy's whereabouts.

'Your housekeeper said that the captain called this morning.'

'Yes. They'd known each other for years. He and Dad served in the Boer War together, though they never agreed about it. Lucy and I got so bored when that came up over the roast beef, and the salt and pepper pots moved around the table, replaying battles.'

'How did they disagree?'

'Oh, you say it, they disagreed. The captain said the war was necessary for the good of the Empire. Dad said it was all about gold. Mother used to get upset. She said our soldiers burned down the farmhouses and destroyed the animals and crops, so that the Boers would have to surrender. She said they put the women and children in camps, horrible places called concentration camps.'

22

English Teachers

'English teachers do not try to teach Boer children to be English, but to know the English as their friends.'
—*Command Paper 934*

South Africa, 1900

Captain Wolfendale cursed his luck. He had given the order to blow up a cartload of Free State ammunition that they did not have the capacity to carry. Some fool of a private had been too hasty with the charge and killed himself. The blast threw Wolfendale into evil red rocks. It knocked his shoulder out. When he regained consciousness, the pain stopped him in his tracks. That he escaped that damned hospital without catching typhoid was a miracle. His new posting made him wish for the battlefield, or for typhoid.

Tailed by Sergeant Lampton and two privates, the captain gazed on the rows of white bell tents with half-closed eyes. If he looked slantwise, he could fool himself that it was a stop-over, a temporary camp on the dusty veld. The putrid stench of latrines gave a lie to that pretence. No soldiers' camp ever stank to high heaven as this did. He waved a hand at his batman. Sergeant Lampton produced a handkerchief. The captain held it to his nose and mouth.

'Dammit, we should number these rows. And why don't they raise their tent flaps in this heat?' He stopped at a tent with an open flap, thinking this must be the right place. The woman might be a traitor to her country, but an Englishwoman would have the sense to want fresh air.

Three adults sat listlessly, gazing at nothing. One nursed a child. Another child lay motionless on a mat, flies buzzing around its face.

It was not the right tent. They kept going.

Further on, the sergeant stopped. The captain opened the flap with his stick. Flies buzzed inside the tent. Three women looked up. At the back of the tent, two young children lay on a blanket. A fly landed on one of the children's eyelids. The younger of the women waved a scrap of material across the children's faces, as if to cool them.

As his eyes grew accustomed to the gloom of the tent, the captain could see that the tiny bodies were covered with red spots. One of them had yellow puss oozing from a scab.

The captain leaned into the tent and addressed the younger woman. 'Are you Elizabeth Bindeman?'

She did not budge, but glared at him defiantly. 'Yes.'

'Your husband is on commando.'

'He is. And when this war is over, you'll answer to him.'

The captain turned to his batman. 'Send for a stretcher.'

The sergeant passed the order to a private, telling the second private to stay by the tent. 'Make sure these two kids aren't disappeared into some other tent.'

'I'll take care of my own children!' The woman placed

her fingertips on the forehead of the smallest child. 'Just get me some fresh water, some calamine lotion.'

The captain said, 'You won't be taking care of anyone. Not for a good while.'

'Don't send them to that damned hospital to die.'

One of the children moaned, more like the hurt cry of a small animal than a human sound.

'They'll be better off there. You're coming with me.'

'Don't take them.' The woman pleaded now. 'Children die in there. Go in with measles, come out dead from typhoid.' She came to the front of the tent, blocking the children from view.

How did you deal with these people? That was the question the captain asked himself. If she were a soldier, there'd be rules. He knew better than to send her off to the magistrate in town. It would reflect badly if he could not keep order in the camp. Better to deal with this himself.

She stared at him in sullen silence. She was a fine-looking woman, a bit scrawny but good bones.

'You were seen, leaving the camp. Supplies went missing. You were giving succour to the enemy.'

She stepped from the tent. 'So shoot me. You've just condemned my children to death.'

From a shadowy corner of the tent, a woman raised her head and in broken English said, 'You mad. What Elizabeth give? Nothing. No food. No wood for fire, nasty, nasty . . .'

Elizabeth Bindeman said, 'She's right. What succour can any of us give? We queued six hours for mouldy horseflesh that we can't cook. There's no fuel to bake bread with your rotten weevil-ridden flour, even if we had clean water.'

'I'm not here to listen to complaints,' the captain said calmly. 'I'm here to investigate.'

If she would vehemently deny giving help to the enemy, he could go back and write in his report that he had investigated and found no evidence. If these foolish crones would give her an alibi instead of coming out with a battery of complaints, he could say that his informant had been mistaken.

'You were seen leaving the camp, madam.'

'And where did I go on these mysterious escapades? Do you think I would stay here if I knew how to leave?'

'I did not mention more than one occasion. You have just done that yourself.'

'Who accuses me?'

Another reason not to send her to the magistrates. That would suit her – to demand in court to know who were the camp informers.

'Escort this lady to my office,' he said to the sergeant.

Let her kick her heels for an hour, then he would give her two weeks' detention in the cage, keeping a watch in case her Boer husband or his friends came to her rescue.

In the camp office, Captain Wolfendale made a great show of looking at his notes. 'You were seen by the camp fence two nights ago, passing food through the wire. Last night you were watched going through a gap in the fence.'

Fires had been lit on the hillside. Scouts were sent but, as usual, found no one. Brother Boer, as ever, disappeared into the heart of the mountains, following the Pied Piper. Before dawn, the explosion from the railway track had lit the sky. And this was the shame of it, he believed it was not the men on commando who had done that, but Elizabeth Bindeman.

She did not deny it. 'Your trains won't fetch any more souls here to their slow death,' was all she said.

'For breaking camp regulations, your punishment will be two weeks' detention. Sergeant, escort Mrs Bindeman into detention.' He could not say, to the cage.

'Say it,' she said. 'Say that an English officer condemns an English woman to be caged.'

She fixed herself to the spot and closed her eyes. Her fists clenched. When the sergeant touched her arm, she would not move. The sergeant sighed. He turned to the private. 'If she won't walk, carry her.'

The women started to sing as she passed by, one of their Boer hymns.

A sullen silence hung over the concentration camp as the captain walked his rounds. This wasn't what he'd signed on for, to be a prisoner himself in this stinking hole, this town of tents. Tents were all right for soldiers who struck camp and moved on. How long could this continue? Was every Boer woman and child to be holed up, and forever?

In a clearing by the fence, two dead children lay on a blanket. A group of women sat weeping.

How he hated these scenes. Fortunately, his batman had found him again. 'For God's sake, get those kids buried.'

The sergeant paused and spoke to the women. He had picked up a little of their language.

To the captain he said, 'They won't bury them without coffins.'

The captain and the sergeant exchanged a look. For a brief moment, each knew what the other was thinking:

of their comrades left behind at the foot of a hill, not marked by the smallest of crosses.

'Tell them there are no more coffins. If we had wood, they could have fuel. Tell them I'll speak to the hospital. We'll find them shrouds.' The sergeant did not respond. 'What? What's the matter?'

'I don't know how to say shrouds in their language.'

The captain strode on, leaving him to it. He had a report to write. The powers that be wanted to know how lessons progressed in the school tent. They seemed to think this place was a Sunday school outing.

He stood in the doorway of the designated tent. Miss Marshall had her back to him. A dozen children sat cross-legged. One or two looked at the teacher. The others, skeletal and hollow-eyed, existed in a kind of trance. Did they all have dysentery? A foul stench filled the tent.

She had not heard him, or affected not to. She spoke in English, with a Cape twang, and was reading to them from *Alice in Wonderland*. 'If everybody minded their own business, said the Duchess in a hoarse growl, the world would go round faster than it does.'

Feeling his presence, the woman turned. She had light curling hair, the colour of burnished gold. Her skin was pale with a faint sprinkling of freckles. In the half light of the tent, he could not make out the colour of her eyes. Blue? He should remember. He had boldly remarked on their loveliness the last time they spoke. Her lips were full and ready to go on speaking of the Duchess.

She turned back to the children. 'Excuse me one moment, class.'

Outside the tent, the teacher stepped onto the dusty track. As she did, the heavens opened. Rain came in a great sudden pelt so that for a moment she seemed to lose her balance. He reached out a hand to steady her.

Through a sheet of rain, she said, 'Captain, one of the children is upset.'

Upset? They stank, they sickened, came out in scabs, their bellies swelled, they caught measles, typhoid, were bitten by snakes. In the hospital and out of it, they died like flies.

'Upset?' Captain Wolfendale repeated, wondering had his ears deceived him.

'Yes. One of the boys. Young Bindeman.'

The captain put his hand lightly on her waist and guided her back into the tent, out of the rain. 'It would be a help if you would come to the office, Miss Marshall, after your duties. I should like to hear about the little chap who is upset, and to know how your classes progress.'

She blushed at his interest.

He spoke in a low voice, almost cajoling, as if his life depended on her answer. 'You will come to see me?'

'At what time should I come?'

'Would six o'clock be convenient?'

'Yes, I think so.'

'Good.'

Women were such fools. All an officer had to do was swear undying love and eternal fidelity and the manoeuvre was more straightforward than an Aldershot field day. But a school teacher. This would be a challenge, he could tell. He smiled at her, looking adoringly into her deep-set eyes. A washed-out blue. She was not in the first flush of youth. Perhaps a proposal of marriage would be number one priority. He felt sure his reputation had not reached the well-meaning school teachers of Cape Town.

23

*Clouding: cloud borders at the top of a scene, may change
from calm to stormy*

Rodney walked me through the motor showroom. We
paused by a shining Wolseley 10, highly polished paintwork, glossy mudguards and gleaming lamps.

'This was Dad's favourite.'

On an impulse, I opened the door, stepped onto the
running board and climbed in. 'She's a beauty.' I patted
the driver's seat beside me.

As Rodney got in, the tension slid away and he
smiled. 'My mother said cars were better standing than
running. No noise, wind, smell, and you didn't have to
put on goggles and a big coat.'

'She had a point.'

He reached out and held the steering wheel. 'Who
would have killed him, Mrs Shackleton?'

Good question. I shook my head, and kept my
thoughts to myself. You are not a bad actor, Rodney. It
could have been you. Your way is clear to take over the
firm and marry Alison. Be rid of the man who
tormented your mother and belittled you. Alison
herself? Milner stood in the way of her happiness. Or
Lucy, sick of Lawrence Milner's pestering. And what

200

better and more dramatic diversion than to take herself into hiding, as a kidnap victim. All four young people had stuck together in the theatre bar. Rodney, Alison, Dylan and Lucy. For weeks they had rehearsed, perhaps in a hothouse atmosphere that led them to compare notes about more than the play. Three of the four, Rodney, Alison and Lucy, would have easier lives as a result of Milner's death.

Either of the Geerts could be the murderer. He because cuckolded, she because she knew he made love to her while hankering after a girl half her age. Or the captain. The man I could not fathom. Did he want Lucy off his hands to the highest bidder, or resent Milner's interest in her?

I looked at Rodney, holding the wheel like a little boy pretending to drive. 'The investigation is in good hands. Inspector Charles will get to the truth.'

His hands dropped to his sides. 'I suppose so. I don't know what to do now. It seems so strange that I'll be going home without having to give a full report to Dad on who came in to look at what motor. I made most of my sales on a Saturday, while he was playing golf.'

'I'm sure when you go home Mrs Gould will look after you.'

'I'm wondering about Alison,' he said. 'And I'm surprised that Lucy hasn't been round to see me. I mean if the captain knew, she must.'

'I happen to know she hasn't been home yet.' I hated to do it, but I was here to find Lucy. 'Alison stayed at the Geerts's last night. Lucy didn't.'

'Really? That's where we left her last night, me and a chum of mine who was at the play.' The surprise looked genuine, but then he had spent several weeks under Meriel's theatrical tutelage.

'Do you know where else she might be?'

He shook his head. 'No. Some other friend perhaps. I hope she's all right.'

'I'm sure she will be.' On an impulse, I said, 'Why don't you go find Alison, at the Geerts's? I saw her earlier, and to tell you the truth she looked a little under the weather. Go there, and drive her home. Her mother's at a church fete his afternoon, you'll be able to have a good chat.'

And it would be better for her to be out of the Geerts's house before the police came asking questions of Madam Geerts, if they had not already called.

He climbed from the shiny Wolseley. 'Do you know, I think I will.' The resolve changed his appearance. He looked more like the young man I had photographed a few weeks earlier.

'What about you, Mrs Shackleton, may I drop you somewhere?'

'I wouldn't dream of asking you to chauffeur me about. You have enough on.'

'Could Owen take you somewhere? We keep a couple of motors on stand-by for visitors to hire. I'd be glad to help. I was completely at a loss before you came today.'

'Well yes, since you mention it. That would be good.'

'Owen!'

And so I found myself on the way to Pannal, hoping that I should have more luck in locating Miss Vanessa Weston, who had pawned a watch chain, than I had in failing to find Mrs deVries, owner of the diamond ring.

Owen drew up outside a newsagent's before we left

Harrogate, for me to buy a couple of boxes of choco-lates, which always come in handy. At least I was not now drawing entirely on my own income. I had the cheque from Mr Moony to cover this particular extrav-agance. If I solved the case, which was looking unlikely, I might eat the other box myself. It irked me to be acting as a messenger for Mr Moony, rather than an investigator, but there was so little to go on.

The ride to Pannal along the quiet road was pleasant. I wore the spare motoring goggles, which were too big and kept slipping down my nose.

'It's Church Lane,' I said, lifting the goggles to check the house number in my notebook.

'Well then, that'll be near the church I presume,' Owen said cheerily. It is surprising how sitting in the driving seat can change a personality, for better or worse. In the showroom, Owen had seemed quite downtrodden, at least until Rodney had assured him that he would keep his job.

The elegant stone house looked too grand for someone who would visit a pawn shop. A slender, faded woman looked at me suspiciously as I approached the gate. She snipped the dead head from a rose. I apologised for disturbing her and asked for Miss Vanessa Weston.

'I'm her mother,' she said. 'Miss Weston is indoors.' Her look asked me my name and business.

It is always best to get in quickly, with an introduction, and a story. If you say something with sufficient authority, it comes out with a ring of truth. With as much verve as I could muster, I brandished a box of chocolates. 'I'm Mrs Baker, from the Beckwithshaw ladies' friendship commit-tee. Miss Weston bought a raffle ticket from one of our members and has won third prize.'

'Ah, thank you.' Mrs Weston prepared to take the chocolates.

'Would you mind very much if I deliver them personally? I said I would.'

Mrs Weston frowned. She placed her secateurs in the trug.

'Oh please don't trouble,' I said hastily. 'I hate to be interrupted in my gardening. It will take me a moment and I can report back to my ladies that I have hand-delivered the prize.'

I could see someone in a shady spot at the front of the house, reading. As luck would have it, it was Miss Weston. Unsurprisingly, she had no recollection of buying a raffle ticket. She looked at the chocolates with suspicion, as though I might be a mad poisoner. Briefly, I told her the real reason for my visit, adding, 'And Mr Moony would like you to go to the shop on the day the watch chain is due to be redeemed. If the stolen items have not been recovered, he will make restitution.'

She glared at me. 'I must have the same watch chain. It was my uncle's, my mother's brother's. She doesn't know I pawned it.'

'I'll tell Mr Moony. He'll do his best to find something similar.'

'Dash it all. How could the stupid man let himself be robbed?' She ripped violently at the chocolate box lid. 'If dressmakers didn't charge the earth I would not be in this pickle.'

Mrs Weston was approaching at a grand pace. I escaped, leaving Miss Weston to think of her own explanations about the winning raffle ticket.

24

The Key Players

Owen dropped me off on Leeds Road, at the end of St Clement's Road, which was now becoming more familiar than I could have wished. I was no nearer finding Lucy than when I started my search. To put off the moment of reporting to Captain Wolfendale, I strolled slowly past each immaculate dwelling, from number one to number twenty-nine. With its unkempt garden and peeling paint, the Wolfendale house stuck out like a sore thumb on a well-manicured hand. It felt fanciful to think this, but it gave off an air that I could not fathom. Captain Wolfendale and Miss Fell were relics of an earlier age. Meriel was immensely talented, a liar and a thief, clawing her way up. Beautiful and ruthless Lucy held those around her in thrall. And then there was Dan Root.

It still niggled with me that 29 was the reverse of 92, Mrs deVries's address. Let the captain wait. I would speak to Mr Root, and get another look at the coin on his watch chain. He was a good actor, quite capable of becoming the stooped clerk who had robbed Mr Moony.

205

Something else felt odd. Lucy could have asked Dan, the captain's favourite tenant, to pass on the message that she would stay with Alison. By not asking him, she had kept him out of the picture. It crossed my mind that he might be hiding Lucy, and that the ransom notes had been posted in the pillar box on the corner.

It was time for me to have a chat with Mr Root. The previous afternoon when my feet hurt and I was tired out from looking for the elusive and probably non-existent Mrs deVries, he had all but snubbed me. This time, he would not shrug me off so easily.

I caught a glimpse of him through his window. He stood at his worktable, head bowed as he gently replaced the back on a fob watch. Several clocks and watches stood at one end of the long table.

The door to his flat stood open, to let in air I guessed.

I tapped as I stepped inside.

For a moment, he looked surprised at my boldness, then he smiled. 'I needed a little break. Shall we sit on the wall and have a cigarette?' He removed his eyeglass, and took off his apron.

Why did he not want me to be inside? Perhaps he was a very private person, or did not want me in his workplace. His anxiety to go out increased my determination to stay in.

'I've always wanted to see how a watchmaker does his work,' I said, with what I hoped was a charming smile. Moving further into his room, I examined the eyeglass he had just removed. 'How on earth do you keep this in place, Mr Root?'

As he picked up the eyeglass to demonstrate, I quickly looked round the tidy room.

He held the eyeglass between finger and thumb. 'You

206

place it on the lower lid, like so. It rests under the bone of the eyebrow.'

'It suits you very well. May I try it?' He passed me the eyeglass. I wedged it in place. The small screwdrivers and tweezers looked suddenly larger when seen through the glass. So did the gold pond on his watch chain.

Averting my gaze to the bench, I asked, 'What are these little wooden cups for?'

'Oh they're to sit the movements on, keep them steady while I work. And this little vice is to hold things in place.'

He half turned to show me the vice, and as he did I swept a wooden cup into my satchel. He had half a dozen, and would not miss one. If he had helped Lucy write her ransom note, I might find his fingerprint.

He had also moved something out of view, a book of some description.

Concentrating on the workbench, I said, 'It's such precise work. It must have been hard to learn.' I removed the eyeglass and placed it on a mat.

The mat was part of an ingeniously arranged wooden box with small drawers which slid out, and one of them unfolded as a mat. A man whose tools could be carried in such a compact fashion could flit from one town to another with ease.

'What age did you begin this work?'

'Twelve. I was apprenticed to an old watchmaker in Covent Garden,' he said.

'Then you must be a master of your craft by now, and enjoy it I should think.'

'A man is never out of work if he can repair watches and clocks. Every job is the same, yet every one is different. Take this clock, for instance . . .'

While he explained about a balance mechanism, I glanced around the room. He must have been a handy person altogether. A length of metal pipe leaned against the wall, parts of a crystal set and a listening trumpet lay on a table. Had Dan Root not looked so very English, he would have been suspected of being a spy during the Great War.

'Isn't this an odd lodging for you, Mr Root? Surely a watch mender needs light. Yet here you are, halfway below ground. Have you lived here long?'

'Long enough. And there's enough light for my purposes.'

What are your purposes, I wondered. There was something in his tone of voice that belied the lightness of his words.

'The captain says you're his best tenant.'

'Because I'm the only one who pays rent. And the only chap. He prefers his own sex.'

I looked at him quickly to see what meaning lay behind his words, but he concentrated on his cigarette, drawing deeply.

The house door above opened and slammed shut. Miss Fell going out, or the captain returning?

'The play must have been a great diversion for you, Mr Root.'

He smiled. 'Have you tried resisting Miss Jamieson once she gets an idea in her head? She was short of males. Living next door to her, I had no chance of avoiding conscription.'

The captain's footsteps thumped the ceiling, then came to a stop. I pictured him standing by the tigerskin rug. A moment later a tap-tap sounded down the chimney as the captain emptied the ash from his pipe, and coughed.

'It must have brought you closer, three of you from this one house taking part in the play, you, Meriel and Lucy.'

'I was very useful to escort the ladies home, mostly Lucy because Meriel would stay behind to write her director's notes.'

So he had walked Lucy home from rehearsals. They must have got to know each other very well.

He moved towards the door. 'Let's sit outside. I spend far too much time in here as it is.'

That left me no choice but to follow him. Yet if he had been hiding Lucy, I would have heard or seen some sign. There was only one door, apart from the cupboard, which I guessed led to a kind of keeping pantry.

We sat on the low garden wall. 'It must be a solitary business, working alone down there.'

He shrugged. 'The watch and clock business in Harrogate is all tied up by the jewellers in the centre. People take their timepieces there, not knowing that they're sent to me. I don't complain. My living is reasonable.'

'Have you been in Harrogate long?'

'I've travelled about,' he said. 'Harrogate suits me. Plenty of watches and clocks here, plenty of work, and the air is pleasant. Do you know, the humidity here is lower than anywhere else in the country?'

'For a man who is conscious of health benefits, I'm surprised you work in a basement. It must put a strain on your eyes.'

'I'm by the window, and I have gas light.' He stubbed his cigarette. Turning the subject away from himself, he asked, 'Will you be taking the waters while you're in Harrogate?'

'I have booked into a hotel, so I may just do that.'

He smiled. 'Sulphur or iron?'

'I don't know. What do you recommend?'

'Neither, to drink. They stink and are vile. But to bathe, either is very pleasant, especially when warm.'

In a moment he would go back to his work. What was keeping me from asking him about Lucy? The thought that the more people knew she was missing, the more her reputation might suffer. I had a shrewd suspicion that Dan Root knew more than he was letting on.

'You and Lucy were very good in the play. Do you think you'll be in another?'

'No!' he said emphatically. 'Not if I can help it.'

'I sat next to Mr Wheatley in the theatre last night. He was very complimentary. He seemed to think Lucy might have the talent to go on stage.'

It was a wild try, but it worked.

Dan smiled, and there was a gleam of something like pride in his eyes. 'Is that what he said?'

'Yes. I think he meant it too.'

I wanted to know why she needed a thousand pounds. And I wanted to know what Dan Root was keeping quiet about. I pressed on. 'All of the other players have occupations, but not Lucy. I should think she's at a bit of a loose end now.'

He said softly, 'You've guessed haven't you?'

'No.'

'We walked home together most nights. Lucy loved being in the play. She's quite stage-struck.'

'Ah, of course. And that would not meet with the captain's approval.'

'Hardly.' He sucked in his breath. 'It must be the worst-kept secret in Harrogate that she intends to become an actress. I said I wouldn't tell, but I don't see what harm it will do if you're going back to Leeds after you take the waters. She intends to go to London, to study acting. She has been offered a place at the Royal Academy of Dramatic Art.'

Suddenly it made sense that when Lucy thanked me for the spare photographs she said they were 'useful'. She had sent, or taken them with her, for an audition at the drama school.

'How could she have done that without anyone knowing?'

'I didn't say no one knew.' He jerked his thumb towards the flat above. 'Captain Wolfendale doesn't know.'

Dan Root stretched to his full height, ready to go back to his work. It amazed me that this tall, well-built man could have played the crafty old miser, and the hunched revivalist preacher, and the doomed manufacturer who took his own life. 'Sorry. I have watches to attend to. If I don't get them back to the shop before teatime, I shall be disappointed with myself.'

I stayed put on the wall. 'Hang on, you can't tell me half a tale. If Lucy plans to run off to the thespians, what would she be running away from?'

'You'd have to ask her.'

There was a challenge in his voice, and a sad smile. He knew she was missing, I felt sure of it. The thought of that gave me goose bumps. It made me wonder whether he had gone to Moony's, offering his watch chain, robbing the man, sharing the loot with Lucy. And now, she was on the next phase of raising money. This time from her grandfather.

Or perhaps the shock of finding a body was sending me peculiar and there were no connections whatsoever.

I persisted, keeping up my end of our conversation. 'But you have a good idea of what she'd be escaping.'

He sighed. 'Like you, I'm only guessing. A dull marriage perhaps?'

'To whom?'

He shook his head enigmatically. 'I could not possibly say.' He smiled. 'Now if you'll excuse me.'

I felt like Alice in Wonderland, being toyed with by the Cheshire cat.

I watched him turn away, go back into his room, and close the door firmly behind him.

Something was nagging away at me, something to do with Dan Root. And then it clicked. Dan was an eavesdropper. He listened in to what went on in the captain's flat. That was why he did not want me to stay in his room after the captain had returned just now.

It had been the same yesterday when I was desperate to take the weight off my feet and he would not ask me in. I remembered where he had been sitting, and how it had seemed slightly odd at the time that he was by the hearth, leaning forward so intently. The metal pipe I had seen by Dan's fireplace was part of a listening device. The sound of the captain walking across the room and knocking out his pipe had travelled down the chimney. All Dan had to do, to hear more, would be to attach the listening trumpet to the metal pipe. He could then overhear whatever went on between the captain and Lucy. But what would be of interest about that? Presumably he would know that Lucy expected an inheritance, and was not about to receive it. He would know that Lucy refused the idea of being bartered into marriage.

Dan would also know what had taken place between the captain and the late Mr Milner. He had listened in when the old comrades played their board game of *Called to Arms*. That was how he knew that Lucy was set to have a "dull marriage" as he put it, though I would have said horrendous.

Was Lucy connected with Milner's death? Milner certainly would have let her come close enough to put a dagger through his heart.

For a few moments more, I remained on the low wall, taking out my notebook, jotting down what I had learned so far, along with the names of people who could know more than they were telling.

Meriel Jamieson
    If true that Lucy has place at RADA, Meriel must have helped – audition piece, etc. Has she put her up to demanding money?

Rodney Milner
    He and Lucy friends since childhood. But not in Lucy's confidence.

Dylan Ashton
    Knows more than he admits? Check for his prints on the ransom note and envelope. House agency – empty properties for hide-out?

Captain
    Why so against involving police? Because of Lucy's reputation, or darker reason?

Dan Root

Lucy confided in him about drama school. Knows more than letting on.

Geerts, Loy and Olivia

Unlikely to be involved in ransom, but Monsieur Geerts strong suspect in Milner's murder.

Alison Hart

Too upset about own situation to lie. Rule out.

A.N. Other

Who?

I snapped the notebook shut. Eliminate the obvious. If I were Lucy, where would I hide? I would not risk being seen out and about, but would keep the plan simple. There was an uninhabited top floor in the house that Meriel had said the captain used for storage. Where better to hide than the last place her grandfather might think to look?

I walked up the stairs to the front door and through into the hall.

With the thought that Dan Root might be downstairs listening, I gave up on the idea of knocking on the captain's door and instead climbed the stairs, past the first floor where Miss Fell's Pekinese yapped a warning, and up to the top floor and the unoccupied flat.

25

Tragic Carpet

Tragic carpet: placed on stage so that tragedians would not dirty their costumes when dead

The simplicity appealed to me. Lucy could be here in this very house, on the unoccupied top floor. The last place her grandfather would think to look.

The Pekinese yapped with every step I took on the narrow runner of threadbare carpet that led me upwards. A large spider web covered a corner of the stained-glass window on the landing. The lock to the top flat was the old-fashioned type that did not take much picking. Closed curtains made the room dark and stuffy. My task would not need much light, but I drew the curtains back all the same. The furniture, covered in dust sheets, offered hiding places.

I walked through the drawing room, where the paintings on the wall were covered with sheets. Arranged between the paintings was an array of British weaponry, with labels attached. It struck me that these could be valuable, as a job lot. Did Lucy think her grandfather could pawn or sell them, and raise her ransom? I jotted down the names: Lee-Enfield Cavalry Carbine 303"; Martini-Enfield Artillery Carbine 303"; Long Lee-Enfield Rifle MkI 1902; Webley Revolver MkIII calibre

455"; Webley WG Army Model Revolver. On another wall were mounted swords, some very old, sabres with curved blades and elaborate handles. Two other swords were straight and plain. A rifle sword bore the supplier's name, Gordon Mitchell & Co., Cape Town. A display cabinet held a bone-hilt dagger with wood scabbard. It was about nine inches long, the blade comprising two thirds of the length. It had what looked like a sharp diamond cross-section blade. Although I had not got a close look at the knife that killed Mr Milner, I found myself examining this one closely. The shelf of the cabinet where it lay looked cleaner than the others, as though someone may have wiped a cloth across, concealing the fact that dust may have gathered around a missing knife. But surely that was fanciful. Dust would not gather on a closed cabinet shelf, would it? All the same, something looked out of place. In this jam-packed room, the solitary dagger looked lonely.

On a table, several items were displayed, as if the captain had once intended to create a private museum. It was an odd assortment: an emergency ration tin had been welded closed; there were pieces of shrapnel shell. A nasty-looking piece of metal with pointed edges bore the label *'Caltrops thrown on ground to cripple horses of attacking Boers'*.

The weaponry and detritus of a long-ago war both fascinated and repelled me. How had Lucy borne life in this house? Small wonder she wanted to escape.

Forcing myself to continue, I lifted the dust covers on the furniture. Speaking her name softly, I checked to see whether she had heard me approaching and was hiding under the sideboard or behind a sofa. She was not. Nor was she under the bed. A large wardrobe stood against the wall.

I opened its door. An army greatcoat swung on its hanger. Any dresses and coats that had belonged to the captain's aunt must long ago have been purloined by Miss Fell, or given away to some deserving person. I moved the great-coat, not expecting Lucy to be lurking behind it, but to see what else might be there. Two uniforms hung side by side. One bore a captain's pips, the other sergeant's stripes.

I remembered what the captain had said, so modestly, regarding his Victoria Cross. 'When you reach a certain rank, there are all sorts of things you just don't have to deal with. I had a wonderful batman, never properly appreciated him. He was with me that day. He should have got that medal.'

Could there be some clue lurking in this wardrobe, between the two side-by-side uniforms? It had crossed my mind that it was odd for a captain to play a board game with a corporal, as Milner had been. Officers and other ranks do not mix, just as society snakes do not rub shoulders with their parlour maids, except in the relationship of mistress and servant. Perhaps Milner had been the batman. But if Milner were a corporal . . . I examined the uniform again. Sure enough, there were three stripes. Perhaps I had been mistaken and Milner was a sergeant; or had been promoted later. But why would his uniform hang in the captain's wardrobe? It did not make sense.

An old cigar box on a sideboard contained a few photographs, of uniformed men in a barren place. The captain and his batman? Men on a hillside, by a tent, by a river. The light was dim and the photographs not very clear. There were papers in the box, beneath the photo-graphs, two sets of army discharges, one for Rowland Oliver Wolfendale, another for Henry Lampton.

Since this flat took up the entire top floor, it

217

surprised me that there was only one bedroom, and then I saw the other door.

A huge cast-iron bath held a covered shape. Lucy? A body was covered in ragged old towels and a torn sheet. The shape did not move, not the slightest twitch. I forced myself to look closer: a head, a shoulder, legs — the outline was clear enough. A body. I froze. Watching, I hoped for the slightest movement, a sign of life, for it to be a young woman who had heard me, and was hiding. No movement, not a breath.

Could it be Lucy, dead? Murdered by her own grand-father, who had himself written the ransom note.

'Lucy?' I went right up to it, and touched the shape. Lifeless.

But there was no blood, no whiff of death.

I pulled back a worn towel, a torn sheet.

It was a figure, not unlike the tailor's dummy that stood in the downstairs window of the captain's flat. That one sported a Boer uniform. This one had worn khaki. The uniform had been cut to shreds. A bone-hilt dagger protruded from the chest. Straw, not innards, tumbled out.

I shut the bathroom door quietly and leaned against it. Just my luck that the first time I get a chance to use my illicit skill of lock-picking, I enter a flat where some maniac has been before me. Was this Lucy's work? If so, what had led her to be so thorough in her destruction of the soldier dummy?

The sound startled me. A great roar made me believe that a tiger rug had come to life or some long-dead elephant had returned demanding its stolen tusks.

'What the devil . . .!' It was the captain, brandishing his sword stick.

'I thought it best to eliminate the obvious,' I said calmly. 'Who has murdered your soldier doll?'

My question diverted him for a moment. I opened the bathroom door wide so that he could see for himself what havoc had been wreaked on the life-size boy soldier. He leaned down and touched the damaged thing, a moan escaping from him.

He rounded on me. 'Who let you in here?'

'Myself.'

'Then let yourself out, and don't come back. I don't need you. I never should have trusted you.'

'As you wish.'

'Yes, as I wish. I don't need a bit of skirt with a high opinion of herself poking her nose in where she doesn't belong. Get out, and when you see your adventuress friend, tell her she can pack her bags. We were all right till she rolled up.'

Retreat was most definitely in order.

He rushed ahead of me to the door, flung it open. 'Out! Out!'

The captain did not follow. I guessed he would be checking his precious museum pieces to ensure there was nothing missing. His fury had unnerved me. I held onto the banister. The dog barked again. I hurried down the stairs, not wanting to be there when he completed his inventory of secrets.

A mighty yell of fury came from above. The door slammed shut. Half expecting to be run through with his sword walking stick, I reached the landing as his footsteps pounded down the stairs.

26

Behind the Mask

A concerned Miss Fell stood at her open door. She hurried towards me, and hastily drew me inside. Mistress of under-statement, she whispered, 'The captain doesn't like anyone looking at his military accoutrements.'

'He must have incredibly sharp hearing.'

'It's a sixth sense he has for protecting his weaponry.'

The dog darted at my ankles, yapping a warning to his mistress not to be so naïve as to invite me in.

'Shut up, Peeko, dear,' she said soothlingly. 'This is an emergency. The captain is raving.' With the triumph of a lonely person who has finally found a captive audience, she shut the door behind us.

I followed her into a large sitting room, furnished with an overstuffed sofa and chairs, smelling strongly of dog and weakly of lavender. The small creature dogging my heels, herding me in, might look like a muff. Its manner, yap and stink told a different story.

It leapt at my leg, demanding attention, its eyes saying with a mixture of pleading and arrogance, 'I'm a proper dog, so watch out.'

Flattery is one of my stocks in trade, especially when

I find myself in a tricky situation. 'Fine fellow,' I said, stroking the dog's silky head. Peeko was not impressed. I tried again. 'Clever fellow.'

That did the trick. Here was a dog that knew well enough he was a fine fellow and only wanted to have his intellect admired.

'Peeko likes you,' Miss Fell said. She waved an arm for me to take a seat.

I perched on the sofa. Matching her for understatement, I said, 'I've upset your landlord.'

'Take no notice. You were only looking for the bathroom I'm sure.' She dismissed the captain with a flick of her wrist. 'Now tell me what you thought of the play. I saw it twice. Haven't seen a finer piece of theatre since the old queen was on the throne. Goodness me, it brought tears to my eyes to see Lucy taking her part so magnificently. It was like seeing a stranger, though I've known her since she was a tot. Do sit down, though it won't be for long. He's restless.'

I did not know whether she meant the dog or the captain who was now marching so loudly across the floor above that the light fitting shook.

My hostess glanced up. 'He'll be muttering and cursing,' she confided sagely. 'I've seen him this way before.'

'It's good of you to offer me sanctuary,' I said. 'You'll risk the captain's wrath.'

'Huh! There's nothing he can do about me,' Miss Fell said confidently. 'I've been resident here for many years. I came as companion to the captain's aunt, a dear lady, the genuine article.'

'Then you must like Harrogate, and this house . . . to have stayed, I mean.'

221

She sighed. 'Harrogate is a wonderful place to live. So healthy, so very refined. But I'm afraid the house is not what it was in Miss Wolfendale's day.'

Miss Fell settled herself for a Good Chat. The dog snuggled up to her. She tickled his head. As she did so, I noticed her hands. They were old, wrinkled and speckled, the nails ridged with age. On each of her ring fingers, she wore a buckled silver ring. The silver ring on her right hand was doing a job: it was holding secure a ring that was one size too big. I stared at the ring. I am no expert but felt sure that this was 18-carat gold. In a concave setting glittered three diamonds and, on either side, three raised bars. The ring exactly matched Mr Moony's description of Mrs deVries's ring.

So perhaps my hunch about the transposition of the house number had not been so wild after all. We were in 29 St Clement's Road. The address for the mysterious Mrs deVries was 92. That would explain her odd behaviour yesterday at the mention of the name deVries. She *was* Mrs deVries. Who had she asked to collect her ring from the pawn shop? If Miss Fell herself had something to hide, she would not have invited me in.

As my mind ran over these details, I tried to think of how to tackle her. I must tread carefully. If she simply denied being 'Mrs deVries', there would be no trail for me to follow. While she went to make tea in her small kitchen, I looked at the photographs on the sideboard. One photograph showed a much younger Miss Fell, and her older companion, who held a walking stick. They wore tweed skirts, stout shoes and berets. The two of them were perched on a boulder, legs outstretched, knapsacks by their feet.

'That's me with Miss Wolfendale,' Miss Fell called from the kitchen.

'The captain's aunt?'

'Yes. And next to that, Miss Wolfendale with the captain, when he was a boy.'

I picked up the second photograph.

The woman and boy, aged about sixteen, looked out at me, the boy posing with a self-conscious air, looking into the lens and half-smiling into an unknown future. He stood to attention, wearing long trousers and a check shirt open at his smooth young neck. The woman wore a print dress and cardigan. Her hand rested affectionately on his shoulder. She had a longish face, slightly horsey. He had the same characteristic, but less markedly, which made me think he would have turned out classic-ally handsome.

'I believe that's taken locally?'

'It is indeed. On The Stray.'

The resemblance between the woman and the boy was clear.

'So the captain is Miss Wolfendale's brother's child?'

'Yes.' She brought in a tea tray, her rings glinting. 'And her only relation. When Miss Wolfendale died, she left the house to the captain with a proviso that I be allowed to remain as a grace and favour tenant. I did not then expect that he would rent out the lower level which does rather give the old place the atmosphere of a lodging house. Not that I dislike the tenants.'

And one of those tenants was Dan Root, owner of a watch chain hung with a South African coin, just like the one Mr Moony's assailant pretended to pawn. Being his own master, Dan would be free to take Monday

223

morning off for a little light robbery in Leeds. But why would he have returned the ring to Miss Fell?

Of course I could be entirely mistaken. No ring is totally unique unless specially made. Having asked her yesterday about Mrs deVries, I tried to think of a way to raise the subject again. I did not need to. It was on her mind.

'You rather threw me yesterday, dear, when you asked about your mother's friend. I'm afraid I wasn't very helpful. This area teems with spinsters and widows, and we don't all know each other. If we were younger, there would be some plan to ship us to the colonies without ado.' The tea came from the fluted china pot so weak it looked in need of help. 'Not too strong for you?' Miss Fell asked.

I assured her it was not.

'Of course it's different for young women nowadays,' Miss Fell said, offering me sugar. 'Take Lucy, how wonderfully well she took her part in the play, not in the least self-conscious. But you see she acted in school plays and was fond of reciting. Even as a wee child she would climb on the table and give us a lyrical ballad or a comic verse. I taught her some poems myself.' Miss Fell waved her hand towards a well-stocked bookshelf. As she did so, several volumes fell from the arm of her chair. I moved to rescue them. They were detective stories from a private lending library. 'Thank you, my dear. On the table please.'

As I stacked the novels on the table, I imagined Lucy, as a precocious child, reciting her heart out. Lucy could have been the robber. She could easily have dressed as a young man, borrowed Dan Root's watch chain. Lulled poor Mr Moony into believing her just another customer, and then made her move.

224

Miss Fell waited until I had set the novels in a neat pile and then continued her praise of Lucy. 'Her memory has always been phenomenal. She claims to remember her mother, though between you and me I believe it's her nursemaid she recollects. I don't disabuse her, though it's odd that she should think of such a woman as her mother.'

'Why odd?' I asked.

Miss Fell stiffened suddenly as we once more heard footsteps on the stairs, and then on the landing. She waited. 'He's calmed down. Something in him snaps if he thinks anyone is delving into his precious junk room up there. We had it as our sewing room years ago.'

'It sounds as though you and Miss Wolfendale got on very well.'

'Oh we did. She was more like an older sister to me than an employer. We went on holiday each year, out into the countryside, staying on a farm, walking in the hill country. I came here in 1897, in answer to an advertisement in *The Lady*. And Miss Wolfendale was a lady. Of course I was a young woman then, thirty years old. Didn't think myself young of course. Thought myself old and past it.' She laughed heartily. 'Don't we always think that we're as old as we're ever going to be? I was companion to Miss Wolfendale until her death in 1903, at the age of sixty-six.' She sighed. 'I did think I might have to find another place when she died. But the executors of the will asked me would I stay on, until matters were settled.'

'And here you are still.'

'As it transpired, Miss Wolfendale kindly made provision for me to receive a small annuity.'

A little piece of the jigsaw fitted into place. Mr

225

Moony had said that Mrs deVries pawned her ring annually. No doubt this coincided with the period just before Miss Fell's annuity went into her bank account.

Peeko perched himself on the window ledge, looking down into the street below with the appearance of a creature expecting an important delivery of horseflesh.

'And you haven't regretted staying on, Miss Fell?'

'Not a bit of it. I felt I owed it to dear Miss Wolfendale, especially when the captain arrived with his granddaughter in tow.'

'Lucy must have been very young?'

'She was two years old, and the prettiest little creature you ever saw. The nursemaid became homesick and went back where she came from. I've since wondered whether she might have stayed on if he'd paid her more. But of course she did attract rather a lot of attention in Harrogate.'

'Why was that?'

'Didn't I say? She was African, what they used to call a Kaffir girl.'

'Poor Lucy, to lose her parents and her nursemaid so young. And it can't have been easy for a man of his age to bring up a child.'

'He could not have managed without me. Forgets that now when he's busy resenting my very presence. Lucy spent more time with me than downstairs when she was little. And it is such a pity that Miss Wolfendale wasn't aware of the existence of her great niece, or if she was, she never mentioned her to me. The captain said his son made an unsuitable match you see, as did the captain himself from what I can gather, though of course he doesn't say so outright. That would explain why Miss Wolfendale never mentioned family.'

The more she talked, the more the questions raced through my mind. Whose was the other uniform hanging in the wardrobe upstairs? An uneasy feeling stirred inside me. When I had told Inspector Charles about Monsieur Geerts seeing his wife with Mr Milner, I thought I had done the right thing. But perhaps I had sent the enquiry off in a wrong direction. It seemed that there might be a stronger connection between Milner and Wolfendale than any of us guessed.

The captain had something to hide. If Milner knew what that something was, it would have given him a powerful lever. Powerful enough to induce the captain to part with money and to be forced into renting out rooms. Milner had blackmailed Wolfendale. And the clue as to why lay in the attic, and this explained his fierce reaction to my poking about there.

I took another look at the photograph of Miss Wolfendale and her nephew. 'How sad for Lucy, to be orphaned so young and not to have met her great aunt.'

She sighed, and offered more tea. 'Who can fathom God's mysterious ways?'

'What happened to Lucy's parents?'

I knew the captain's account of what had happened, but wondered what he had told Miss Fell, when he first arrived in Harrogate.

'Lucy's mother died of typhoid. Her father in some sort of accident.'

So he had been consistent.

Miss Fell leaned forward in a confidential manner. 'When she was small, the captain told Lucy that her mother had left her a letter, to be read when she was twenty-one. When she came of age, on the sixth of this month, she asked him, and he said it wasn't true. There was no letter, no money, there was nothing. That infuriated her, naturally. She became very hard about it. Wouldn't sit and chat. Oh she would walk Peeko, but further than the poor little chap wanted to go. She would end up carrying him back in a state of exhaustion. Her hair all over, losing her gloves, acting like nobody's child. If she hadn't put her energies into the play, I do believe she would have run mad when she found out there was no inheritance.'

It seemed treacherous to involve Miss Fell in a scheme to unmask her darling Lucy as a robber, but I had to do it. 'Miss Fell, I'm going to confide something that may shock you. And I shall ask you to help me.'

Miss Fell turned pale. 'It's to do with your question yesterday. Did I know a Mrs deVries.'

I could have gone all around the houses, but I decided to be direct. 'Yes. You are Mrs deVries, I believe. You gave a false name and address to Mr Moony to hide your embarrassment at pawning the ring.'

It felt cruel. My words hit her hard. In an involuntary movement, she drew her hands to her chest, twisting the diamond ring on her finger. 'I thought pawnbrokers kept a person's confidence.'

'They do, as a rule. But Mr Moony was robbed of his pledged items, and no ticket was presented for that ring.'

Her eyes widened in astonishment. 'That can't be possible. I gave the ticket and the money to Lucy. She told me she had collected it. Last Monday.'

27

Full of Smoke and Embers

March 1922

Captain Wolfendale sat by his hearth. Wind rattled in the chimney and blew smoke back into the room. His visitor, Lawrence Milner, had brought a drop of something warming, a good port wine. He raised his glass thoughtfully. 'We'll have cause for celebration later this year.'

'Oh?' The captain poked the fire. 'I don't know what's to celebrate.'

'Why, of course you do. Your Lucy comes of age in August.' Milner took it on himself to pour another two generous measures.

The captain placed a shovel in front of the fire, and a newspaper over it, to draw smoke up the chimney and get the coals cracking. He watched carefully, snatching the paper just as it scorched. Smoke still curled into the room.

In a reminiscing vein, Milner said, 'Do you remember that old tobacconist fellow? His son-in-law was a Kent man. He boasted that with eyes tight shut, this son-in-law could name any English apple by its smell. Cox, Bramley, Russett, any of them and more. Well, that's you and baccy, eh *mein Kapitän*?'

'Less of that.'

'Less of what?'

'That *mein Kapitän* business.'

'Insubordination, beg pardon, Captain. And me a lowly corporal. Shame, eh?' Milner plonked his glass on the *Called to Arms* board, on the square titled 'Court Martial'.

The captain moved the glass, leaving behind a small red circle of port. It would stain. 'What are you leading up to, Milner? You know it's finished. You know I've not a penny left.'

'We've done well, my friend. We've done well. Look on these years as an investment. And now it's time to make something of it.' Milner had that bantering mood on him, teasing the older man. He had let the old fellow win two games of *Called to Arms*. Butter him up now, do no harm to butter him up. 'I bet you can guess the name of this twist of baccy I've brought you.'

'Bugger off with your tests. We're not schoolboys.'

'Humour me. I've a little bet with myself.'

Wearily the captain closed his eyes. 'Go on then.'

How had he let this idiot get the better of him all these years? There was a rustling as Milner brought out the tobacco. The captain recognised the blend straight away. It was a mix he had bought from that tobacconist years ago, his favourite. Milner was reminding him, reminding him of the chains that bound. One of these days he would get the better of Milner.

'Well? What does your snitch say?' Milner asked.

Just for devilment, the captain wanted to come up

230

with some nonsense, as if he did not know. But his pride would not let him. 'Light Virginia, mixed with Latakia.'

'Exactly! It's your lucky day, Captain.' Milner put the tobacco on the table.

The captain picked it up and placed it in his jar on the shelf. Milner was a lout. A bloody jumped-up corporal, he now had minions doing his bidding, in his car showroom, his motor repair works, and at his home. He had driven his wife to the grave and now kept his son under the thumb. He wanted to be liked too, damn his eyes. He not only wanted to bleed the captain dry – well, he had done that – but he wanted to be liked for doing it. The captain moved the board. He took it to the kitchen and wiped at the wine stain.

The captain returned the *Called to Arms* board to its box, along with dice and tokens.

Milner lit a cigar. 'And how is our Lucy?'

'She is doing well enough. Has ideas to find work, like her friend Alison.'

'Lucy won't have to work. Lucy will be a prize for any man. She'll be a lady of leisure, in the old pre-war style.'

The captain resumed his seat. He wanted to smoke the tobacco but would not give Milner the satisfaction. 'She may have to find something to do.' He looked steadily at this enemy of his who took the guise of friend. 'You've bled me dry, Milner. I have nothing left. That means there is nothing for Lucy.'

Milner leaned back in the big armchair. He held the cigar casually, like a man who is wealthy enough to let it burn out and fling it into the grate. 'There is everything for Lucy, if you will let me offer it to her.'

Some part of the captain knew straight away what

Milner implied. But he would not let himself believe it. 'You would employ a girl?'

'Hardly a girl, but no. I would not dream of employing Lucy.'

'You're thinking of a match between Lucy and Rodney?' Hope lifted the captain's voice. What Milner robbed him of he had put to good use in his business. That business would come to Rodney. If Lucy and Rodney married . . .

Milner raised the cigar almost to his lips, and then laughed. He sucked on the cigar thoughtfully, shaking his head at the imbecility of this old man. 'Look at me. I'm still a young chap. I'm forty-five years old, in my prime. Lucy is too good for Rodney. And they don't regard each other in a romantic way.'

'Never happen, Milner. Forget that . . .' the captain said in a low voice. He knew what Milner did not know. Every time Lucy heard Milner's step, his ring of the bell, which she always recognised, she would fly upstairs to the old woman and stay there until he had gone. 'She does not see you in that way, and never will.'

'Why whisper? Are you afraid I'll tell her the truth about you-know-what? I never would breathe a word, if she were mine. I'd cherish and protect her.'

It came out before the captain could stop himself. 'Like you cherished and protected your wife.'

'Come, man. This is different. Lucy is different. At least say you'll think about it. She would be taken care of. And as my . . . well, let us say grandfather-in-law, so would you be. Believe me. I would cease all claims. I would make recompense.'

The captain stood up slowly. He took the tobacco

from the jar, the mixture of light Virginia and Latakia that stirred so many memories. He began to fill his pipe. 'She would never agree.'

'You know,' Milner said softly, 'I always get what I want. I would court her. I would bring her round, but I need you to be on my side.'

The captain's flesh crawled. He would never be free. This would go on and on, until the grave. His face took on the blankness of misery.

Milner spoke with vigour, leaning forwards, pressing his point. 'Don't look like that. This will be the very last thing I ask of you. Depend upon it.'

28

 No Pension

'No pension, an' the most we'll earn's four hunder pounds a year.'
— *Rudyard Kipling*

London, 1903

When they left the army, Captain Wolfendale took rooms in Bloomsbury for himself and his loyal batman, Sergeant Lampton. This was the plan: the captain had enough put by to take over the tobacconist's shop on the corner. It would be a better gold mine than The Rand, the captain reckoned. Men could live without gold, but not without a smoke.

Every day, Lampton walked to the tobacconist's, talked to the old fellow, learned about a decent mix of Light Virginia, delightful Latakia and a pinch of something from the top shelf. The fussy, musty window display filled Lampton with new ideas.

Walking back to the lodgings, he marvelled at the length of his own shadow on the pavement, the freedom of being his own man. Here he was, treading a proper street at the heart of the Empire, hearing the traffic and the call of the newspaper boy. Never again would he march across a dust-blown cursed land to the tramp of boots and the cry of baboons.

Back in the rooms, he said to the captain, 'We'll put our medals, crossed daggers, souvenirs and such in the window on display. It'll be a draw, sir. Men will flock to our tobacconist shop to reminisce about the old campaigns.'

'Good thinking. But drop the sir. Just call me Captain. We're civilians now.'

It was on his daily visit to the tobacconist's shop that Lampton bumped into Corporal Milner, now also out of the army. The man stood on the corner by Coram's Fields, cap on the ground at his feet. Lampton looked away, so as not to embarrass him, and to give Milner time to pick up his cap and put it on. Milner's face was grey, unshaven, and his cheeks were sucked in with hunger. Lampton walked him along Millman Street, looking for a café. After sausage and mash, Milner looked more his old insolent self.

'Come and look at our new setup,' Lampton said, and walked him to the tobacconist's shop. 'It'll be yours truly behind that counter in a few weeks' time.'

There they parted, shaking hands, Lampton slipping a half crown into Milner's pocket.

Lampton felt cheerful. Life had been kind. The next day, he set off for the shop, intending to try a new tobacco, perhaps the Perique.

The old tobacconist with his parchment face and yellow moustache took a pinch of snuff. 'Some people call this a filthy habit. There's worse habits in my book, like procrastination.'

'Oh?' asked Lampton, wondering what the fellow was getting at.

The tobacconist tapped the counter with his nicotine-stained fingers and ridged brown nails. 'When will the captain sign on the dotted line?'

Lampton frowned. The business should have been done and dusted by now. He lit his pipe. Out of long habit, he spoke loyally, 'The captain won't be tardy, it'll be in hand.'

To sit on the other side of the tobacconist's counter, on a high stool, would be very heaven. He would do all the work of course, but he didn't mind that, was used to it. Let the captain take his strolls, drop into public houses, visit his lady friends to his heart's content.

Lampton had stopped playing the rolling stone. He never wanted to leave England again. He'd had enough of countries where you boiled or froze.

The tobacconist snooked and gobbed into his spittoon. 'I'm glad to hear you say that, Mr Lampton. The solicitor's confidential clerk was in this dinnertime for his Cut Cavendish. He has that snide clerk's way of letting on to something he won't properly tell. Hintful like, that something's gone wrong with the sale.'

Lampton's answer came out with more confidence than he felt. 'Oh, you know these clerks, jumped up fellows with no excitement in their lives. They always reckon to know something that puts a chap out of humour. Helps pass their dull days.'

Lampton gazed into the shop window. In his mind's eye, he set up his new display. The longing to be settled came over him. Who knows, perhaps he would find himself a wife, some quiet creature who would put his dinner on the table every night, do his washing and polishing as he had washed, cooked and polished for the captain all these years.

As he walked back towards the rooms he shared with the captain, Lampton heard someone call his name. It was Milner. Lampton expected to be tapped for another bob or two. But Milner said he had found a couple of days' work. The meal and the half crown Lampton gave him had changed his luck.

That evening Lampton set out the table for himself and the captain: a pork pie apiece, pickled onion, bread and butter, glasses of ale. When they were in service, he and the captain had not eaten at the same table.

'You must do it, man, if we're to be in business together,' the captain had insisted. 'Changed times call for changed manners.'

After their meal, the captain left, to visit his lady friend, the widow. It was Lampton's guess that the captain would move in with the widow, eventually.

Lampton cleared the dishes. He rinsed the plates over the tin basin with water poured from the jug. The tobacconist's shop had excellent facilities – an indoor tap and a privy out the back that was shared with only three other shops. If the captain did set himself up with the widow, Lampton would have a place all to himself when the shop door closed at night.

There was only one comfortable chair in the Bloomsbury rooms. Lampton sat in it when Wolfendale was out. So it was a fluke that he found the letters – not one, but two. At first, he took them to be something to do with the business over the tobacconist's, and that the captain had forgotten to mention them, pushed them down by the side of the cushion out of absent-mindedness. He never was good at attending to brown envelopes. But if they were to do with the purchase of the tobacconist's, then Lampton had a right to know.

The contents of the first letter did not perturb Lampton. Trust the captain to play cards close to his

237

chest and not reveal where he got the wherewithal to buy the shop. It had been forwarded from army headquarters.

Beresford & Black
Solicitors
27 Albert Street
Harrogate
19 June 1903

Dear Captain Wolfendale

It is my sad duty to inform you of the death of Miss Hilda Wolfendale of 29 St Clement's Road, Harrogate.

You are the sole beneficiary under your aunt's last will and testament, excepting a small bequest and proviso for her lady companion.

While we could arrange for the execution of the will through a London solicitor, you may wish to visit Harrogate so that you can view the property willed to you, and give us your valued instructions.

Assuring you of our condolences and best attention at all times.

We remain,
Yours faithfully
S Beresford
Beresford & Black

The second letter, dated two days ago, was brief. Mr S Beresford thanked Captain Wolfendale for his letter. He looked forward to seeing him at 4 p.m. on the 17th instant. Mr Beresford was pleased to hear that the captain would be taking up residence in Harrogate — such a fine and healthy place. A clerk would be at the

238

station by 3.20 p.m. to meet the 11.20 a.m. train from King's Cross.

At first, the sergeant could not keep still. He seemed to be in a dream where nothing was quite real. For twenty-five years he had been batman to Captain Wolfendale. When Lampton was a private, Wolfendale was a lieutenant. He had washed the captain's underwear, tended his wounds, fed him, saved his life, watched him claim the VC. And he did not resent any of that. He thought he knew Wolfy. He did know him. Inside out. He knew his likes, his dislikes, the stories of his boyhood, his way with women; and his one weakness of always betraying the women who fell for his charms. That Cape Town schoolteacher. What was her name? Miss Marshall. That was a bad do.

The soft old chair cushion sagged under Lampton's sparse weight.

One enormous question threatened to burst his brain. But no. The answer must be no. The captain would not betray him. The captain would not betray his own batman, the person who knew him best, who knew him longest.

A railway timetable had lain on the sideboard since they took the rooms. A strip of newspaper marked the King's Cross to Harrogate page. There was a question mark next to the 9.50 and a tick against the 11.20.

When the captain came back, three hours later, Lampton was still sitting in the big old chair. He had pushed the letters back into their place at the side of the cushion.

'Dozing are we?' said the captain.

That was the kind of banter they had developed since leaving the army. The 'we' had lulled the sergeant into

239

a false sense of security. Now various little telltale signs came back to him. When he had spotted the captain consulting a railway timetable, the captain had looked up and said, 'The widow Philomena has it in her mind to have a day by the sea.'

Lampton made a move to get up from the chair, but his heart and his hopes held him there. He said, as lightly as he could, 'Did you and the widow arrange your little outing?'

'We did not,' said the captain. 'She nags so, you know. Did I say that before?' Without waiting for Lampton's reply, the captain said, 'It's all washed up between us. She'd be a millstone around my neck.'

'What now then?' asked the sergeant.

'I shall take that day out on my own, tomorrow, have a breath of bracing sea air. I'll take meself off to Brighton in the morning on a ten something train. Stop the night there if the fancy takes me.'

'Brighton?' said Lampton in a flat, unenthusiastic voice, still hoping that he was wrong about the captain's betrayal. 'Bit of sea air might do us both good. Shall I come along with you for company?'

'Why no, old chap. We live too much in each other's pockets. Let me go there and stride by the sea, and think of how we shall get on when we have the tobacconist shop.'

'Will you be signing the lease and such shortly?' Lampton asked.

The captain waved his hand. 'It's all coming along nicely.'

'If you're stopping the night, I'll pack a bag for you,' said Lampton. 'You'll want your shaving kit.' The captain had never packed a bag of his own.

'No need. You can't play the batman forever. All that's behind us now. Let's have a toast to me being fancy-free again. The widow Philomena, she'd got too bossy by half.' The captain had already had a skinful. But he seemed in jovial mood and not to notice that the sergeant had little to say and no enthusiasm for raising a toast.

Wolfendale poured whisky and handed a glass to Lampton. 'We've seen a lot together, and I'll never forget it. I couldn't have wanted a better batman.'

Lampton gulped down the whisky. This was where the captain would break the news about his inheritance.

'And by God, we saw a new kind of war altogether with the last show.'

'We did,' Lampton agreed.

'You shouldn't have resigned just because I did,' said the captain. 'Do you have regrets about leaving?'

The sergeant shook his head.

'Come, man, yes you have. You're a natural for the army. You could sign on again you know. Any regiment would open its arms to you, with your record.'

So that's it, thought Lampton. You are just going to leave without a word, after all these years. Why?

It is because, he answered himself bitterly, he is as tired of me as he is of that putrid widow. He looks at me and sees the ravages of war, dead men's eyes, lost limbs, a small dark hole in a young man's forehead.

And because he understood him so well, he could almost forgive. But Lampton thought of that tobacconist's shop; its blue wispy fragrance, and the gentle touch of tobacco leaves, so soothing to fingers used to loading a gun. The sense of loss hit him with the force of a bayonet in the gut.

241

The captain reminisced through a full bottle of whisky. On the stroke of midnight, he staggered to his bed. At the doorway, he turned. 'I've ordered a cab to take me to the station in the morning. For the Brighton train.'

For a long time, the sergeant sat like a man in a trance.

When the captain began to snore, the sergeant opened the door to his room and looked in. Wolfendale's portmanteau was already packed. When had he done that? Earlier in the day, perhaps, when Lampton was reassuring the tobacconist that all would be well with the exchange of contracts. The sergeant carried the case into the other room and set it on the table. He opened the catches. Naturally, it was badly packed. Item by item, he emptied the case: good suit, best shoes, three shirts and six collars, underwear, socks. The batman neatly repacked the case.

How long he sat there, Lampton could not have said. The gas mantle popped and spluttered as the captain called out. He was being sick, he wanted the basin.

Dutifully, Lampton picked up the basin and carried it into his captain's bedroom.

The man looked a mess – pale sweaty face, a hairnet keeping the black waves in place. He was just about to vomit. His eyes met the sergeant's and his mouth opened, expecting the basin to be there for him. Suddenly, he was black in the face, his eyes filled with terror and pleading.

Lampton pushed him back, quite calmly, so the captain, used to such ministrations did not object. When the sergeant put the pillow over his head and held him very still, he barely struggled.

*

During that long night, Lampton thought carefully about what he had done. 'Do it to them before they do it to you,' had been his captain's mantra. Was this worse than killing the smooth-skinned young Boer, against whom he bore no malice, who had done him no wrong, a young man fighting for his own land?

Lampton did something he had only ever done once before, and that in secret. He put on the captain's uniform.

He was still wearing it, and had not slept, when the young woman arrived at the door early the next morning, carrying an infant.

'Captain Wolfendale?' she asked.

'Yes,' he said boldly, for that was the only course.

'Mrs Granger sent me. You've to take care of the child.'

'Mrs Granger? I don't know a Mrs Granger.' A pang of misgiving made him hold his breath. Perhaps he did not know everything about the captain after all.

'Miss Marshall as was. She has made a good marriage with a clergyman. If he finds out her sin, all that will go to the bad.'

'Look here, this won't do.'

The Cape Town schoolteacher had come to England to have her baby. That was meant to be an end of it.

'I'm not to take no for answer,' the nursemaid said.

'It's the only answer.' Lampton heard himself adopt the captain's tone of voice. But somehow the voice did not convince. He would have to try harder.

'I'm to say,' said the nursemaid stubbornly, 'that she doesn't want to make a clean breast to her husband, but she will, rather than see the child be farmed out. She said to remind you that your name is on the birth certificate.'

He would have to get her out of here. 'Look, you can't stay. There's been a tragedy.'

The nursemaid had her orders. And she was used to tragedy.

'Don't you want to know your daughter's name?'

'No.'

'It's Lucinda Wolfendale. I call her Lucy.'

29

Miss Fell's Supporting Role

'I need your help, Miss Fell.'

We were strolling in the small park, Peeko sniffing at wallflowers. Miss Fell moved more and more slowly as though her legs and her brain refused to work.

'I can't take it in. It seems impossible to think Lucy would have offered to make the trip into Leeds to fetch my ring, and then for such a thing to happen.'

Miss Fell had seemed so distressed at the thought of Lucy being dishonest that I had told her a little more about my investigations, and had quickly invented some plausible explanation that cast suspicion on that eavesdropping master of disguises, Dan Root.

The afternoon was a warm, but she tightened the scarf at her throat. 'Mr Root seems so upright, quite a religious fellow. Always off to some service on Sundays. Of course you can never tell with young men. Chapels are where they do their courting.' At a cast-iron bench, Miss Fell came to a halt. 'I usually sit here.'

Peeko circled us expectantly, making small leaps at Miss Fell's pocket. She peeled off her gloves and took out a ball, tossing it along the path. Peeko raced towards it. Miss Fell held her gloves carefully, gazing at her diamond ring. 'I am sure you are wrong about Lucy being involved in this matter. It's true that I gave her the pawn ticket, and she agreed to redeem the ring. As to her going missing, there must be some simple explanation.'

'Then let us try and find that simple explanation,' I said gently. Peeko brought me his wet ball. I threw it for him with a bit of a bowler's spin, sending him racing across the grass. 'All I want to do is get to the truth.'

'Very well. What do you want me to do?'

'I would like to see whether Dan Root has any jewellery hidden in his room. When you go back, and you take Peeko upstairs, find some task that you can ask him to help you with. Perhaps you have a gas mantle that needs changing?'

Miss Fell's eyes suddenly sparkled. 'I'm assisting a detective aren't I? I shall be helping prove Lucy innocent.'

'I hope so.'

'Now what can I ask Mr Root to do? My mantles are all in perfect order, unlike the captain's. He has been threatening to put a new light in the hall for six months.'

'Something on a high shelf, perhaps, that he could reach for you? As long as you keep him talking. Keep him out of the way for about fifteen minutes, if you can.'

'I do have an obstinate jar of piccalilli that I can't open. And two of my curtain rings have come off.'

'Perfect.'

'And there's a case on top of the wardrobe he could lift down, while he's about it, and when I have what I want he can lift it back.'

'Excellent. And Miss Fell, there is one other thing, if you would be willing.' I had not yet finished searching the captain's attic. I wanted to take a careful look at his cigar box of documents and photographs. 'After you have finished with Mr Root, I should like you to go downstairs, and keep Captain Wolfendale occupied.'

She looked alarmed. 'Oh dear. Are you risking returning to the lion's den?'

'Yes. And I should like to borrow that magnifying glass of yours.'

After our walk, I loitered in the park, and then walked back slowly. I watched as Miss Fell knocked on Mr Root's door. The two of them went up the front steps and into the house.

Root had not troubled to lock his door. Why should he when he expected to be gone for only a few moments?

I hurried into his flat.

I searched under his worktable, the pantry, and the cupboards. Quickly I went to his chest of drawers. In the top drawer were a couple of old pocket watches, not from Moony's list, along with a set of plain gold cufflinks. The other drawers held neatly folded shirts and socks. If he had robbed the pawnbroker, then he had found some other hiding place for the goods.

Out of curiosity, I picked up the book he had moved to one side when I had visited him earlier, as if trying to keep it from view. It was a bible. Written on the flyleaf was the name Gideon Bindeman. At first glance, I thought the language Dutch. Then I realised that it must be Afrikaans.

Chimneys sometimes provided a hiding place.

Reluctantly, I searched the hearth. Covering my hand with a handkerchief, I felt into the cold chimney breast and then checked the ash pan. Nothing.

Relying on Miss Fell's talking powers to keep Root out of the way, I glanced at the speaking trumpet I had noticed on my earlier visit. The metal pipe that lay near it intrigued me. It was turned at a forty-five degree angle. The end of the speaking trumpet, when I tried them together, fitted perfectly. The trumpet was edged in soot. I put it into the hearth and raised it into the chimney breast.

Silence. And then, the unmistakeable sound of the restless captain, blowing his nose. So I had been right about the eavesdropping.

The house door slammed. Root would be here any second. Quickly, I dismantled the trumpet from the pipe, and hurried out of the flat. But he was already coming down the steps from the house. There was nothing for it but to stand by his door. I raised my left hand to knock, because that was free of soot.

As I tapped on the door, I felt the warmth of his body right behind me.

'Mrs Shackleton. To what do I owe the honour of another visit?'

I stepped aside, to give him the freedom to open his own door. He did not, but waited.

'I thought you might be able to help me,' I said, making a fist of my sooty hand so that he would not see it. 'Do you know where Lucy is?'

'Always searching for someone,' he said with a smile. 'Yesterday Meriel Jamieson, today Lucy. I must put a new sign on my door, enquire within for missing persons.'

His arrogance and the smile irritated me. 'Lucy *is*

missing, as I'm sure you know.' I watched closely, waiting for some reaction.

The look of concern seemed genuine. He could have feigned surprise but did not.

'I haven't got her hidden here, if that's what you mean.' He flung open the door. 'See for yourself.'

My withering look stopped him in his tracks.

'Sorry,' he said. 'But you seem to be blaming me.'

He was playing games with me. It was my guess he had heard every word that passed between me and the captain. Well, let him see the soot on my hands. Let him know his dirty little secret was out.

'Do you mind if I wash my hands?'

'Be my guest.'

For a South African, his accent was perfect. Occasionally his words had a slightly chopped sound, but not enough to draw attention. What was it that Mr Moony had said? The man's accent was neutral, not local. In height and looks Dan Root did not look the part of Mr Moony's robber, but his voice certainly fitted. On stage he had acted his parts to perfection: stooped for the miser, with a disappearing neck for the revivalist, and a shuffling, defeated gait for the despairing manufacturer who hangs himself. Dan was indeed a master of disguise.

He was acting now as he graciously passed me a clean hand towel, saying, 'Lucy's probably with a friend. I wonder if she has heard the news about Milner? I expect you have.'

There was something in his voice that was almost triumphant. It frightened me. Why was he here, a Boer in the house of the enemy, listening in to what went on in the flat above?

'Yes, I have heard.'

'I was in town earlier. People are talking of nothing else. I expect the police will want to interview all of us who saw Milner last night.'

The way he enunciated Milner's name betrayed his dislike of the man. But it was less noticeable the second time he spoke the name than the first. Perhaps he was practising. Dan Root was such a good actor that he would do shocked horror to perfection, and play innocence with utter conviction.

I handed back the towel. 'Thank you.'

'Not at all. And I shall keep an eye out for Lucy.'

I left his flat and went back into the house. The captain had interrupted my search of his attic with such vehemence that I knew he had something to hide. Miss Fell, good as her word, was waiting at her door. She passed me her magnifying glass, and wished me luck. As I began to climb the stairs, she went down, to tap on the captain's door, and keep him talking.

30

Enter the Cavalry

When I left number 29 after my second sojourn into the attic, I desperately needed to think, to make sense of what I had seen. Wanting to walk, I set off for the railway station, taking my time, paying little attention to my surroundings as I made my way down the Leeds Road. I turned onto York Place, and then Station Road, beginning to get the hang of Harrogate, whilst still juggling pieces of an extraordinary puzzle.

The double wooden doors of the red-brick railway station stood wide open, releasing a newly arrived torrent of visitors. An elderly porter pushed a trolley loaded with trunks, hatboxes and portmanteaux, wheels squeaking as he headed for the taxi rank.

Sending for the fingerprint kit had seemed a good idea. It was now two o'clock. I hoped that Sykes would have put the kit on the train at about noon, and so it should be ready for me to collect. Then I might discover who else besides Lucy had handled the ransom note. My first guesses had been Dylan Ashton, Rodney Milner or Alison Hart. After speaking to Alison and Rodney, I felt sure they were not in Lucy's confidence. That left

Dylan, a young chap whom I should be able to crack between finger and thumb. But Dylan had proved surprisingly stubborn. Another distinct possibility now seemed to be Dan Root.

So far, so uncertain. There was also the small matter of my lack of expertise in dealing with the loops and whorls of fingerprints. Jim Sykes had given me a demonstration. I had tried it myself – once, but my confidence took a dip as I entered the station.

Through the barrier, I watched happy shoppers stepping off the York train. A young man beamed at the sight of his lady friend alighting from a first-class carriage. The porter hurried to help an old lady.

Everyone had something to be pleased about: their visit to the Spa; coming home; a successful shopping trip; a reunion. Trust me to be there to meet a wooden box.

Before I had time to check at the parcels office, someone from an inch behind my head said, 'Mrs Shackleton!'

I nearly jumped out of my skin. If he had said, 'Hello, I am your local murderer,' I could not have been more startled.

'Mr Sykes! Where did you come from?'

'Sorry to creep up on you. I saw you walking along but could not get near for the taxi cabs, and the crush.'

'How did you get here?'

'Drove across in your Jowett, Mrs Shackleton. You said I could make use of the motor while you were away. And I have visited all the gentlemen customers on Mr Moony's list.'

Sykes had only just learned to drive. With him at the wheel in the emergency that followed our last case, we had crawled home at the pace of an arthritic snail.

He seemed terribly pleased with himself, practically bouncing as we threaded our way through the busy station.

'After the telegram yesterday, and your telephone call to Mrs Sugden this morning, thought you might appreciate reinforcements.'

Sykes's presence made me feel better. I did not turn to detection in order to become expert at analysing fingerprints and was more than glad to leave that to him. All the same, it would not pay to let him think he had the better of me. 'If this is a contest in handling the mysterious case of the pawnshop robbery, you will have a great deal of catching up to do.'

He had parked the Jowett in James Street, perhaps on account of worrying about having to reverse if he drove to the station. As we crossed the square, I told him all about unmasking Miss Fell as Mrs deVries, the fact that the pawned ring was back on its owner's finger, and that the person she had entrusted to redeem it, namely Lucy Wolfendale, had gone missing.

He let out an astonished whistle. 'You have been busy.'

'That's not half of it.'

James Street bustled with shoppers. We paused to let a woman and her daughter totter in their heels to a motor whose chauffeur opened the door smartly. They were followed by a shop assistant, heavily laden with parcels and hat boxes.

As we reached the Jowett, Sykes asked, 'Why did our mysterious gentlewoman go all the way from Harrogate to Leeds, so as not to be known, and then go to the trouble of supplying a false name and address?'

'She is embarrassed by her poverty,' I said in a low

voice. 'I'm sure that Miss Fell has no connection with the robbery. As far as she was concerned, Lucy Wolfendale simply offered to do her the favour of redeeming her ring from Moony's pawnshop.'

When we were sitting in the car, this time with me back in the driving seat, he asked, 'But who else was in on it? Who was the young man who throttled Mr Moony?'

Not wishing to shout above the engine noise, I waited before starting the motor. 'Good question. There is a Mr Root, Dan – originally from South Africa. I believe his real name is Bindeman. Either for his amusement or some other purpose, he listens in to what goes on in the captain's flat. I hope I'll have his fingerprints on a watchmender's cup. Who knows? Perhaps he'll be on police records.'

I started the car and began to drive up the street, towards the Valley Gardens, and past the Royal Pump room. Once on Cornwall Road, in a quiet spot in sight of the Grand Hotel, I stopped the car.

Sykes picked up where we had left off. 'What sort of figure does this missing Lucy Wolfendale cut?'

'I wouldn't have thought she could be mistaken for a chap, though she is a budding actress, and a good one. Her height would be about right.'

Sykes barely kept the envy from his voice. 'No wonder I drew a blank in Leeds. This is a ladies and gentlemen of Harrogate job. Is this Lucy part of some criminal ring?' He turned to me, with a please-tell-all look on his face.

'I doubt it. Her ransom note to her grandfather had a distinctly amateurish look about it. I would not say we are looking for a mastermind.'

He smiled. 'Ransom note? Tell me you're joshing.'

'I wish I were. What does leave me feeling uneasy is that the man who doted on her was murdered.'

The smile vanished. His look became suddenly serious. 'The motor trade man?'

'You know about it?'

'Heard it from the beat bobby in Woodhouse this morning. I never dreamed there might be some connection with the robbery.'

'We don't know that there is, yet.'

'But you suspect?' He was staring hard at me. I could hear his brain ticking, and anticipated the next remark. 'Have you told the police?' he asked, in a sombre voice.

'I'd better tell you everything from the beginning.' In a methodical order that would suit Sykes's tidy mind, I told him everything that had happened since I arrived in Harrogate. He listened with rapt attention, his mouth opening now and again, until I had to remind him that it was summer, and there were flies about.

'Is that it?' he said.

'No. One more thing. Half an hour ago, I asked Miss Fell to go down and keep Lucy's grandfather, Captain Wolfendale, talking while I searched his attic for a second time, looking for the jewellery, and checking on something else that had intrigued me. There was no stolen property – or at least not what we are looking for. But I did find something else. The captain has a cigar box, with photographs from the Boer War, and some documents. One of the photographs shows the captain and his batman. And what is very puzzling is that having seen a photograph of Wolfendale as a lad, and having got to know him as he is today, I am almost certain that the man calling himself Captain

255

Wolfendale now is the sergeant in the photograph.'

Sykes shook his head. 'This is too much for me to take in. You've lost me.'

'The young Wolfendale in a photograph with his aunt has the same shape face as you, longish, and he is recognisable in the photograph in uniform, taken twenty-odd years ago. The man beside him in that photograph, in sergeant's uniform, has a round face.'

'Perhaps they changed caps, for a lark or something.'

'That's possible, I suppose. But the man calling himself Wolfendale now has that same round face, quite chubby. There is a death certificate for Henry Lampton, who died of suffocation whilst inebriated. There are discharge papers for the two men, Sergeant Lampton and Captain Wolfendale. I think that the person who died was Wolfendale, and that Lampton took his place.'

The afternoon sun shone brightly, turning the motor into an oven. 'Let's walk for a while,' I suggested.

Sykes did not budge. 'I don't know how you do it.'

'I can't quite take it in myself. I almost picked up the cigar box and made off with it. But I don't suppose Inspector Charles will be too delighted if having pointed the finger at Monsieur Geerts I now tell him that perhaps he has another suspect.'

Sykes sighed. 'And, of course, you could be mistaken. Perhaps the chap just put on weight. Men do when they get older, and aren't living an active life any more.'

In the bright sunshine of the afternoon, my interpretation of the photographs seemed less convincing to me. And I had certainly not convinced Sykes. He was impatient to be doing, not talking.

'If it's all the same to you, I'd just as soon get on with

256

this fingerprinting. Because I feel I've contributed nothing, apart from being Mr Moony's messenger boy to his customers.'

I started the motor. As I did, my stomach rumbled.

'Was that you or me?' Sykes asked.

'Me. I haven't eaten a thing since my shared duck egg this morning. We can have a bite to eat, you check the fingerprints – see whether we can find out for sure who has been helping Lucy in her ransom efforts. Once I find her, I can get to the bottom of what is going on. Then I'll go to the police, if needs be.'

I stopped the car at the entrance to the Grand Hotel.

The hotel doorman doffed his cap and got into the driving seat, ready to park the motor. He spoke to Sykes. 'Need any attention to the motor, sir? We have a pit in the garage.'

Sykes looked at me.

'Just petrol. Thank you.'

'Very good, madam,' he said in a slightly offended voice.

'Hold on,' Sykes said, hurrying round to the rear of the car. 'There's something I need from the boot.'

He lifted out the fingerprint kit. We entered the hotel and I picked up my key from reception. Then we found a seat in a quiet corner of the dining room, away from the string quartet, beside a verdant palm, designed to calm the spirit.

Sykes claimed to have eaten and said that he would start straight away checking fingerprints. He jotted down the names and items as I reeled them off. 'Dylan Ashton's prints should be on the note. I got him to write some addresses this morning when I visited the house agent's office. Alison Hart's are on the drinking glass I lifted from the room she was in at Madam Geerts's house. Rodney Milner's will be on this business card. Dan Root has handled the little egg cup-style item that he uses in his watch mending. Captain Wolfendale's prints should be on the matchbox.'

Having purloined so many items, I was wishing I had lifted the cigar box from the attic. But if the captain had something to hide, then it was best not to give him reason to become more jittery than he already was.

'What about Lucy's own prints, for elimination?' Sykes asked.

'There's a perfume bottle I picked up from her dressing table.'

A waiter took my order for ham sandwiches. When he had gone, Sykes said, 'Regarding Captain Wolfendale, your London cousin telephoned earlier with a message for you. Mrs Sugden took it down word for word.'

'Excellent. What's the gist of it?'

Sykes is not a man for giving the gist. He took out a notebook and read what Mrs Sugden had written. 'Your cousin says nothing on Corporal Milner. Records on enlisted men do not come under his jurisdiction. As to Captain W, as he called him – I expect he didn't want to give the full moniker in case anyone was listening in – Captain W, of the Yorkshire Light Infantry, served in India before shipping out to Cape Town from Mauritius on the HMS *Powerful*. He served in South Africa in the war against the Boers, 1899 to 1902. Awarded VC. Marital status single . . .'

'Single? That must be a mistake.'

'Don't think so. Says here, Next of kin Miss EW, paternal aunt, of Harrogate.' Sykes looked up from the notebook. 'Those were the facts. The next part is hearsay. Your cousin adds that his superiors in India were glad to see the back of W. There was a scandal in Calcutta involving the gentleman in question and the wife and daughter of a highly placed official. In South Africa a schoolteacher made a fuss after an encounter with him, and had to have her passage paid to England.' Sykes closed the notebook. 'Want to see for yourself?'

I shook my head. 'He's a widower, supposedly, with a son and daughter-in-law who died in South Africa – hence Lucy. And all this scandal and womanising, that's not like him. He says himself he is hopeless with women. You realise what this means?'

Sykes looked miserable. 'I'm sure you're going to tell me. Don't forget this is the first I've heard of this and I don't know any of these people.'

I felt a mounting excitement. 'I think it means I could be right, that the captain is not who he says he is. He came to Harrogate with a pack of lies.'

Sykes returned the notebook to his pocket. 'All very odd. I'll leave you to puzzle that out while I check fingerprints.'

The checking did not take long. The revelation was less than startling. Lucy's prints, taken from the perfume bottle on her dressing table, were all over the ransom note. She had cut and pasted the message herself. Nor was it a surprise to see that Dylan Ashton's thumb-print appeared on the note. I could hear their voices in my head. 'How does this sound Dylan?' 'Perfect, Lucy.'

We left the dining room.

'I'll go and visit Dylan again. He works at the house

259

agents, Croker & Company. This time I'll have good reason to make him squeal.'

Sykes looked at his watch. 'It's four o'clock. Will they still be open, on a Saturday?'

'Meriel told me that Dylan lives in rooms above the office. I shall disturb his peace and demand answers.'

'Do you want me to come with you?' Sykes asked.

'No. What would help is if you could find out more about Captain Wolfendale and his links with Mr Milner. Ex-corporal, or ex-sergeant Milner, whatever he was.'

'Why do you say sergeant?'

'Because I think Milner was a corporal, but there's a sergeant's uniform hanging alongside the captain's uniform in his attic. My guess is that it belonged to the late Sergeant Lampton, and I wish I could be sure.'

'Why would Wolfendale keep a sergeant's uniform?'

'Because he was that sergeant?'

'Then why would he keep the captain's uniform . . .?' A light went on in his eyes. 'Because . . .'

'Because he was the sergeant until Captain Wolfendale came into an inheritance, and then he became the captain. Is there anyone in Harrogate who knew the captain and the sergeant when they were still in uniform?'

Sykes looked doubtful. 'I'll see what I can come up with. But I don't know the watering holes in these parts, or where old soldiers are likely to congregate.'

'This is a small town, and everyone is going to be talking about the murder. Milner must have mixed with the Harrogate well-to-do.'

'How long have I got?'

'I should be back within the hour.'

He nodded.

'Oh, and one other thing I should probably tell you, Mr Sykes. I was the one who found Mr Milner's body.' Before he had a chance to express his concern, I said, 'But it's all right. I'm over the shock. Almost.'

As I left the hotel, I tried to concentrate on how best to make Dylan confide in me. But instead my brain would not let go of the information about Wolfendale. I could hear my cousin's voice as he dictated his message to Mrs Sugden.

'Captain W, of the Yorkshire Light Infrantry, served in South Africa in the war against the Boers. Awarded VC. Marital status single. Next of kin Miss EW, Aunt, of Harrogate.

Had Wolfendale lied to the army command, or to everyone else?

31

Resting

Resting: what an actor does when not working

The best way to find Lucy Wolfendale would be to shake the truth from Dylan Ashton. Now that I knew for sure that his prints were on the ransom note, he would not be able to deny having helped in the scheme to fleece her grandfather.

I had expected Croker & Company to have the sign on the door turned to 'Closed', and it was. But Mr Croker was still there. We stared at each other through the glass door. His frown deepened as he looked at me, one hand on the 'Closed' sign. Would he remember me as a prospective client?

'Mr Croker,' I mouthed. 'I was here earlier.'

He opened the door a fraction. 'I'm so sorry. We're closed.'

'I'm Mrs Shackleton. Is Mr Ashton available?'

My questioned deepened his frown. 'Sadly, no.'

'Do you know where I may find him?'

'He's in the infirmary. Goodness knows what state he's in.'

'Poor boy! What happened?'

A snake-oil salesman would have been proud of the

way I got my foot in the door. Mr Croker gave me his businessman's eye for spotting a time-waster.

'Has he been taken ill?' I asked.

'Involved in an accident. He was knocked off his bike by some blighter who didn't stop.'

His words left me feeling light-headed. It seemed too strange that something had happened to Dylan so soon after Mr Milner's murder. Perhaps his reluctance to talk this morning had been because there was something he needed to keep quiet about. And now someone had tried to silence him, and make it look like an accident.

Mr Croker picked up his hat. 'So now not only am I without my assistant but the police insist I go over to the infirmary, to make sure it's him, so if you don't mind . . .'

'Is he dangerously hurt?'

'By the sounds of it, yes. He can't muster himself to say who he is.'

I felt responsible in some vague way I could not define. 'Let me do this for you,' I said. 'I know Dylan well, through my friend Miss Jamieson who directed the play. If you'll allow me, I shall visit him and report back to you on his condition.'

Relief flooded Mr Croker's face, but almost immediately he thought better of his near capitulation. 'No, no. This is my responsibility.'

'Are they sure it is him?'

'Our business card was in his pocket. And he has been missing for hours, and such a busy day, and I have an appointment on my way home and . . .'

It seemed treacherous to sow seeds of doubt. 'It may not be him. Your business card is in my bag, and I daresay in many other pockets.' The thought gratified

263

Mr Croker. I pushed my advantage. 'I'll come back directly and tell you if it's him, and glean what I can about his condition. I was a VAD nurse.' The number of times I bandy that about, I ought to be ashamed. We weren't even proper nurses if the truth be told. Lightly trained and heavily worked.

Mr Croker weakened. 'The thing is, I have a call to make and the chap does not have a telephone. It will go badly if I do not keep the appointment. And ...' He almost checked himself. I gave my most sympathetic nodding smile to encourage him to go on. 'It is my wedding anniversary and we have a motor booked to take us to the Café Imperial, and on to a concert at the Royal Hall and a theatre supper afterwards at the Prospect.'

'You must not let your wife down. What anniversary is it, may I ask?'

'Silver. Normally, I would not dream of taking up your offer, and really no. I must not.'

'Please. I can assure you that I will carry out the task with great delicacy and let you have the information straight away, if you'll give me your address, or a telephone number.' I produced my card: *Kate Shackleton, private investigator.* 'Tact is my stock in trade and I would be happy to do this for you, Mr Croker, and for such an obliging young man as Dylan Ashton.'

I had him. Relief flooded his face. My private guess was that relations with his wife were less than perfect and to let her down on her wedding anniversary would be a step too far.

'Agreed?' I held out my hand. He took it.

Mr Croker opened a drawer and produced a letter heading. He scribbled a note. 'Show this if there is any reluctance to let you act on my behalf.' He turned the page and wrote his address on the other side. As he held the door open for me, concern gave way to something approaching annoyance. 'If it is Dylan and if he is conscious, you might ask him where had he been, to be riding back along Stonehook Road when he was supposed to be calling at a property in Cowling Avenue.'

Approaching the solid stone-built infirmary brought back memories of wartime, and injured men trying to be brave. This conjured up my sense of hopelessness, at being able to do so little for those men. My steps slowed. I pictured Dylan in the play, as the doomed youth, Willie Price. His stock in trade a lost and yearn-ing look; loving his hopeless father; hopelessly loving Anna. Pincers of fear gripped my belly. You don't know him, I told myself. He's nothing to you. It wasn't true. He mattered. Don't worry, I told myself. Wait. Every event is worse in the thinking about.

The porter on the door looked up expectantly. Weekly visiting hours were clearly signed on the notice board. This was not a visiting time.

I introduced myself. 'I'm here on behalf of Mr Croker, Dylan Ashton's employer. He was admitted after a road accident and I've been asked to confirm his identity.'

'Are you a relative?'

Idiot. If I were a relative, I would be here on my account, not the house agent's. I produced Mr Croker's note. That did the trick.

A moment later, the porter returned with a young policeman.

'You're sure you'll be able to identify the chap, madam?' He spoke with a Leeds accent, and must have been drafted in to help in the murder investigation.

'I will if it is Dylan Ashton.'

The constable seemed relieved not to be the only fish out of water. 'I'm here for when the young chap regains consciousness. We'd like to . . .' He stopped himself from saying the word interview, which would connect his presence with the murder investigation. 'I have to get some details from him.'

'So he hasn't spoken yet?'

'Not anything that makes sense. He had a Croker & Company business card in his pocket. Of course, that could be there for any number of reasons, that's why I went round to the house agent.'

Walking the infirmary corridor towards the ward felt so familiar from my VAD days, almost like a slip in time. A nurse went by carring a bed pan covered with a cloth. The constable led me along the ward to a bed with screens drawn around, which made me fear the worst.

The ward sister gave a disapproving glance as she strode towards us purposefully. We cluttered the top end of her ward. She kept her annoyance barely under control as she said, 'Still here, constable?'

'Until ordered otherwise, sister,' the constable answered mildly.

'And I'm Kate Shackleton.' I tried to put on my best nursing manner. 'Here to confirm the patient's identity. His family would wish to be informed of the accident as soon as possible.'

'Just so,' the policeman said.

His back-up proved unnecessary. The ward sister nodded to me to go around the screen.

Poor Dylan. He lay there pale as alabaster, his head bandaged. One arm was tucked under the sheet, another lay bandaged on top of the cover. His eyelashes flickered.

'Dylan? It's Kate Shackleton. Can you hear me?' I reached for his hand. 'Squeeze if you can hear me.'

Did his fingers move? I could not be sure.

The ward sister touched my shoulder. 'That's enough for now.'

Feeling heavy and useless, I slowly walked back to the ward office, deliberately not looking at the sick men on either side of the ward.

'Well?' The policeman looked up expectantly.

'He's Dylan Ashton, employee of Croker & Company. He lives in the upstairs rooms at the house agent's premises.'

He took out his notebook, and licked his pencil.

'Do we know his next of kin?' the ward sister asked.

'Mr Croker will have that information. I'm sure he'll telegraph Dylan's family,' I said. 'What's his condition?'

The ward sister seemed easier now that we were off her ward and in the office. 'He's concussed, and has a broken wrist and bruising. It might not be as bad as it looks. We gave him a sedative.'

It seemed heartless to pass on the next request, but I needed to know for myself as much as for Croker. 'Did Mr Ashton have details of a property in his pockets, or keys that should be returned?'

The ward sister consulted her notes. The policeman did likewise.

'No,' said the sister.

'No mention of any keys here,' said the constable.

'Pockets empty bar a comb, a handkerchief, two ciga-
rettes and a couple of matches. There was a broken
bottle of tea on the road. He must have had his lunch
with him. Birds had finished off most of his sandwich.'

'Do we know what happened?' I asked. 'Were there
witnesses?'

'Another cyclist heard a crash bang. When he
rounded the bend, there was the cycle and rider in the
ditch. A car had stopped but the blighter must have got
in and set off again without staying to help.'

'How do we know he'd stopped?'

'Cyclist chappy said. He rounded the bend and the
car was stopped – next thing it was pulling away. We do
have his statement. He had the presence of mind to
attempt first aid and go for help. Might have saved
young Ashton's life.' The constable looked hopefully at
the ward sister. She remained non-committal.

'What sort of person would just leave him there?' I
wondered aloud.

'Some sort of person who drove a De Dion motor,'
the constable answered before snapping his notebook
shut. 'Now if I may use your telephone, sister, I can
confirm the lad's identity to my sergeant. And Mr
Croker needn't worry about notifying the relatives.
We'll be in touch with the nearest local station and send
someone round.'

'Where precisely did the accident happen? For Mr
Croker's information,' I added quickly.

'A mile out of Harrogate, along Stonehook Road.
The lad's bike was in a ditch.'

'Do we think he was cycling to or away from
Harrogate?'

The constable frowned. 'Most likely on his way back

to Harrogate. Bike was on the easterly side of the road.'

Only as I left the infirmary grounds did it hit me between the eyes that there might be some connection. The two young men most likely to have helped Lucy were Dylan and Rodney Milner. Rodney Milner and his father held the dealership for De Dion motor cars. Rodney had driven away from the showroom in a De Dion this morning. But he was going to collect Alison from the Geerts, wasn't he? Had Rodney gone out driving to distract himself, to seek out Lucy, and accidentally or on purpose run down Dylan Ashton? The idea seemed too preposterous, and yet it stuck.

Madam Geerts came running towards me as I left the infirmary. One thick strand of her hair had come undone and fell over her left eye. She was without her handbag and her arms seemed not to know what to do with themselves. She charged at me and I put my hands up to grab her and stop her knocking me to the ground.

'Madam Geerts, what's wrong?'

'Is it true? Is it true that Dylan is in this 'ospital?'

'Yes.'

'Then I must speak to him.'

'Why?'

''e alone can save my Loy, my 'usband.'

'What on earth do you mean?'

'The inspector ... ah, Mrs Shackleton, you do not know the anguish. My Loy would not 'arm a soul. Many lovers I 'ave 'ad and not one 'as my sweet Loy murdered. Now they say it is a *crime passionel* and 'e kill Mr Milner. They 'ave arrested 'im.'

She was shaking. I gripped her shoulders. 'The police

have to take everything into account. If your husband is innocent, he'll be released.'

'We foreigners, we take the blame for everything. This is what it is like. The police they 'ave set up question station at the Prince of Wales Hotel. All Harrogate will point the finger at the foreigner.'

'Surely not. You're very highly regarded here.' I did not know whether this was true so gave my words great emphasis. 'And where does Dylan come into this? Why is he so important?'

'Dylan and Loy leave the theatre together. Loy is with Dylan until midnight. I must see Dylan.'

'They won't let you see him. He's unconscious.'

She threw up her arms in a gesture of despair. 'Tell them. Tell them my man is innocent.'

'Madam Geerts, I have no connection with the murder investigation.'

I did not tell her that my own statement had led to suspicion falling on her husband. It was cold-hearted, but my main concern was to go on looking for Lucy.

32

A Delayed Entrance

Here is my situation, Lucy told herself. It is Saturday afternoon. My watch has stopped. Granddad has received two notes – how much to pay, and where to leave the money, if he wants to see me again alive. Dylan has turned yellow belly and abandoned me. My ankle throbs, sprained or broken. I feel poorly. Perhaps I will die. Then they will be sorry – Granddad that he did not give me my inheritance, Dylan that he did not stand by me.

This magical tower from which she would emerge triumphant was no longer magical. Those were bats hanging in the corner. She had not noticed them before because of the nests and cobwebs.

'I am locked in, with no key,' she thought. How ridiculous.

She could move best by sitting on her bottom and shuffling. She had made painfully slow, inch-by-inch progress back up to the floor below the battlements where she had her ground sheet and blankets. Sitting with her back to the wall, she kept her painful leg extended, hoping that this was just a bruise and the throbbing would stop.

Not yet would she give in to the humiliation of clambering up to the battlements and waving a white petticoat flag of surrender. She had come this far and could not bear the bitter taste of defeat. Dylan would come back.

If she hadn't dropped the key, she could have got to the stream and plunged her ankle in icy water. She could have had a cool drink. Damn, damn, damn. When would Dylan come back? If he was working all day, she may not see him until this evening. Perhaps he would turn sulky and leave her alone altogether. She would never rely on anyone ever again. How long would an ankle take to heal? She did not want to hobble into RADA in October. As an actress, she must turn this injury, this setback, to her advantage.

Suffering. Pain. Fury. Frustration. What was the difference between a powerful emotion and an ordinary, everyday feeling? Without a mirror, she had to imagine her own pale face, drawn with pain, her pretty mouth turned down at the corners. This is how I should look if I ever play a part when my character has suffered an enormous setback, she thought. A character abandoned by the world would feel as I do now.

Her ankle gave a sudden throb. What if sometime she were cast as a character who suffered constant pain? There were such people. At the dancing classes she had heard Madam Geerts whisper with girls' mothers about prolapsed wombs and ulcerous legs. Miss Fell, a martyr to rheumatics, never a day without a twinge. Grandfather and his old war wound that kept him awake at night.

She would need to be able to convey emotion through her movements, too. Facial expressions were all well and good for the other actors and the front rows of the stalls. An artist must play to the gallery.

If she ever got out of this damned tower alive, her acting would improve no end.

Surely Dylan would come back, saying sorry, bringing water, bread, a Cox's pippin. Don't think of food, she told herself. Her tongue stuck to the roof of her mouth. He had lied when he said he had nothing with him – no bread, no cold tea. She could bet a shilling that he had something on his bike. He had lied so that she would give up, be starved out.

Once she had watched a horse licking a stone to cool its tongue. She gulped, trying for saliva, knowing how the horse felt. She began to count how many stones there were between floor and ceiling. This tower was older than people thought. Here and there were the marks of the builders. She had learned about that at school when they visited an old tithe barn. The illiterate builders had made their mark, to show how much work they had done in a day, and what wages they had earned.

Lucy shivered. She pulled her blanket closer. If Dylan had really fallen out with her, it could be Monday before she escaped from here. Surely by Monday, if she did not collect the ransom, there would be a hue and cry.

What if she died here? Mr Milner had died. Perhaps this was her turn. What if Mr Milner was waiting for her in eternity, a foul grin as he reached out for her saying, "Come, Lucy, take my hand."

He was here! There was a noise at the door, someone trying to get in. Oh God, what if it was the ghost of Mr Milner? She would have to stay here another night, and there were cracks and places for a ghost to enter. Forgetting to breathe, she listened.

Someone was outside. Someone was at the door. Someone was trying a key in the lock. Having longed for Dylan's appearance, now she felt angry that he had taken so long about it.

Then, silence. She wondered had she imagined the sound.

33

Improvisation

Sykes and I monopolised a bench at the edge of the Valley Gardens, our backs to the Grand Hotel.

When I told him that Dylan Ashton was unconscious in the infirmary and unable to help us locate Lucy Wolfendale, he thumped the bench so hard he grazed his knuckles.

'Damn his eyes. Excuse my language. What's he doing coming off his bike? If he'd led you to Lucy we could be recovering stolen goods by now.'

Sykes nursed his sore knuckles in the palm of his left hand.

The evening was turning chilly. I put on my costume jacket. 'I don't suppose he came off the bike on purpose. And I'm wondering whether someone knocked him down deliberately.'

'Unlikely,' Sykes grunted. 'And where do you think Dylan was going when he took the tumble?'

'According to the police, his bike was in the ditch, on the way back into town, along Stonehook Road. My guess is that he had been to warn Lucy, tell her that we know about her ransom caper.'

Sykes let out a sigh and stared at his knees. 'It's frustrating. I'd love it if we recovered Mr Moony's goods where the Leeds police failed.'

Of course he would. Sykes had been a policeman whose face did not fit, and who fell foul of his bosses. My own father, a superintendent, admired him but he would never be part of the police force again.

Sykes seemed so sure that Lucy and Dylan were in on the robbery together, because Dylan's thumbprint was on the ransom note. To me that did not ring true. I could not quite make a connection between the robbery and the ransom, but it was difficult to justify that feeling to Sykes. The way he saw it, Lucy took the pawn ticket, and now Miss Fell was once again wearing her ring. There had to be a link.

He put the case for the prosecution. 'She had the pawn ticket. What other conclusion can there be?'

I put the case for the defence. 'If Lucy has a stash of jewellery tucked away, why is she trying to fleece her grandfather?'

'If you are right about the old man's past, and he *is* the sergeant who did for the real captain, then who's to say he is her grandfather? Maybe she found that out for herself. Wants to cash in, and cut the ties.'

So at least he did not dismiss my interpretation of the photographs I had seen, and the oddity of the captain keeping two sets of army discharge papers, Sergeant Lampton's death certificate, and two uniforms.

'Did you pick up any gossip about the captain, or Milner?'

I felt Sykes bristle. He disliked the word gossip, and preferred to think of himself as a gatherer of useful information.

'I talked to an old soldier in the hotel bar. He reckoned Wolfendale and Milner were strange birds. Nobody likes Milner. He's successful, rich, lacks social graces, but he's influential. A man who gets his own way – or did do up to last night. As Milner rose, the captain fell. Like a set of scales. The captain is a recluse. No close friends or associates.'

It all fitted. The more I thought about it, the more I felt sure: Milner had blackmailed the captain. But Sykes was still focusing on the robbery. Quite right, since this was our case.

'If Dylan and Lucy are in cahoots, which they obviously are, then he could be the person who robbed the pawnbroker.'

'He is not the type.'

'What type is that?' He gave me his annoying stare of forbearance.

'Don't look at me as if I expect someone to wear a black mask and carry a bag marked *swag*, but he seems so ... I don't know, innocent. And the robbery took place on a Monday morning. When I parted company with Mr Croker, he could not understand why Dylan had been on Stonehook Road. He said it was entirely out of character for Dylan to be somewhere where he shouldn't be. He has not missed an hour's work since he started there – including all of last week, when he was in the play. That rules out his disappearing on Monday.'

Sykes gave a disappointed groan. 'We could take a drive up Stonehook Road, try to locate where Lucy is hiding.'

'Yes, and we could search a haystack for a needle. I would prefer to have something to go on.'

A sudden yelp from behind us made me jump. I half

expected Madam Geerts to have returned from the Prince of Wales Hotel, having discovered that my statement had led to her husband's arrest for murder.

Hands covered my eyes. 'Guess who?!'

'Meriel!'

'Spoilsport!' She hopped, skipped and beamed round to the front of the bench, eyes shining with delight. 'Kate darling, what news what news!' She grabbed me, kissing both cheeks.

Sykes stood up, and put a little distance between himself and Meriel.

'This is Mr Sykes, Jim Sykes. Meriel Jamieson.'

She grabbed Sykes's hand as though she were heaving him from a lake half drowned and she held the life jacket. 'Congratulate me, darlings. You're looking at an assistant producer. My dear sweet badger boy has offered me a job in his theatre. I'll be leaving Harrogate on Monday.'

'That's great news, Meriel. I'm so pleased for you.'

'I wish I had a magnum of champagne on ice. I would invite you back into the Grand . . .'

'Well, I do have a room there, but my bag is still at your place. In fact, I was thinking that would be my next move, to go collect it.'

'Then I shall book in at the Grand too. I won't spend one more night at number 29.'

Sykes took another step back, keeping his distance. 'I'll fetch the car, shall I?' He spoke to me, but she answered, grinning, cupping her hands over his ears and gently rolling his head from side to side. 'Glee is required, Mr Sykes. Can you do glee?'

'Not as a rule,' Sykes said. 'But I can laugh in French.'

'Then please do so.'

He made an exaggerated O of his mouth and gave a deep belly roll that resulted in a Santa Claus ho-ho-ho.

Passers-by were beginning to stare at us.

'Excellent,' Meriel smiled. 'I like a man who can produce a sound from his belly. Were you ever on stage?'

'If I were I wouldn't put it forward in evidence.' Sykes turned and walked towards the hotel.

Meriel whispered to me. 'What a dark horse you are, Kate. He's adorable.'

'Mr Sykes is an ex-policeman and works with me.'

'Oh yes,' she said, arching her eyebrows.

During the short ride back to St Clement's Road, Meriel regaled us with theatre stories, and how she and Mr Wheatley had talked about which Ibsen play she might choose to direct.

Stepping from the car, I glanced up at the captain's bay window. He was not looking out. Sykes stayed close behind me as I followed Meriel round the path and down the steps to her door. No sign of Dan Root at his workbench either.

'Isn't it glorious?' Meriel said, unlocking her door. 'At last my life is taking a turn for the better.'

'You deserve it, Meriel,' I said, 'after all your hard work.'

She was already rooting behind a curtain that covered the space under the sink. 'I'm sure I have a drop of cooking sherry here somewhere.'

'Before we're into celebration mode, there's a couple of things I should tell you, Meriel, and something to ask.'

'Oh?' She straightened up. 'Better take a pew then, both of you. Don't tell me you intend to get hitched and you're asking me to be maid of honour?'

'Mr Sykes is already hitched.'

'Ah.' She sighed. 'Life can be so difficult can it not?'

'It's not good news, Meriel. Poor Dylan was knocked off his bike and is in a bad way in the infirmary.'

Meriel's expression turned to pained shock and she let out a cry as though she herself had been mortally wounded. 'The poor boy. I must go to see him. Take him flowers.' She looked with a brief glimpse of satisfaction at the stolen Belladonna lilies, perhaps mentally congratulating herself on her foresight, but then shook her head. 'They won't do. Hospitals call for lilac — that's past isn't it? Are we too early for chrysanthemums?'

'And there's more bad news. Monsieur Geerts has been arrested for the murder of Lawrence Milner.'

I wanted her to protest his innocence, to come up with some miraculous little comment that would shed a new light on the situation.

'How awful! I hope people won't think there's a jinx on taking out advertisements in theatre programmes. Poor Mr Milner took a full-page advertisement. It paid for the set. And the Geerts advertisement, well, that was a very useful contribution. And Croker & Company also took a half page, and there's poor Dylan lying in hospital. Do you think the Harrogate papers will make something of it, Kate?'

Sykes looked from her to me. He does not usually betray his feelings, but I could see he regarded Meriel with the same kind of astonishment a child might view a performing seal.

I said, 'I don't know what the papers will make of it. It's not exactly the best kind of publicity for the Spa.'

She sighed. 'Ah well, never mind. Perhaps it's just as well that I shall be crossing the Pennines.'

I would not let her get away with pretending to be entirely flippant. 'It was kind of you to call and see Rodney earlier.'

In her most sincere voice, she said, 'Well of course I had to offer condolences to the poor boy. Though what can one say? It's not my place to speculate whether poor old Geerts tipped over the edge and did for Milner. Everyone knew Mr Milner and Olivia Geerts were . . . close. It may have been that Monsieur Geerts could tolerate adultery but that the public humiliation of Olivia pouncing on Milner in the bar was quite another matter, from a male point of view. Isn't that so, Mr Sykes?'

Sykes looked for a way to escape her question, but she fixed him with a stare. 'I wouldn't like to speculate, Miss Jamieson.'

'Besides,' she added, 'Mr Milner had kindly offered me a loan and Rodney was a real gent and came good for me on it. I said he shouldn't, what with his raw grief and the shock, poor lamb, but he insisted on opening the safe and giving me twenty guineas.'

More fool him, I thought.

My bag was already packed from this morning. I placed it by the door. Meriel successfully laid her hands on the cooking sherry and found two glasses and an egg cup.

'Not for me thanks,' Sykes said. 'I'm not a sherry drinker.'

She poured the sherry.

We clinked glasses. 'To your new job, Meriel. I hope it will be a great success.'

'I shall make sure it's a success.' She took a sip. 'Vile isn't it?'

'Not too bad,' I lied, valiantly. 'Now there's something else I have to ask you. About Lucy.'

'What about her?' Meriel asked.

'She didn't stay with Alison last night and we don't know where she is. Do you have any ideas? It's very important that I find her.'

'Good for her,' Meriel said. 'I told her she should strike out on her own. But I'd be sorry to lose touch with her.'

'If she's safe, that's all well and good. But I still need to speak to her, just to make sure.'

'Doesn't Alison know where she is?'

'No. Meriel, you've worked with Lucy for weeks and weeks. You're in the same house. You know all the cast, her friends, her comings and goings. You must have some idea where she may have gone, even an inkling. Anything.'

Meriel scratched her head with both hands. 'Such as?'

'Where did they rehearse, I mean when they went out and about?'

'Oh that! I couldn't say. You see, I have this technique. I set the cast the task of being in the role of their characters, in different settings. I might say to Lucy and Alison, meet up as Anna and Beatrice. You have agreed to make – I don't know – lace for an antimacassar, or a Berlin woolwork creation for the chapel sale of work. Do it in character. Choose where and when. Leave Lucy and Alison behind and become your new selves. That kind of thing. I had them all at it. I know they went on a picnic – supposedly the chapel picnic. They were full of that. But I said "I don't want to know where you were and what you did. I only want to see the results in rehearsal". It's a brilliant technique. I picked it up from a Hungarian Jew in Switzerland.' She paused, as if expecting admiration.

'Meriel, you know where Lucy is, don't you?'

'I really and truly don't know. Swear on my mother's grave, wherever that may be.'

'If she doesn't know ...' Sykes began, watching Meriel as she smiled and sipped at her sherry. Meriel fascinated him, and for some reason that irritated me enormously.

When I didn't speak, she said, 'Oh dear, poor Kate. You really do want to find Lucy and I'm no help. Well, I shall think about starting to pack.' She stretched out her leg and kicked the tea chest. 'And in my next digs I shall have a chest of drawers. Now what's this about a champers in our room at the Grand Hotel? My badger boy has gone back to Manchester so I'm free as a bird and open to all invitations. You and I should visit the Turkish baths, Kate. Bit of a splash, eh?'

'We have to go. Meet you in the hotel later, Meriel.' I glanced at Sykes. 'We've got one or two things to attend to.'

A loud knocking came from the front door. For a second Meriel froze. Then she said, 'Why doesn't the captain answer?'

'Perhaps he's not in.'

'He's always in.'

As the knocking started again, Miss Fell's Pekinese began to bark.

Meriel scooted up the back stairs, shot back the bolt on the inner door, and listened. A moment later, she ran back downstairs.

283

'Miss Fell's answered them. It's the police, asking to talk to me.' Alarm flickered in her eyes. 'What do they want now?' She moved the flower vase from the table to the corner of the room.

'It won't be about that,' I said. 'Perhaps because they've arrested Monsieur Geerts, they have further questions.'

'Why me?'

Footsteps came along the hall, followed by a gentle tapping on the door at the top of the back stairs, 'Miss Jamieson?' Miss Fell's voice trilled. 'A visitor.'

'We'll go,' I said. 'Leave you to it.'

'One sec,' Meriel said. 'Take something to the Grand for me would you? Save me breaking my arms carrying all my worldly goods.'

She grabbed a carpet bag, dropped a pair of shoes into it, scooped skirts and blouses from the tea chest, a small attaché case and theatre scripts from a pile on the floor. 'Just save me a trip. I shall collect it later, when we meet up for our drink.'

Sykes took her bag, and picked up mine. 'Of course, if it helps.'

'Shoo, shoo,' she said. 'I'm sure you don't want to be caught up.'

'It's all right,' I said. 'They'll probably want to speak to me again too. Good luck.'

We left by the side door, walking up the outside steps as she mounted the inner stairs to let the policeman come down.

'What's she up to?' Sykes asked as we walked to the Jowett.

'Search me.'

'I'd rather search this bag. I know she's your friend . . .'

'I don't fool myself that she's my friend. When she soars in theatrical circles, I'll never hear from her again.'

Sykes laughed. 'Unless you book a room at the Grand Hotel.'

'And champagne. Though I'm sure she'll have her fill of that from her badger boy.'

We got into the car. I sat in the driver's seat, Sykes in the passenger seat. The carpet bag loomed between us.

'You or me?' Sykes asked.

I pulled on my gloves. 'If you'll put the clothes in the back . . .'

With the shoes, clothes and scripts removed, the attaché case sat lonely at the bottom of the bag. I lifted it onto my lap, half-expecting to find a set of matching knives, missing the one which had been left in Mr Milner's heart. Though what motive could Meriel have had for murdering Mr Milner? After all, he had taken out a full-page advertisement in her programme and his son had proved an able leading man, as well as stumping up twenty guineas.

The catch did not give.

Sykes went to the rear of the car, taking the carpet bag and the clothing with him. He returned with a set of small keys.

The fourth key opened the case. The two blue cloth bags contained three watch chains, a diamond bracelet, two wedding rings, an emerald and pearl ring and a set of gold cufflinks and tie pin, and two pocket watches.

34

Tireman: in Elizabethan theatre, the man in charge of the wardrobe

I started the car. The last thing we needed was to draw attention to ourselves.

'Where are we going?' Sykes asked. 'The bobby will already have spotted the car.'

'Yes but we needn't rub it in. Don't want to be sitting here admiring stolen jewellery when he comes out.'

I did not drive far, turning the corner and drawing in a few yards, towards the gates of an athletic club where two other cars were parked.

Sykes climbed out and retrieved the carpet bag. Carefully, I replaced the attaché case in a nest of skirts and dresses next to a pair of dance pumps.

'Do you remember that Mr Moony described a heady smell, like polish and roses, when the robber brought out a handkerchief to wipe his brow?'

'Yes,' Sykes said.

'It was from Meriel's Darjeeling tea chest.' Fury with Meriel tightened every muscle in my body. Stealing milk, eggs, flowers, I could understand. I had even pitied her poverty. But this was in a different league.

'And the false address she gave Mr Moony when pretending to pawn a watch chain – she knew I lived in Headingley.'

'Yes,' Sykes agreed. 'It was the first thing that came into her head. Your friend's next theatrical production will be in Holloway. Do they have a theatre there?'

'Not last time I looked. Anyway, she's not my friend. She made use of me – to provide free photographs for her production, chat to her main programme sponsor and butter up her producer friend. The captain's right. She's an adventuress.'

'But you can't help liking her,' Sykes said.

'Is it that obvious?'

'A lot of criminals are charming, Mrs Shackleton,' Sykes said gently. 'Not the everyday fools and knaves, but the smart ones.'

'Our priority is to return the goods to Mr Moony. Ask him to confirm that these are the stolen items.'

'And have Miss Jamieson arrested on suspicion,' Sykes said.

A whopping snowdrift of reluctance hit me in the chest. 'I want to confront her about this now, but without the complication of a Harrogate bobby on the scene.'

'He'd be a good witness,' Sykes said thoughtfully.

'We're the ones holding the stolen goods. She'll deny all knowledge.' I could picture the puzzled shake of Meriel's head, and hear her denial, "Nothing to do with me. Can't imagine where that's come from."

'Mr Sykes, I'm getting to know her. Too well. I don't want her to have the opportunity to wriggle her theatrical bottom out of this one.'

Sykes jumped out of the car. 'I'll tell you when the coast is clear.'

After a few moments, he returned. 'The bobby's gone.'

I turned round the car and headed back to number 29.

I walked slowly round to Meriel's flat, Sykes behind me. Through the window, I saw that Meriel was packing a second bag. The dismay at seeing me and Sykes lasted no longer than a fraction of a second. A glowing smile lit her face as she opened the door.

'Kate, do you mind if I see you down at your hotel? Apparently I'm wanted at the Prince of Wales for a further interview. The police have set up an HQ there. Don't they just like to be mysterious? I expect they'll want you too. I'll need to tell the police where I can be contacted in case I'm needed for poor Mr Milner's inquest or anything of that sort.'

'Just a couple of questions first, Meriel.'

Reluctantly, she opened the door.

Sykes swung her carpet bag onto the table. He opened it. I lifted out the attaché case.

'Goodness me, what dramatic gesture is this?' Meriel asked.

Sykes stepped back, leaving the two of us to confront each other across the table.

'What were you doing last Monday morning?'

'Monday morning? Having my breakfast probably.'

'Meriel, you know what's in this attaché case. Do you have anything to say about it before we call the police?'

'No idea what's in it. I'm looking after it for someone.'

'Who?'

'I'd rather not say, especially since it's causing you to turn puce and nasty.'

Sykes stepped behind Meriel and silently delved into the tea chest. Meriel had begun to transfer its contents into a suitcase. He held up a man's suit jacket in a thin grey stripe, a pair of grey flannel trousers, and a pair of Oxford brogues. 'Were you going to leave these behind?' Sykes placed the jacket, trousers and brogues on the table. Meriel dropped the shoes onto the floor. 'It's unlucky to put shoes on a table.'

'Only new ones,' I said. 'And I think your luck's run out, Meriel. Mr Sykes, check the suitcase for a man's shirt and tie. Oh, and there should be a darkish raincoat and a homburg.'

'Oh for heaven's sake, Kate, it was a spur of the moment action. I went to the pawnbroker's as a favour to Lucy. She told the mad old bird upstairs she'd redeem a pledge for her. I wanted Lucy to rest and not break her concentration. She's worked so hard on being Anna. I couldn't risk her turning in a bad performance because she'd been trotting about all day on the old fool's errand.'

'So you dressed up as a man, got a watch chain from somewhere . . .'

'Borrowed it.'

'Borrowed from?'

'From Dan Root.'

'Did he know you'd borrowed it?'

'I don't have to answer all these questions.'

'Oh but you do. And straight answers too, for once. You even gave Mr Moony an address in Headingley, near me.'

'Well, I didn't know you'd come hunting me down. I was going to pawn Dan's chain till we had our week's takings, that was all. He kindly said I could. You don't

289

know what it's like to be on your uppers. Dan does. You can't imagine how hard it is to put a production together when you're hungry and don't know where your next meal is coming from. And you're being hounded to pay the rent by a mean old tartar. Do you know how much our dear sweet captain of a landlord tries to extract from me for this place? Eight shillings a week! That's robbery if you want robbery.'

'You terrified Mr Moony.'

'Never. I wouldn't hurt a fly. Honestly. I just gave in to temptation, seized the opportunity.'

'You throttled him.'

'What?' She looked genuinely surprised. 'I studied stage fighting, it's true, but I never throttled anyone in my life. That I do swear to. He was fiddling about with his bags, and I'd got myself into this pickle because I'd paid some small bills from the money to redeem the diamond ring, and while he was fiddling I just . . . well, it took me two minutes to nip round the counter and snatch the bags. It was temptation. He should have been more careful.'

I felt like hitting her. 'You committed a serious crime. These are precious items, entrusted to the pawn-broker because the owners were hard up. Don't you feel any remorse?'

Remorse. The word touched a chord in Meriel. She knew how to play remorse. Her hand went to her heart. 'I've had an ache here ever since it happened. Didn't you notice last night how I tossed and turned? Why do you think I entrusted this damned attaché case to you? I couldn't think what to do with it.'

Sykes cut through in his flat matter-of-fact police-man's voice. 'It can be tricky, divesting yourself of stolen goods. And you don't get a fraction of the true value.'

Meriel placed the palm of her right hand on the table, as though it were a bible and she were swearing her oath. With deep earnestness, she said, 'I am truly so glad you opened that case. I was working out how to return the goods. It's hard to know how to go back on something, change the past, turn around a situation.'

Sykes looked at me quickly. I knew what he was thinking. All thieves squeal, he would say. This was a just a variation on the theme. All shoplifters ask to be let off because of their special circumstances.

'I'll be back in a minute. Something I have to get from the car,' I said.

Meriel's sheer effrontery and her manipulative way of pretending remorse infuriated me. She had played me for a fool.

Well, it was completely straightforward. We must return the recovered pledges to Mr Moony, and inform the police.

Meriel looked askance when I returned with my camera and handed the flash gun to Sykes. She was not the only person who could act a part. In my best prison wardress voice, I said, 'Mr Sykes, please turn your back while Miss Jamieson dons these items of male attire.'

'No! I won't do it. What are you playing at?' She took a step back.

'I'm not playing. Just put on your robber costume, Meriel, and I shall take your photograph. Or would you prefer Mr Sykes to catch up with the constable? It'll thrill him to bits to arrest a jewellery thief when he was only here to deliver a message. Promotion in no time.'

Sykes turned his back.

291

Meriel said, 'Kate, I'll do anything if you'll just understand that it was completely out of character for me to steal those jewels.' She divested herself of her skirt and pulled on the trousers, hitching the braces over her shoulders. 'And there was nothing sinister about my dressing up like this. I often do it. Makes it so much easier to travel about without all the restrictions and stares that attach to being female.'

'The tie,' I said. 'Same kind of knot as last Monday. Windsor knot, probably. Funny isn't it how it's the knot we women always go for. And slip on the jacket. We'll have the attaché case in the picture. And now, the raincoat.'

Once fully dressed in her jewel thief outfit, she thought better of the situation. She shook her head. 'Dear Kate! You can't do this to me. Take the jewellery, just take it and go.'

'I don't think so.'

'Can I turn round now?' Sykes asked.

'Yes,' I answered.

'Two choices,' Sykes said, raising the flash gun. 'Do as my gaffer says or I'll manage to find a pair of hand-cuffs in one of these pockets and we'll drive you to the station.'

Meriel gulped. 'I can't!'

'Yes you can.'

'Dash it all, Kate. You're supposed to be on my side.'

'I'm working for the pawnbroker. Where's the hat? A homburg, I think?'

'Haven't got it. Left in wardrobe at the theatre. Wish I'd done the same with this lot.'

'Ready, Mr Sykes? Miss Jamieson only has to put on her shoes and open the attaché case. I'll set the attaché case just here, in the centre of the table. We'll have a fine shot. In fact, it would be rather good if you'd sit on the edge of the table, then I get the shoes in. Where's the key?'

She drew a slender chain from her neck and lifted it over her head. 'This is it.'

'Then open the case.'

Her face turned to stone. She did as I asked.

Sykes clicked the flash. I took the photograph.

She said, 'You're trying to humiliate me.'

'I think we'll have a signed admission, too. Photographs aren't always trusted these days.'

Meriel reached for my arm. 'If I help you to find Lucy, will you let me off?'

'I don't need to find Lucy, not now that we've recovered the stolen property. Lucy's out of the picture.'

'What are you going to do?'

'Escort you to the police station,' Sykes said sharply.

I cleared my throat. 'Mr Sykes?'

We stepped out onto the path into the stillness of the evening. Somewhere a fire had been started in a back garden. There was a faint whiff of smoke.

I told Sykes my idea. 'I think we should deal with this matter ourselves. Mr Moony wants his pledged goods returned. He may not want publicity, not to say the ridicule of having it known that he was robbed by a woman who denies she did any more than snatch and run.'

He shook his head emphatically. 'No, Mrs Shackleton. We can't let her off. She's committed a felony.'

'Let's not be hasty. We need time to think. Our priority is to return the goods to Mr Moony. He will have his first good night's sleep since the robbery. Let him decide whether to press charges.'

'With all due respect, that is no way to go on. The woman's an out-and-out thief. And if we don't grab her now, she'll be gone by tomorrow.'

'I will know where to find her.'

Sykes gritted his teeth.

I went back inside. 'You're not out of the woods, Meriel. I'll talk to you tomorrow.'

As I closed the door and stepped outside, I caught the smoke, which gave off an acrid stench. Sykes beckoned to me from further along the path. I followed him to the rear of the house, hearing the crackle of a fire.

'Is that the captain?' Sykes asked.

'Yes.'

The old man stood by a fiercely blazing bonfire, piled with flaming papers, scorching coats, boxes and caps. A strong whiff of paraffin told me he meant business. As we moved closer, he tossed the last contents of a cigar box into the flames. Photos curled at the edges and turned black.

'You were right about him,' Sykes said softly. 'He's burning the evidence of the past.'

'And we're too late to do anything about it.'

Although I had asked Miss Fell to keep him talking while I had taken my second look at the secrets in the attic, his sixth sense must have come into play. No longer would he leave himself open to discovery.

It was still a puzzle to me. If he really were the batman who had taken the place of his captain, who was Lucy?

I stepped up to the fire. Red sparks flew skywards as the captain poked a half-burnt sheet of parchment with a stick. It flamed and turned to ash.

'What are you doing, Captain?'

He glanced at me. In the absence of a hat to raise, he touched his forehead in a polite gesture. 'Sorry I was a little hasty earlier, Mrs Shackleton. I know you were only doing your best. Only you see, I don't need your help now.'

'Have you heard more from Lucy?'

'No.' Once again, his attention was on his fire. 'But I shall be at the designated place on Monday, at the designated time. I know what to do now.'

35

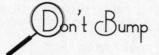

Don't Bump

Don't bump into the furniture: advice to an actor

I let Sykes drive back to Leeds in the hope that it would keep him quiet. As a learner driver, he had not fully mastered the art of driving and talking. For a while, that worked – until we reached the turnoff to Pannal where I had visited Miss Weston earlier in the day, bearing chocolates and the news that she may never see her uncle's watch chain again. Just as I considered a detour to reclaim the chocolates, Sykes, unfortunately, found his tongue. He returned to his theme.

'Meriel Jamieson is a thief, Mrs Shackleton. We can't let her get away with it.' With an air of great patience, he began to explain why. 'This isn't like searching for missing persons, where no crime has been committed. Miss Jamieson attacked Mr Moony. And don't let her kid on it was spur of the moment, otherwise why did she go in disguise, dressed as a man?'

'It could have been spur of the moment. Don't think I'm defending her actions. But all her life, Meriel has waited for someone to give her the opportunity to prove her ability. Last night, that happened. A theatre producer is going to give her a job.'

Sykes made one of his dismissive noises.

It would be such a waste if after all her hard work, Meriel Jamieson ended up in prison. 'She speaks five languages.'

It was not an appropriate testimonial. Quick as a flash, Sykes muttered, 'And probably lies fluently in each one.'

'She plays the violin, the harpsichord. She's lived hand to mouth. If you'd seen *Anna of the Five Towns*, you'd appreciate her talent, what she has to offer.'

Sykes gave wide berth to a rabbit that hopped across the road. The excitement of that manoeuvre kept him quiet for several minutes.

'I know she's your friend . . .'

'You said that before. She is not. I don't even like the woman. But I can't bear the thought of her rotting in gaol.'

'Then with the greatest respect you are in the wrong business. Seek employment with the League of Nations as some sort of peace broker. I'll go back to being a security man for the boot manufacturers.'

'If you're so keen on applying the law, you should have stayed in the police force. Anyway, you hated the boot manufacturers.'

We found ourselves behind a hay wagon. Sykes slowed to crawling pace but stayed too close to see whether he might be able to overtake.

'I hate seeing criminals get away with it.'

'Mr Moony wants his pawned items back. He didn't ask us to make an arrest. Meriel won't do it again in a hurry.'

'Not in a hurry, no. She'll take her time. People don't change, except to get worse.'

A bale of hay on the wagon swayed precariously.

'She has huge ambitions. Once she's a respected person in British theatre, she won't risk falling foul of the law. With her talent . . .'

'With her talent it'll be the Bank of England next. There's no doubt in my mind she's corrupted young Lucy Wolfendale. Do you think there would have been a ransom note if . . .'

And so it went. The hay wagon turned off. We had a clear road as far as Harewood. A dark-red sun hovered on the horizon, threatening to disappear from the world.

'Mr Sykes, do this my way. We return the goods, and then see. I don't believe Meriel did throttle him. I think she really did intend to redeem one item and pledge another. Let us get the truth out of Mr Moony. Did she use violence? He'll admit that to you, but not to me. I'm sure you can coax that out of him.' I thought that was a good ploy. Give Mr Sykes something to probe.

'Whether she was violent or not? You mean . . .' Sykes asked.

'The Harrogate side of the case was my operation. I had the success.'

Sykes braked suddenly to avoid an elderly clergyman who had stepped into the road without looking. Contemplating tomorrow's sermon and collection, he continued to the other side without a second glance. It was close. My heartbeat increased. I thought of poor Dylan Ashton, lying pale and injured in the infirmary.

'Go on,' Sykes said with some bitterness. 'You take over the driving then. You make it plain you're the boss.'

'Don't be silly!'

He got out and set off walking. The idiot. I had half a mind to speed past him, let him walk the rest of the way. I watched him for a hundred yards. He looked every inch the bobby on his beat. I set off and drew alongside.

'Get in!'

He did so. Making sure I put on enough speed that he could not jump out, I said, 'Mr Sykes, would you please not behave like a schoolboy.'

'I am behaving like a police officer who knows the law.'

'You are not a police officer now.'

'My circumstances have changed, but the law hasn't. Police officer or not, what's right is right.'

A black horse raised its head on the other side of a wall and looked at us with great interest.

'You have said "police" twice in the last thirty seconds. Why do I have a feeling that you are fighting some old battle?'

That remark hit the spot. He shut up. I did not know for sure the circumstances of his departure from the police force, but I knew there was a principle at stake and that he had become very prickly. So nothing new this evening.

After a long time, he said, 'I got back in the motor because I don't want to walk back to Leeds. Not because I will ever come round to your way of thinking.'

'Very well. You have made your point.'

Sometimes I know for sure he is the ideal partner for me. Other times, the man turns handcuff mad. I admire his passion for justice. It is his obsession with comeuppance that I find hard to take. The worst of it is I know he is right, and I am being far too lenient towards Meriel Jamieson. On the other hand, there are so many ways in which women have to find their feet in the world, claw their way into some kind of life. Who am I to send Meriel hurtling back onto her knees?

Believing Mr Sykes would not appreciate that point of view, I kept it to myself.

When we were five minutes from his house, he said, 'Your friend won't wait patiently to be arrested. She'll have done a bunk by now.'

He was right of course.

'Stop calling her my friend. And she won't do a bunk. She hopes for a sparkling career in the theatre. I've told you, if she leaves Harrogate, I shall know where to find her.'

'It galls me to think she could skip away scot-free.'

I felt too tired to argue.

It was almost nine o'clock when we reached Woodhouse. The sun had set long ago. A small group of girls still played out, turning a rope under the street lamp.

I pulled up outside Sykes's house. 'It's too late to call on Mr Moony tonight. I'll telephone him when I get home and lock the stuff in my safe, make an appointment to see him.'

'Very well. You'll let me know?'

'Yes. I'll get a message to you.'

Poor Sykes. He wanted the job. He liked working for me, and the freedom it brought. The fly in the ointment was me. This journey home was the nearest we had come to a parting of the ways, and the day was not over yet.

One of the girls left off waiting her turn to jump rope

and came running to the car, calling 'Dad!'

Sykes clambered out of the car. 'This is Irene. Say hello to Mrs Shackleton, Irene.'

Irene turned suddenly shy. I knew she was twelve, but looked younger with her curling light-brown hair and bright eyes. As though to distract my attention from herself, she said, 'Our Thomas has summat for you, miss.' She ran into the house.

Sykes paused on the kerb. 'Thomas is my eldest. He's thirteen and our visit to Robin Hood's Bay is the first time he saw the sea. He connects it to you – my working with you.'

A studious-looking boy stepped cautiously from the house, carrying a parcel. He was gawky, all elbows and knees. Sykes said proudly, 'The cabinet maker in Robin Hood's Bay took a shine to him. Thomas got it into his head to make something for you.'

Faces appeared at windows. Half a dozen other youngsters, some in their nightshirts, came out of their houses to admire the car. Thomas pushed his way through. He handed me a brown paper parcel neatly tied with string. 'A present from Robin Hood's Bay,' he said solemnly.

'Thank you very much. May I open it now?'

'Yes.'

A dozen children crowded close, peering. Thomas stood very straight, shoulders back.

I undid the knot. The flat of my hand touched smooth wood, cool to the touch.

'It's English oak,' Thomas said.

It was a block of light-coloured wood, about six inches by nine, and an inch deep. In the top left corner he had carved out a tiny bat, stained brown. At the bottom right corner, a dark green ivy leaf looked to have been blown to a halt by the wind. Across the centre of the block of wood was the carved name, *Pipistrelle Lodge.*

For a moment I did not know what to make of it, and glanced at Thomas, not daring to ask what it was supposed to be. Then it dawned. 'You've named my house.'

'I told him he should have asked you first,' Sykes muttered.

'No. It's perfect. Thank you so much, Thomas.'

Thomas gave the most perfunctory of nods and something like a smile played on his lips but he tried not to let it. 'I've been in the woods behind your house when it's coming dark. Them pipistrelle bats go fluttering about in droves.'

'They do,' I agreed. 'One flew through the window the other evening. I had to catch it and set it free before the cat got it.'

Thomas forgot himself and laughed. All the children laughed, though the younger ones did not know what they were laughing about.

'Well, clear the way,' said Sykes. 'Let the lady go.' The children moved away, though I knew they would run after me when I set off.

I looked at Sykes to say goodbye, but he turned and went into the house without speaking.

36

Pipistrelle Lodge

My housekeeper, Mrs Sugden, is in her mid-forties. She wears her long salt-and-pepper hair in plaits, wound around her head, dipping below her brow as though her tresses become embarrassed by the height of her forehead. Metal-rimmed reading glasses slid down her long nose. 'Kettle's on,' she said. The kettle is always on.

She admired the house nameplate which I set on the kitchen table. 'Well, I think that's just grand. Mr Sykes has a talented lad in young Thomas. I'll have Ernest put it up.'

Ernest was the wizened old chap for whom Mrs Sugden dashed out to collect manure whenever some passing horse left its gift in our road. I used to think he had an allotment, but with the amounts gathered I began to suspect some other purpose. Perhaps he was a secret alchemist and had discovered a spell for turning horse muck into gold.

'I hadn't expected you back tonight.'

'It's a long story. We've recovered Mr Moony's stolen goods. I know it is late, but I shall telephone him now and arrange to see him in the morning.'

Mrs Sugden tilted her head enquiringly. 'That was fast work.'

'Yes.' I suddenly realised how exhausted I felt.

'You look to me as if a Robin Hood's Bay kipper and a slice of bread and butter wouldn't do you any harm.'

'Well it might not.'

'Right. I shall see to it.'

I picked up the telephone and after a moment spoke to Mr Moony. His silence when I broke the news, in as discreet a way as possible so as to fool any listening operator, made me believe he had suffered a heart attack.

Finally he said, 'Am I to believe, Mrs Shackleton that the goods are safe?'

'Yes. And tomorrow morning, I shall return them. Unless you prefer me to wait until Monday and come to the shop?'

'The sooner the better. Tomorrow will be admirable.'

'What time would suit you?'

We arranged that I should call to see Mr Moony in the morning at nine o'clock. By the time I hung up the receiver, Mrs Sugden had supper on the table. She sat opposite me at the kitchen table while I dealt with kipper bones. 'You said you'd stop at the Grand Hotel in Harrogate tonight,' she said accusingly.

I groaned. In the haste to return Mr Moony's goods, I had forgotten all about my booking at the hotel. 'I had better telephone and cancel.'

'Your mother was on the phone. I told her you were booked in there. She has it in mind to come over and join you tomorrow. She's booked into the Grand.'

'Did you not tell her that I was working?'

'I suppose I might have done. But as she says, you can't work all the time. She says she has fond memories of Harrogate. Besides, there was a murder there you know.'

'Yes I know.'

'She'll be worrying for you. It's in tonight's paper.'

She looked at me over her glasses and I knew there would be no peace until she heard at least something of the story.

Forty minutes later, after my telling of the tale, I pushed back the kitchen chair and stood up. 'Well, must get on. I have a report to write.'

'It's nearly eleven o'clock.' If Mrs Sugden were a member of parliament she would make it her business to regulate the working day. She devotes each evening to her pastimes of reading, knitting, crocheting and writing letters to her daughter and cousins.

'You're right. But I just want to jot down one or two points, to sort out my thoughts.'

The dining room doubles as my office. I have a new cherrywood filing cabinet, index card filing system and month-by-month engagement calendar. Having only two truly professional cases under my belt, it occurred to me that there may never be another job for Kate Shackleton, private investigator. It is not the money I would miss, but the work, and the excuse to be nosy, to swan into others' lives and make a difference. A couple of months ago it may not have mattered a sheep's shimmy whether another job came my way for months. Now it mattered. It would be one thing if Mr Sykes left my employ because his scruples would not allow him to stay. It would be quite another if I had to let him go because of lack of work.

Seeing his children reminded me of the great responsibility of taking on an employee.

First I wrote out a bill. The cheque given to me on Friday morning would suffice as payment. Next I wrote a brief report to Mr Moony, naming the people visited and the arrangement made that they would come to enquire about their items on the due date. It was slightly tricky to describe recovery of the goods in a way that did not name either Lucy Wolfendale or Meriel Jamieson. I did not want to incriminate Lucy without speaking to her. And although I knew Sykes was right, and Meriel ought to answer for her actions, I could not bear the thought of her going to gaol. Never having done anything like this before, I was not sure what might need to be said to the insurance company and the police. It would be useful to speak to my dad, who is superintendent of the West Riding Constabulary. This was not something that could be done over the telephone. Oh for the simple days when I tracked down missing men for mothers, sisters and deserted wives.

Sookie, my black cat, rescued while I was in Bridgestead on the Braithwaite case, was a scribe in a previous life. She watched closely as I dipped my pen in the ink. I had the feeling that if my writing was not up to scratch, she would send the inkpot flying.

It was almost midnight when the telephone rang. Mrs Sugden had gone to bed. I did not immediately recognise the confident masculine voice.

'Mrs Shackleton?'

'Yes.'

'Inspector Charles here. I'm sorry for the lateness of my call. Did I wake you?'

'No.'

'I did not know you intended to return to Leeds today.'

'Should I have informed you?' My words came out more sharply than intended.

'No, of course not. We had your details.'

It was bad enough having my mother checking up on my whereabouts without a police inspector. 'Can I help you with something, Inspector?'

He hesitated. We all knew how difficult it was to talk on the telephone.

'Possibly. Are you planning to return to Harrogate?'

'Possibly,' I said, echoing his cautious tone.

'Then perhaps you would be good enough to call at the Prince of Wales Hotel, at about eleven tomorrow morning, if that is convenient.'

'Noon will suit me better. I have an appointment in the morning.'

'Very well.'

'Can you give me a clue?'

There was a pause. 'It is regarding a third party whom I have yet to locate. I hope you may be able to help.'

So he wanted to find Lucy Wolfendale.

'I see.'

'Tomorrow, then,' he said with an air of finality. 'Good night, Mrs Shackleton.'

'Goodnight, Inspector.'

37

Scissor Crossing

Scissor crossing: the crossing of two actors from opposite directions

Bees buzzed in and out of the hollyhocks in the Moonys' garden on Street Lane. Sykes and I strolled up the path together, still a slight awkwardness between us. He cleared his throat. As I rang the door bell, we exchanged a look. He met my gaze, and glanced away, knowing that he must leave the talking to me.

Mr Moony opened the door, smiling a good morning, eyeing the attaché case that Sykes carried.

We followed him into his study. The velvet drapes were hooked back from the bay window and weak sunlight played through the stained glass.

He bounced like an excited child as he watched Sykes set the attaché case on the desk. 'It is only forty-eight hours, and you have . . .' Mr Moony's words failed him as Sykes clicked the back the catches and lifted the lid to reveal the objects within.

Mr Moony stared. 'Remarkable. Such relief!'

'Would you please identify these items, Mr Moony?' I asked.

He did not hear me, but stood, gazing down at the contents, his mouth open in astonishment. 'I never thought . . . This is a miracle.' When he turned to look at me, his eyes were moist. 'My wife said to come to you. She was right. Mrs Shackleton, how can I ever . . .'

'We did our job, Mr Moony, and had a little good fortune on the way.'

Slowly, his hands trembling, Mr Moony checked the contents of the case against his list. 'The diamond ring?' he said finally. 'Everything is here except Mrs deVries's ring.'

Sykes did his best to suppress a triumphant smirk. Returning the goods was the easy part. Explaining could take a little longer.

'That is back in the owner's possession.' It suddenly occurred to me that it was in the possession of Miss Fell, and Mr Moony had not received the money loaned on it. 'You'll want to know all the circumstances,' I said. 'Do you have a safe to . . .'

'Ah yes.' He seemed reluctant to lose sight of the items, but after another moment's amazed gazing, he opened a safe and locked his prized goods away. 'And I'm sure you'd like some tea. My wife longs to meet you.'

The four of us moved into the drawing room. Mr and Mrs Moony sat side by side on a well-stuffed couch. Sykes and I sat opposite them. The low table between us was set with a teapot, small square china plates and home-made biscuits.

I gave a touching account of 'Mrs deVries' and her deception in adopting a false name. 'She entrusted the pawn ticket to a young friend, who then entrusted it to another who intended to pawn a watch chain. It was that person, a young woman, previously of good character, who momentarily succumbed to temptation and snatched your pawned goods, Mr Moony.'

'A woman?' He began to choke on his oatmeal biscuit. Mrs Moony hurried to tap him between the shoulder blades and urged a sip of tea.

'A woman?' he repeated.

Sykes concentrated heartily on the pattern in the rug.

I continued, trying not to sound either lame or fantastical. 'She disguised herself by wearing gentlemen's clothing. And she has now left Harrogate.'

This was a little disingenuous, but probably true.

'The cold-hearted minx!' Mrs Moony's cup trembled in its saucer. 'My poor dear Philip. Such a shocking ordeal.'

Mr Moony could not take in the story without a second and a third explanation.

'And now you must decide, Mr Moony, what is to be done. You have your goods returned, and restitution will be made for the amount you loaned against Miss Fell's diamond ring. I have not revealed the name of the perpetrator.' Mr Sykes looked at me across his cup. I ignored him, or tried to. 'This young woman is at your mercy if you wish to press charges.'

Sykes could contain himself no longer. He picked a crumb from his trouser leg. 'She committed a felony.'

Mr Moony looked from me to Sykes and back to me. 'Would it reach the newspapers if I go to the police about this?'

'It would,' I said in a definite tone.

Sykes was about to speak when I sent a severe thought wave in his direction.

'It is an awful lot to take in, my dear,' Mrs Moony said quietly to her husband. She looked at me. 'My husband believes it better to think things over. It is Sunday after all. I am sure he will want to take the

310

matter to church with us later, perhaps to evensong.'

Mr Moony agreed that this was exactly what he had in mind.

This seemed a good moment for me to make a move and depart. Yet there was a feeling of unfinished business hanging in the air. Something more needed to be said, and I was not sure what.

Mr Moony tilted his head and looked at Sykes. 'You were about to say something, Mr Sykes?'

Sykes looked at me. 'No. Nothing, sir.'

Mr Moony gave a noisy expelling of air that you could not call a sigh. 'I am very grateful for your success, and for your speed.'

I took the envelope from my bag. 'Here is a brief written report, and the settled account.' I set it on the table. 'Apart from ourselves and the police, the only people who know about the robbery are three of your lady customers and the gentlemen Mr Sykes visited. I am sure they will be discreet, for their own reasons.'

Mr Moody nodded. 'I am very grateful for everything that you have done. I shall report to the police and the insurance company that the goods are recovered.'

For a few moments, the conversation became circular. The desire for prosecution of the perpetrator was weighed against the bad publicity of a trial.

Making a valiant attempt at changing the subject, I looked through the drawing-room window into the long back garden, crowded with flowers and vegetables. 'You have an industrious gardener, I think.'

Mr Moony smiled. 'I like to be in the garden. Plants makes a refreshing change from jewels. If ever I retire, I shall take on more myself. As it is I have an old chap who gets his hands dirty for me.'

'I'm growing marrows,' Sykes said, glancing with envy at the serried rows of vegetables. 'Just taken on an allotment.'

Mrs Moony said, 'Show Mr Sykes your marrows, dear.'

When the men had excused themselves and left the room, Mrs Moony gave me a challenging look. 'You don't wish for a prosecution against this ... this person,' she said with distaste.

I felt myself become suddenly warm. Had it been so obvious?

She went on, 'Why is that, may I ask?'

'Sometimes I think it is better to draw a line. It has been a terrible experience for Mr Moony and to go to court would be to relive it. From what little I know of him, I believe it would be mortifying if news of this got out.'

'Surely there could be some confidentiality for him, some protection.'

'That is not how the legal system works, Mrs Moony,' I said with all the conviction that comes from having read Charles Dickens on the matter. 'Once the law begins to roll along its relentless course, there is no protection of that kind for anyone. There would have to be a trial, a jury, reporters would be present in the court.'

'So it is entirely for my husband's benefit?' she said coolly.

She was far more astute than I had expected. There was nothing for it but to be frank. 'Mr Sykes disagrees with me, although he is loyal enough not to say so.'

She nodded, hands folded carefully in her lap, waiting for me to continue.

'The decision will be Mr Moony's. But if you are

asking why I feel as I do, although I hate what this woman has done, and it was an appalling crime, I understand how she came to do it, out of desperation.'

Somehow I did not think that an account of Meriel Jamieson's prospective brilliant career in the theatre would hold much sway with Mrs Moony.

'You make it sound as though she is previously of good character. I believe that is the phrase sometimes used in mitigation.'

Whatever Meriel's qualities, I did not for a moment entertain the thought that being of good character was one of them.

'She is a most personable and intelligent individual with sharp insights into human nature.'

'Then it seems incomprehensible that she could stoop so low.'

'It does indeed.' Looking over Mrs Moony's shoulder, I could see Mr Moony in the garden pointing with pride to what was probably a giant marrow. Sykes glanced through the window at me and Mrs Moony. He knew exactly what I was doing. 'I believe there are occasions, Mrs Moony, when even a person who has committed a wicked act deserves a second chance.'

'Is she sorry?'

'Oh yes.'

Meriel Jamieson would be very sorry to end up picking oakum and sewing mailbags.

'I do not believe Mr Moony will want to prosecute,' Sykes said gloomily as he drove back to Woodhouse, having claimed he needed more motoring practice.

'Oh?' I said in as neutral a voice as it is possible to utter that syllable.

313

Sykes had become very confident at driving along a straight clear road. 'I left the force because I didn't fit. When they got something wrong, I said so. I stuck my neck out.'

'Yes I know.'

'You're the boss, you pay my wages. But know this, Mrs Shackleton ...' He veered onto the edge of the pavement as he turned a corner.

'Careful. Mind the lamppost.'

Sykes returned his attention to the steering wheel and his eyes to the road.

'What did Mr Moony say, while you were inspecting marrows, that makes you think he will not prosecute?'

'Nobody throttled him. He was just too slow. While she snatched his bagged items, he was too open-mouthed to do anything about it.'

'Poor Mr Moony.'

'He is embarrassed by his actions – or lack of action.'

'Thank you for not trying to influence him, when you were in the garden together.' It struck me how large a part embarrassment had played in this case. Miss Fell's at her poverty. Mr Moony's at being robbed.

Sykes shrugged. 'All I have to say is, I can have no truck with compounding felonies.'

I sighed. 'No. I don't suppose you can.'

Sykes's driving had improved to the point where it surprised him that he had reached his destination without having to think about it.

He got out. I climbed into the driver's seat and set off for my appointment with Inspector Charles.

38

$\mathcal{M}$ystery Play

Mystery play: English medieval religious drama

Inspector Charles had said he would meet me in the Prince of Wales Hotel where he had set up an investigation room on the first floor.

From my chosen seat in the lobby, I could see the staircase and the lift. The same police sergeant who had escorted me and Meriel on Friday evening plodded slowly down the stairs, stifling a yawn. A short, sturdy workman, whom I guessed to be one of the Milner & Son motor mechanics, pressed for the lift and seemed to enjoy the disapproval of the lift attendant.

Coming down the stairs slowly was Inspector Charles. He gave me the briefest of acknowledgements and held up a finger to indicate that he would be one moment. He disappeared into the hotel's telephone cabinet, closing the door behind him.

Five minutes later, the inspector reappeared and apologised for keeping me waiting. As we walked up the stairs, I was very conscious of his closeness, the easy stride, an air of concentration. We walked along a corridor, hung with views of old Harrogate in the coaching days.

A door stood slightly ajar. I glanced in at a room set with two trestle tables and a few chairs. His back to me, a stout plain-clothes man in shirt sleeves spread index cards on the table, like a man playing Solitaire.

Inspector Charles took a key from his pocket and unlocked the door to another room. This one was smaller, with a desk and two chairs.

He pulled out a chair for me, and took a seat himself.

'Thank you for your written statement. I did take the Belgian chap, Monsieur Geerts, into custody. But we have now released him.'

This news made me feel awkward, at having pointed a finger at the wrong man. 'It was helpful to talk to him all the same,' the inspector said quickly.

'I was doubtful that he was our man, even before we checked his alibi.'

'Oh?'

'Geerts hasn't a scratch on him. The evening dress clothing that he wore is in pristine condition. I believe he genuinely did not know how Mr Milner was killed, or that the tyres of the car had been slashed.'

'And he has an alibi?'

'Young Dylan Ashton recovered consciousness long enough to confirm Geerts's story. They left the theatre together. Geerts had been agitated to discover his wife carrying on under his nose. He went into the gentlemen's cloakroom to compose himself. Young Ashton was there, feeling unwell. Geerts walked Ashton home and went in with him. He had a hip flask and dosed Ashton with whisky. He left Ashton's rooms just before midnight. On the way home, he said goodnight to a chap who was walking an old sheep dog. We have confirmed that.'

'And Dylan Ashton?'

'With his friends, up to the point of leaving with Geerts.'

'That will be a relief for Madam Geerts. She was most upset yesterday. And I'm glad to hear Dylan Ashton is recovering.'

'We have the reckless driver who knocked him off his bike. Blighter left him by the roadside, panicked and went on his way. Fortunately, the local sergeant had circulated the description of his car, given by a fellow cyclist. A garage owner spotted it, with a damaged wing. The driver was a flighty young fellow who'd been carousing all night.'

So Dylan's accident had no connection with Milner's death, or with Lucy's disappearance.

'Mrs Shackleton, you know we do from time to time in the force ask for female assistance.'

'Yes.'

'Of course, you would know that, being Superintendent Hood's daughter.'

So he had done his homework. 'I joined the women's voluntary police myself for a brief time at the beginning of the war, before I deserted for the VAD.'

'Then I'll come straight to the point. We're pursuing a wide range of enquiries, talking to the deceased's business associates, customers, and so on. But I'm naturally interested in the people who saw him last – theatre patrons and performers, and there is one young lady we have not spoken to yet.'

'Lucy Wolfendale.'

He gave me an appreciative bow of the head. 'You are two steps ahead. Just as you were at the Geerts' dancing school yesterday, where I understand you were asking

317

about Lucy Wolfendale, and Alison Hart.'

'Yes.' I decided against volunteering further information. I waited.

'You found Miss Hart, but not Miss Wolfendale. Why were you looking for her?'

That is the trouble with policemen. They are entitled to ask awkward questions. I felt some sympathy with Lucy and her vaulting ambitions and was reluctant to get her into trouble. At the same time, I would not lie for her.

'Lucy's grandfather was worried. He asked me to see whether she really was at Alison's house, as she had said.'

'Go on.'

'She was not, as you know. Alison had stayed with Madam Geerts.'

'Go on'

How irritating he could be with his go on, go on. 'I did not find Lucy.'

He chewed thoughtfully on his lower lip, realised he was doing it and stopped. 'Why did the grandfather ask you?'

I felt myself blush, which was very annoying. 'Because he knows that I am a private detective.' A stroke of genius occurred to me. I could hint at Lucy indulging in some forbidden romantic liaison. 'Captain Wolfendale knew I would be discreet regarding Lucy's reputation.'

'So . . . you think . . .?'

There he was, at it again. In my excitement at recovering the jewellery, I had abandoned my threat to go to the police if Lucy was not found by the end of Saturday. Now I regretted it, but I did not want to give chapter

318

and verse about Lucy's phony ransom demands.

Mr Charles pressed his hands on the table. 'Does it not occur to you she could have come to harm, or be responsible for harm?'

It had not. The idea seemed absurd. Besides, I had been too busy solving my own case. With confidence, I said, 'I don't believe she has been murdered, if that is what you are suggesting. Or that she murdered Mr Milner.'

'Then where is she?'

My annoyance levels rose. It was suddenly time to get off the back foot. 'Inspector, I was in Harrogate from Friday afternoon to Saturday evening. Captain Wolfendale asked me to look for Lucy, which I spent a few hours doing. He then changed his mind. You asked me here today to help you, and all that has happened so far is that I have been cross-examined myself.'

He gave me a candid look, tilting his head to one side, as though undecided about something. Then he smiled. 'I'm sorry. Mrs Shackleton, I asked you here because I hope you may be able to help us, if you are willing.'

'What is it you wish me to do?' I knew exactly what he wanted me to do, and he knew that.

'Since you began to look for Miss Wolfendale, would you kindly go on doing so, try and find her for me? I believe you may tread more delicately and with greater success than some of my men.'

'Very well. But I will do it in my own way, a way that does not damage her reputation. Harrogate is a small place.'

His jaw tightened. 'Reputation?' he said coldly. 'A murderer is on the loose, a girl is missing since Friday evening, and you talk of reputation, and worry about gossip.'

'If you are asking me to help you, please trust my judgement.'

Let him order his sergeants and constables to do things his way, but he would not order me.

He sighed. 'Of course. Thank you for agreeing. We have a standard rate of payment for such engagements. I could . . .'

I interrupted him, not wishing to discuss pounds, shillings and pence. 'Your standard rate will be acceptable.'

It suited me very well to continue looking for Lucy, to finish what I had started. The only looming difficulty was my mother's impending arrival. I kept quiet about that.

The inspector had a way of filling a pause with expectancy and meaning. There was something else he wanted to say. I waited. He flexed his fingers as though playing the piano. It made me think of a theory of Gerald's, that the Druids and the poets of old had a memory system for stories that depended on their fingertips.

He said slowly, 'I am not cross-examining you. Please do not think that . . .'

'But?'

'There is one other matter.' He was slightly embarrassed and this led him to sound a little brusque, which was oddly endearing. He continued 'Madam Geerts is naturally very defensive at present, and emotional. She seemed equally upset about Mr Milner's demise and her own husband's arrest. It would be useful to know from her, or from other quarters, whether any other lady . . . this is rather delicate.'

His tactic seemed to be a pretend hesitation, or

perhaps it was genuine. 'Are you asking me to find out from Madam Geerts what other mistresses Mr Milner may have had?'

Now it should have been his turn to blush. He did not oblige. 'I suppose I am. There are husbands who would not be as tolerant as Monsieur Geerts.'

'Madam Geerts would probably be in the dark about other women. But I have another suggestion. There was no love lost between Mr Milner and his housekeeper. She might be able to help.'

'Good thinking. I don't believe that line of enquiry was followed up when the housekeeper was inter-viewed.'

'Also, Milner played golf every Saturday. His golfing partners may know something of his amorous exploits.'

The inspector leaned back in his chair in a relaxed manner, as though trying to banish the earlier awkward-ness there had been between us. 'I am going up to the golf club myself later. Not much golf being played there just now. It was flooded last week.'

'Yes, I heard that.'

'But I'll talk to the secretary and the staff.' He smiled. 'Do you play golf? A lot of ladies do these days.'

I shook my head. 'We played tennis at school. That's the extent of my prowess in ball games.'

'And I don't play tennis.' He gave me a quick glance from unfathomable hazel eyes.

It was one of those moments when we each knew there was an undercurrent, a tension between us that might go one way or another. He held my gaze for just a fraction too long. But there was no overture, nothing more than a ripple in the air between us.

'I expect it would be a pleasant change for you to

come to Yorkshire without a murder having happened,' I said, sliding over the moment as quickly as he had himself, yet wanting to mark it in some way.

'It would,' he said, giving me a penetrating look that almost made me forget I was here to help the police with their enquiries.

In that moment, something was understood between us, and it was nothing to do with a murder investigation.

The moment passed. He took a small key from his pocket and unlocked the desk drawer. 'I have something to show you.' He drew out an evidence bag, and tipped it. Something slid from the bag onto the desk. It was a bone-hilt dagger with a sharp diamond cross-section blade, more blade than hilt. As I looked closely, I saw that blood had dried on the blade.

'Do you recognise this?'

It looked familiar, and yet I could not be sure. 'It's the murder weapon?'

'Yes. One of our chaps says the dagger is most likely from central Africa.'

'It was dark when I saw the body. I couldn't really have made much of the dagger handle.'

'No, I suppose not.'

'Are there fingerprints?'

'We think the perpetrator may have worn gloves. The only clear print is Mr Milner's. There were signs of a struggle, a mark on Mr Milner's right-hand knuckles as though he had hit out at someone.'

Slowly and reluctantly, my words came out. 'I've seen a dagger similar to this. When Captain Wolfendale asked me to search for Lucy, I took a look round. He has a collection of weaponry. One of his daggers could be the twin to this.'

322

The inspector nodded. 'I've made enquiries about him. He and Milner served in South Africa at the same time. We found a similar weapon in the Milner house.'

So Rodney had not been exaggerating yesterday when he kept denying to me that he had killed his father. For all I knew, he was still a suspect. 'Mr Milner and the captain, they know . . . knew each other well. It's possible that Mr Milner had some kind of hold over him.'

'Oh? Go on.' The inspector leaned forward.

'On Friday afternoon, when I arrived in Harrogate, I believe it was Milner I saw through the window, with the captain, playing a board game.'

The inspector looked surprised. 'That sounds a rather friendly kind of activity. Wolfendale said that Milner called regularly. Milner had served under him and was fond of the old chap. Brought him tobacco.'

Of course it sounded friendly. Having been wrong about Geerts, I hesitated to jump in with my suspicions about the captain not being the captain. Without evidence, it would seem far-fetched.

'Wolfendale would bear a closer look,' I said finally. 'He has something to hide.'

'He claims rarely to leave his flat. He was at home all Friday evening, if we are to believe him.'

'And do you believe him?'

'I keep an open mind. The full picture isn't in view yet by any means. We know from enquiries that there is one person whom Milner would have let close enough for her to put a knife through his heart and, at the last moment, he could have struck out.'

'Lucy?'

'Yes.'

'But the cufflink . . .'

'That could be the killer's, or it could have lain there unnoticed for a week.'

The inspector's eyes locked mine. 'When you look for Lucy Wolfendale, Mrs Shackleton, if you find out where she is, or even where you think she may be, please tell me. I know you think it unlikely, or even impossible, but she may be dangerous. May I rely on you to do as I ask?'

'That sounds more like an order than a request, inspector.'

His look had an unsettling, searching quality as though he were throwing out another kind of challenge.

'If she hears that we want to interview her, she may well become alarmed and disappear.' He returned the dagger to the bag, placed it in the drawer and locked it. 'We have fewer men on the case than I would wish, but if you need assistance, ask. Do not take risks. Please.'

It was the please that did it, and his smile. It struck me that he would have a whole battery of ways of achieving exactly what he wanted.

'I don't believe Lucy has anything to do with the murder,' I said, with more confidence than I felt. Yet having taken such an instant and powerful dislike to the late Lawrence Milner, I now felt a sudden surge of pity for him. 'I shall do my best to find Lucy.'

I had said the same words to Captain Wolfendale a little over twenty-four hours earlier, and look where that had got me. Precisely nowhere.

39

Corsican Trap

Corsican trap: ingenious mechanism for bringing on a ghost

Dylan had not returned, even though he must know she had nothing left to eat or drink. Lucy refused to give in. He would come this morning, she had felt sure. He would see she was not at church, and he would come.

Now all the church bells were long silent. Her ankle hurt worse than ever. It was the size of a balloon. Her tongue felt swollen. Her head ached. It was too bad of Dylan, mean, cowardly.

Somehow, she must get to the top of the tower and attract attention. There must be a person walking along the road who would see her petticoat waving. This was like a nightmare. It could not be happening. But it was.

More than once she had thought she heard a noise. It turned out to be the wind, or the old tower groaning at her folly.

She reached the parapet by going up the stairs backwards, sitting on her bottom. Once at the top, she felt exhausted, hardly able to stand. She leaned against the wall, pushed herself up and stood on one leg, to look out towards the road. Deserted.

She needed to rest. Sliding down the wall, she sat

with her back against the cool stones, gently bringing herself onto her bum bones, shifting her position as best she could.

She stared at the sky for inspiration. Tiny fluffy clouds that might have been painted by a child went racing by. The clouds were her dreams, speeding away.

Taking off her petticoat, a flag of surrender, took an age. She cried tears of frustration and rage at the stupidity of it all. If only she had put the key on a ribbon around her neck. As the petticoat reached her calves and she had to raise an ankle, she started to laugh. It was so ridiculous, completely ridiculous. How had this ever seemed a good plan?

Once again she pushed herself up, trying to keep weight off her throbbing ankle. Her leg hurt. Her whole body hurt.

And there he was, before she waved the white petticoat, the answer to a prayer, striding across the field.

She cursed him for keeping her waiting, for leaving her all this time. He had better have a good excuse.

As he came closer, she saw that it was not Dylan. It was Dan Root. Was he out for one of his famous walks? If he did not look up, he would miss her.

Forgetting that she was supposed to have been kidnapped, a person being held for ransom, she waved her petticoat and called to him frantically. 'I'm locked in. I've lost the key!'

He did not answer, merely raised a hand in greeting as he came nearer, and then reached the door. She listened to thumps and bangs, as he fought the lock. It would be so humiliating if a locksmith had to be called.

The noise stopped. Once more he came into view, stepping back from the door, giving her the thumbs-up

326

sign. She heaved a sigh of relief, and then came the light tread of his footsteps on the stairs.

'Hello, Lucy.'

'Hello, Dan.'

She dreaded questions. He asked none, but handed her his water bottle. Never in her life had she felt so glad to see a familiar face.

She took the top from the bottle and drank greedily.

Bobbed down beside her, Dan shot her that look of his, a crafty glance he had used when he played the miser. He was the only person in the cast whose talent came close to her own. What was the matter with him that he looked at her so strangely? She must look a sight.

'It's lucky you came along. Or did you know I was here?'

'You took some finding. But I remembered where you came to rehearse, and how you talked about the tower.'

She licked a drop of water from her lips and replaced the top on the bottle, but did not return it to him. 'Good thing you did. Dylan has deserted me.'

'He would never desert you. He was knocked down, not far from here.'

Her hand flew to her mouth. 'No! Poor Dylan. Is he badly hurt?'

'I don't know yet. He is in the infirmary. When I found out where he came off his bike, I knew my guess was correct. What did you do to your ankle?'

'I tripped on the stairs.' She started to shiver. 'But Dylan. He wanted me to give up . . .'

'Wait!' Dan said. He leapt to his feet and disappeared down the stairs.

'Don't leave me!' she called, all courage deserting her.

He came back with one of her blankets. 'Here, wrap yourself in this.'

'Are you sure about Dylan? How do you know?'

'I saw one of the assistants from Wood & Tophams. He had heard from his manager who had heard from Mr Croker.' Dan put his hand in his inside pocket and brought out a teacloth, unfolded it and produced a sandwich. 'It's potted meat.'

'You've saved my life.' She began to devour the sandwich. 'I should give up, because of Dylan being hurt. But I won't, not now, not after everything. I can hold on, until tomorrow.'

'Lucy, I have something to tell you. I have a lot to tell you.'

'Do you? I want to listen, Dan. But my ankle throbs. My throat's dry. My head spins. And you haven't asked why I'm here.'

'I know why.' A little involuntary twitch happened at the side of his mouth. He had used that twitch as the preacher. Lucy copied the gesture. When she did, some feeling she couldn't name caught her chest and stopped her breath. She wondered whether he looked in the mirror as many times in the day as she did herself.

'How did you know?' Dylan was supposed to have kept her secret.

'Something I overheard, leave it at that,' Dan said. 'Everything has changed,'

'Will you stop being mysterious, and just tell me?'

'Your ankle needs bandaging. Let's get you to the stream. Cold water will help. We can use your petticoat.'

So that was his game. He was trying to get her home, make her give up. First the stream, then the road, then the back of his bike and a return journey: defeat.

'I'm not going back. If you really do know why I'm here, then you'll know that in just twenty-four hours, I will collect some money . . .'

'You need to go home.' He sighed. 'It's complicated.'

His words made Lucy anxious. 'Has something happened to Granddad?' Her mouth fell open, her breathing became erratic. 'What are you not telling me? I've killed Dylan. And my note gave Granddad a heart attack.'

'No. Nothing has happened to him.' He turned his glance from her and looked at the opposite wall of old grey stones, and seemed to look through them to some distant place.

'What then?'

'I saw the captain first in my own land, in Africa.'

'That's not what I asked you. And how could you have?' Lucy said sharply. 'That was years ago. And you're not African.' She took another sip of water. Something about Dan began to frighten her. He was so good looking, but strange. Girls came to the theatre hoping to get to know him, but none of them did. He always went home straight after the performance. On Sundays, his one day off, he went out walking alone for hours. Then she realised. So many men who had fought in the war were damaged, not always on the outside with a shorter leg or a missing arm, but inside, in their minds.

That would explain why Dan could sit hour after hour after hour mending clocks and watches. It would also explain why he was so good at pretending to be other people on stage. Because he was not happy being himself.

'Listen, Lucy. I have something to tell you.'

40

Blocking

Blocking: process of arranging moves to be made by the actors

Alison was sitting in her garden. She was not alone. Rodney Milner sat beside her, shooing away a wasp that buzzed near Alison's hair and made her squeal. He gave me a quick smile as he stood up. 'I'll fetch another chair. Take mine, Mrs Shackleton.'

'Save me from this wasp!' Alison shrieked, ducking her head as it returned.

I waited until Rodney was out of earshot. 'How are you feeling, Alison?'

Far from the wan worn-out creature of yesterday, she looked a picture of health. 'I ache all over,' she complained. 'Mother thinks I'm tired from the play.' She glanced quickly at the house, as though half expecting her mother to be spying through the window, and lip reading.

'Any ... repercussions from your episode with Madam Geerts?'

'None.' She gave a sigh of relief. 'So I suppose that means ...'

'It means you need to see a doctor without delay.'

The wasp returned. Alison flicked a handkerchief at

330

it. When it flew away, she beamed at me. 'I've told Rodney,' she whispered quickly. 'He says confound the mourning period. He'll marry me by special licence.'

I smiled. 'There you are. What did Gypsy Kate predict? And you didn't even have to buy my lucky heather.'

She returned my smile, reached out and gave my hand a squeeze. 'I haven't told my mother yet. We're going to wait until after Mr Milner's funeral, to show respect. But I'm glad you called. It was so good that you came to the Geerts's yesterday. When I think what could have happened . . .'

'Try not to think about it. Write to me when you have a bouncing baby. One of the photographic magazines has a happy family competition. I will do you a family portrait, and use it as my entry. How does that suit?'

Alison gave a pretend pout. 'Oh dear. I should hate for us to lose, or get the booby prize.'

Rodney appeared from the back of the house, carrying two more deck chairs. 'Your mother will be out shortly.' He looked questioningly from Alison to me as he unfolded the canvas chair.

'Alison's told me,' I said. 'I wish you both much happiness.'

'Thank you.' He placed his chair next to Alison, and reached for her hand.

'Now I need your help. Lucy is still missing. You must have some idea where I could look for her.'

'Gosh,' Rodney said, biting his lip. 'I don't know where she could have got to. Does Meriel know?'

'I have a feeling Meriel will have taken the train to Manchester yesterday evening.'

'Lucy is invincible,' Rodney said, 'I'm sure she'll be all right, wherever she is.'

'Rodney, she has not been seen since she left the Geerts's house late on Friday evening. It's now Sunday. The police want to talk to her. Everyone else has been interviewed . . .'

'I haven't,' Alison said.

'You will be.'

The implications of this made Alison's lower lip quiver. Rodney reassured her.

My impatience rose. That is the trouble with lovers. They cannot see beyond their own cocoon. 'Will you two please just think for a moment? Is there anywhere she may have gone to hide?'

'Hide?' they said in unison.

'Yes. I didn't want to tell you this, and I hope you'll keep it to yourselves.' I gave Alison a look. 'There are some things best not talked about.'

'You can rely on us,' Alison said, looking to Rodney for confirmation.

He nodded agreement. 'Of course. Lucy's our friend.'

'I have reason to believe . . .' Listen to yourself, I thought. You are beginning to sound like a policeman. 'Lucy sent her grandfather a ransom note, demanding money. She's pretending to have been kidnapped.'

Unexpectedly, Rodney started to laugh.

'Rodney!' Alison rebuked him sharply, a slap of the wrist in her voice.

'No, but it's just like her,' Rodney said. 'I could just imagine that. And the poor old boy probably doesn't have a bean. How much is she asking for?'

'Never mind that now. But Dylan helped her and he

332

is in the infirmary. So it is important that I find her. Do you have any idea where she may have gone to hide?'

Alison looked at Rodney, willing him to be the one to come up with an answer. He obliged.

'When we rehearsed, going out as our characters, there was a spot, wasn't there, Alison?'

Alison blushed. 'You mean . . .'

'Yes.' For a moment they forgot my presence and gazed at each other. Rodney continued. 'We were supposed to meet Lucy and Dylan, only we were late, and they didn't wait.'

'Where was this?' I took out my notebook.

The wasp returned. Rodney picked up the Sunday paper and swatted it away. 'Out on Stonehook Road, way past the park, just an open area of ground where visitors don't go. We didn't want to make spectacles of ourselves, you see.'

Alison gazed at him dreamily. 'There's a stream, a meadow. It was supposed to be the chapel picnic, from the story of *Anna of the Five Towns*. We had a lovely picnic,' Alison said. 'Lucy and Dylan missed it because they went off on their own. You tell her, Rodney. You can describe it better.'

'They went into an old tower, an abandoned windmill, or a folly, I don't know. They pretended it was the premises of Price and Company . . .'

'In the play, you know,' Alison added. 'Willie Price's father falls behind with the rent.'

Rodney said, 'Dylan told me that Lucy took a great fancy to the tower. Dylan planned to tell Mr Croker about the place, so that they could find out who owned it and perhaps Croker & Company would get the business, seeing who might want to buy it, or the land.'

Alison smiled. 'Lucy said he must do no such thing. She would buy it when she became rich and famous.'

Or, she would use it as a hideaway. 'Where is it?'

'Do you know Stonehook Road?' Rodney asked.

That was where Dylan had come off his bike. I handed Rodney my notebook. 'Would you draw me a map?'

'She won't be there,' Alison said. 'Not in a million years. It's horrible and smelly. Dylan said so.'

'Is there anywhere else that you can think of, Alison?' I asked.

She shook here head.

'Then this is worth a try.'

'Do you want me to come with you?' Rodney asked, looking up from his sketch, showing no great enthusiasm.

'Of course not. Stay with Alison. You've both been through far too much.'

At that moment, Mrs Hart toddled from her front door. 'Mrs Shackleton! I do hope you've come to join us for Sunday dinner.'

I leapt to my feet, ready for the off. 'No, this is just a flying visit, Mrs Hart. Was your church fete a success?'

'It was indeed. The fallen women have a lot to be grateful for.' Her hand flew to her mouth, as she realised her faux pas in mentioning fallen women in the presence of a gentleman. She drew me aside, to the shade of the pergola. Unable to resist, she dead-headed a faded white rose. 'Poor Rodney. I insisted that Alison telephone and ask him over for Sunday dinner. You're very welcome to stay yourself, Mrs Shackleton. A roast will always offer another slice.'

'Thank you but my mother will be coming over and

meeting me at the hotel, otherwise I would have loved to.'

'Some other time?'

Over her mother's shoulder, Alison made great eyes at me, demanding silence. That irritated me.

'Rodney, dear, would you be kind enough to take my chair into the shade of the pergola? This sun is rather too much.'

Mrs Hart was a woman in need of a son-in-law. The alacrity with which Rodney complied showed that she had found one.

Before he obliged her, he returned my notebook. I made my goodbyes. Alison walked me to the gate.

'When Dylan comes out of the infirmary, I think he'll be in need of his friends,' I said. 'Don't forget him, will you?'

Alison smiled. 'Of course not. I think those of us who were in *Anna of the Five Towns* will always have something a little special between us.'

You certainly will, I thought. Murder, blackmail, pregnancy, an engagement, extortion.

'And just in case I don't find Lucy in the tower, is there anyone else she might have confided in?'

'Can't think of anyone.' Alison pouted. 'She didn't confide in me about her ransom plan. I should have told her not to be so silly.'

Alison closed the gate. As I walked toward my car, she called, 'Of course there is Dan Root. He walked her home most nights. But I don't see her confiding in him. He's a funny chap.'

I took a couple of steps back towards her.

'Funny in what way?'

'Oh, for instance today, he'll be at some church or

335

chapel and nobody will know which. He's tried them all, from All Saints on Harlow Hill to the Railway Gospel Mission Hall. That's why he was so good at playing the preacher if you ask me. He's listened to them by the cartload.'

As I followed Rodney's perfect map and found my way to Stonehook Road, I thought about Dan Root. No Church of England congregation would suit him, draped with its union flags and banners. Wesleyan hymns would not be to the taste of a Boer boy, a young man, loose in the world with his watchmaker's case and his family bible. Again I asked myself the question, how and why did he find his way to Harrogate?

41

Bar Bell

Bar bell: Warning: The interval will end shortly.

Rodney's map gave no idea of distance. The landmarks were an abandoned cottage, the brow of a hill, and a clump of trees. I was to look out for a round tower.

Hoping the small copse that came into view was the clump of trees Rodney had mentioned, I slowed down. Soon I had to gather power for a hill. He had not mentioned how the road twisted and turned. Small wonder poor Dylan had been thrown off his bike. More trees then, sure enough, the tower came into view. I pulled in at the roadside.

Someone had walked across the meadow flattening grass and flowers in a straight line between hedgerow and tower. The scent of grass and clover made thoughts of ransoms seem madly melodramatic. The tower gave off such a forbidding silence that surely no one could be in there.

The heavy door creaked open. It smelled damp and stale. The stink of rats' urine and rotting vegetation rose in a dizzying perfume from the deep drop below broken floorboards. The place was dangerous. It should be razed to the ground or boarded up and padlocked.

Only someone young and romantic would see enchantment here.

I wanted to call Lucy's name but something about the atmosphere silenced me.

Foot on the first shaky step, I began to climb, as quietly as I could. If I surprised her, she would have no time to gather her thoughts and come up with some cock-and-bull story.

It took a little while to become accustomed to the gloom. Straight stairs, with one tread missing, led to a first floor. An old blanket lay in a crumpled heap in the centre of the circular room.

At the foot of the spiral staircase that must lead to the top of the tower, I paused. A voice broke the silence, a man's voice. One or two more steps and I could begin to make out the words. Was he talking to himself? No. He must be talking to Lucy, but she was not responding. A feeling of panic tightened my heart. Another step. I could hear his words clearly now. But surely he must hear my breath, and the pounding in my heart, the throbbing in my temples that sounded as loud as a train? I took a few deep breaths. Don't panic.

Of everyone that might have been an ally of Lucy in her little game, Dan Root had not been near the top of the list. He had at first seemed aloof and self-contained, above the petty concerns of other mortals, until I realised that he listened in to what went on in the Wolfendales' flat.

Being in the dark about so much made me feel like a mole crawling through an earth tunnel. But when I raised my eyes, the light from the top of the tower urged me on.

First, I listened.

338

Dan said, 'I decided to kill him because of what he did.' His voice was entirely at odds with the words. He spoke with reassurance, a hot water bottle of kindness in his tone.

Silence from Lucy. Was he talking to a corpse? A confession of murder could not safely be made to a living, breathing human being.

Dan said simply, 'I hated him.'

Still no answering word.

I could tiptoe away. I could hurry back the way I had come and fetch help. But why should I be afraid of a man who had sat on the wall and talked to me in such an ordinary everyday kind of way, who had let me try his eyeglass and who mended clocks and watches with such skill and care, love even?

It occurred to me that I was doing to Dan Root what he had done to the captain, listening with rapt attention. Had he listened because he was obsessed with Lucy? After the performance of *Anna of the Five Towns* he had walked Miss Fell home. A perfect alibi. Then he had gone back and murdered Milner for pestering his true love, for wanting her. And now what?

There was the smallest sound. It could have been the words 'Help me'.

Sykes, where are you now, I asked. What is the point of having an assistant if when you need him most he is twenty-odd miles away tending an allotment. Nothing for it but to press on.

'Hello!' I called as I climbed the last few stairs to the parapet. 'Is anyone there?' I asked, hoping to allay the suspicion that I had heard a confession of murder.

'I hope the view will be worth it,' I said, trying for a light-hearted tone as I came onto the parapet.

339

The first sight of Lucy startled me into freezing on the spot. She was seated, facing me, her back to the wall, legs outstretched. She looked exhausted and dishevelled. Her ankle was swollen to tree-trunk size. Her face was hot and red from the sun, yet she had a blanket draped round her shoulders.

Dan Root sat in a similar position. He was to my left which was why I did not see him straight away. The sun played on his broad handsome face and lit his mop of fair hair.

'Come and join us, Mrs Shackleton.' He waved me in. 'Will you sit by Lucy, or near me?'

'Lucy, what happened? You look terrible.'

She glared at me. 'Who asked you here? Can't a person have a little privacy?'

'Charming.' I turned to Dan. 'What's going on? I heard the two of you talking just now.' I kept my voice light and even, not wanting to give away that Dan's words had shaken me. That it had sounded like an admission of murder.

Dan shrugged. 'You tell her Lucy.'

Lucy made no attempt to speak.

I stood over her. In my schoolteacher's voice, I said, 'You owe me an explanation. I was the one who carried the lying message to your grandfather on Friday night.'

'And she does know all about your ransom notes,' Dan said. 'Your grandfather asked her to find you.'

Lucy glared at me. 'Why did you have to stick your nose in?'

I sat down beside Lucy. 'That is what I do. I find people who have gone missing.'

'I'm not missing.' She turned her attention to Dan. 'And how do you know about my notes, and where to find me? I didn't tell you what I planned to do.'

'I guessed,' Dan said, not very convincingly.

Neither of them moved from their positions.

'Tell her how you really found out, Dan. I expect you listened in while she and Dylan were upstairs from you, plotting this grand adventure.'

Dan shrugged, obviously not willing to admit to Lucy that he had eavesdropped. I wondered how I could ever have thought him attractive. He looked sulky, like some boy caught with his fingers in the sugar. He was not going to own up to his sneaky ways. I turned to Lucy.

'Inspector Charles of Scotland Yard wants to talk to you, Lucy . . .'

Lucy groaned. 'Why is everything going wrong?'

'And the inspector knows I'm here,' I added for good measure, and self-protection.

Dan glared at me. 'If that is supposed to be a threat, then I am quaking in my boots.'

'It means you better not try anything silly.'

'I hate that word,' Dan said. 'Silly. It is overused by schoolteachers and people who like to make you feel small. Tell Mrs Shackleton what I was saying, Lucy. I don't mind.'

'Oh shut up for heaven's sake,' Lucy said. She looked like someone suffering from shipwreck. 'I think I've broken my ankle.' She licked her lips. 'I probably won't hold out till Monday. That's when I told him I'd collect the money, give him time to go to the bank or round with the begging bowl somewhere or other.' She sighed. 'Do you have any sweets on you, Mrs Shackleton?'

'You're throwing in the towel pretty quickly,' Dan said. 'You won't earn any medals.' He stood up.

341

I did not like the way Dan Root edged to the door. It looked as if he intended to stop any attempts to leave. If he had confessed to murder, perhaps Lucy would not get a new life, or any life at all. Neither would I.

In my most confident manner, I said, 'You have a choice, Lucy. Come home now and get tidied up. Let's bandage that ankle.'

'What is the other choice?'

'The alternative is to wait for the police to come and find you.'

'Everything's gone wrong,' Lucy wailed. 'And it was such a good plan.'

'My plan isn't going very well either.' I seized the moment. 'Time to go.' I stood up, and held out my hands. 'Take the weight on your good ankle. Put an arm around my shoulder.'

Dan watched us for a moment as Lucy struggled to her feet. Then he stepped across, picked her up as though she were an infant and carried her down the stairs.

I hurried after them with a sudden fear of being left behind, locked in the tower.

A strange trio, we trod across the meadow to the hedge. 'There's a gap somewhere,' Lucy said. 'It will save you lifting me over the gate.'

'I know,' Dan said. He found the gap and made straight for my car. 'Hold on,' I said. 'Slide Lucy in first. You can get in the back, Dan.'

But Dan turned away. By the time I started the motor, he had climbed on his bike and sped off down the hill towards Harrogate.

Had he murdered Milner? I glanced at Lucy, as she

grimaced in pain. She looked a mess, and she was still beautiful.

There was a mark on the bodice of her dress. It looked like blood. 'Lucy, what was Dan saying to you before I arrived?'

42

Curtain Call

My sense of direction had deserted me. I found myself on the far side of The Stray, behind a chauffeur-driven family who had instructed their driver to go at two miles an hour.

If at a disadvantage, pretend that you know what you are doing. 'I'm driving you to the infirmary, Lucy. They can take a look at your ankle.'

'No! I just want to go home! Look at the state of me. I'd be embarrassed to go in the infirmary.'

She had refused to say what Dan had been talking about earlier. All that I could get out of her was that he was just trying to make her feel better about things. When I asked what things, she simply said, 'Oh Mr Milner and everything, and me wanting to get away.'

I would take her home, and let her and Dan Root explain themselves to Inspector Charles.

She waved her arm. 'It was left, Mrs Shackleton! You should have turned left there.'

'All right. Don't yell. I'll turn left at the next corner.'

She glared at the meandering visitors. 'Look at them gawping at everything and everyone.'

'That's what people do on a Sunday.'

'Stupid idiots. I used to like to give visitors the wrong directions, if one of them asked me the way.'

'Why?' I asked.

'It amused me. That's why people come here, to shop and to be amused. Well, some of them can amuse me.'

'I thought visitors came here for their health.'

'That's the old ones who always want everything to be "like before".'

'Before what?'

'Oh, you know.' She put on a shaky voice, full of regret, imitating some old person. 'If we still had King Edward and we hadn't had that war, everything would have been all right.' In her own voice, she said, 'Now it's left. Now!'

Dan had made quick progress on his bike. I did not overtake him until we reached Leeds Road. I sounded the horn and waved, acting as if I had not heard him confessing to murder in the tower. What had he been telling Lucy that she was so cagey about? Why had he stayed at the top of the tower with her, instead of helping her down straight away?

'Good,' Lucy said. 'We'll be there before him. I don't want to be shown up by him thinking he has to carry me in, having the neighbours staring.'

'Seeing how much trouble you've caused, you are just a little too full of yourself, Lucy Wolfendale.'

She let out an angry growl. 'I'm fed up to the back teeth. Everything's gone wrong.'

I refrained from saying that the weekend had not gone according to plan for Lawrence Milner either. We drove back to St Clement's Road in silence.

I stopped the car outside number 29.

Captain Wolfendale stood in the window, next to the suit of armour. A second later, he was gone. The front door flew open. He hurried down the steps.

'Lucy!' The captain helped her from the car. 'What's happened to you?'

He thanked me over and over, while trying to support Lucy up the front steps.

'I'm all right. Don't make such a fuss, Granddad. Just let me lean on your arm.'

The captain shook his head despairingly as he helped Lucy into the house. 'You look as if you slept in a hedge. Where have you been?' He led her into the flat.

Slowly, she crossed the room, holding onto furniture and her grandfather. She dropped heavily into the velvet chair.

He found a footstool for her. 'Better raise that leg.'

She smiled sweetly. 'Thank you, Granddad. I've had a terrible time. And I'm so hungry.'

The captain jumped to it. He disappeared into the kitchen.

I perched on the arm of the leather chair. As soon as he returned, I would go. A few moments later, he reappeared, with a glass of water and a hunk of bread spread with dripping. His initial relief at seeing Lucy safe and sound had evaporated. He was frowning, and short of breath.

'Thanks.' Lucy bit into the bread. With her mouth full, she said, 'Mrs Shackleton, you were a nurse.'

'Yes.' This was not a moment for disclaimers or provisos.

'I know I've been a bit rude to you, but do you think

you could tell me, have I broken my ankle?'

'It looks like a sprain.' I turned to the captain. 'Do you have a crepe bandage?'

The pleasure and relief at seeing Lucy safely home now turned to anger. 'Ankle? Crepe bandage?' He did something approaching a mad Morris man dance. 'Two ransom notes. Written by you, sending me half mad. What's your explanation?'

Lucy spoke to me. 'First aid box is on the shelf in the hall.'

The old man had aged since I saw him first on Friday night. He had helped Lucy into the house with a small burst of energy. Now, his breathing was heavy and he could not keep still. 'Have you nothing to say, Lucy?'

Lucy stared at him. 'I don't suppose you've ever done anything wrong in your life. I don't suppose you ever needed to get money to do something you desperately wanted to do.'

The captain stared at her, his mouth open. Suddenly he seemed to shrink from her, as from a monster.

'You told me, you always told me I'd have a legacy.'

They no longer noticed me.

When I came back with the bandage, dripping from the bread had dribbled onto Lucy's chin. She wiped at it but only succeeded in smearing it across her face. 'I asked you nicely, Granddad. I asked you for my inheritance, but no. You wouldn't give me a penny. You forced me into this.'

For two pins I would have left them to claw at each other but the nurse in me could not leave the ankle untended.

The captain watched as I applied the bandage. He said gruffly, 'The police want to talk to you, Lucy. There was a nasty incident after the theatre on Friday night, concerning Mr Milner.'

Lucy gulped. 'I've nothing to say to them. I don't care that Mr Milner's dead. But I didn't stab him.'

The captain stared at me. I refused to catch his eye. In a low voice, he said, 'How do you know he is dead?'

Her eyes darted from the captain to me, and back to him. 'Dan told me he was murdered, and I'm not sorry about it. He disgusted me.'

For a moment no one spoke. If the souls of the dead hover to watch the effect of their departure on the living, Milner would be in torment. His son, his housekeeper, the girl he dreamed of possessing, none mourned his passing.

The captain sat down on the chair arm beside Lucy. His voice came out in a whisper. 'Did Mr Root tell you that Milner was stabbed?'

'I don't know.' She bit into her bread, chewed and swallowed. 'Well, he would be wouldn't he, or shot or something?'

This time I did catch the captain's look. He stood up and walked into the kitchen. I followed him along the dim hallway. He held onto the kitchen table for a moment, before sitting down heavily. I took the seat opposite him.

'I talked to the police earlier,' he said. 'They came to find me because Milner and I were comrades in the Boer War.'

'Did they tell you the cause of death?'

The captain shook his head.

I waited for him to ask me whether Milner had been stabbed. He did not. He knew without my having to say.

348

He folded his hands and looked down at them, as though he had never seen hands before. 'What will happen now?'

'She will be interviewed.'

My mind was racing. Either Lucy had murdered Milner, or someone had told her that he was stabbed. That was possible. Dylan might have told her, if he got as far as seeing her yesterday, or it could have been Dan. The police wanted to keep information back, but they were not always successful in doing so. All it would take would be an early-morning cleaner with sharp ears and a wagging tongue and the information would be out.

The overheard conversation from the tower came back to me. Dan Root, saying to Lucy, 'I hated him', and 'I decided to kill him because of what he did'.

'What are you thinking?' the captain asked.

'When I found Lucy, Mr Root was already there. I wonder exactly what he said to her.'

'We can ask her again,' the captain said eagerly, making as if to leave the kitchen.

'No. If we go back into your living room, Dan Root will listen in. He has a device that he uses to eavesdrop on the conversations you have.'

The captain stopped in his tracks. He looked at me in amazement, and then sat down again. 'The sneaky blighter. Why would he do that?'

'Captain, does the name Bindeman mean anything to you?'

'Bindeman? I don't think so.'

It was the name I had seen in Dan Root's bible. A person who travels light would not normally carry a bible that belonged to a family other than his own. 'I think Dan Root is not his real name. I believe he is

Afrikaans. Try and recall. Is there anyone of that name, Bindeman, who might bear you, or Mr Milner, a grudge?'

At first, the captain shook his head, and then a flicker of remembrance changed his expression. 'Yes. It comes back to me now. During the Boer War we had to herd the civilians into camps. Nasty but no choice about it. They gave succour to the enemy you see. We had to burn them out of their farms. There was someone of that name. She was an English woman married to a Boer. Rebellious type. You had to admire them in some ways. Brother Boer came all the way to the camp. We suspected her of passing them food – not that there was much to pass. And sabotage. She had a hand in that. The captain . . . The thing is, she died under detention. But I don't see what . . .'

'Who was in charge of the camp?'

'The senior officer of course . . .'

'You?'

He hesitated before answering. 'Yes.'

I gazed at him steadily. If I were right and he were an impostor, what a strain it must have been all these years, waking every day, wondering would he be found out.

'Did Mrs Bindeman have a son?'

'She had children. I remember that.'

'A son?'

'Do you know, I think she did. Two of her children died. I felt sorry for her. And there was a boy. I remember because the schoolteacher made something of a pet of him. Took him to Cape Town when the camp closed.'

A piece of the jigsaw fell into place. For the captain,

350

also. His breathing became more rapid. He wiped a hand across his forehead.

'You have it, Mrs Shackleton. Root was too good to be true. The perfect tenant. Polite, rent on time, walking Lucy home from rehearsals. And all the while . . .'

All the while what, I wondered. What wrong had Milner done to this young man? What puzzled me was that if Dan Root had arrived in Harrogate intending harm to Milner and the captain, he had taken a long time about it.

'You had better tell me everything, Captain. So far I've had less than half a story from you. I've had to work out a great deal for myself.'

'What are you hinting at? I've been entirely candid, madam.' His voice carried no conviction. He knew the game was up.

I wanted to know the connection between him and Milner. I wanted to test my hunch that the man opposite me, his hand trembling slightly, was not who he claimed to be.

'Who came to Harrogate first?' I asked in a light, conversational tone. 'You or Mr Milner?'

'I did.'

'Milner & Son. That sort of company would require capital. Where did he get the money to start his business?'

The captain took out a handkerchief and blew his nose. Clearly, he did not intend to answer.

'Will you let me ask a different question, Captain?'

'Very well. Only because you have brought Lucy back.' He was trying to put on a brave face, but I felt sure would have ordered me out if he felt secure enough to do so.

351

'Did Mr Milner come to Harrogate because you were here?'

'Yes, if you must know.'

I barked out one more question. 'Army number.'

He rattled off his number.

'Thank you, Sergeant Lampton.' It was not quite a shot in the dark, but my jab hit home. The captain would never turn pale, but a little colour drained from his round, ruddy cheeks.

'What are you driving at?'

'That you impersonated the captain and took over this house, and his inheritance.'

He seemed to weigh up what I had said, looking me in the eye. 'You won't be able to prove it.'

'Perhaps, perhaps not.'

'You are too clever for your own good.' He lowered his head. 'Only one other person knew.'

'Two people knew: Mr Milner, who blackmailed you, and Dan Root whom I suspect became very confused when he came to find the captain, and found you.'

He closed his eyes for a moment, and bit his lip. This is the moment he must have dreaded, ever since he claimed another man's inheritance, another man's life. 'How did you work it out?' he asked quietly.

'You gave lots of hints yourself.'

He shook his head. 'No. Never did.'

It seemed an incongruous conversation to be having at a kitchen table on a Sunday afternoon. 'When you told me about the war, and your part in it, you said, "That was all so long ago. I was a different person then." You really were. A different man. And your photographs confirmed it for me. I never have understood

352

why some chaps have prominent Adam's apple and others none at all, just one of nature's little variations. I saw a photograph of Miss Wolfendale's nephew as a young man. His throat was smooth as a girl's.'

His hand went to his throat. 'That's nothing to go on.' He looked slightly sick, and uncertain. I guessed that he had forgotten how to be his old self.

'Young Rowland Wolfendale had a longish face, like his aunt. Miss Fell has a photograph. You have – or had until your bonfire yesterday – a photograph of the two of you together, wearing your caps and badges. Side by side, it is very clear who is the captain, and who is the sergeant.'

He wet his lips, and for a moment looked as though he would protest. When he did not, I continued. 'Two uniforms in your room upstairs, one with a captain's pips, the other with a sergeant's stripes. Two sets of discharge papers. I wasn't able to learn anything of the batman's service record, but Wolfendale was not married. And army tittle-tattle names him as a ladies' man.'

He gave a bitter sound that could be taken as a laugh. 'Oh he was that all right.'

'Unlike you. You confessed you were at a loss in dealing with women and girls. Besides, not many officers would admit that their batman should have received the honour of a VC. But of course, you *were* the batman, Mr Lampton. Or would you prefer I continue to call you Captain?'

He stood up quickly, holding onto the back of the chair. 'I must lock the front door. If Root killed Milner, I could be next. If this is some vendetta . . .'

I walked out of the kitchen with him, and along the hall.

'Captain, what wrong did Milner do to Mrs Bindeman that her son would want to murder him?'

'None that I know of.'

'When Dan listened in, would he have discovered that Milner was blackmailing you, had blackmailed you out of everything you falsely inherited?'

He hesitated. 'You can't prove anything.'

'No. You made sure of that when you destroyed your papers and photographs. But you and Lucy could be in danger. Please tell me the truth.'

A shudder went through his frame. Just as yesterday, he seemed on the point of suffering a seizure. I moved a hand to touch him, to steady him, but he shook me off. 'If you are right, and he listened in to what passed between me and Milner, he would know that Milner came to Harrogate to bleed me dry. And that having taken every penny, he wanted Lucy.'

'And what is Lucy to you? Is she really your grand-daughter, Mr Lampton?'

After an endless pause, he sighed. 'She is nothing to me, and she is everything. She is Captain Wolfendale's illegitimate daughter, by a schoolteacher, Miss Marshall, born on the crossing from Cape Town.'

Another part of the puzzle fell into place. 'Is this the same schoolteacher you spoke of, who made a pet of young Bindeman, or Dan Root?'

'She must have been his starting point for tracing me.' It wasn't so much fear in his eyes, as some emotion I could not quite fathom. He looked like a man whose chickens have all come home to roost at once, and have dropped a message he does not understand slap bang on the smooth crown of his head. Finally, he said, 'Young Dan Bindeman was orphaned. His father killed in the war, his mother died in the punishment cage. Put there by ... by Captain Wolfendale. The schoolteacher planned to adopt the boy. The poor fool, she thought Wolfendale would marry her.'

So Dan Root was the nearest Lucy had to a brother. Had he come to Harrogate out of love, or hate? Or both?

43

Limelight: brilliant white light from lime or calcium flare, used for beams of sun, moon or lamplight

I walked down the front steps of 29 St Clement's Road, ready to fulfil my obligation to Inspector Charles, and tell him that Miss Wolfendale was at home and available for interview.

After that, I would banish all thoughts of crime and detection and escape to the hotel, to meet my mother.

It was not to be. Or at least, not yet.

When I went outside, Dan Root was sitting in the driving seat of my Jowett.

In a flat, matter-of-fact voice, as if he jumped into other people's cars all the time, he said, 'I would very much like to go for a drive.'

Was this an admirer's opening gambit, or was he trying to prevent me from telling Inspector Charles about Lucy?

'Some other time, perhaps.'

He slid across to the passenger seat. 'Will you give me a lift to police headquarters?'

'Why?'

'Because you're going there I think. And wouldn't you like the notoriety of delivering up Milner's killer?

After all, you found the body. It would be a nice touch of symmetry.'

Put like that, it was difficult to refuse. But I hesitated. What kind of trick was he pulling?

'Come, Mrs Shackleton. I'm sure you heard me confess when you arrived at the tower.'

'No.' I said too quickly.

He smiled sweetly, held out empty hands, and made a fist of turning out his pockets, to show he carried no weapons. 'You're not afraid of me are you?'

'Of course not,' I lied. 'Push up a bit.' I climbed into the car, next to someone who was cold-bloodedly sane, or barking mad. Which?

'To whom am I giving a lift? Dan Root, or Dan Bindeman?'

'You're clever, Mrs Shackleton, or nosy.'

'Both I'd have said. Like you.'

'Root was the name Miss Marshall gave me. She was the schoolteacher who adopted me. She thought I would put down roots in England.'

'And do you think you ever will?'

'Not now. Not after having killed Lawrence Milner.'

Everything was so Sunday-afternoon normal. A nursemaid wheeled a pram in the direction of the little park. A young couple with a child and a dog in tow strolled arm in arm.

'How did you find your way to Harrogate, Dan?' I asked in a conversational tone as I turned the motor around and drove along St Clement's Road.

'It took some doing. I found out from Miss Marshall that the captain was in London, and then that he'd gone to Harrogate. It took a lot of searching, asking questions, making up stories to get information.'

'Why did you come here?'

'I wanted to kill the captain, to avenge my mother. I'd vowed to do it as a boy, that I would remember his face, that he would die for what he did. Of course, he was already dead, and Lampton wore his shoes.' He took out a cigarette. Shielding it from the breeze, he struck a couple of matches and lit it on the second attempt. 'Don't ask me too many questions. Let me have a pleasant last drive at least. It's not you I'm confessing to.'

Dan took out his watch for a quick glance. I wondered had he decided on a time limit, that he would make his confession to murder by a certain hour? He returned the watch to his waistcoat pocket and sat back in a relaxed manner, looking all around him, as though savouring his last moments of freedom.

As luck would have it, we found ourselves on the Leeds Road behind a Boys' Brigade brass band, who were playing *Look for the Silver Lining*.

'I could turn off and do a detour,' I said, thinking aloud.

'No it's all right.' Dan puffed on his cigarette and spoke almost cheerfully. 'This is an important journey for me. My last as a free man. I like the idea of its being something of an occasion, serenaded down the road in good company.'

The band marched onto West Park, and then onto The Stray. I parked on the corner, opposite the Prince of Wales Hotel.

Dan stepped out slowly, as though suddenly having second thoughts. He took a deep breath and threw back his shoulders.

The Boys' Brigade Band had two collectors, one in

the front and one pulling up the rear. Dan slid a hand in his pocket and brought out a coin. It jingled as it fell into the box. I wanted to speak, but could not find words.

He said, 'There's no need for you to come any further. Thank you for bringing me. I should have been sorry to hang without ever having ridden in a motor car.'

He shook my hand solemnly, and then crossed the road, almost ending his life there and then as a horse-drawn carriage was overtaken by one of those eight-horse-power Coventry Premiers.

I waited, and then followed at a discreet distance.

In the hotel, head high, Dan spoke briefly to the doorman, and then walked up the stairs and along the corridor hung with its pictures of old Harrogate. He did not see me as he opened the door and turned into the room with trestle tables.

I walked along the same corridor, glancing at the old coach-house scenes on the walls, wondering what it is that makes us look over our shoulders all the time, as though we are caught with invisible threads to a past that never quite was what it should have been, and we would like to try again.

I tapped on the inspector's door. No answer.

It would not be a good idea to follow Dan.

At the reception desk, I asked when the inspector would be back. No one knew. Nothing for it but to wait.

I took a seat in the lobby, on a small sofa, keeping to one side as though to give the impression I expected company. Normally I would be happy to sit and watch the world go by, speculating on passers-by. This time, I felt heavy and weighed down by feelings I could not quite define. Yes, I had overheard Dan confessing to Lucy that he had killed. But it did not seem to fit. He had harboured his vengeful intentions for years. And yet now he was confessing to having quite deliberately walked back to town, after escorting an old lady home, lying in wait for Milner, and killing him in cold blood. What had suddenly prompted him to act when he had procrastinated for so long?

'There you are!'

A whirlwind blew through the lobby, her round, smiling face crowned by a be-ribboned picture hat. She wore a low-waisted slip-over type dress in silk crepe, the bodice and skirt panels embroidered in brilliant colours, scrolls and stars. My mother.

'I might have known you'd be here.' She sat down beside me, lowering her voice to a triumphant stage whisper. 'The instant I heard that the police had taken over part of the Prince of Wales, I thought, I know where I'll find Kate. Look at you. Have you seen how lovely everyone looks out there? Why are you wearing a beige costume, and those shoes?'

'Hello, mother.'

'Don't sound so pleased to see me! Have you had Sunday dinner?'

'Not yet.'

'Darling, it's almost two o'clock. Back to the Grand with us, this instant. They are holding dinner. Your father is waiting.'

'I can't. I'm working.'

'What do you mean, you're working!'

'Shush.'

A man and woman on their way to the lift turned to

gaze in disapproval. There was only one type of work a woman alone in a hotel lobby could be engaged in.

Fortunately at that moment, Inspector Charles strolled through the entrance doors, and spotted us. He made a beeline for me, raising his hat. 'Mrs Shackleton.'

'Mr Charles. Mother, this is Inspector Charles of Scotland Yard. My mother, Mrs Hood.'

'Marcus Charles at your service. Delighted to meet you.'

It was exactly the kind of response my mother loves. She gave her winning smile. 'Sometimes Lady Virginia. This is Harrogate after all. One's title is allowed an outing here I think.'

I suppressed a groan.

'My daughter has over-democratic sympathies. But really, Kate, a title will get us far better treatment in the spa, believe me.'

'Mother, I need to talk to Inspector Charles now. Please tell Dad I will come if I can. Otherwise I will call and see him next weekend.'

'And what about . . .?'

'I'll see you this evening. Promise.'

Inspector Charles took in the situation at great speed. He motioned to one of his men who was beside us in an instant. 'McDonald here will escort you back to your hotel, Lady Virginia.'

'Thank you but I have a car waiting.'

'Then would you oblige me by letting me give you and your daughter supper this evening, at your hotel?'

Mother looked from him to me and back again. 'That would be delightful. Would nine o'clock suit?'

'Yes.'

'I look forward to it.' She leaned towards me, for a kiss on the cheek, and then was gone.

The inspector lowered himself onto the sofa beside me. 'You have news for me?'

'Lucy Wolfendale is at home now. She has a swollen ankle, but apart from that is all right, and could be interviewed.'

'Thank you.'

'And one other thing. Dan Root – he lives in the flat below the Wolfendales, and played three roles in *Anna of the Five Towns* . . .'

'Versatile chap.'

'Yes, an exceedingly good amateur actor. He's with one of your officers now, confessing to the murder of Lawrence Milner.'

'What?! But my men saw him earlier.' He shook his head and gazed at me in amazement. 'You've cracked it again. Do you have some kind of sixth sense?'

He looked almost elated. I felt entirely miserable. 'This doesn't make any kind of sense to me.'

The inspector practically rocked on his toes in his eagerness to get to Dan. 'Do you mind waiting a little longer, Mrs Shackleton? I should like to hear how you reeled this chap in.'

I watched the inspector disappear upstairs, wondering just who had done the reeling in, Dan or me. I plumped for Dan.

44

Get Out

Get out: dismantling and packing up the set

For twenty minutes, I stuck limpet-like to my sofa in the lobby of the Prince of Wales Hotel, pretending to read the Sunday paper, alert to the comings and goings from the first floor.

As the inspector came down the stairs, he caught my eye. I folded the newspaper carefully as he crossed the lobby. The man in the chair nearest to me put down his book, pricked up his ears, and stared. Police activity had aroused a good deal of interest.

The inspector gave nothing away by his look or a word. 'Shall we go?' he said pleasantly. As we left the hotel, he shot me a quick, concerned look. 'I'd very much like you to be with me on this next interview. If you feel up to it.'

My whole body felt somehow dried out. My eyes itched, my mouth felt dry, there was a prickling on my skin and a faint feeling of nausea. The day did not feel real; it was a carousel of uncertainty. 'You have a car, I think,' he said.

'Yes.'

'I still want to talk to Lucy Wolfendale,' he said

quietly. 'Do you feel up to driving? It may be kind not to arrive at 29 St Clement's Road in a police car.'

We walked to my car. He climbed into the passenger seat without a murmur about Dan Root's confession.

'Are you all right?' he said, when I did not start the car.

'No. I have just spent the morning with a man whom I then drove to your rooms to let him confess to murder. And you haven't said a dickybird. I have to know.'

He sighed. 'Dan Root had a good deal of information about the killing, tells a persuasive tale, and has the impeccable motive of coming between a lecher and a young lady he is fond of.'

'But?'

'He didn't do it. I got the impression that he wished he had. One motive is usually enough, but he had two. Says he cared for Lucy and warned Milner to keep away from her, then stabbed him. Says Milner was a soldier in the Boer camp where his mother died, and he bore a grudge.'

'Isn't that good enough?'

'Root fought in the Great War. He's as British as I am, though he might not like it. He's wasted an hour of my men's time.'

'How can you be sure?'

'He claimed to have used a kitchen knife, knew nothing about the parked car, or the damage to it. I've told the sergeant to let him stew for another half hour and then send him on his way. I'll deal with him later. My interest at the moment is in talking to Miss Lucy Wolfendale.'

'You suspect her?'

'I want to talk to her, that's all.'

I started the car, suddenly not fully trusting myself to drive. A pressure in my head made me feel my brain would burst. I took a few deep breaths, and drew away from the kerb.

We drove in silence, thoughts spinning in my head. If Dan Root were not guilty, and he was protecting Lucy, then what they must have been talking about in the tower was her having killed Milner. And Dan could have been offering some understanding, saying that he himself had once intended to kill. Engrossed in my thoughts, I almost passed the end of St Clement's Road. I would have liked to have driven on, and away, and out of all this mess. I signalled right, and turned.

By now I was heartily sick of this road, and the sight of shabby number 29. If I never saw it again, that would be too soon.

The main door was open. I tapped and entered the Wolfendale flat. Miss Fell was seated in the captain's chair. She held a finger to her lips and came towards us.

'Lucy's sleeping. The captain has gone out. He said he may be some time.'

'Miss Fell, this is Inspector Charles of Scotland Yard. He needs to speak to Lucy. I know it's a shame to wake her . . .'

'Scotland Yard?' Miss Fell's eyes widened.

'Perhaps you and I could have a brief word, Miss Fell, while Mrs Shackleton rouses Miss Wolfendale.'

He led Miss Fell into the hall.

As the inspector and Miss Fell left the room, I sat down in the chair opposite Lucy. She lay like Sleeping Beauty, waiting to be awoken by a prince. Still wearing Friday night's dress, she had a faintly earthy whiff about

365

her from having slept in her clothes all weekend. She had managed to keep her ankle raised. On the low table beside her was an unappetising jam sandwich.

The clock on the mantelpiece ticked loudly. It struck half past two.

She opened her eyes. 'You can eat that blackberry jam sandwich if you like. I'm not asleep. Auntie Ada fusses so much I had to shut her out.'

'What's that you have?'

A fat envelope lay on her solar plexus.

'Granddad gave it to me. It's a mass of money. Haven't counted it. If he'd done this on my twenty-first as I asked, I could have saved myself an awful lot of trouble.'

'Where did he get it? How much?'

'It's lots. Nice big fivers. He said it came from Mr Milner. But how could it, when Milner's dead?' She pushed it behind the cushion. 'Why does the policeman want to talk to me?'

'Why do you think?'

'About Mr Milner I suppose. Does he think I stabbed him?'

I was saved the trouble of answering.

The inspector walked in, introducing himself.

Lucy's manner changed. She stiffened and sat up. 'I didn't do it,' she said straight away. 'He was a nasty man and I hated him, but I didn't kill him. Why should I? I want to go to drama school. I have a plan and it did not include marrying or murdering anyone.' She swung her legs to the floor and faced him, wincing in pain.

He motioned me to stay in Wolfendale's big leather chair, and brought a carver across, placing it between me and Lucy.

'What happened to your ankle, Miss Wolfendale?'

'I fell.' She nodded towards me. 'Oh I expect she's told you about my little escapade. I know I shouldn't have done it.'

The inspector's attention remained on Lucy. 'What escapade is that?'

She looked at me in surprise, and gratitude. 'You didn't tell?'

'No. Perhaps you should do that. And while you're about it, put your leg back on that footstool.'

There was something about Lucy that brought out a protective instinct in me. Now, of course, the inspector would wonder what else I had not told him.

He showed great patience as he drew Lucy's story from her. He asked her about the play, and the final performance on Friday evening. 'Don't plays usually run to a Saturday?' he asked disarmingly.

'They do. But the Opera House is a professional theatre and although they have a space for amateur groups to perform, they had a variety show touring in for the Saturday, and so we had to get out on Friday night, gather up all our props and costumes and so on.'

'What props did you have to carry?'

'I'd borrowed Auntie Ada's sewing box. My character, Anna, she went without needle and thread to a sewing evening, and her friend provides her with what she needs. Alison Hart played my friend. Well, Alison's mother said she wasn't parting with her sewing box for love or money, and so I had to take one.'

'Tell me about that Friday night, after the performance.'

As she spoke, she painted a picture of the party that I recognised – the admiration of the cast for Meriel, how she and the other young people formed a clique, the shy way in which Dylan stuck by her, how relieved she was when I kept Mr Milner talking, and when Madam Geerts drew him away.

She left the theatre at about 11.15 p.m. with Madam Geerts and Alison, and walked back with them to Madam Geerts's house. Rodney and his friend were with them. She went into the house for a few moments, left her props there, and then pretended that she would catch up with Rodney and his friend. Instead, she went to the backyard of Croker & Company, where she had arranged to meet Dylan. When she heard another voice, and recognised it as Monsieur Geerts, she hid in the outside lavatory until he had gone. Then Dylan got out his bike and cycled her to the tower.

Just as the inspector was about to ask another question, we were interrupted by a loud knocking on the outside door.

I stood up. 'I'll go.'

It was a short, stocky plain-clothes policeman, a little out of breath. 'Inspector Charles here? I need to speak to him, urgently.'

The inspector had heard, and came out into the hall. I left him and the constable to talk, and went back to Lucy.

'He's nice,' she said. 'And I don't think he thinks I killed Mr Milner.'

'No.' I had no idea what was going on in the inspector's mind.

'He likes you,' she said confidently, trying to scratch her ankle under the bandage. 'The inspector likes you, Mrs Shackleton. I can always tell.' She dropped her voice to a whisper as he came back into the room. 'You like him too.'

The inspector looked suddenly grey-faced and grim. He did not sit down but gripped the back of the chair. 'I've sent the constable upstairs to tell Miss Fell something, but it's something very bad, Lucy, and you must know it first.'

Lucy ran her tongue around her lips. 'Is it Dylan? Has he died? He was only trying to help me . . .'

'Not Dylan. Your grandfather. There is no easy way to say this. He is dead.'

'No. He was here, he . . .' Her eyes widened. She clenched her fists.

'He just came to our headquarters in the Prince of Wales. He made a confession to having killed Mr Milner . . .'

She stared at him, her mouth open, as if she suspected this might be some horrible trick.

Inspector Charles continued, 'From what your grandfather said, the details he gave, we have every reason to believe that he did murder Mr Milner.'

Her head dropped forward. She began to shake convulsively. I feared she was about to have a fit. In movements that seemed like slow motion, I went across to her, sat on the arm of the chair and took hold of her.

After a few moments, she stopped shaking. With tears on her cheeks, she looked up. 'But you said grandfather is dead. And now you say he is a killer.'

His look was full of compassion, his voice gentle. 'He brought with him a revolver. When he had signed the confession, he turned the revolver on himself.'

Lucy's voice was little more than a whisper. 'He wouldn't. He . . .'

'Death was instant. He shot himself through the temple. I'm sorry, Miss Wolfendale.'

I shut my eyes, willing myself not to be sick. When I opened them, I looked at the photograph of Lucy that the captain had placed on the occasional table. There was the clearest thumb mark where he had held it while admiring my photographic skill and Lucy's translucent beauty.

It shook me to the core to think that when I had come in here late that evening after the theatre, after sitting in the police station giving my story, the captain had blood on his hands. Coolly, he had handed me the telegram from Sykes about Mrs deVries and her address. Unblinking, he had, the next morning, sought my help in finding Lucy. All the while I had been dealing with a cold-blooded murderer.

Miss Fell came bustling in. 'My poor Lucy.' She rushed to Lucy and folded her in her arms. Lucy began to sob.

'Will you be all right?' the inspector asked me.

'Yes.'

'I have to get back to the Prince of Wales.'

'Of course.'

I followed him into the hall. The front door stood open. The two men were about to leave.

'Wait!' They turned back to look at me. Now was not the time, but I had to know. Because something did not ring true. I remembered the expression on the old man's face earlier, when he looked at Lucy and realised that she knew how Milner had died. 'Did he really do it, or was this another false confession?'

The inspector looked at me in great surprise. One false confession would be unusual. Two would be extraordinary. He nodded to his subordinate. 'We can trust Mrs Shackleton.'

The plain-clothes man cleared his throat. 'Captain Wolfendale had all the details correct, the time, the weapon, the slashed tyres. He even said he had lost a cufflink and disposed of its match down a drain.'

That should have convinced me. My nagging doubts were based on flimsy thoughts that would sound ridiculous if I put them into words. The old man was not capable of changing a gas mantle in his own hall. Could he be so thorough as to almost get away with murder? And why confess?

The inspector was impatient to be off.

I wanted to stop him, to say that there was something wrong. 'One more question. What was his motive?'

The plain-clothes man relaxed a little now. It made me wonder if he, too, thought the captain's account of the murder had been too tidy.

'He was being blackmailed by the victim. It had gone on for years. On Friday, Mr Milner had come round in the afternoon and asked him to sign over the house. That was the last straw.'

I did not believe that. Milner wanted Lucy, not a dilapidated house with a sitting tenant.

Inspector Charles asked the next question for me. 'What was the captain being blackmailed about?'

'Something that happened during the Boer War, sir. Apparently, the captain was decorated for his bravery. He took credit for another man's courage, and after the war, he killed a man. Killed his own batman. It reads very convincing in his statement, sir.'

It would have been more convincing, I thought, if he had confessed to being the batman who had killed his captain. But then, Lucy would be left homeless. There would be no provision in law for this house to be inherited by Miss Wolfendale's nephew's illegitimate daughter. That would be a Dickensian suite in chancery.

The three of us stood in silence for a moment. The detective constable put on his hat and left. Inspector Charles looked at me with respect and admiration. 'You said it this morning. You said we should take a closer look at Captain Wolfendale. You were right.'

With that, he left.

I returned to the room. Lucy and the ancient Miss Fell were locked in a tragic embrace.

I barely trusted myself to speak. But there was one question I needed to ask.

'Lucy, when Dan was in the tower with you, was he confessing to murder?'

She looked up. Tears smudged her cheeks. 'No. Why would he?'

'I overheard him.'

She stared at me for a moment, then a flicker of recollection came to her. 'Oh that. No. He was saying that he wanted to kill someone he really and truly hated, and so he knew how I felt.'

'About what? How you felt about what?'

She burst into a fresh bout of weeping. 'About killing Mr Milner. I told him I murdered Mr Milner.'

My mouth felt so dry I could barely get the words out. My top lip stuck to my teeth. 'And did you kill Mr Milner?'

'No!'

'Then why did you say you did?'

'Oh I don't know. I wanted Dan to help me. I wanted him to look after me, and collect the money from the hollow tree on Monday.'

Suddenly it made sense why Dan had confessed to murder. I had felt protective towards Lucy, he felt the same, and in spades. 'So you really told him that you killed Mr Milner?'

'Yes. I thought if Dan was on my side, everything would be all right.'

What I did next was not like me at all. I bore down on her, kicked the footstool from under her sprained ankle so that her leg dropped and she let out a cry. I grabbed her and shook her. 'And your grandfather. Did you tell him the same thing? That you killed Milner?'

'No!'

'Are you sure?' I kept on shaking her. Her head flopped back and forth like a rag doll's. She was wailing.

'Of course I'm sure, I swear it.'

Miss Fell pulled at my arm. 'Stop it! Leave the child be. Don't you see how upset she is?'

'Did you kill him, Lucy? You had good reason to stick a knife in Milner's heart.'

Miss Fell began to pull at my clothes, trying to drag me off. Lucy became a dead weight. I had stopped shaking her and held her by the arms, to keep her from falling. I let her drop back into the chair. She looked up at me, dislike and resentment in every feature.

'I didn't kill him. Granddad asked me had I done it. He said to not be afraid to say. But I didn't. I told him, it wasn't me. Ask Alison. She was with me the whole time. We went to the dressing room together, so that he wouldn't get me on my own.'

She was telling the truth. She looked too exhausted to lie. I turned and left the room. Now I was the one who had begun to shake.

45

Revenge Tragedy

Revenge tragedy: bloody deeds from the past demand retribution

I shut the front door quietly and walked down the steps, not sorry to be leaving 29 St Clement's Road behind.

In my mind's eye, I saw what might have happened on Friday night: the captain, hailing Milner as he walked towards his motor on Cheltenham Parade. What words had he uttered as he plunged the knife into Milner's heart? In a slow dance, had he guided Milner up the alley to the doorway and let him slide into oblivion?

My hands began to shake as I made to open the car door. I leaned slightly, supporting myself as my legs turned weak.

'Mrs Shackleton!' Firm hands gripped my upper arms.

I turned to see Dan Root.

He released me. 'Sorry, saw you through my window. Thought you were going to faint.'

I shook him off. 'I'm not the fainting type, Mr Root.'

'All the same, won't you come in for a moment?'

'No. Thank you.'

'I've something to tell you.'

'You had something to tell me before. It was a pack of lies.'

'Only the part about killing Milner was untrue.'

'Only!' Everything in my body screamed at him to keep his nonsense to himself. 'I don't want to hear any more from you.' But that was not true. Given his habit of eavesdropping, there might be something he could tell me that would help make some sense of the captain's confession.

'Let me at least offer you a glass of water, and an apology. Come in and sit down, just for a moment, until you feel ready to drive.'

I did not have the energy to refuse, but told myself this was work. In his confession, the captain had given an account of what passed between him and Milner on Friday afternoon. Eavesdropper Dan would be able to confirm or deny that. If what the captain said was true, about Milner wanting the house, then perhaps the rest of his statement was also true. There was the advantage that Dan could not have heard my conversation in the hall with the two policemen.

His bench and work in progress was covered with a darned white sheet. Otherwise the room was just the same as when he had given me a demonstration on how to use an eyeglass, and as it had been when I returned to search hastily, looking for some clue to Lucy's whereabouts, and finding his telltale South African bible.

The old speaking trumpet and pipe were connected and lying on the hearth. 'So you have heard the news about the captain's confession and suicide?'

He had the grace to blush. 'Sit here.'

It was the only chair – a metal-frame contraption with large flat cushions that would extend to a narrow bed. He turned on the tap, and filled a glass with water.

'And did you hear me just now, trying to shake the truth from Lucy?'

He handed me the glass of water. 'No,' he lied. 'I've been seeing to my stew.'

Something was cooking in a pot.

He lowered the flame on a gas ring. 'I bought myself this contraption. It comes with a gas canister. I go to Mr Preston, the butcher in Lowther Arcade. Neck of mutton makes a good stew, with onion, pearl barley, a carrot and a potato, salt and pepper.'

He could stick his lying head in the stew for all I cared. With a good deal of effort, I kept my voice steady. 'I'm not interested in recipes. Why did you confess to a crime you didn't commit?'

He picked up a ladle. 'Will you have some stew?'

'If I ate, I'd be sick. Just tell me. Why did you make a false confession?'

'Can't you guess?' He lay down the ladle reluctantly. 'All these months I've been too cowardly to act. I came here to avenge my mother. The man I wanted to kill, the real Captain Wolfendale, had been dead for two decades. You can't imagine how that felt. Like walking into a brick wall. When I heard Milner was dead, I wished I'd killed him. And when Lucy said she'd done it . . .'

I had slid back in the chair.

'Please. You look pretty done in. A bite to eat will do you good.'

'Offer it to Lucy and Miss Fell. Just tell me. Why would you go to the gallows for Lucy? I know you believed her when she said she killed Milner.'

He pulled out a straight chair and sat down, tilting it, balancing on the chair's back legs, drawing up his knees against the edge of the table. 'Because . . . because it was a miracle to me to find Lucinda, after twenty years. She was born on the ship that brought me to England. Her mother was the schoolteacher who adopted me, Miss Marshall. Miss Marshall would have kept Lucinda, and me, if she could. But I was apprenticed to a watch mender, and she despatched to her father, so that Miss Marshall could marry her upright clergyman, the only man who would have her.

'I did not expect Wolfendale would have taken care of Lucinda, of Lucy. I thought she might have died, like my little sisters died in the camp, or been put into an orphanage. So when I saw her, the first moment I saw her, when I enquired about a room here, I loved her. I don't mean in the way Dylan dotes on her, or the way Milner wanted to have her. I just loved her. And I stupidly believed her when she said she'd murdered Milner.'

He brought the chair to an upright position. The table was set with a single spoon and dish. It struck me that he had an air of loneliness all around him, like a cloak.

'You were listening, Dan, when Lucy talked to her grandfather. Did she tell him she had killed Milner, as she told you?'

'No.'

Perhaps she had not needed to, I thought. Perhaps the captain made that assumption because Lucy had known Milner was stabbed.

Dan picked up the spoon and twiddled it in his fingers. 'Will you tell me something?'

'What?'

'How did the police know I was lying in my confession?'

'You missed out some details, such as the type of knife.'

'Ah,' he said. 'Of course,' as though suddenly realising what type of knife he should have described. 'What other details?'

'The damage to Milner's motor.'

'And the captain.' He jerked his head in the direction of the flat above. 'He got all his details correct?' he said, almost with a slight touch of resentment.

'So it would seem.'

'And by shooting himself did not allow for cross-questioning.'

'Are you suggesting that he did not do it?'

Root shrugged. 'He must have. I did not hear him go out that night, after I had walked Miss Fell home.'

'Did you hear me and Meriel return?'

'No. Perhaps I sleep better than I think.'

I stood up. 'Thanks for the glass of water.'

He walked me to the door, and out to my motor. I turned to him. 'What did the captain and Milner talk about on Friday afternoon?'

He shook his head. 'Not much that day. About the play, about tobacco.' He gave a rueful smile. 'It wasn't worth listening to.'

'I know what I think Milner's hold was over the captain. But will you tell me what you think?'

He looked up to the room where Lucy was nursing her sprained ankle and her great ambitions. 'You won't tell Lucinda? It would destroy her.'

'This isn't for her to know. It's for me.'

'Promise?'

'I can't promise, but if I can keep it to myself, I will.' He remained silent. 'All right, Dan. Let me tell you what I have worked out. The real Rowland Oliver Wolfendale, VC died, either of natural causes or, more probably, foul play, twenty years ago. His batman,

Sergeant Henry Lampton, took his place, inherited this house, and brought up Wolfendale's daughter as his own granddaughter. Am I correct so far?'

Dan looked at me steadily. 'There is nothing I would contradict.'

'And Milner, who had served with both men, came up to Harrogate with an eye to sharing in his old comrade's good fortune.'

'That's one way of putting it.'

And now all three of them were dead, and here was Dan who had come for revenge. Instead he had taught himself to make stew, and an efficient listening device. I had been angry with him earlier. Now I felt pity.

'Go up and see her, Dan. Throw that damn speaking trumpet in the ash pit. Talk to her. You are the only link now between Lucy and her mother. Some day she might be glad of that, and so might her mother. She must wonder every day what happened to her daughter, and to you.'

'Do you think so?'

'I know so.'

46

Cup and Saucer Drama

Cup and saucer drama: plays with a domestic setting

Lively strains of music floated to meet me as I walked into the lobby of the Grand Hotel. The orchestra played the tune my mother always requested, "Have you seen me dance the polka? Have you seen my coat tails fly?"

I glanced into the Palm Court room where afternoon tea took its stately course, the chime of cups and genteel chatter underscoring the music.

My mother was seated under a huge potted palm, at a small round table, with two other matrons. She caught my eye, waved and beckoned. I knew exactly what she would have been saying to her companions. *My daughter, Kate, a war widow . . . I should so like to see her settled.*

Unable to face small talk, I waved in a jolly manner, pointed upstairs, and did an about turn.

At the foot of the staircase, a page approached. 'Mrs Shackleton?'

'Yes.'

'Lady Virginia has arranged for you to move into a suite. May I show you?'

I thanked him, and we climbed the stairs. Sliding my hand along the solid polished banister, I attempted to turn myself from detective into not-so-dutiful daughter.

Just like mother to wangle improved accommodation. My father had always insisted that we live on his police superintendent's salary. His job came with the requirement that he rent a designated constabulary house, which was where I had been happily brought up. It followed that whenever mother felt herself let loose, she would waste no time in throwing her own inherited money at the nearest luxuries.

The accommodation was suitably grand. We had a sitting room, with a bedroom on either side. I kicked off my shoes and went to see which of the bedrooms had been allocated to me. Mother had the biggest of course. Her fox fur, a stole and the day dress I had seen earlier lay discarded on the bed. Afternoon tea had naturally required a change of outfit.

Mother was probably glad I had not ventured into the Palm Court room wearing the crumpled costume I had dressed in since first thing this morning. I looked out of the window across the Valley Gardens. Human dots moved slowly around the grounds of the Royal Bath Hospital and Convalescent Home.

Her voice startled me. 'Poor things,' my mother said blithely. 'We have a view of two convalescent premises and the home for incurables. It makes one appreciate life in all its glory. If ever I become incurable, you must bring me here.' She sat down on the chintz-covered sofa and tapped the spot beside her.

I sat down. 'How did you wangle this suite at the height of the season?'

'Oh, old chum of mine. She and her husband came for the golf. I know there are other courses about, but they decided in view of the floods to take themselves to Lossiemouth. But never mind that. Your father told me before he left that this dreadful murder has been solved.'

'There was a confession, followed by a suicide.'

Mother shuddered. 'How appalling! No wonder you look so washed out. Now this is my plan. I shall order tea to be brought up. You look too exhausted to go downstairs. After tea, you must have a bath, and then a sleep.' She patted my hand.

'No tea for me. A glass of gin would go down nicely.'

'No sooner said than done. What will you have as a mixer?'

Ten minutes later, I lay in a tepid bath, feeling exhausted enough to slide under the water. Concentrating very hard on the bath tub's enamel surface and the glint of the brass taps, I tried to push everything out of mind. It worked for several seconds at a time.

Lucy had not killed Milner. She was not a mastermind by any means but she would have known to behave normally, and go home – not spark suspicion by disappearing into her tower and proceeding with her ransom demand.

It was perfectly plausible that 'the captain', Lucy's 'grandfather', had finally snapped. Blackmail ends in one of three ways: prosecution, continued payments or death. The dilemma was whether I should tell Inspector Charles what I knew about the background of Milner, the real Wolfendale, and his impersonator, Lampton. The man I had thought of as the captain had somewhat redeemed himself in my eyes by taking care of another man's child, and doing his best for her. If I revealed what

I knew, and there were investigations, army records opened up, then Lucy and Miss Fell would forfeit their home. Rodney Milner would remember his father not just as an unpleasant bully, but as a blackmailer. If all this came out, Rodney and Alison's life in Harrogate might prove intolerable.

By the time my bath water turned cold and I pulled the plug, I knew I would not tell.

When I got back to the room and climbed into bed, I discovered hot-water bottles.

My mother smiled. 'I know it's August, but you've had a shock.' She had also sent for hot water and poured a tot of gin and hot water in equal measure. 'Drink that down.'

'You've hung up my clothes. Thank you.'

My evening dress was hooked onto the wardrobe door. I had popped the Delphos robe in my suitcase, because it packs so well. Made in Paris, it is a pleated silk tunic, in fabulous colours, turquoise, purple and orange. My aunt gave it to me when I admired it.

Trying not to sound critical, my mother said, 'Berta bought that gown in Paris in 1908. That makes it fourteen years old.'

'No one will know that, will they? I always feel happy in it. It makes me feel that I'm in Paris.'

She tucked me in, as she used to when I was a little girl. 'But tonight you will be in Harrogate, having supper with our charming police inspector, and that will be so much more satisfactory than looking back to some long-lost time in Paris.'

She closed the curtains, and went quietly from the room.

I appreciated her thoughtfulness, having expected the

usual grilling, and plans to take me shopping. She would have thought ahead to Lawrence Milner's funeral, what I would wear and whether there would be some eligible mourner for me to latch on to. That made me smile. There would doubtless be compulsory shopping trips between taking the waters and sampling the delights of an Electrothermic or Chromopathic bath. I tried to imagine how much Mother would pack in to the next few days.

The door opened again. 'Before you drop off, I've arranged to have Emmatt & Son bring some gowns and daywear to the suite, at about ten-thirty tomorrow.'

She shut the door gently.

In spite of my mother's interventions, Lawrence Milner's dead face floated before my eyes in the moments before sleep, followed by the captain's as I had seen him last, his ruddy cheeks pale, his eyes haunted, and his forehead creased with a frown. He was trying to tell me something.

I wished I could be as confident as the inspector and the constable that the captain had, indeed, murdered Milner. Perhaps I would grow used to the idea.

47

The Scene Draws Over

*The scene draws over: two flats are drawn together to hide
the scene set behind them*

After a sleep, I felt refreshed, hungry, and ready for
company. I was in my trusty Delphos robe, but my
mother had refused to dress. 'Give Mr Charles my
apologies. This has been a long day for me and if we're
to be up before seven in the morning to take the waters,
I must have my rest.' Since she was already in her satin
nightgown and robe, there was no arguing with her.
'Have a lovely evening, dear. I won't wait up.'

At five minutes to nine, a hotel page knocked on the
door of our suite to tell me that Mr Charles waited on
Mrs Hood and Mrs Shackleton's convenience in the
hotel lounge.

What I love about my Delphos tunic is that it seems to
let me float in a touch of magic, caressing and propelling
as I walked down the stairs to the ground floor.

The inspector stood as I entered the lounge, and for a
moment gazed at me wide-eyed. 'Mrs Shackleton, you
look wonderful.'

'Thank you, Mr Charles. My mother sends her apologies. She has a headache and decided to have an early
night.'

If he guessed that it was a diplomatic headache, he gave no sign. 'Some other time, perhaps?' His look was suitably, but not too, regretful. 'Shall we go in to supper, or would you like an aperitif?'

'Let's go in.'

Our table was by the window, at some distance from the string quartet and shielded by a potted palm. The waiter gave us menus. I glanced at Mr Charles while he ordered wine. Wearing an evening suit emphasised a quality in him I had half noticed when we first met. There was something about him that made me intensely aware of him, aware of the movements of his body under his clothes, the sense of something powerful being contained, not just physically but in other ways too, mental, emotional. It was a rare quality.

We both chose lobster bisque. I went for the venison, he for jugged hare. The wine waiter hovered as he poured, waiting for an opinion. When he had gone, the inspector asked, in a solicitous yet professional tone, 'How are you feeling, after everything? It's been an ordeal for you.' He looked at me with grave concern and total attention that could have been disconcerting if it were not so broadly edged with kindness. I would not have liked to be on the receiving end of an interrogation by him.

'It was a shock, hearing about the captain's confession, and that he shot himself. It did leave me shaken.' I did not tell him that I had also made sure Lucy Wolfendale was shaken, by me.

'I'm sorry that I dashed off like that. Did you stay long with Miss Wolfendale and the old lady?'

'No. They had each other. And Mr Root gallantly came to my aid.'

Mr Charles gave an unexpected laugh. 'Good for him,' he said ruefully. 'It almost prompts me not to charge him with leading us up the garden path with his false confession.'

'Will you pursue him on that?'

He shook his head. 'I made it my business to call him in and give him a ticking off. He was suitably chastened.'

'I suppose you soon realised that he was not telling the truth.'

'It has been known for an inaccurate confession to be made by a killer – inconsistencies and so on – only to throw the hounds off the scent, but usually in detective stories rather than in life.'

'He was protecting Lucy Wolfendale because he thought she was the murderess.'

'That girl does elicit powerful emotions,' he said, with a puzzled look.

'You've seen her only in the dragged-through-a-hedge state, with a swollen ankle and dirty face. She polishes up in spectacular style. And Scotland Yard better watch out. She will be coming to London to study drama this autumn.'

The inspector mockingly put his head in his hands. 'That'll give my boys something to look forward to.' He suddenly gave me a serious look that made my heart skip a beat. Was I to be berated for not saying what Lucy was getting up to? 'I do not blame you for covering up for her,' he said kindly. 'She is young, ambitious, and foolish. And she did take some smoking out of her hidey-hole . . .'

'But?'

'You should have told me about what she was up to.

As it turned out, there was no connection between her disappearance and the murder, but there might have been.'

'I suppose you're right. But I was fairly sure one had nothing to do with the other.'

He leaned across the table and took my hand in his. The events of the last three days had set emotions racing. It was a little like wartime, when we lived in a heightened state of tension. 'If ever we work together again, promise me you'll keep nothing back.'

I avoided making any such promise. 'That sounds like the offer of a job at Scotland Yard. I did not realise I had applied.'

He smiled. 'All right. I give up. For now.'

When he let go of my hand, I could still feel his touch.

During the soup, we deliberately left behind the subject of the murder, and got on first-name terms. I learned that Marcus Charles was forty years old, and a widower. He had joined the CID at the age of twenty-two, after a year as a beat bobby.

My question surprised me. It must have been lurking there all along. I was thinking about having let Meriel off for thieving from the pawnbroker – an action that threatened my professional relationship with stalwart Jim Sykes.

'Have you ever,' I asked in what I hoped was a throw-away manner, 'ever turned a blind eye when an offence has been committed?'

'If it is some minor infringement, there may be discretion. At other times we are left with no choice in the matter.'

'Say, in a robbery or something of that sort,' I said,

immediately regretting my choice of example. It would not surprise me in the least if he had heard that I was in Harrogate to investigate Mr Moony's pawnshop robbery.

There was a pause while the waiter gathered up our soup plates.

'It's my job to enforce the law, and that is what I do.'

I had the feeling that he was reluctant to go in the direction I was leading. The waiter set our plates of venison and jugged hare on the table, and dished out potatoes, carrots and cabbage.

I poured some gravy onto the venison. 'Do you not sometimes feel pity for the perpetrators? An understanding of what drove them to the act?' I turned the handle of the gravy boat towards him.

'Oh yes, of course. All sorts of emotions come into play. Shock, as with this crime here in Harrogate — particularly in such a tranquil setting; anger and, yes, pity. The captain was a frail old man.'

In as light a tone as I could muster, I asked, 'So his confession convinced you?' I glanced at Marcus's hands, his shirt cuffs, his cufflinks, which were gold, with a tiny embossed pattern in one corner. It made me think of that other cufflink, lying in the gutter. It suddenly struck me that it was not the kind of cuff-link I would expect an old man to wear. And if it indicated a scuffle, then there would be no doubt who would come off best. Milner was younger, heavier, fitter.

'Without doubt I believed the captain's confession,' the inspector said, in a gentle, reassuring voice. 'He could not have made it up.'

I remembered that Meriel and the captain had both

389

called on Rodney to offer condolences on Saturday morning, Meriel first. 'Miss Jamieson could have let slip to Rodney some details about finding the body, and about the motor when she called to see him on Saturday. I know she shouldn't have, but it's possible. And then the captain called. For all we know, Rodney may have told him some details.'

Again, he took my hand. 'Kate, Kate. Don't worry. You were right when you said I should pay attention to the captain. Believe me, he was the man. It was his knife. He described it. Now can we change the subject?' It was as if he were saying 'Don't worry. There is no mad murderer loose on the streets of Harrogate.'

The string quarter struck up a waltz. By the time our plates were whipped away, I had talked of my passion for photography. Marcus confided that he enjoys sketching, when he can find the time. This comes in useful at the scene of a crime when he can make a speedy visual record of whatever may catch his eye. Committing it to paper helps him make sense of what he sees. I learned that he lived in North London, walked on Hampstead Heath and swam in the pond there early in the mornings, and that this helped him think when he was stuck on a particularly difficult case.

Over dessert, we conjured a romantic notion of swimming together one day soon. It would be a fine day in September or early October when we decided that there would be a spell of good weather, and we would take a picnic and set out a blanket like two people without a care in the world.

'Would you care for brandy?' he asked as we left the dining room.

'Good idea.'

The lounge was crowded. One or two people cast glances in our direction as we hovered for a moment in the doorway, looking for a free space. Were the glances because we were a striking couple, or because some of the guests had recognised the police inspector? We turned away.

'I have a better idea,' I murmured. 'My mother never travels without brandy. Will you come up to our suite?' I said the words calmly, without betraying the inward tremble.

'There's nothing I would like more,' he said softly.

We climbed the staircase side by side, not speaking. There was a touch of madness about what I intended, what I hoped would happen. This may break the spell my missing husband still held over me. Marcus touched my hand very lightly as we walked along the landing. At the door, I fumbled for the key.

He had a boyish, almost hesitant look as he stepped inside. 'Won't we wake your mother?'

'Not unless you plan to be very rowdy. That's her room.' I waved to the door on the right of our sitting room.

'And yours?' he asked gently.

We forgot about the brandy. It was still there the next morning when Marcus had gone, leaving on the bedside cabinet a small thick envelope.

The short letter, if such it could be called, was on hotel notepaper. It contained no endearments, but he had whispered enough of those in the small hours for that not to matter. Then we had slept soundly, or at least I had, curled in his arms and feeling safe from the haunting images of Milner's staring eyes and the even more horrifying picture of what I had not seen: the captain, blowing his brains out.

The reason for the thickness of the envelope was that it contained a medal — Captain Wolfendale's (the real captain Wolfendale's) Victoria Cross. Marcus's note was written in a way that would withstand scrutiny should it fall into the wrong hands. It read:

Dear Mrs Shackleton

Thank you for your assistance. I am in two minds about leaving this VC with you. By rights it should go to the late Captain Wolfendale's next of kin. However, after he signed his confession, the captain said to Sergeant Walmsley that this medal must come to Mrs Kate Shackleton, and that she alone would know who to give it to.

I did not hand the medal to you yesterday evening. It was not the right moment. If you do not accept the burden of this responsibility, please return the enclosed to the Harrogate police.

If you are inclined to take up my invitation to visit Scotland Yard, I should be pleased to show you around by appointment. I can recommend a very good place to stay in Hampstead.

Yours sincerely
Marcus Charles

I read the letter, once, twice, three times, and weighed the medal in my hand.

My mother was moving about in the next room. We had an enjoyable day planned. Nothing would get in the way of that. I put the letter and the medal in the back of a drawer and slammed it shut.

Captain Wolfendale, Sergeant Lampton, whoever you are and whatever hell you are in, I do not want to know. Leave me alone.

48

Radiant Heat and Light

Mother is not exactly a stickler for following directions. She appeared to be making an exception in relation to the Harrogate waters. It was 7 a.m. I was bleary-eyed, exhilarated and exhausted in equal measure, and still reeling from being given the dubious honour of taking charge of the captain's Victoria Cross.

Every action seemed clumsy. I could not find the heel in my stocking. A garter was missing. While I dressed, or tried to, in my bedroom, mother sat in our shared sitting room, reading to me from a guide book.

'All the hot sulphur waters ought to be drunk quickly, or else the sulpheretted hydrogen blah-di-blah escapes. What is sulphuretted hydrogen, Kate?'

'Don't know.'

'Ah, wait a minute, listen to this. "It is better to drink all the iron or chalybeate waters through a glass tube." Which will we be drinking, chalybeate – how do you pronounce that? – or iron?'

'Don't know.'

'Let's see. Oh, it's all so complicated. Did you know the waters were unpleasant?'

I laced up my new, sensible walking-about-Harrogate shoes. 'I guessed they would be.'

As I walked into the sitting room, mother stared at my feet. 'What on earth are those?'

'I had to have a pair of comfortable shoes.'

'Why?'

'I'll change later.'

Mother eyed the two brandy balloons and raised an eyebrow. 'You haven't told me yet how you got on with that nice inspector last night.'

'His name is Marcus Charles . . .'

'What a wonderful name! He sounds like a Roman senator.'

'We hit it off admirably.'

'How splendid!' Mother unscrewed the top on the brandy bottle. 'Do you know, I think if we are going to drink what sounds like fairly disgusting water for the good of our health, we ought at least to fortify ourselves. I mean we only have these medical men's words that this water is any good, and they'll say anything to line their pockets. Whereas we know for certain that brandy is efficacious.' She poured two tots of brandy. 'Here's to Marcus Charles.' We clinked glasses. 'I am so pleased you hit it off. And is he, is he all right? I mean if a man gets to that age, what is he, forty?'

'Yes.'

'And he is still available at forty, it could indicate a peculiarity or two.'

'He is available, and I did not notice any peculiarities.' Far from having peculiarities, Inspector Marcus Charles seemed to me to personify near perfection in a man.

To ward off further questions, I sank the brandy, stood up and offered my mother a hand.

In good spirits, mother clutching her furs against the early-morning chill, we set off for the Royal Baths Pump Room.

Only later, as I gave myself up to the Dowsing Radiant Heat and Light bath, did my mind go blank and all thoughts vanished in a weirdly combined sense of discomfort and wellbeing. Perhaps this was how to grow a second skin: have long moments when nothing at all mattered, except your own physical self. But as I stepped out and began to dress, the thoughts flooded in. Like the police, all I wanted was to say case closed. Questions that I hoped to keep at bay popped up, demanding answers. What had Lampton, or the captain as I was used to thinking of him, tried to tell me? There could be some Lampton relation he wanted me to search out, and give that person the award that should have gone to the captain's batman.

I dismissed the idea as unlikely. All his actions had been directed towards keeping quiet, keeping secrets. The confession had convinced the police. Perhaps they had wanted to be convinced, including my estimable Marcus Charles.

As I laced up the sensible shoes, something clicked. The batman, Lampton, should have got the VC in the first place. It came into his hands when he killed his captain, along with the captain's identity and inheritance. In other words, the medal came to him because he committed murder.

I tied my shoelaces in a double bow.

That same man, Lampton, had gone on pretending to be the captain, had falsely confessed to murder, and taken his own life. He did not believe Lucy to be the killer, or the medal would have stayed with his effects and gone to her. He thought that I alone would be able to work out who really should get the VC. Who really killed Milner.

But why? I could not fathom his reasoning. I had out-manoeuvred him, and now he was setting me a challenge.

When we returned to our suite, a powerful scent of roses greeted us. An enormous vase of red and white blooms sat on the occasional table by the sofa. A small card read simply, *To K from M.*

'Well,' my mother said, breathing in the scent and sighing deeply. 'You did make an impression on Mr Marcus Charles. When will you see him again?'

'He has asked me to London, promised to show me Scotland Yard.'

'I hope he's interested in you for yourself and not in your . . . I don't know, fingerprinting technique.'

'I don't have any fingerprinting technique.' I slit open the envelope I had picked up at reception.

Mother asked, 'Is that from him, too?'

'No. It's from Alison, one of the actresses in *Anna of the Five Towns.*'

Dear Mrs Shackleton

I thought you would like to know that Mr Milner will be buried on Friday at 9.30 a.m. at Christ Church, High Harrogate, and a funeral breakfast at the Queen Hotel. Rodney respectfully hopes you will accept this invitation.

Yours sincerely
Alison Hart

Good for Alison. She had wasted no time in getting her feet under the table. After the funeral, it would be a short step to the special licence and a wedding.

I decided to attend the funeral, to pay my respects. I told myself that I was not carrying on any investigations.

But if I were correct, Lawrence Milner's murderer could still be at large, going about his or her business, perhaps even attending Milner's funeral.

I passed Alison's note to Mother. 'I'll stay on in Harrogate until the end of the week.'

She beamed. 'That is just perfect. As it happens, I took the precaution of asking Emmatts to include some suitable outfits for a clement-weather funeral.'

At eleven-thirty, we took our seats to watch two hapless young assistants from Emmatt & Son parade their wares. This was not something I would ever have arranged myself, and I felt that mother hoped fervently one of her old cronies had caught sight of the shop assistants making their way to our suite. But it did result in my putting on account a wide-sleeve long shawl collar dress with a low waistline, along with a modest hat, suitable for Mr Milner's funeral. It was not all I bought and when the assistants had gone, mother was delighted.

'You will have some good pieces for your visit to London. But don't go to Scotland Yard, dear. I have been there myself. It's a very dusty place. The cleaners would not last two minutes if they had a woman in charge. Now – about shoes . . .'

By mutual consent, we decided one day taking the waters had been quite enough. The mental relaxation they had afforded lasted for at least another couple of hours. Only as I sat in Applebys, trying on shoes, did my thoughts return to the question of who really killed Lawrence Milner. As I paced the floor, testing the fit, I had an unaccountable feeling that somewhere in the dramatisation of *Anna of the Five Towns* lay a clue to the murder of Mr Milner. But what was that clue?

Part of me simply did not want to know. And since there had been some connection between my putting on shoes and my mind going over clues and possibilities, I seriously considered going barefoot.

I replayed the drama of *Anna of the Five Towns* in my mind's eye. I thought of every character, every actor, every scene. And then I remembered that some scenes had been cut from the play. Madam Geerts had said so when we were in the train together. Mr Wheatley had admired Meriel's skill in knowing what to leave in and what to cut. And someone – I racked my brains to think who and when – had said that the scene where Mr Price, Willie's despairing father, hanged himself had been left out, so that he was not seen being cut down from the noose, but the event was reported. If originally, in rehearsals, he had to be cut down, someone must have had a knife among their props.

49

Tabs: stage curtains

Sitting in a rear pew on the pulpit side of the church, I glanced through my discreet veil at the arriving mourners. Mr Croker was among the businessmen, flicking dust from his top hat. Caps in hands, mechanics and Owen the labourer, from Milners' motoring firm, filed into a pew. Mrs Gould, the Milners' housekeeper, in a black felt hat and serge coat, far too hot for the day, was accompanied by a ruddy-faced man, and a young woman smartly dressed in a dark costume.

The Geerts, neat and trim, stepped with graceful dancers' movements down the side aisle, looking neither right nor left. They glided into a pew at the half-way point.

Miss Fell, head held upright, carrying her missal, looked even tinier beside Mr Root. He had slowed his steps so that she could keep up with him.

The surprise mourner was Meriel Jamieson, in flowing black dress, full veil and elbow-length lace gloves. She spotted a place beside me, and squeezed in as the organist struck up.

'Bloody train driver. Over-stopped in Todmorden to

wait for some farmer. We had a German in the carriage. He looked at the station sign, muttered in these horror-stricken tones, "Todmorden? Death, murder?" Well I had all on not to say, better go to Harrogate if that's what you're after.'

Bearers entered the church in solemn procession. Rodney followed the coffin, head bowed, Mrs Hart and Alison behind him. People turned to look, not just out of respect for the dead but in surprise at the living. This was Rodney's public statement of loyalty to Alison, and I admired him for it.

The craggy-faced clergyman conducted a dignified service, eulogising an enterprising man, an asset to the town, a loving father, cut down in his prime, gone to join Jesus, and his own late wife.

'Lucky her,' Meriel whispered.

The service over, Meriel and I hung back, letting the rest of the congregation make their way to the church-yard.

In the porch, I said to Meriel. 'I didn't expect to see you back here, Meriel.'

'Nor did I expect to be here. But Rodney was such a good chap in the play, and Mr Milner backed us to the hilt. I felt I had to pay my condolences.'

'What was the other reason?' Knowing Meriel, I felt sure there must be something in this for her.

'Oh Kate. I wish you didn't see through me. I'm to direct *A Doll's House*. Both Mr Wheatley and I think Lucy would make a perfect Nora. I thought she'd be here.'

Outside, the sun shone, noisy birds serenaded us mourners, a bright and cheerful day. We fell into step with Dan Root and Miss Fell.

'Where's Lucy?' Meriel demanded, as we four formed a slightly self-conscious band of outcasts – representatives in some odd way of the confessed murderer.

'She sprained her ankle,' Miss Fell said, a little defensively.

'I shall visit her,' Meriel announced.

Miss Fell shot her a suspicious glance.

We took our positions at the edge of the group around the grave. Through a gap in the mourners, I watched Alison dab at a tear. The housekeeper blew her nose.

Being on the back row, we were not offered earth to sprinkle on the coffin.

'Meriel.' She stiffened as she turned to me, perhaps still expecting to be apprehended for robbery.

'What?'

We edged a little further apart from the other mourners. 'On Saturday morning, when you went to pay your condolences to Rodney, did you tell him the details of how we found the body?'

'I might have done,' she said warily. 'Why do you want to know?'

'Please. It's important.'

'I told him that you and I found his father. He asked me about it, naturally. I know the police said not to say anything, but I thought he should know.'

That answered one of my questions. Meriel had told Rodney about the dagger, the tyres, the cufflink. Rodney's next caller that day was the captain, his father's oldest comrade. What more natural than to pass on the information; information that would clinch a confession.

'Excuse me.' Meriel moved gracefully through the throng, made a beeline for Rodney and shook his hand. The poor boy looked surprised and gratified. I supposed I should do the same and walked over. Meriel tried to shake Alison's hand. Alison ignored her, and turned to me.

'Don't let Meriel Jamieson come to the breakfast, please,' she said in a low voice. 'It's too upsetting.'

'What is?'

'She only wants money. And I'm glad Lucy's not here. It would be so awkward.'

Alison and I moved aside, as Mrs Hart and Mrs Gould flanked Rodney, his twin guardian angels.

Alison glared at Meriel. 'I can't forgive her. Apparently she came last Saturday, told Rodney every gory detail about the death, and then touched him for twenty guineas. And in his distress, my poor lad left the safe unlocked and the captain, who called next, robbed him, helped himself to a wad of notes from the safe while Rodney was out of the room.'

'Has Rodney told the police?'

'He won't. Honestly Mrs Shackleton, I shall have my work cut out taking care of him.' We shook hands as Alison was approached by another mourner.

Alison need not have worried about Meriel's tagging along to the Queen Hotel. Meriel took Miss Fell's arm and they headed for the lichgate.

Dan Root fell into step with me. We waited by the gate, and in turn shook Rodney's hand. I would have liked to ask Rodney whether he gave the captain Meriel's account of our having found Milner. But now was not the time. Besides, I felt sure I knew the answer.

Dan and I watched Rodney, Alison and Mrs Hart

being driven off in the mourners' carriage. Others set off walking to the nearby Queen Hotel.

My only difficulty in questioning Dan was that he, like me, doubted the veracity of the captain's confession. He may guess what I was driving at. But I would take that risk.

He gave me an opening, saying, 'I thought I would leave Harrogate, but I have decided to stay a while longer, and be a big brother to Lucy for a short time at least, if she will let me.'

'I'm glad to hear it. But you may have to do that in Manchester, if Meriel gets her way.'

'Oh?' He looked a little put out. 'Lucy said she would have the attic cleared for me. That I could move up there.'

'Good.' It was now or never. There was a slight noise behind, and I turned. Already the gravediggers were at work, shovelling soil back into the grave. 'Dan, there is something I wanted to ask you, about the play.'

He groaned. 'What now?'

'Just a small thing. There were some scenes Meriel tried out and then discarded.'

'She cut a couple of scenes, yes.'

'The scene where you played Mr Price, when he committed suicide, I believe that was one.'

He laughed in spite of himself. 'Do not remind me, please. You mean the one where I hanged myself.'

'And your son Willie found you, too late.'

'Yes. Both Dylan and I dug in our heels over that. It would have brought the house down in gales of laughter. Even Meriel had to agree. She said it was a mite too Lear and Cordelia. He was to have cradled me in his arms!'

'Was there a prop involved, to cut you down?'

He paused. A butterfly landed on the gate, realised its mistake and made off in a ray of sunshine. Very quietly, Dan said, 'There was a prop, yes. We all brought props of various kinds. Not all were used. We took them home afterwards, when they weren't needed.'

'Who brought the knife to cut you down?'

A late straggler came from the churchyard. We parted, to let her through.

'I can't remember who brought the knife.' He took out a cigarette.

'This prop. Was it an African dagger?'

Not looking at me, he lit his cigarette. 'I can't remember what it was. As I say, we never used it.'

So there had been a knife among the props to be gathered up from the dressing rooms after the performance. Dan was lying. It was the African dagger that Marcus had shown me, taken from the attic at number 29 St Clement's Road. Four people would have had reason to see and handle that knife. Lucy, who brought it, Meriel as director, Dan as the chap to be cut down, and Dylan Ashton.

50

Saved by the Clapper

A fresh light breeze fluttered the leaves as I left the churchyard and walked to my car. There was one person whom I had been busy suspecting of aiding and abetting Lucy but had not considered as the murderer. I drove back through the now familiar streets and parked near the police station, so as to be at a little distance from Croker & Company.

I cut through Princes Street, ignoring my surroundings, desperately hoping to be wrong about Dylan Ashton. He seemed such an unlikely candidate, unassuming, a bit of a weakling, and with an alibi. Monsieur Geerts had latched onto him after the party, and had walked him home. But why would a young man need walking home?

It was time to take a closer look at young Mr Ashton. I would start by searching his room, above the house agent's premises, keeping my fingers crossed that Mr Croker had gone to the funeral breakfast.

I was not sure what I would find. A cufflink matching the one in the gutter would be far too much to hope for. But as I pictured the cufflink left behind at the scene of the crime, I felt sure I was right in thinking it had not belonged to the captain. It was too modern for a man who had probably not shopped for himself in a couple of decades. Marcus had been remiss not to bring it with him to show to Lucy. Perhaps my inspector friend's attention to detail was not as good as it ought to be.

The notice on Croker & Company's door read: "Closed Friday morning – funeral". After counting the number of shop premises, I walked round to the back alley, and counted again.

An imperious cat watched from the roof of next door's outside lavatory. What excuse could I come up with if caught entering premises in broad daylight? 'Thought I spotted an intruder, your honour.'

Once again I brought out my trusty penknife. The inventor of sash windows bestowed a boon on private detectives. The catch shot back with ease.

Carefully, I closed the window behind me. I stepped into the shabby downstairs back room of Croker & Company, with its sink, cupboards, oilcloth-covered deal table and battered filing cabinets.

The door to the upstairs accommodation was shut, but not locked. I climbed the stairs, noticing that the third stair creaked.

Dylan Ashton's room bore the reasonable tidiness of a person who did not have sufficient belongings to become untidy. There was a washstand, a bedside chair, but no wardrobe. On a hook behind the door hung a dress suit, the one Dylan had worn after the play, the trouser bottoms muddied. A little shabby, the jacket had been skilfully mended under the right arm. A slight stain by a button hole could have been anything. But if it were blood, it could be analysed and identified. A pair of good black shoes was tucked under the bed, still marked with clay from Dylan's nighttime trip to the tower with Lucy when he had crossed the field.

The green candlewick bedspread had been hastily pulled up to cover the pillow. A couple of threads of white cotton lay on the bedspread, along with an expensive white knitted silk scarf that a house agent's clerk could ill afford. I remembered a gesture from the play when Rodney, playing the businessman Henry Mynors, threw the scarf across his shoulder in an easy gesture. If I were right, Dylan had helped himself to the scarf. He could have taken the scarf when collecting props because he coveted it, or because wearing it would allow him to hide something, such as a bloodstain on his jacket.

On the washstand there was an ashtray, a twist of tobacco in a jar, and a finely painted Potteries dish that held collar studs and a pair of cheap enamel cufflinks. The absence of shaving kit and hairbrush made me guess that Mr Croker had been in here, and delivered these to Dylan in the infirmary.

The washstand cupboard contained nothing remarkable: undervests and writing materials; two shirts, five collars, one of them a dress collar.

On the landing, a closet held broom, dustpan and brush, mop and cleaning cloths. It was the smell of starch that made me pick up one of the dusters, which turned out to be a shirt sleeve. I pulled out all the cloths. A dress shirt had been ripped up for rags. Either the front had already been used, or not been put there in the first place. Why? The obvious answer was that it had been splashed with blood. The clapper on the shop door sounded, halting my search.

I froze. Unsure whether to go up or down, I stayed put. Coming in through a downstairs window was one thing. Getting out through an upstairs window and shimmying down the drainpipe in broad daylight was altogether a different caper. Slowly, I came down, step by step. The telephone rang. Mr Croker answered it. How miserable of him to rush back to work and miss the funeral breakfast.

His telephone conversation gave me the chance to escape the way I had come. I hurried down the stairs into the back room, and across to the window. Just as I was about to push it open, Mr Croker said 'Thank you', and replaced the receiver. Confound the man for having no conversation.

And now he was on his feet and walking into the back room. Trying to still my heart, I fled across the room and stood behind the inner door as he entered. He walked towards the filing cabinet. As he bent his head to flick through folders, I quickly moved round the door, into the outer office, to the main door, and opened it to make my escape. The clapper sounded, but I was gone before Mr Croker could reappear.

51

Manet: a character remains on stage

At the infirmary, I was shown into the matron's office, a bright south-facing room. The matron greeted me warmly. 'Yes, sister mentioned you, Mrs Shackleton. You're the lady who identified Mr Ashton.'

She sat across from me at a desk that held a vase of white roses and a framed photograph.

'How is he, matron?'

'Better than expected. That's youth for you. As well as the wrist and the bruises, he broke a couple of bones in his left foot. He took a bad bump on the head. We cannot be sure whether he will suffer from that in the days to come, but he quickly recovered from concussion.'

'I wonder if I might see him, before I leave Harrogate?'

'Yes indeed. Perhaps you may be able to help.'

I braced myself for a plea to contribute to the upkeep of the hospital, but it was not that.

'The thing is, Mrs Shackleton, Mr Ashton needs time to convalesce. We can keep him here if needs be. I cannot discharge him to go back to a room above business premises.'

'I believe his family is in Staffordshire.'

She frowned. 'Too far for him to travel. Local people have kindly offered to take him in and allow him to recuperate, but he flatly refuses. He is insisting on going back to his own room, which is out of the question.' She pulled a folder from her drawer and looked for the names. 'Here we are, Mr and Mrs Geerts have offered to take him.' She ran her finger down the page. 'Mrs Gould also called. She is housekeeper to the Milners. What a horrific crime that was. Mrs Gould believed it would do Mr Rodney Milner good to have another young person in the house, that it would take his mind off the tragedy of his father's death. Now would you not expect Mr Ashton to say yes in that situation? I hope you may be able to convince him.'

'That is difficult,' I said, avoiding the question. My mind raced. Was Dylan reluctant to accept hospitality out of shyness, to avoid answering awkward questions, or did he desperately need to return to his own room to check that he had not left evidence that would connect him to the murder? After all, he had not had a great deal of time to cover his tracks.

Matron stood up, satisfied to have got her point across with such force. 'I will have Mr Ashton taken into our small private room. I hope you will have more success with him than I.' She gave me a meaningful look as though expecting after a five-minute interview I would request a wheelbarrow to take him off her hands.

Dylan, wearing hospital pyjamas and dressing gown, sat in a wheelchair, one leg raised. He looked up as I entered the room, his face pale, head swathed in bandages, arm in a sling. A flicker of a glance told me that

411

he had hoped the footsteps along the corridor would be Lucy's.

'You've been in the wars, Dylan.'

'Yes.'

'How are you feeling?'

'Bit of a headache. But I think that's because my bandage is too tight. I told the nurse, but they know best.' He smiled weakly.

'Do you remember what happened, where you were going?'

He blushed. 'I was coming back from seeing Lucy. Is she all right?'

'Yes.'

He pushed a finger under the bandage, to scratch his temple. 'I don't remember the accident. The nurse told me someone knocked me off my bike and drove off, but that another cyclist stopped to help.'

'Matron tells me you refuse offers from the Geerts and from Mrs Gould to take care of you.'

'I just want to go back to my own room,' he said stubbornly, refusing to meet my eye.

'Then it is not because you would feel awkward at being in Mr Milner's house?'

Now he was on his guard. He glanced at me cautiously before looking away and taking a great interest in the colour of the paint on the wall. 'I don't want to be obliged to anyone. I can take care of myself.'

'But you can't. That's the point. Thirteen steps up to that room of yours, with the stained suit hanging on the back of the door, and Rodney's silk scarf thrown across the bed.'

He stared at me, his lips parting, like a frightened animal in a corner. Then he clamped his lips tight shut.

But he had given himself away. I said, 'It must have been quite a rush after the performance, picking up the props. Not that you had much to collect, and really it should have been Lucy who took the dagger that was to have been used in the scene where you, as Willie Price, found Mr Price hanging from a beam. But you took that dagger, didn't you, Dylan?'

'I can't remember what I took. I must have picked up Rodney's scarf by mistake.'

'Or to cover the mark on your shirt. You had no time to clean yourself up, what with Monsieur Geerts insisting he walk you home, probably complaining about his wife.'

He jumped on this too quickly. 'Monsieur Geerts was with me all the time.'

'He found you alone in the gents, being sick. What made you sick?'

'Something disagreed with me, I expect.'

'Was that something murder?'

My words hit home. If it were possible, his pale face turned a lighter shade. He was small-boned, delicate almost, a creature half formed, and deeply vulnerable. He did not answer me; ran his tongue over his lips, gulped, but did not speak.

'You wonder where your cufflink got to. The police did find one, in the gutter near Mr Milner's motorcar. You will be hard pressed with your arm in a sling and a broken foot to go round tidying up evidence. And it's too late.'

'I need to get back to normal, that's all.'

'But you never will. The small stain on your good suit is hardly noticeable. I have asked for it to be analysed. I think it will turn out to be blood.' He gripped the arm

413

of his chair tightly, but said nothing. 'Your shirt was also stained, wasn't it? You had just one dress shirt, and two collars for it. One of them is still in the washstand cupboard. You burned the shirt front because it was bloody, and tossed the collar on the fireback for good measure. You tore up the rest of the shirt and put it in the bag for the cleaner to use as dusters. She'll think it odd. Starched material does not make a good duster.'

'It was muddy. My shirt was muddy, from taking Lucy to the tower.'

'Mud washes. You would not have thrown away a good shirt. And the police have the cufflink that was found by Mr Milner's motor. Someone will recognise it as yours.'

He pushed his wheelchair to the other side of the room, and flung open the door. For a moment, I thought he would make a dash for it, but he was checking that no one was listening.

Slowly, he wheeled himself back. 'Lucy's grandfather killed Milner. The nurse told me he confessed. Everyone knows.'

'But we know differently, don't we, Dylan? You see, you and Monsieur Geerts are the two people who had no one to vouch for them. He is in the clear now. You are not. Far from it.'

'But Captain Wolfendale . . .'

'The captain knew it was all up with him. He had reasons of his own for wanting to bring an end to his life.'

And part of that reason was me, I thought. I was the one who had unmasked him. I was the one who told him about Dan Root. I was the one who let him know his secret was no longer safe.

It was not cricket, but I bowled Rodney underhand. 'Have the police taken your fingerprints yet?'

'No.'

'Oh they will. You see, there is that little question mark over the captain's confession. Because the prints on the dagger are not his.'

Finally, he gave in. He lowered his bandaged head and cradled it in his hand.

He moaned but did not speak, so I pressed my point. 'You left the theatre by the rear entrance, where the loading and unloading goes on. You murdered Mr Milner, and then you went back through that same entrance and up to the dressing rooms. You thought you'd be missed if you ran off, although I expect you wanted to. The white silk scarf that belonged to Rodney, you took it when you went back to the dressing room because you saw blood on your shirt. There'll probably be a trace of blood on the scarf. Police scientists are very clever these days.'

His lips quivered. He looked wretched. His voice came out as a whisper.

'You can't prove any of this.'

'No? Fingerprints, traces of blood, the torn-up shirt. And someone will recognise that cufflink. It was very convenient that you were asked to provide an alibi for Monsieur Geerts. It gave you one for yourself, but it won't hold water.'

None of the things I had challenged him with would stand up in a court of law, not if he had a good barrister. To get to the truth, I must make him confess. It was touch and go. Lucy would be the last weapon in my armoury.

'You killed Milner with the captain's dagger. Lucy

had brought it for you to do just that.'

'No! Not Lucy. Don't say Lucy. She'd forgotten all about the dagger. I got it as a prop when I was at her house, weeks ago.'

'Then you had better tell me. If you tell me exactly what happened, perhaps I will be able to help.'

He brightened just a smidgen, like a man who has been told he has weeks to live and then the prognosis is lengthened to months.

'You mean if it was self-defence? Because that's what it was, truly.'

'Tell me then.'

After a long time staring at his bandaged foot, he said, 'Mr Milner was leaving the bar. I was waiting for Lucy and Alison in the doorway. Mr Milner said, "Don't hang about, lad." He said, "*I'm* taking Lucy home. I'm fetching the motor round." He went sauntering off, in that way he had . . .'

I could picture Milner's style of walking very well, like a man who owned the world, a man used to getting his way. 'Go on.'

'Lucy had asked me to help her. I knew if Mr Milner barged in he would manage to get his way. Lucy relied on me. I thought if I can do something to his motor engine, break something, he would have to attend to that while we dodged him. I had the knife in my pocket – that was the only prop I had to pick up, that and my Sunday school bible. I knew he parked on Cheltenham Parade, so I went out the back way. But I don't know anything about cars, how to damage them so they won't run. So I went for the wheels.'

'And?'

'It's not as easy as you think to rip at a tyre. I was still

416

at it when he came running at me like a mad man, diving on me, pulling the knife from me. I was scared. I ran up the alley, to get away. He came after me, saying he'd show me who was boss. We struggled. He pulled me into a doorway, I think so we would not be seen, so no one could come to help me. He was trying to cut my face. He did, just here.' He pointed to the spot under his chin that I thought had looked like a shaving cut when I had questioned him that Saturday morning.

'Go on.'

'I thought he would cut my throat. Because he is taller than me, when I twisted and turned and tried to get free of his hold, I must have forced him to turn the knife towards himself. He went still, and sort of slithered down. He lay there, in the doorway, the knife in his chest. I leaned down. There was a trickle of blood. I knew he was dead.'

'What did you do?'

'I went back into the theatre, to the dressing room. I didn't know whether I had blood on me or not. I picked up Rodney's white scarf, just as he was coming along the corridor. The girls were in their dressing room. I could hear them talking. Rodney said something like, "I knew you had your eye on that scarf. You can have it if you want." Then I made a dash for the washroom. I was sick. Mr Geerts came in. He thought I was poorly.'

I stared at him. Three people had confessed to murdering Mr Milner. Dan Root, the captain, and now the mild and lovelorn Dylan Ashton.

A nurse put her head around the door. 'Matron said to ask, would you both like tea?'

'Yes. Thank you.' I did not want tea, but it would

give me longer with Dylan, time to think.

'Does she know?' Dylan asked.

'Do you mean matron?'

'Lucy. Does she know I killed Mr Milner?' He was crying, like a little boy. 'I was only trying to help Lucy. I never meant to kill him. But it's murder all the same, isn't it? I was going to say what I'd done, but I let Mr Geerts walk me home. When Lucy came to be cycled up to the tower, I just did it, as if I were some machine without a mind of my own.'

'Lucy does not know. No one does.'

'Not the police?'

'No.'

Dylan's mouth fell open. He looked like a cod writhing and gasping in the bottom of a boat.

My dint of pity came not in a drop but in an avalanche. Dylan Ashton would have to live with this forever.

As I left the infirmary grounds, I recited a mantra. *Must grow a second skin. Must grow a second skin.*

But not today.

Epilogue

It was early evening when I returned to my house in Headingley. I parked my car in a converted stable that belongs to the big house just up my road. I stayed inside the garage for a few moments, not wishing to be spotted by the neighbour who wants to draw me into conversation about dandelions in the professor's garden.

When the coast was clear, I walked the few yards home. On the wall to the left of the front door was fixed the neat house name on its block of English oak: *Pipistrelle Lodge*.

Mrs Sugden was sitting at the kitchen table, absorbed in the *Evening News*. After we exchanged greetings, I asked, 'Who put up the sign young Thomas Sykes made?'

'Mr Sykes came round this morning, asking after you. He said he might as well put it in place.'

'Ah. And how did he seem?'

'His usual self,' she said enigmatically, folding newspaper carefully.

So he had decided not to take his ball home over my failure to pursue Meriel Jamieson and have her boiled in oil.

Over a cup of tea, I caught up with the post. One item was a confidential hand-written note from the manager of Marshall & Snelgrove. He asked for help in detecting a suspected shoplifter or shoplifters who were costing the store a great deal of money. Mr Moony had recommended me.

I passed the letter to Mrs Sugden. 'What do you make of this?'

She adjusted her spectacles and read it, twice. 'The blighters. Makes me sick that crooks get away with such villainy, when honest folk have to pay every inch of their way.'

The following morning, I discussed the letter with Mr Sykes. He was willing enough to take on the task, but pointed out an obvious truth.

'It will be very well me going into furnishings and male attire departments. I'd be a sore thumb in ladies' wear and haberdashery.'

Mrs Sugden was outside, emptying the teapot in the garden. I looked at Sykes, he looked at me, and nodded.

When Mrs Sugden joined us, I asked, 'How would it suit you to work with Mr Sykes in spotting shoplifters – to be a store detective for a short time?'

She grew in height. Her shoulders moved back several inches. 'It would suit me very well.'

I pulled out a chair for her. 'Mr Sykes will lead this operation.'

'Now the thing is, Mrs Sugden . . .' He propounded his theories about how to approach the work. 'And when you collar a thief, he or she will always squeal out a tale to break your heart. But it must not wash. These are criminals. We will be in the store to enforce the law. We must give no quarter.'

'Absolutely not,' Mrs Sugden said, with utter conviction. 'A thief is a thief, a villain is a villain.'

They made their plans. I watched and listened, envying such certainties.

When they had gone, I opened the bottom drawer of my new filing cabinet. Mrs Sugden had thoughtfully placed manila filing pockets in alphabetical order. I held the Victoria Cross awarded to Captain Wolfendale in the palm of my hand. If ever Lucy Wolfendale asked me for it, she should have it. For now, I would file it, under M.

M for Medal. M for Murder.

Acknowledgements

Thanks to George Cairncross whose family archive and photographs helped inspire this story. The characters bear no resemblance to your relations, George. Thanks to Jean Coates for her good company in Harrogate; Jan Coates for typing up notes; Sylvia Gill for listening; Ann Hazan for sharing the trip to South Africa, and to Stephen Wright for leading me through the art of repairing watches and clocks.

The Cairncross South Africa medals were not available for display when I visited the Cape of Good Hope Museum in Cape Town, but a wealth of other materials brought the past to life, as did diaries, photographs and memorabilia in the Royal Armouries, Leeds, where Stuart Ivinson searched out just the sorts of papers I needed. At Harrogate Library, Samantha Findlay found background material that had not been packed away during library renovations. Margaret Power was also on hand, to answer some of my questions. Not every Harrogate street and landmark mentioned in the story will be found on the map.

Thank you to a very special editor, Emma

423

Beswetherick, for such spot-on insights and patience, to Lucy Icke and staff at Piatkus who provide sterling support, and to my agent Judith Murdoch for her continued encouragement.